# The Wrath of Weasley

## A Tale from the Realm of the Blind

## William Wilkin

Bell Street Publishing, LLC

This is a work of fiction. Names, characters, places, and incidents either are the product of the author's imagination or are used fictiously. Any resemblance to actual events, locales, organizations or persons, living or dead is entirely coincidental and beyond the intent of either the author or publisher.

Bell Street Publishing, LLC

*Published by Bell Street Publishing, LLC,*
*7360 Middlebrook Circle*
*Nashville, TN 37221-6545*

ISBN: **978-0-9600387-3-2**

*First Published in the United States, 2019*

# Contents

# Foreward

I owe an immense debt of gratitude to several people who have contributed substantially to this book's artistic integrity.

There are my two sons, James and Matthew Stone.

James contributed the digital painting on the cover which captures as I never could my vision of the sense of the book. He also made a number of graphic design suggestions that are incorporated in the cover design and interior of the book.

Matthew Stone made manTy suggestions for the layout and design of the interior as well as completing the cover layout.

My wife, Lou, contributed in both obvious and subtle ways to the completion of the book. She is a Spanish teacher and has extensive experience editing and correcting texts – both student and professional. Any remaining grammatical and spelling errors must not be accounted to her. They proceed from my eccentric ideas about the value of deviating from standards occasionally to accurately portray a state of mind or emotional content. A subtle way that she supported the completion of this book was her endless patience with those eccentric ideas.

In addition, she was willing to endure the many, many times that I worked into the early morning hours pursued by my characters who insisted on telling their stories at the most inconvenient hours.

She has always been emotionally constant in the shifting winds of our lives throughout the long thankless years of the struggle to bring these stories to print. Bravo Lou!

# Preface

For those who are not familiar with Hogwarts School of Witchcraft and Wizardry, I provide a brief resume of the recent history of the venerable school that precedes this tale and the most important dramatis personae.

Following the tumultuous events surrounding the death of Tom Riddle, the most powerful dark wizard of the age and possibly of all times, the world was attacked by an interstellar traveling race of parasites (known to themselves as "Souls" and to humans as "Ghosts") that could infest and control intelligent and semi-intelligent species. This invasion was thwarted by the combined efforts of wizards and Muggles.

Hardly had the world recovered from this invasion, than an even more mystifying series of events happen. A small group of AWOL US soldiers assembled and launched a faster than light interstellar ship. James Wendt, leading a team of wizards and Muggles, pursued this group to attempt to learn their purpose and stop it. Their failure to do so was fortunate as subsequent developments (and stories) show.

The Ghosts returned to beg the help of humans in solving a mysterious series of widespread deaths on some of their colony planets. The solution uncovered a different race, the PAK, that was determined to completely annihilate the Ghosts because they regarded the Ghosts as a pestilence on all intelligent races. Wendt assembled a team and prevented the destruction of the Ghosts' home world.

In a subsequent story, we discover that the Ghost's problems have not ended. Those problems continue in stories where the Ghosts' home world is discovered by the PAK and that world is targeted for total destruction along with its entire solar system. This time, a team lead by Jaimie Brewster prevented that from happening.

Jaimie Brewster is a witch who happens to share the memories of James Wendt. The way that this strange symbiosis came to be is related in full detail in the book, *The Curse of Souls*. However, for the present story, it is more than enough to know that Jaimie can call up Wendt's memories in time of need.

In the story preceding the present one (*The Doppelganger*), the Ghosts' home world has not been attacked, but still seems to be in danger. The danger was temporarily averted by an even bigger imminent disaster—the utter destruction of the entire universe. This story begins shortly after that disaster is averted.

The main characters whom you would have encountered in previous stories and the present one are:

- James Wendt an English literature instructor at Hogwarts. He has been married to the
- Headmistress of Hogwarts, Minerva McGonagall. However, she died in trying to save the Ghosts. Wendt was the victim of an experimental Polyjuice potion, which altered his DNA to match that of a witch at Hogwarts.
- The result was a witch, Jaimie Sinistra, who none-the-less retained all Wendt's memories. This person had all of the genetic capabilities of a witch. This resulted in the formation of a new personality that was female. This new person decided that she did not want to be sent into oblivion to give back the male Muggle, James Wendt, his life. She fled and went into hiding. She named herself, honoring both of the people who went into her creation. She applied for and got James Wendt's teaching post. She met and married
- A widower, Edward Brewster, who had a daughter at Hogwarts,
- Cecilia Brewster, who is a brilliant student, a highly accomplished chess master, and something of a preprubescent know-it-all.
- Dudley Dursley is the cousin of Harry Potter. Everyone thought he was a Muggle until shortly after the defeat of Riddle. He applied for and got the post of apprentice to
- The Janitor of Hogwarts, Argus Filch. Filch is of the old school who think that Hogwarts ought to go back to the old punishments—like hanging upside-down.
- Aurora Brahms (nee Sinistra) was almost the first person Wendt met at Hogwarts. She is the astronomy professor there. They had a lengthy and sometimes troubled relationship. Her marriage to Nicholas Brahms largely put an end to the troubling part of that relationship.
- Nicholas Brahms, the husband of Aurora Brahms, has the nickname, the Boy Genius (aka B. G.). He runs a computer security consultancy from the Shrieking Shack, an old house on the outskirts of

Hogwarts. It had a checkered past and an undeserved reputation as a haunt of ghosts.

- The Headmaster of Hogwarts is Professor Horace Slughorn who took over after the death of Headmistress McGonagall. He was both the Headmaster and the Potions instructor. Now Dudley Dursley has become the Potions Master of Hogwarts.
- The Minister of Magic has been for a number of years, Pamela Moertl. She became Minister of Magic shortly before the invasion of the Ghosts.
- Ginny Weasley entered the Auror Academy shortly after her graduation from Hogwarts. She distinguished herself in the fight against the occupation by the Ghosts. She has advanced in her career, and at the beginning of this story, she is a chief inspector, who is frequently consulted by the Minister of Magic on issues involving Muggles.
- Jaimie Sinistra existed in another universe as well as the one that "our" Wendt lives in. She wandered into our universe through the vanishing cabinet in the Room of Requirement. Although this universe's Jaimie can't coexist with this universe's James Wendt. Jaimie's from other universes can. One does.

For a more thorough history of James Wendt, read the first subchapter of the chapter of this book titled, *Heathrow Again.*

# Weasley

I had just finished lunch on the first day after the end of Fall term. There were still several teachers around in addition to staff. We had had lunch in the Great Hall at the Huffelpuff table. Everyone had scattered quickly, but I was not in a hurry to get back to my office. So, I lazed along as I left the hall.

Jaimie and I were continuing the fiction that we were only sharing the office of the English Department. Supposedly, my quarters were shared with Dursley. In the years that she had spent in that other universe where she used to live, she had developed some friendships outside Hogwarts. She was trying to renew them by spending time with them during the Christmas Holiday. To me it seemed a hopeless case—like carrying coals to Newcastle. She was determined to do it, though. She was traveling to visit them—without me—thank goodness.

As I was about to turn toward my office, I noticed the main door of Hogwarts open, and a figure enter. As she approached, I was pleasantly surprised to see that it was Ginny Potter. It took me a minute to recognize her because she had changed substantially from the last time I'd seen her at her wedding. Of course, at that time she was wearing a wedding dress and was at the height of her beauty. However, now she was very different. She seemed almost gaunt. Her fiery red hair was pulled up in a severe bun at the top of her head. I probably wouldn't have recognized her if it had not been for that head of hair. I changed course to approach her.

When I got within easy speaking distance, I said, "Ginny. What brings you to Hogwarts?"

She hadn't been paying much attention to me until I spoke. When I did, she took a closer look and almost gasped. Then she said, "Is it Professor Wendt?" Her tone was incredulous.

"You bet it is. How is married life treating you?"

4

Rather than answering, she stared at me and seemed deep in thought. I joked, "I hope it isn't that hard a question to answer?"

With that she seemed to come to a decision. She said, more to herself than to me, "He's good enough, I suppose."

I said, "I should hope so."

She said something that in other circumstances would have seemed crazy, but here, maybe not so much. "I want you to fill me in on recent history—say the last ten years or so."

That set me to scratching my head. I said, "Before we begin that, I'd like a cogent and believable reason that you need the Cliff Notes on recent wizard history."

She sighed a sigh that made me think that she might have given up on it as a bad idea. Then she said, "You're a Muggle."

I said, "Always have been always will be."

There was a little color in her cheeks, and her lips twisted in a way that made me think the time for joking was past. She asked, "Can you be serious?"

"Yes, ma'am."

"I just mean that you know about science and physics and things. You might just believe what I'm going to tell you."

I considered the possibilities. You didn't want to trifle with a witch with a wand, so I said, "This sounds like it might turn into a lengthy discussion. Why don't we go to my office. Oh, also, a stiff shot of something good might not be out of line as well."

She nodded. So, we walked up to my office. We went in. I stood by the door and said, "With your permission, I'd like to lock the door. I think that we don't want to be interrupted, right?"

She nodded again, pointed her wand at the door and me, and spoke a silent spell. The door slammed shut and locked. She commented. "That should keep most witches out."

I invited her to take the old red leather chair. She did and commented, "I've heard about this chair. I never thought I'd sit in it." This was ever more puzzling. She had certainly sat in it a number of times. I took my desk chair and asked if I could pour us drinks. She nodded. I decided that this was not a problem that required my special JB Blue, so I got out a bottle of Jameson and poured two good shots. She took a good sip and sighed, "This is better than I've had in a long time."

I said, "OK. This is your nickel; make it good."

She smiled at that. The first real smile I'd seen from her so far. She leaned back and asked, "Do you believe in parallel universes?"

With that question, everything became much clearer. I asked her a question in return. "You're from an alternate universe, right? You came through the vanishing cabinet in the room of requirement?"

Her mouth fell open. I said, "You're not the first to come through from a different universe. What brings you here?"

She said, "Answer my question."

"OK. Well, let's see. A lot has happened in the last ten years. I'll give you the top ten events, and we'll see if that satisfies you. Starting with number one:

- Tom Riddle was defeated and killed by Harry Potter.
- Hogwarts has been restored and is in businesses.
- The Earth was invaded by aliens, calling themselves Souls, who almost put an end to the human race. As you see, we won. And on a personal note, Minerva and I got married.
- Some humans developed faster than light travel.
- The Souls returned to beg for help. We provided it, but Minerva died helping them. She was killed by the antagonists of the Souls. We call them the PAK.
- The PAK came back to us asking for help against another race who wanted to destroy the Universe.
- We helped them and saved the Universe.
- You got married to Potter.

"I guess that's not ten, but it gives you the dragon's-eye view."

She said, "You mentioned my marriage. Is that earth-shaking?"

"I guess not, but then I mentioned my own marriage as well."

She nodded. I said, "How about mentioning the top ten events in the last ten years in your universe."

She finished off her glass and asked for another. I complied. Then she said, "OK. Here goes:

- Tom Riddle defeated and killed Harry Potter.
- DeathEaters finished taking over the Ministry of Magic.
- They conquered the rest of the magical governments.
- When the Souls came, there was a terrible war. A large fraction of the world's humans died.
- I don't know anything about faster than light travel.
- No alien races have come to us for help.
- The Universe hasn't been destroyed.
- I haven't married.
- I don't know what happened to you. I strongly suspect that you died somewhere along the way.

- Riddle discovered how to travel to other universes. He is trying to rule other Earths where he died. He came here."

That last statement scared the pants off me. I said, "Oh, shit." I finished my shot and poured another. Then I said, "So you've come here to try to . . . what?"

"It's obvious, isn't it? Here he's far more vulnerable than back in my universe."

I asked, "I suppose that Potter didn't get all the horcruxes in your universe. Did he get any?"

She finished her drink and took the liberty of pouring herself another. "All but one."

"It's not a big secret, but there are a number of people who know where all the horcruxes were in this universe. Which ones did he not get?"

"It was the one that was hidden somewhere in Hogwarts." She suppressed a sob and went on. "I'm determined to find it and destroy it."

I said, "Well, it's easy to tell you where it was—in this universe anyway." I started to say the location when Ginny put a hand over my mouth.

She said, "Don't say it."

I didn't say anything. I just looked the question. She asked, "Do you know how saying You-Know-Who's name was dangerous at the end?"

"Sure. The first rule of our opposition was: Use his real name—Tom Riddle."

She gasped, "I wish that we'd thought of that. Anyway, the Order of the Phoenix decided not to say his preferred name or any critical information aloud."

I nodded. I pulled a piece of parchment out of my desk and wrote the name of the horcrux and its location down. I was about to hand it to her. She grasped my wrist and held it away. "Don't do that unless you want to sign up for this job."

I said, "Everything else you've said is reasonable, but you're going to have to explain this."

A grim smile creased her lips. She said, "Do you know the first rule for underground revolutions?"

"Maybe. What's your #1 rule?"

She relaxed the grimace and said, "Everyone is organized in small cells. There's no central control. No one knows the identity of anyone other than other members of their cell and one member of one other cell."

"OK. It's a good rule. The Order of the Phoenix here didn't follow it. So, keep going."

She leaned back in the red leather chair and took a sip of the Jameson. Then she said, "I'm only having one other member of my cell. If you give me that information, you're in my cell for better or worse—no dropping out. Do you still want to hand that parchment to me?"

I topped off my glass and took a generous drink. I leaned back and thought with eyes closed. I pursed my lips. Then, I came to a decision. I laid the parchment down. I got my purse out and opened it. I fumbled around in it looking for a small Muggle artifact. I finally found it. It was in a resealable plastic snack bag. I handed it to Ginny. She took it in her hand and stared at it. "What is it?"

I smiled a grim smile that matched hers from earlier. "I doubt that your Dad ever showed this to you. I gave it to him as a souvenir after he helped me acquire this." I reached into the purse and drew out another Muggle artifact. I handed it to her. "Do you recognize that?"

She nodded with a light of understanding in her eyes. "It's some kind of hand gun. Is it an uzi?"

"Not a bad guess, but it's actually a Glock. How do you know about Uzi's?"

"There was a lot of Muggle resistance to the takeover by Deatheaters. Some of the most persistent were the Israelis." She smiled again, and her eyes lit up. "There were a lot of Deatheaters who died in Israel."

I nodded. "I imagine there were." I took the Glock back and said, "That object that you hold is a bullet for the Glock. I gave it to your Dad." A sudden lump had appeared in my throat. I hadn't thought until then of what probably happened to Ginny's family.

She noticed and said, "No. He's OK. As a matter of fact, after Potter died, Riddle was almost generous with wizards—even those who had opposed him. Wizards didn't even have to become Deatheaters."

I went on. "I gave it your Dad the first year that we met. He kept it for a long time. Then last year, I got it back at Christmas as a present."

She gazed at me questioningly. "Why?"

"I can't say."

She thought about that for a while. I went on. "Anyway. It seems to me that it'd be a just act to kill him with that bullet. I'd like to be the one to do that with my Glock."

She stared and said, "I think you really mean that, but I can't guarantee you the chance. Can you tell me what you specially have against Riddle? There are a lot of people who would line up for that chance."

I started to talk about Cedric. She stopped me with a hand over my mouth. I said, "OK. You know, you're awfully free with that hand and my mouth. What's the problem now?"

She had her very serious face on again. "If I'm going to take you on as a member of my cell, you're going to have to do a real interview. I want to

8

know that you can handle yourself in a fight. I want to know that you're in for the long haul. I want to know that you're not going to sell me out."

I sighed. "Don't tell me that I have to fight you."

"Don't be stupid. The only real proof of all those things is past performance." I was about to make an objection when she raised The Hand. I leaned back and signaled with my hands that I wouldn't say anything.

She said, "The only proof of past performance is your own testimony under *Veritas Serum*."

I nodded contemplatively. "You've got a good point. I suppose that you've used it before."

She smiled a wicked smile. "Yes, but I don't have any with me. It's not very easy to make."

I said, "There's probably some in the potions Classroom."

"Good. Is it still the same place?"

I put my hand up this time. "Look. You're in my universe now. We do things my way. I happen to have a good friend who's the Potions Master. I think he's still in the castle. We can go find him and find out if he's got any."

She took a quick sip and swished it around in her mouth before swallowing. "Do you really, really trust him?"

I smiled, "With my life."

She nodded. "OK. Is it Slughorn? Because if it is, I'm not so sure how trustworthy he is."

I smiled. "No. No. Actually, Slughorn is better than he used to be. The fire of the war with Riddle seasoned him. However, there's a new Potions Master. He's really good. I've been with him in life and death situations."

"Do I know him?"

"I don't know. His name is Dudley Dursley."

With a sudden motion that put her wand against my throat, she said, "Don't tell me he's the same ass-hole who was Potter's cousin."

I moved the wand away from my throat. I said, "Hear me out. I wasn't kidding when I said that I would trust him with my life. And, yes, he is Potter's cousin. I'll be happy to talk about him in the 'interview'."

She shook her head slowly. "You will talk about him. Lots. *Veritas Serum*. Do you still want to have the interview?"

I finished my drink and said, "Yes. Let's go find him right now."

☐

She agreed. I got up and led her out of the office and down the staircases until we got to the basement where the Potions classroom, the Slytherin Dorm, and Filch's Office was. She instinctively turned toward the Potions Class-room. I said, "No."

She spun around in confusion. I said, "Dursley's Office is over here."

She frowned, "The only office that way is Filch's."

I said, "It's now shared by Dursley."

Her mouth did something that I'd not seen yet. It opened into a wide, perfect "O". I said, "Yes. Dursley started off as the Squib's Apprentice and worked his way up to be the Potions Master. They actually became pretty good friends, so they continue to share the office."

She shook her head sadly, "Why does that not surprise me? OK. Let's go."

I knocked on the door. Filch said, "Come in. It's not as though I could keep anybody out."

We went in. Filch was leaning back in his desk chair with his feet up on his desk. Dursley was facing him. He had leaned over his desk writing on a parchment. When he saw Ginny, Filch jumped up and said, "Oh, ma'am. Sorry. I didn't know we had any student parents visiting." With that Dursley stood and swung around.

He was even more surprised. He said, "It's . . . It's Mrs. Potter, isn't it?"

She turned to me and asked, "I don't look that bad, do I?"

I shrugged and took over the conversation. "Sorry to bother the both of you. Her name is Ginevra Weasley. We won't keep you long. Mr. Dursley, we need a little help from you if you wouldn't mind coming down to the Po-tions classroom with us."

He smiled, "Of course. Always a pleasure to give you a hand, Professor. What can I do for the two of you?"

We left and headed for the Potions Classroom. I said, "Let's wait until we get there before I tell you what we want."

He shrugged. We were inside quickly. I motioned all to sit at student benches. Ginny started to say something. I cut her off. "We'd like to have a little *Veritas Serum*, please."

He stared at me as though I'd grown a second head. "What in the world do you want *Veritas* for?"

I smiled. "Well, Dudley, Ginny and I have a little difference of opinion about something. I offered to tell her the story under *Veritas* so that she'd believe me."

He shook his head. "Well, that's a funny use for *Veritas*, but if you re-ally want some, I won't stand in your way. How much time do you want to be under *Veritas*? I need that for dosage."

I looked to Ginny. "Would five hours be enough do you think?"

Ginny thought about it and said, "Why don't we make it a round eight hours?"

I agreed. Dudley gawked at us. "You're both crazy. You should be able to settle any bet in much less than an hour. You're not thinking of giving this to more than one person, are you?"

I said, "I swear to you that the only person who will take this is me. It will be in one sitting—that is if it's safe to take that much all at once."

Dudley said, "I've never heard of any problems with *Veritas*, but I doubt that anyone has taken that much all at once." He paused. "OK. For you, Wendt, I'll give you that much. How much do you weigh? Ten or eleven stone?"

"I'd say that neighborhood. Definitely less than eleven."

Dudley nodded and unlocked a cabinet. He took out a small bottle. He found a clean graduated cylinder and measured out a quantity. He then transferred that into a clean sample flask. He handed it to Ginny with the admonition, "This is only to be used on Professor Wendt. When you're finished, destroy what's left. And for God's sake, be careful with it."

She nodded, and we all left the classroom. Dursley headed down the corridor toward Filch's Office. Ginny turned to me and said, "To your office."

I shook my head. "I don't think so. I have a roommate who might return before we're done. Let's go to . . ."

Her mouth dropped open, and she said, "I didn't think that you'd ever be with anyone other than Minerva."

"I'd rather not talk about that, but under *Veritas*, you can certainly ask me."

She frowned at that. Then she said, "I'll stay away from that topic if I can, but I offer no guarantee. You might have to talk about it before I'm done."

I shrugged, "Fair enough. Let's go to a Muggle hotel and rent a room for the afternoon and evening. I would go someplace where you won't be recognized. I don't want anyone to think that you are being unfaithful to Potter."

She gasped, "Potter really survived in this universe, and I . . . uh . . . she married him?"

I nodded. Then she said, "Good idea. You're the Muggle. Where would you go?"

I thought a moment. "Let's go to Newcastle. I'm sure that we can find a decent hotel there. It's off the beaten path. It should be good."

She asked, "Disapparate?"

"Certainly, it would be too dangerous to take the floo someplace in Newcastle."

We walked up to the main floor, left the castle, and walked down the path toward the gate. I saw Hagrid's hut and shuddered. She asked, "Something wrong?"

11

"I'm alright. It's just that I never see Hagrid's hut from here without thinking of the last time I saw Snape in life."

She smiled. "I suppose I should hate him, but somehow he always seemed to me to be a tragic figure who could have ended up so much differently."

"Right."

⊓⊓

We appeared in a back alley of a street that I supposed must be in Newcastle. I brought my phone out and called directory assistance. I asked, "Is there a Hilton in Newcastle?" The answering voice said, "Yes. I'll complete your call."

Ginny asked, "Well?"

I tried to shush her as the front desk of the Hilton came on. I explained that I needed a room for one night. No, I wasn't a member of their club. No, I wasn't a Triple-A member or any other club member. She quoted me a nightly rate of eighty-five pounds plus taxes and fees. I accepted and finished by saying, "We'll be there in about fifteen minutes. Will it be too early to have our room?"

She assured me that I could go directly to the room. I hung up and held my hand out to Ginny. "Take us to the Airport Hilton." She took my hand, and we spun out of the ether in the ladies' loo in the lobby. Luckily no one was in it, and no one saw us leave it.

She said, "You take disapparation pretty well for a Muggle."

"Yeh. I've had lots of practice."

We walked up to the Lobby Desk. The pert lady manning it asked if we had a reservation. "Yeh, I just made it. My name's James Wendt."

She consulted her computer and said, "Yes. I'll put you in 315 if that's alright with you and your companion."

"Sure."

She prepared a couple of electronic keys and took my passport and credit card. Then she said, "I hope you both have a pleasant stay. Do you need help with your bags?"

I said, "No. We'll go up and look at the room first and then get our bags from the rental car."

She said, "If you park at the east end of the lot, you can go up the stairs at that end."

"Thanks."

We walked to the elevator. Once we were inside and on our way up, Ginny said, "That was smooth. Do you take single witches on this sort of trip very often?"

I laughed. "Since Minerva, I don't remember more than two or three occasions. Of course, you can always . . ."

"Ask. Yes, I know."

Despite her knowledge of some Muggle inventions like uzi's, she was not familiar with modern hotels. I handed her one of the electronic keys. She asked, "What is this?"

"I'll show you. It's an electronic key to an electronic lock." I swiped mine and the door lock clicked. I opened the door and said, "*Entrez-vous.*" She did. Once inside, I shut and locked the door. Ginny did something with the wand, and I knew that it would take something serious to get into our room from the outside.

She looked around the room swiftly and said, "I wish that we had some whiskey. This stuff goes down better with that."

I said, "Just a spoonful of Dewars makes the medicine go down in such a delightful way."

She just sneered while I opened the frig and found several mini-bottles of whiskey. I held two up and asked, "Will you join me?"

"No thanks. Just take one of those glasses and mix this *Veritas* with one of those whiskeys and bottoms up."

I did. However, just before I swallowed, I asked, "Should I be seated? How long does it take to work?"

She was all business and answered, "A good idea. Probably less than a minute. Get to it."

I opened the bottle and mixed the concoction. I sat in the one armchair in the room and held the glass up. "Ready?"

She sat close to me on one of the double beds in the room. "Get comfortable and go ahead."

I took a deep breath to center myself. Then I drank. I couldn't swallow it all in one gulp. It wasn't the *Veritas Serum*. It was the whiskey. I don't see how people can do that. Anyway, it took me three good gulps. I wondered how long it would be before I was affected. Suddenly, I realized that I wasn't going to be affected at all. As a matter of fact, I had this feeling of omnipotence. No *Veritas Serum* could make me reveal anything that I didn't really want it to.

At about that point, Ginny said, "I see that you're ready."

"Damn right, I'm ready. Do your worst."

She asked, "Tell me about how you got started at Hogwarts."

I scoffed. "You should start with a hard one. This is as easy as pie. I had a Master's degree in English literature from Stanford University. I'll bet you don't have a Master's from anywhere. Anyway, I decided to go to the seat of all English literature—England. I was going to visit all the big places—Stratford-upon-Avon, the poet's corner, you know, all the big places."

Ginny said, "Yes. I do know."

"Anyway, I ended up working in a Starbucks in London. I wasn't really making enough to support myself, so I decided to try to get a job teaching English literature. Teaching English literature in England—like carrying coals or Muggles to Newcastle, eh?"

"That's right. Go on."

"Anyway, I read the want adverts in *The Times of London*. There was a position for an English lit teacher in a public prep school. I applied for it. There were a couple of nice teachers who came to interview me. Do you know who they were?"

"No, I don't. Why don't you tell me?"

"It was none other than the Headmaster and Assistant Headmistress of Hogwarts. Dumbledore. A great man. And Minerva, a wonderful woman. I think I fell in love with her the second time I saw her—at Hogwarts."

She started to ask, "What did you find attractive about her?" However, she stopped in mid-sentence, so I didn't have to answer that. Then she asked, "Did they hire you right away?"

"Oh, yes, yes. No delay. I started the Fall term of 1990."

She asked, "OK. Give me an example or two of courage on your part."

Examples immediately popped to mind. I said, "At the end of the second year that I was at Hogwarts, Dumbledore suggested that we attend a chamber music concert. I met him there and bought our tickets because he didn't have enough Muggle money. At the end, he suggested that he could give me a lift home. I took the Underground instead.

"On the train I found a couple of Deatheaters following me. I tried to escape from them, but was petrified and taken to someplace where they tortured me with the *Cruciatus* curse. At one point, there was a sound in another part of the building. One of the two went to investigate.

"The Deatheater who was left wanted me to open my moke-skin purse. He thought there was money in it. He was right. I opened it, but instead of taking money out, I took my Glock out and held it this way." I opened my purse and grabbed my Glock by the barrel and swung the handle like a hammer. "I hit him and knocked him out. Then, I broke his wand. I told him to get up and stand between me and the door. If he did anything that I didn't like, I would decorate the room with his brains."

Ginny asked, "Could you do that with your Glock?"

"You bet I could. Anyway, the other Deatheater came back. I told her to drop her wand or there would be brain wallpaper."

Ginny chuckled. "You didn't actually say exactly that, did you?"

"Maybe not, but that was the gist of it. Then, I crushed her wand with the heel of my shoe. I told her to lead the way out to the street and reminded her that it was not too late to do redecoration with brains. We slowly inched out of the room, down the hall, to a door. I reminded them about what would happen if anyone tried to get away on the street. By this time, it was beginning to be light. There still weren't any people on the street that happened to be Knockturn Alley. We walked slowly up to Diagon Alley. When we got there, I had everyone turn around so that the three of us were pointing into Knockturn Alley. I told them to count to ten. If they moved before ten, I'd shoot them. I turned and ran. I don't know what happened to them."

Ginny smiled and said, "Very impressive. Any other?"

I said, "Sure. During my third year at Hogwarts I made friends with Cedric Diggory. I helped him with his chess. In my fourth year, we went to tournaments, and he became an International Master. In my fifth year, I wanted him to enter a terrific tournament where he'd been invited to play. He chose to play in the Triwizard Tournament instead. In the final round of the Tri-wizard tournament, he was killed by . . ."

Ginny interrupted me. "I know. He was killed by Riddle. You don't have to tell me more about him."

I said, "I do. I became so angry that I got your Dad to help me steal some hand grenades from a US Army arsenal in Germany. They almost caught me at that."

She asked, "What would have happened to you if they'd caught you?"

"I'd have been put on trial and sentenced to prison somewhere."

"Like Azkaban?"

"Probably not as bad as Azkaban."

"What happened then?"

"I returned to Hogwarts and experimented with hand grenades in a cave nearby. When I was confident, I made a vest covered with hand grenades. I thought I knew where Riddle was. I went there. I entered the mansion. I found the room he was. He was there with Peter Pettigrew.

"I ran toward him and pulled the pin of a hand grenade in the process. Riddle saw in my mind his death. He fled. I withdrew."

Ginny tapped the bed coverlet with the palm of one of her hands and looked down at the floor. She said, "I can't believe that you built an IED and tried to kill Riddle by suicide. I can't fault your courage." Then she asked, "What have you done since then?"

I said, "Well, I went on a vacation with Minerva in the States and was almost captured by DeathEaters who petrified me."

She asked, "What was courageous about that?"

"I was 'rescued' by doctors who tried to 'cure' me of petrification. It was mostly torture for weeks. Minerva rescued me, and I was 'cured' by

Healers. After the end of that ordeal, I returned to Hogwarts for the next term."

"I see why you think that's courageous. Putting your life in the hands of those 'doctors' is courageous. Keep going."

I said, "No. No. The courageous thing was going back to Hogwarts."

"At the end of the next year at Hogwarts, Riddle took over the Ministry. Minerva forced me to try to leave England. I was captured by the English military who tried to get me to help them fight Riddle. I could have sat behind bars and not taken risks. Instead, I organized a raid on Azkaban to release political prisoners."

Ginny exclaimed, "What!"

I thought what I'd said was clear, but she wanted it repeated, so I did. "I organized a raid on Azkaban led by your brother and me. We attacked Azkaban from a nuclear submarine and evacuated by it to a base in the States."

Her mouth fell gaping open. She said, "How is that possible?"

"Well, I talked the government in the States to loan us a nuclear submarine to be used to help protect the United States from Deatheaters."

Ginny's mouth was open again. "Nuclear submarine?"

"Yes." I added, "Oh, you know how to pronounce 'nuclear'. Most wizards don't."

Ginny's eyes were brimming with tears. She said, "I had friends who died in a nu-cle-ar explosion. They were trying to fight Deatheaters." She emphasized each syllable. Then she said, "What else?" with a dull voice that seemed to say that she expected more.

"I returned to Hogwarts and began teaching again. During that year, Dudley Dursley, who it turns out was a wizard after all, came to Hogwarts. I helped him when he decided to work with Professor Slughorn to publish a revision of the latest version of *Advanced Potionmaking*."

She just could not stop interrupting me. "That's impossible!"

"What's impossible?"

"Oh, just everything! Well, the big one. What am I saying? They're all big." Ginny shook her head. "Shit. What about writing a book? You can't tell me that Dursley's capable of writing postcard, but a book?!"

I said, "He didn't do it by himself. Slughorn helped him. They used Snape's notes in the book that came out of Slughorn's library given to Potter. They tested almost all the revised spells themselves. Dursley insisted that they not significantly harm any test animals."

"Bully for him. I thought I'd gotten rid of that book forever. But, where do you fit in?"

"When the book was published, the brother of the Muggle Studies teacher tried to destroy all copies of the book by kidnapping and threatening the life of Dudley's girlfriend."

"Why would he do that?"

"Like everyone, he believed Snape killed his sister. He wanted to obliterate the memory of Snape as a form of revenge.

"I went to the meeting to turn over all the drafts and the original. The crazy guy wasn't that far from killing us."

I kept going. "The 'Souls' came, and I went on several expeditions away from the secure wizards-only enclaves. In one, Ginny—not you—helped us burn down the department store that used to be above the Ministry of Magic to divert suspicion."

Ginny just shook her head and said, "Stop. When the Souls came in our universe, they were discovered and it was the policy of Riddle that all Muggles would be killed on sight until we found out what was going on. We never did on our own. The aliens finally realized that they would all die with the Muggles in which they were living. They were smart. They left with only a brief assertion that they would never return. Riddle didn't care how many Muggles died while the Souls escaped. In the end, one third of the Muggles on Earth died. I don't know how well you did."

I said nothing. Ginny said with some impatience, "How did you do?"

"I don't remember precisely. I think we lost two or thee percent of the Muggle population."

"Damn that Riddle!" Then, in resignation, she said, "Go on."

"We were approached about a year later to help the Souls when several of their colonies appeared to be suffering an outbreak of a disease. I, Minerva, and the Brahms's agreed to help the Souls track down the problem.

"It turned out to be an attack on the Souls' worlds intended to force the Souls to reveal the location of their home world. They did. Then we discovered that our spaceship was piloted by two members of the race that was attacking the Souls' worlds. They intended to destroy the Soul solar system with a suicide attack using our ship. We all risked our lives to prevent the attack. We were successful in our mutiny. We killed the two alien pilots, but Minerva died in the insurrection."

"Then, after some further time." Here I was interrupted by Ginny.

She said, "All right, all right! You win. I accept you. Now, we need to get started. First up. Where is the horcrux and what is it?"

I had begun to feel less and less invulnerable and more susceptible to undue influence. I said, "Wait one minute. We need to plan our attack before we go off half-cocked."

Ginny looked at her watch. "I see your time is about up. It's just as well. I doubt that I could have taken much more of this detail. I accept that you're a decent cell member."

I agreed to join her cell, but I said, "I want to see a long-range plan for how we're going to attack Riddle before we finalize the deal."

17

She saw how reasonable that was. So, she explained her idea. "We go back to my universe to find the last horcrux. When we have it, we destroy it. Then we return to this universe and hunt Riddle down. When we find him, we kill him."

I shook my head sadly, "Well, your plan raises more questions than it answers. First, how do you plan to destroy the horcrux?"

She nodded. "Yes, I hadn't gotten to that detail. However, I have at least one idea."

"Good. What is it?"

"There are basilisk teeth in the Chamber of Secrets that retain venom that would be capable of destroying a horcrux."

"That's a good idea. Can you get into it?"

"My brother knew how to get in. He and Hermione entered the Chamber of Secrets and retrieved several dragon fangs."

I reflected and asked, "What's your fall-back if you can't get in there or there aren't any fangs available."

She was silent for a while. Then she said, "I don't have a fall-back. Do you?"

"Maybe. I have a long-shot idea. I don't want to talk about it until we need it. I hope I don't have to. So, you've destroyed the horcrux. What next?"

She almost laughed. "We corner the bastard and kill him."

"Oookay. How do we do that?"

"First, we have to find him. Then we kill him."

"Do you have an idea about how to find him?"

She looked down at her feet and reddened. "I will let him find me."

I gasped. "Let me get this clear. Your plan is to let him capture you. Then you'd attack him?"

She sort of nodded her head and said, "I guess it amounts to that."

"I think we can do better than that."

She did laugh this time. "I suppose you've got a better idea?"

"As a matter of fact, I do."

She drilled me with her eyes. "So, give. What is it?"

I shrugged. "I've not given a lot of thought to it, but we know, in this universe at least, that Riddle stayed in a couple of places. One was the abandoned Riddle Estate. Another was the Malfoy Estate. He may not be at either, but I would bet a fair amount of galleons that he is.

"That raises another question in my mind. You came through the vanishing cabinet in the Room of Requirement, right?"

"Sure. So did Riddle."

"OK. You ran into me. How did Riddle get out unobserved, particularly if he arrived a few days ago when a lot more people were here?"

Ginny said, "Sure. That's actually easy. You may not realize it, but after Riddle took over the Ministry, he began flying without a broom. He could have gone to any open window, leaped out, and flown away."

I mumbled, "Better and better."

Ginny grinned. "You can drop out any time you want. Of course, then I'd have to obliviate your memory of all this."

"Oh, I'm not thinking of dropping out. I just like to have a realistic view of what I'm up against."

She chucked me on the shoulder and said, "That's the spirit. Put together a bag with some clothes, and we're on our way."

# Weasley Redux

After, she'd taken me back to Hogwarts, and I'd packed, I asked her, "Are we finally ready?"

She seemed about to say, "Yes," when her mouth gaped open. She asked, "Ginny is alive in this universe, isn't she?"

"Sure."

She struggled for a moment trying to control a sob that seemed certain to come out. She did. Then she asked, "And Potter is alive?"

"Yes."

"And you're sure that we, uh, they got married, right?"

Now, I had to work to suppress a sob, but I did a better job than she had. I said, "I'll tell you why I'm so sure."

□

It was Spring. I'd been teaching two classes of English literature, third and fourth years, while my partner, Jaimie had been teaching the other five grade levels. Life as teaching partners and partners in the bedroom had worked out unusually well. Even though we had different temperaments and different sexes, we shared a fund of life experiences that gave us a perspective that allowed those differences to be merely stimulating rather than disturbing.

One day, we had decided to go out to the lake to enjoy the early spring thaw. We usually started these sessions with a review of our day. It was a mini lessons-learned session. We would first take turns naming our successes of the day. When one ran out, the other stopped—even if she had other successes.

Then we took turns listing our areas where we'd failed. We hardly ever had more than a couple each of lessons to learn. This day, we were celebrating that we had only successes. That was rare enough. When that happened,

20

we rewarded ourselves with a brief snogging session. However, on the lake, in plain view of all students, staff, and teachers, we decided to substitute holding hands surreptitiously.

As we were sitting there enjoying this brief respite before lesson planning for the next day began, we were looking out over the lake toward the north. As we looked, we both noticed a dot near the horizon. I asked Jaimie, "What do you suppose that is?"

She said, "Oh, probably a seagull." After a brief pause she added, "Do you suppose that is an owl?"

"I think it might just be." I wondered where it might be going. Then Jaimie said, "I think it's for us."

"I have a bad feeling about this." Feelings or no, it was not more than a minute or two away from reaching us. We obviously could only wait for its arrival.

Jaimie asked, "Do you suppose it's for me?" In a moment the answer became apparent. It dropped a note in my lap without even slowing down.

I said, "God, I'm glad that I wasn't having dinner in the Great Hall. Can you imagine what that missile would do to a bowl of soup?"

She said, "Oh, just open it up and find out what it's about."

I did. I said, "Here's the scoop:

Mr. and Mrs. Arthur Weasley
and
Mr. and Mrs. Vernon Dursley
request the honor of your presence
at the wedding of their daughter
and their nephew

## *Ginevra Weasley*

to

## *Harry Potter*

Saturday, the Nineteenth Day of April
Two Thousand and Eight
Three O'clock in the afternoon

Hogwarts School of Witchcraft and Wizardry
Hogsmeade, Scotland

Reception to Follow

*rsvp*

Jaimie eagerly pulled it from my hands. "OOOH! Wonderful. A wedding. I wonder how many people are invited? I wonder what her colors are? I wonder who the bridesmaids are? OOH! I wonder who the Maid of Honor is? I wonder who the groomsmen are?"

I said, "That's a lot of wondering." There was another smaller card in the envelope that gave instructions for responding and selections for the meal to accompany the reception.

Jaimie had one more wonder. "I wonder who your plus one is going to be?"

I shrugged. "Does it really matter, since I'm not going?" Jaimie struck me a healthy wallop on the shoulder. My response was, "OK. OK. Sure, I'll go. Now, I wonder whom I should invite? Maybe Filch."

She struck me again on the shoulder and I admitted, "OK. OK. Sure. You're going to be my plus one."

She rewarded that honor with a really decent (or maybe it was indecent) French kiss despite the possibility of our PDA being seen by the impressionable youth of Hogwarts.

⊓⊓

The next couple of weeks some of us had a hard time concentrating on school. That went for Jaimie too. It was a real pain. I had to go with Jaimie to look at dress robes for her and dress robes for me. Did I mention that it was a royal pain?

The Old Boys Club met once during this period. It was a time of genuine mourning. Everyone was present: Professor Slughorn, Filch, Professor Dursley, Professor Hagrid, the B. G., and me. Everyone complained.

Slughorn got the worst of it. Filch started off. "Why did you ever let those two DJ's get married here?"

He asked, "DJ's? What are you talking about?"

"You know both of that Potter and Weasley were Delinquent Juveniles when they were here." Then he lowered his voice and said, "And besides, Ms. Prinz wants me to get new dress robes."

Hagrid was not exactly against having the wedding in the castle, but he didn't want to disappoint anyone.

I wasn't exactly opposed to the wedding being at Hogwarts. As the wedding got closer and closer, I became less and less excited about it. It seemed like an era was coming to a close. The number of students from the good old days of Potter's residency at Hogwarts who were both alive and unmarried was fast declining. Off the top of my head I couldn't think of a single one. I knew there must be some, though.

We were almost all at the point where any of us might have done what I did. I went to Headmaster Slughorn. Sally ushered me in immediately. I guess she realized how disturbed I was.

Slughorn invited me to sit and have something to drink. It was after my last class, but I demurred. He had a small glass himself and bid me talk.

"I want an excuse."

Slughorn laughed and said, "Do you want a note to let you out of school?"

I said, "No. I'm serious. I want an excuse to avoid the wedding. I don't care what it is! Send me to a non-existent conference. If you won't, I'll . . . I'll resign."

Slughorn could see that I was serious. He asked, "What's all this, then? I thought that you and Potter were on decent terms. Has he done something?"

I grimaced. "No. He's just fine."

"Then is it Weasley? She's a peach."

I said with more feeling than I wanted to express, "Yes, she's really perfect."

"Then what's the problem? Is it Jaimie somehow? Does she and Weasley have a feud going?"

"No. No. I just won't tell you. Just do something to give me an excuse."

Slughorn watched me for a few minutes over his glass. Then he said, "You're one of my best teachers, but I just can't go along with your insanity. Please just show up. You can come in just before the actual ceremony starts and duck out after the last of the toasts." He reconsidered and said, "You really should stay for one dance with the bride. She deserves that."

I nodded. "Deal. I'll be there for the actual wedding and the toasts and one quick dance with the lucky bride."

I was dragged away the next week to look for a wedding gift. They were registered at a Muggle home goods store. We disapparated there from just outside the friendly confines of Hogwarts.

After we entered the store, we went directly to the customer service desk to find out about the gift registry. They directed us to a kiosk nearby. Jaimie understood about gift registries from my pre-Hogwarts memories, but she'd never seen one like this. The ones that I remembered from before were paper registries. She was fairly adept with computers, so I let her give it a go. She was stuck at the first.

You had to specify who the bride was to find the registry list in the computer's database. She insisted on using the name Ginny Weasley. After a couple of unsuccessful tries, I said, "Let the pro take a crack at it."

She did. I typed in "Genevra Weasley". Immediately the list popped up. As we scrolled through it, Jaimie gave the occasional exclamation of joy at some item that struck her fancy. The china pattern, a Mikasa, particularly brought joy to her heart. She said, "Oh, let's get her a place setting!"

I wanted more time to browse, so I keep scrolling. We eventually found a silver flatware settings for which they wanted eight settings. That was my choice. Jaimie said, "That is very nice. Do you want to do one or two?"

"I'm going to sign up for all eight."

That made her gasp. "That's so very expensive."

I smiled. "You're aware that I'm fairly well-to-do. You don't really realize just how well-to-do I am. Believe me, that will barely be perceptible in the old Gringotts vault. As a matter of fact, let's go to the department to look at the real thing. I want to make a few small additions to the gift beyond what they've asked for."

When we arrived, I found a salesperson who was more than happy to show us flatware. The first question that the salesperson asked was, "Are the gentlemen and lady considering having a gift registry for an upcoming event?" Jaimie looped her arm through mine, and with a thrill that ran through my whole body, we intertwined fingers.

She said, "Not at this time, although we might be soon. No. We were looking at another couple's gift registry and wanted to see the flatware set that they'd chosen."

He asked the name and looked up the gift registry. Then he said, "I'm sorry. They've all been purchased already."

I said, "Oh, I know. We purchased them."

His eyebrows lifted at that. "You must be very close to them. You surely can't be parents of one of them?"

I said, "No. Ginny was a student at my school. I've had a professional relationship with her off and on across the years. What I'd like to do is to add a few items to the silver—say another four place settings and a few miscellaneous accessories, like serving implements."

He nodded slowly but didn't answer for a moment. Then he said, "Let me suggest an alternative. You would be spending only slightly more if you bought our twelve place setting set. It includes a carving set, a pie server, various serving spoons and forks." He hesitated for effect to bring out the *piece de resistance*. "And, it comes with a mahogany (not veneer) velvet lined storage box."

I said, "That sounds fine." With that Jaimie both kicked my shins and squeezed my hand at the same time. Talk about mixed messages! That was the ultimate.

She said, "Why don't you buy me nice things like that?"

I shrugged. "All you have to do is ask."

The salesperson never missed a chance. He immediately said, "You could start a wedding registry right now. We wouldn't publish it. You could work on filling it out over weeks or months. Could I sign you up right now?"

I said, "Although that's an interesting idea, I'd like to look at other stores' gift selections. I'm rather partial to Harrod's myself." I got another squeeze from Jaimie.

The salesperson would not let go. He said, "Well, there's no commitment. You could start your registry today, and if you really wanted to do it at a different store, you wouldn't even have to do anything with this starter registry here."

Jaimie used her cow eyes on me, but I was impervious to another squeeze or two. We left the store unscathed—other than the cost of a complete silver set.

By this time, Jaimie was definitely thinking about how she would organize her own (I suppose I should say "our own") wedding. She had picked colors and her bridesmaids. It's no surprise to anyone that Sally, Aurora, Dursley's girlfriend Pamela were on the short list. She also wanted the other Jaimie. Of course that was out of the question.

She wanted me to pick best men. Of course, she had been assuming all along that I would be the lucky groom. I have to admit that when we were together in bed, that seemed perfect. However, in my right mind, I wasn't so sure. Anyway, I named Filch as my best man, Dursley, Hagrid, and Slughorn as other groomsmen—the other members of the Old Boys Club. She had no idea of that, I think. She sort of wondered at my choice of Filch as best man.

I retorted, "Filch is always the forgotten man at Hogwarts. People never seem to think of him. He's a squib. I think he deserves a chance at happiness." That brought a tear to Jaimie's eye. It almost brought one to mine.

The night before the wedding arrived, I was not invited to the rehearsal. After all, I didn't have a part in the wedding. Somehow Jaimie thought that I ought to have been. I wasn't invited to the bachelor party. Another omission that I was actually happy about. After all, I'd have been the oldest man standing at the party.

Jaimie was invited a few days before to the bridal shower. I guess that she thought that if she were invited to that, I should be invited to the bachelor party. I pointed out very reasonably that the bridal shower was to collect gifts, so you wanted the widest selection of people that you could have. On the other hand, the bachelor party was for the guys to reminisce about old times together and mourn their end. I didn't have any "old times" with Potter unless you counted the occasional word of advice while he was struggling through Hogwarts. They were neither times that I enjoyed particularly nor times that he did—I suppose.

On the eve of the wedding, Jaimie thought it would be "cute" if we pretended that it was our wedding night and that we were going to bed for the first time (officially). It was not hard to get into the spirit of that but not to actually act it out. I was going to carry her across the proverbial threshold and lay her gently on our "bridal" bed. She said, "No, no, no! We'd be doing a honeymoon. Let's go to a real honeymoon destination."

I said to her,. "OK. You know a little French hotel where you can see La Tour Eiffel from many rooms. Why don't you take us there?"

She clapped her hands in joy. We made it there in two jumps—using the magical travel techniques that I hate—floo to the Cauldron and then disapparation to a Paris alley near the hotel. We walked in and found that the hotel was sold out. However, they did give us a recommendation to a nice four star hotel that was not far off. We disapparated there. They had a few rooms, including one that they called the "suite lune de miel" or honeymoon suite. It was expensive—not as expensive as the silver that we'd bought Ginny and Harry but plenty expensive. It had a view of Notre Dame and the Eiffel tower. We sat out on a small balcony for a little while as the sun set.

We didn't actually spend a lot of time on the balcony. As a matter of fact, the lights of the city weren't very visible when we retired to our "salle de chambre". I think it was as memorable as any honeymoon night is for anyone.

The next morning, Jaimie was anxious to get back to Hogwarts. She didn't want to miss any of the day-of events. She was pretty sure that she could worm her way into the bride's agenda for the day. Her argument was, "We really don't want to miss breakfast at Hogwarts. It will be at least as good as anything that we can get here. Then too, we can catch a glimpse of the lucky groom and the bride, right?"

I wasn't going to argue. So, I nodded. We dropped in at the front desk to drop off our room keys, and we were on our way back the way we had come. The Cauldron wasn't open this early, so we had to do the return to Hogwarts by disapparation just outside the gates. We did arrive in time to catch the end of breakfast. As usual on a Saturday, the crowd was light, there were plenty of slightly cool left-overs, and the meal was scrumptious.

Jaimie excused herself to try to get on the bride's agenda. I happily went back to the office to work on lesson plans. She made a brief appearance at lunch to tell me that she was going to get dressed for the wedding and would be spending the rest of the afternoon with the bridal party. I inwardly gave a small prayer of thanks and returned to the office. It was less than two hours until I had to show up in the Great Hall for the wedding, so I myself got dressed and walked around the office trying to pass the time. I finally walked down to the Great Hall.

I found that the Old Boys Club had gathered there near the main en-trance. I latched onto them as the one fixed point in a world of spinning rela-tionships. Everyone was trying to kill time. Filch was complaining when I arrived. "You'd think that the ladies would just be happy to be at a wedding. I've got to sit by Ms. Pinz and let the rest of you go. And the worst part is that the bar doesn't open until after the wedding and the photographers do their worst. Ugh"

I said, "Well, that's life in this UK."

Filch stared at me as though I'd grown a third eye. "What does that mean?"

"Oh, just that it's the way the world works." At that point, Dursley's girlfriend showed up to drag him away. In a short while, Ms. Pinz showed up. Then I asked Hagrid, "Do you have a plus one?"

He answered, "What would that be Professor?"

"It's a slang term for a date."

He looked down at the floor, hemmed, and said, "Madame Maxime should be showing up sometime soon."

I looked to Slughorn and asked, "You?"

However, just then, Jaimie showed up and took my arm. She asked Slughorn the same question. To which, he replied, "Not really."

She invited him, "Come join us then." So the three of us found seats. There was a question as to which side we should sit on since we'd all had both Potter and Weasley in school if not in a class or two. I insisted on sit-ting on the bride's side, citing my long term relationship to the Weasley family.

Slughorn asked me while we were waiting for the ceremony to start, "He didn't try to show you his awful Muggle artifact collection, did he?" He suddenly remembered whom he was with and said, "No offense intended."

I was easily able with full enthusiasm to say, "None taken."

The prefatory music began. It was performed by a string trio. The works they performed were not familiar to me except that I could swear that one was a Bach string trio excerpt of the *Goldberg Variations.* Slughorn whispered to me that he thought that selection was a salute to Dumbledore. I thought it might be. Jaimie hushed me, of course.

Then, at the stroke of 3:30, the normal things happened: The mother of the bride had already been escorted to a seat on the front row. The bridesmaids processed one by one. I recognized only one, Luna Longbottom. Of course, others might even have been students, but I didn't recognize them. One could hardly mistake Luna's long, dirty-blonde hair. Now, that I thought about it, I realized that among the bridesmaids were a blonde, a brunette, a redhead, and George Weasley's wife .

The color of the wedding was a light shade of green that worked well with Ginny's hair without making one think of Christmas. I recognized Harry's groomsmen. There was Ron Weasley, who was the best man. In addition, there were George Weasley, Neville Longbottom, and amazingly, Dean Thomas who made up the rest of the groomsmen. Their cummerbunds were all the same shade of green as the bridesmaids' dresses.

The ceremony itself was very traditional—no self-composed vows, no strange homily by the Methodist minister, no weird candle-lighting, and no roping together of husband and wife. I'd actually seen all of those in one wedding or another over the years.

After the ceremony there was the endless round of photography. In the mean time, the house elves rearranged furniture for the reception and dinner to follow. The photographs were made all the more lengthy and objectionable by the fact that wizard snaps are actually short videos. So, you had several takes of videos like the bride and groom re-enacting the first kiss as husband and wife. I complained about it to Jaimie. All she would say was delivered in a superior voice. "Wait until you see the photo session for our wedding." Slughorn was nearby. I turned to him and mimicked being hung on a gallows. Jaimie didn't see that.

The reception line was painful. Not only was it long, but there was no opportunity to talk to the victims of the wedding at any length. They probably only heard ten percent of the comments they received. When I arrived at Ginny, she turned a shade of red that rivaled her hair and said to me, "I hope you are well."

I could only nod and say. "You as well." I am absolutely sure that she heard and understood, because she asked, "And your family?"

"Yes."

Before the dinner began, there were the obligatory toasts. After I thought they were completed, I was surprised that Ginny whispered to Harry. He then said, "Would Professor Wendt care to offer a toast?"

I stood, thinking as I rose and walked to the table of the wedding party. When I arrived, I looked Ginny directly in the eye and said as slowly and clearly as I could, "If there is any justice in the world, Ginny and Harry will enjoy all the happiness that this sad world can provide. I give you the bride and groom." With that I raised my glass and drained it to the dregs.

When I got back to Jaimie, she looked at me and said, "Wow. That almost sounded like a dirge. Are you sure you were earnest in what you said?"

"I could not be more earnest than I was."

The string quartet was replaced by a small band, consisting of a drummer, a bass player, a guitarist, and a singer. They performed a lot of standards for weddings even including a Celestina Warbucks song, *A Hot Messy Cauldron of Love,* or something like that. The bride and groom had their first dance.

As the rest of the people who wanted to dance with the bride or groom worked through the obligatory dance, I reconsidered my agreement to dance one dance with Ginny. It had been hard giving that toast. Dancing with her?

As the line of dancers thinned, Jaimie, who had already danced with Potter, nudged me and said, "I know you're not a great dancer. Just go up there and waltz her around the floor once." Slughorn who was sitting at our table threw in his weight, adding, "You know you promised."

"Yes. Yes. I'll do it." I rose and walked up to the line waiting to dance with Ginny. There were just two people ahead of me when I arrived. The time flew by and Ginny was standing in front of me. I hesitantly approached her. She offered her hand. I took it. Then her arm was on my waist and mine on hers. We stood there a moment. I think we were both stunned by the experience. The music was going, but we just stood and looked into each other's eyes. I moved, and we were going. She said, "I'm so happy that you came."

"Me too. It's good to see you happy."

She smiled, "Oh, I'm ecstatic."

I almost said, "Me, too." Of course, that would have been such a blatant lie that I couldn't force myself to say it. Instead, I said, "You know that if you ever want or need anything, it would be my greatest pleasure to provide it." She nodded silently and kept her head down at the end of the nod. I don't know how many times we circled the room.

Eventually, Harry came and tapped me on the shoulder. He said, "My turn." I nodded and left.

I would have left the room that instant if Jaimie hadn't grabbed me before I left the dance floor and insisted on a dance. While we were dancing, she insisted, "We are not leaving the reception until I've seen them open our present!"

I acknowledged the necessity to stay. Then we returned to our seats. Slughorn commented, "I thought the two of you were going to be up there dancing the rest of the night." He wasn't referring to Jaimie and me.

Everything is eventual. Eventually, the presents were wheeled out and the endless process of opening and acknowledging them began. I whispered to Jaimie, "As soon as ours is opened, I'm gone." She grudgingly agreed.

It didn't really matter. Ours turned out to be the last. I supposed that it was saved by the bridesmaids for last because of its obvious value. When Ginny opened it, she stared at the box dumbly for a moment. Then she noticed the catch that kept it closed. She opened it facing her. She gasped and quickly looked at the card that was attached. She turned it so everyone could see the silverware set in it's velvet-lined box. There was a general exclamation at that. Then she announced the donors. She rose, came to where we were sitting, and took both my hands in hers. She said, "I can't tell you how much I appreciate this. It's far more than you should have done."

I simply said, "You know I'm rich. If a man can't spend his money on those whom he cares about, how should he spend his money?" She smiled and bent to kiss me on the lips, briefly. I rose and shook her hands. Then we parted.

Jaimie said, "Well. I suppose considering the gift, a kiss isn't an unreasonable thank you." She added, "Don't let it be a habit."

I simply nodded.

# What Happens in Newcastle Stays in Newcastle

When I ended the recitation, the other world Ginny nodded, keeping her head partially turned from me. When she spoke, it was in a catching, halting way. "Thank you so much. I'm so happy that Potter and . . uh . . . another me had happiness somewhere." She paused and resumed, "But you seemed sad about it—the way you told the story."

I shrugged. "It was the end of an era for me. It was a reminder that I was perhaps the last member of the original Hogwarts group that hadn't married yet." Ginny started to object. I interrupted her. "Oh, I know, there's still Slughorn, and Dursley and so on. Still. Somehow it just seemed very sad to me."

It was near midnight. I said, "Look. It's been a long day. I say that we get a good night's sleep and have a decent breakfast before planning our next steps."

She stared at me. "You aren't thinking of sleeping with me!"

I tried to communicate the insanity of that idea. "No! We've got two beds. I can sleep in my clothes. I'll bet you have to a lot, living in that crazy universe you come from. I'm in love with someone else. As a matter of fact, I don't want her to know anything about this crazy plot. She'd be a bloody nuisance."

She looked at me uneasily. "Well, OK. I always have some necessaries in my handbag. I'll just use the WC, brush my teeth, and so forth. Then you can have it."

After we were both ready for bed, we flung the comforters off the beds and slept in our clothes under a light sheet. We argued a little about the temperature setting of the thermostat. I wanted it a little warmer, she a little cooler. We compromised. I found myself pulling a cover partially over me before the night was over.

In the morning, Ginny was up before I was. She'd obviously redone her hair. It was still in a tight bun of some sort, but it was different. She wanted to go directly to Hogwarts and have breakfast there. I insisted on having breakfast at the Hilton. She argued, "We can get going so much faster. These Muggle restaurants take time to fix a mediocre meal."

I answered, "That's to our advantage. We need time for in-depth planning." She grimaced, and she glared, but she didn't say anything. I elaborated, "Look, we have to have a real plan, not some wishful thinking that anything might work plan. We've got to plan for things we need to do before going to your universe."

She was clearly anxious to start, but within her a war was going on between her natural inclination and the logic of what I said. She said, "Ron told me that, when he was with Hermione and Harry, they always planned things carefully, and then shortly after they started to execute, all hell broke loose."

I shrugged. "Well that was Ron and Harry. I'm different. Most of my plans don't go pflui when a wheel comes off."

She was puzzled, "A wheel comes off?"

"Yeh, you know, something unexpected happens."

She laughed. "I suppose that could happen to a wagon. Do Muggle cars sometimes have wheels fall off?"

"Oh, it's possible. The results are pretty disastrous."

She sighed and said, "OK. Let's do detail planning. I'm sure that you have suggestions." So, we adjourned to the coffee shop of the Hilton. When we were seated and had placed our order, we continued where we had left off in our room.

I said, "I do have suggestions. First. Let me outline what I think we should do. Then we can drill into the details for the first few steps. I think you've outlined our path pretty well. However, I'd add some work at the beginning before we even begin on your plan."

She sort of shrugged. "Go ahead. What's the worst that can happen?"

"Well, I want to start off by getting prepared for the last step—killing Riddle. I know that you're well-armed. I want to be as well."

"Oh, I suppose that's a good idea. I thought that you wanted to use your Glack for that, though."

I smiled, "Yes. I'd prefer to do that, but we may have to fight our way through some Deatheaters to get to him. I want additional weapons ready."

"So, all right. How do you get them?"

I held my breath waiting for the inevitable explosion as I announced, "I want to go to the easiest place in the world to get advanced weapons—the States."

Her mouth dropped open. It would have been funny—she had a mouth-ful of scrambled eggs in it. However, when she closed it, she said in a barely controlled scream, "Are you a moron? That will take forever!"

That made my next words even harder. "I'm afraid that you don't know the third of it. I will need to train on these weapons . . . and . . ."

You have to admit that Ginny is a quick study if she's anything. She said, "I am not learning how to use a Muggle gun. I don't need to, and I won't."

"Well, this may be the parting of our ways, then."

She glared at me and said, "Why?"

I knew I had her then. "Well, how far away can you kill an opponent with your wand?"

She thought a bit and said, "Well, maybe a couple of hundred feet on a good day."

I replied, "There's a Muggle gun that can kill accurately at a mile and a half."

Her mouth dropped open again. This time it held a piece of toast with marmalade. She finished chewing it—very slowly—and said, "Truly?"

I was exaggerating a little, but not much. "Well, I can't do it that far right now, but with training, it's possible."

She didn't say anything and ate a few more bites. Then she said, "Do we really have to train?"

"Sure. How long did you train with your wand?"

She considered and said, "I was pretty damn good within five years. We're not going to have to train that long." It was a statement of fact. She would not tolerate anything near that long.

"No. I don't know how long, but it will be much, much less than that. You can do hundreds of things with your wand. We only are training to do one thing with one rifle—killing at a distance. We'll work on that to the ex-clusion of all else."

That was the end of conversation during breakfast. It was well on the way to lunch before we left the coffee shop of the Hilton. As we walked out, I asked, "Have you got anything in the room that we need to get?"

She shrugged. "No. Where are we going now?"

"I need clothes and some kind of luggage; a few personal items like tooth brush, floss, so on; and some reading material. This project could have its boring phases. You perhaps need some things."

She shook her head. "When I left my universe, I brought everything that I would ever need in my handbag."

I shook my head as well. "What you're wearing worked in a pinch in Muggle settings. You need some pure Muggle clothes for where we're go-ing."

"Where's that?" She quickly took the question back. "Of course, we're going to the States."

"Right. Let's go to Harrod's for both our clothing needs."

I've never met a woman who, once introduced to Harrods, didn't thoroughly enjoy shopping there. As a matter of fact, most women seem to enjoy "helping" men shop at Harrods. Ginny was opposed to buying anything beyond a Muggle winter outfit and a Muggle summer outfit. She claimed that the summer outfit was superfluous because we were going to be done before summer arrived. Besides that, spring in northern Scotland was more like winter than summer. She was especially unhappy that I paid for the outfits. She would have liked to pay herself, but the small supply of galleons that she brought were obviously not Muggle money and even more obviously not wizarding money. They had Riddle's image on one side and the statue of a wizard sitting on a throne consisting of Muggles adorning her version of the Ministry of Magic money.

Happily, she had no such scruples about spending my money to buy outfits for me. I insisted on sticking to my standard of simple solid color dress shirts and jeans with a pair of tan dress slacks and dark blue blazer for formal wear. I doubted I'd need that outfit, but when she saw me try it on, she was absolutely insistent that I had to have it. I bought a small, simple duffel bag to hold them. When we got out of the store and into an alley preparatory to disapparating, she placed an effective infinite extensibility charm on the bag.

I insisted that it was unnecessary because everything had fit nicely in the bag, but she would not hear otherwise. The next order of business was travel plans. Ginny wanted to go to a little wizard inn that she knew for dinner. I reminded her that: First, that inn might not exist here. Second, even if it did, it might not be the little quiet inn that she thought it would be. Third, why take chances of someone recognizing her? Reluctantly she agreed. We went to a restaurant that I knew in Oxford.

It was pretty decent and more importantly, it was quiet. We shared a modest shepherd's pie as we discussed getting to America. My opening suggestion was, "Have you ever flown in an airplane?"

She slammed her hand down and then got control of herself. "I will not fly in one of those Muggle deathtraps. All Muggle inventions have been banned in my universe. Good riddance to aeroplanes is my byword."

I sighed. "And your alternative is?"

She looked furtively around and said, "Port Key."

I rolled my eyes. "You don't happen to have a Port Key on your person that's set up for the States, do you?"

"Well, of course, not. We can get one from the Ministry."

I said, "Maybe you can. But I think you will be noticed immediately." Then the thought hit me. "You aren't an auror in your universe, are you?"

She shook her head.

"Well, in this universe, Ginny is a well-known auror—at least around the Ministry. There would be questions from the get go, especially since Ginny got a Port . . ." With that, a thought occurred to me.

Ginny prodded me and asked, "Have you had a stroke?"

"No. A fascinating idea just occurred to me. I happen to know someone who has a Port Key already set for Dallas, Texas."

"Who?"

"You?"

"What!" She started to remonstrate and then the answer to the conundrum occurred to her. "You mean me here in this universe."

"Right. So, all we have to figure out is how to get it. Really, how to convince her that we want it for an innocuous purpose."

Ginevra—I'd begun thinking of her as Ginevra to differentiate from the Ginny of this universe—said, "I can send her an owl. We can ask her to let you use the port key if she hasn't already used it. What do you think?"

"Who do we tell her is actually going to use it because I can't?"

Ginevra thought. "Not Jaimie, of course. She might well talk casually with Ginny and spill the beans. What about some member of your OBC?"

"What?" I asked.

"Your Old Boys Club."

"How do you know about that?"

She smiled. "You mentioned them once or twice in the last twenty-four hours. Anyway, you could surely get any of them to claim that they were going to take a vacation in the States in Texas."

I thought about that. Yes, Dursley would be someone who might just do that. He'd already been in the States, but only running around the outer rim of the country. I said, "Dursley. I want to avoid anyone finding that Dursley isn't actually going to use it—for a good while. It doesn't have to be forever. Would you send an owl to Dursley, asking him to meet us at the British Museum tomorrow morning?"

She asked, "Are you going to tell him the truth?"

I frowned, "I hate not reading him into the truth about this, but since you don't want anyone to know about our project, I won't. I'll tell him that I'm planning to go to the States during the next Summer Holiday. I'm going to take Jaimie. However, I want it to be a surprise to her."

Ginevra asked, "Then, he'll send an owl to Ginny to sell him the port key?"

"No, I'll ask him to send Ginny an owl with the ask. Then, he'll take me to their apartment at the agreed time."

36

She thought a minute. "Sounds good. You write the question. I'll get it put on an owl's leg. By the way, where are we staying tonight?"

I laughed. "What do you think of going back to Newcastle?"

She made a face. What the heck did she think her better offer was? We had to be somewhere. Newcastle was a great place to hide out. I was pondering this when she made her ask. "Can we have two rooms? I can give you some galleons."

I laughed. "Oh, I'm so, so sorry! Of course, we can have two rooms. I've got tons of galleons and pounds and US dollars. The next time you want something, the last thing you should think is, 'Can we afford this?'"

She stared, unbelieving, and said, "I thought you were exaggerating when you told about buying that silver flatware. That wasn't really silver was it?"

"Sure it was. I have lots of money."

She shook her head. "OK. Just don't be surprised when your vault is empty."

"I won't."

So she agreed to go to Newcastle. We registered into two rooms. Then we had dinner in the hotel coffee shop. She said, "Well, it's not Hogwarts cuisine, but then where I come from, Hogwarts cuisine hasn't been Hogwarts cuisine in a long time. How I wish I could spend some time in your Hogwarts where food is great!"

I shook my head. "Really, I wish you could, too. Maybe after this is all over, IF we're still alive, you can spend some time in Hogwarts." While we were in the coffee shop, I got a scrap of parchment out of my purse and wrote the little note. I handed it to Ginevra and asked, "How are you going to find an owl to tie this to? You didn't bring one, did you—maybe in your handbag."

She laughed her head off. I was afraid that I was going to have to execute the Heimlich maneuver to keep her from choking. I'd never seen her laugh like that ever. Finally, she said, "No. I didn't bring an owl." She giggled some and then said, "Don't worry. I won't worry about your galleons. Don't you worry about my getting an owl."

"Deal." Then we went up to our rooms that weren't even side by side. I saw her into hers successfully. Then I went to my room.

□

The next morning around 6:30 AM, there was a tapping on my door. I was not surprised, just disappointed. How could that stupid owl think this was a good time to come knock, knock, knocking on Heaven's Door? Well, maybe it wasn't Heaven, but I sure thought that any place that I could get a good night's sleep would be a good imitation of Heaven. I didn't bother to put a pair of jeans on. I just opened the door to find a scrawny owl on the floor. I knelt down and took the parchment off. It was addressed to Professor Wendt, Newcastle Airport Hilton, room 378. It said, "10 AM at the entrance, best wishes, D." The owl was hanging around, so I must be expected to provide a response. Underneath Dursley's scrawl, I wrote, "Sounds good. Professor W."

Ginevra and I had arranged to meet for breakfast at 8 AM. I went back to bed to try to catch some more sleep. It was a fitful hour of sleep, but better than nothing. I was down at the coffee shop at 7:55. Ginevra was there waiting for me. We were seated, and I lead off the discussion. "I got an answer from Dursley: 10 AM at the entrance to the British Museum."

She nodded. "Good. That will give you a chance to clean up before we go. What time do you want to arrive?"

"I want to be there around 9:30."

"I'll be at your room at 9:00. By the way, what am I going to be doing while you're meeting with Dursley?"

"You could take a tour of the Museum."

She shook her head. "Never have. I could have until I was sixteen. After that, the Museum was closed. I don't know what happened to the art in it."

"There's no time like the present."

We finished breakfast and went to our rooms. I did take a shower and dressed. Ginevra arrived at nine, and we prepared to disapparate directly from my room. At 9:20, we disapparated. I walked to the entrance to the museum while Ginevra held back. At 9:50 Dursley showed up. We got in line to purchase tickets. We were in the museum at 10:15. I led Dursley into one of the distant parts of the museum. We sat on a bench.

Dursley asked, "Why all the cloak and dagger?"

I smiled at my little joke. Then I explained. "I want to take a vacation in the States over the summer holidays. I'd like it to be a little surprise for Jaimie."

He smirked at that. "You sneaky . . ."

"So, I don't want it known generally. Now, the lucky deal is that I happen to know that Ginny has a port key that is set up to go to the States. I'd like to buy it from her. So, you see that I have to do this very secretly. Could you send her an owl asking if I could buy that port key and asking for a time to do it?"

He thought a minute. "Why don't we just disapparate right now and try her front door. She might be there. It's morning on a Holiday week. She might be."

I shrugged. "OK. Let's go right now."

Dursley looked around and asked, "Do you mind if we disapparate from here?"

"Not at all."

We stood. He reached out his hand. We disappeared from the British Museum. We landed in a suburban mixed-use community with an apartment building. It had some storefronts on the main floor. There were some homes and a block of shops within view. Dursley led me up to the apartment building. We rang the doorbell that had the label, "H. Potter". On the third ring, a voice that might have been Ginny's said, "Come on up."

The door buzzed, and we entered. The apartment was on the second floor. We walked up the emergency stairs, found the door, and entered because it was open. Inside, Ginny was waiting. Her eyes widened. She said, "I didn't realize that it was you."

"Yes. I have a favor to ask."

Ginny's eyes never left me as she said, "What can I do for you—anything?"

"I'd like to buy that Port Key to Texas if you've still got it."

Her eyes were unblinking. She said, "I do have it. You can just have it." She laughed. "Who would have thought that I'd be the first to do a favor for you?" She turned to a table where there was a chair with a handbag hanging on it. She picked up the handbag, opened it, and immediately found an old sock. It was argyle. She held out a hand with the sock in it. I grasped the sock, and we stood unmoving for a moment. I pulled gently on it. She slackened her hold on the sock, but her hand was dragged toward me. She didn't ask me what I wanted it for. Her eyes just never left mine.

Finally, I said, "Would you please not mention to anyone that you gave this to me? I have to go now. It's good to see you."

She nodded, but her eyes still tracked mine. "Have you got one of your secret missions going?"

I shook my head. Then, she said, "Good seeing you. You must come again." It was said tonelessly, but I thought there was more feeling in what she said than I'd ever heard her use before.

Dursley grabbed my arm and turned me. "We really must be going Professor."

I reluctantly turned and followed him out of the apartment. We reached street level and found an alley. We returned to the British Museum in a WC. When we left it, Dursley asked, "Do you need a lift anywhere?"

I shook my head and said, "Go on back to Hogwarts or wherever. Thanks for the lift."

He said, "Any time." He paused and turned, "Is there anything I should tell . . . uh anyone? No one knew you would be gone for a couple of days. Slughorn kind of wanted to talk with you a bit before the next term."

I sighed and said, "Uhm. No. There's nothing that anyone needs to know." I added, "Just in case. Something happens. You know, unexpected. You all should know that I . . ." I stopped, unsure what to say.

Dursley said, "Not necessary. No one will be either surprised or unsure about your feelings." Then he turned and left the room. I knew that Ginevra was somewhere in the building, so I started walking aimlessly, knowing we would catch up with each other some time.

# Deep in the Heart of Texas

When Ginevra caught up with me, she asked, "Well?"

"I've got the port key." Then I displayed the sock.

"Can we leave now?"

"There's nothing to hold us now."

We went back to our hotel. I paid the bill. We packed our bags and met in my room. I asked, "Port Key from here?" Instead of answering, Ginevra held her hand out for the Port Key. We both took it in our hands, and we spun out of the room. The rotation was rapid. At the end we dropped to the ground in a public park. The park was across the street from a large hotel.

After I regained my equilibrium, I asked Ginevra, "Looks like a nice hotel. Is it OK with you to stay there?"

She shrugged. "This is your home territory. I trust your judgment."

We registered and managed to get rooms next to each other. There was a communicating door between them. That allowed us to meet without revealing that we were meeting. When we got into our rooms, I partially unpacked and knocked on the communicating door. She opened the door. She invited me into her room. Once inside, I suggested that we sit around the small table in the room.

She asked, "What are we doing?"

"Planning. I brought the phone book from my room."

She asked, "Phone book?"

"Well, you know about telephones?"

"I knew that Dad had one in his collection. I don't really understand much about them."

I thought for a second about just how much I needed to explain. I decided to go minimalist. "For our purposes, the key is that the phone book has advertising for businesses—all sorts of businesses. We're looking for a particular kind of business. The phone book does a good job of categorizing businesses so that people can easily find the kind of business that they are looking for."

"What are we looking for?"

"We are looking for gun shops."

She thought a second and asked, "I ask your typical question. What's the detailed plan here?"

I opened the bag completely. "OK. We want to kill Riddle."

"I'm with you so far. You want to do it with your stupid Glock."

"I'm reconsidering that. Here's the detailed plan after we've destroyed the last Horcrux. We have to find where Riddle is staying, of course. Once we have, then I have two approaches to killing him.

"The first, preferred option is killing him from a distance using a sniper rifle. You can do that from as far away as a mile. It has all sorts of advantages. Riddle would probably not be aware that he's in any danger, so he wouldn't take any special precautions. If we don't succeed on the first shot, subsequent shots are probably possible before he realizes how much danger he's in. If he does elude us, he probably won't know what direction the attack is coming from, so we have more opportunity to escape. Of course, it might just not work out, so I have the second option, which is much more difficult, dangerous, and likely to fail.

"The second option is to disapparate into the place where Riddle's holed up and kill him at short distance. I don't see any way to know what room he's in, so we'd have to disapparate from room to room until we found him. When we disapparate, we'll have to do it back to back. That way we can locate him the most quickly. With luck we eventually find the room he's in and then kill him before he either kills us or disapparates."

Ginevra's lips curled up. "I like the second possibility. I know you want to kill him, but I want to do it too. That's the only way that I can."

I smiled. "Au contraire. If you learn to use the rifle, we both can kill him."

She stared at me in amazement, "Come on. How is that possible?"

"If we both fire at the same time." I could see that she was preparing a reply. "Now, hold on. Hear me out. If we both fire at the same time or approximately the same time, and we both aim at different vital organs— maybe you the heart and I the brain—then it's impossible to know which killed him. It's possible that both did."

She watched me as I flipped through the pages of the gigantic yellow pages of the Dallas-Fort-Worth area. She said, "Could be. You're forgetting that I've never fired a gun before, and you are a past master of that Glock of yours."

"Not at all. I may be fairly good with the Glock at short range, but I've never fired a rifle with a sniper scope. I need to train with that kind of gun just as much as you do."

I had found a page of gun shops. I was reading the adverts and comparing them. She asked, "Look, I still think I like the first option. I want Riddle to know that he's about to die and at my hand. But he's always got Deatheaters around. What if the first room that we go into has got a couple of Deatheaters? Aren't we toast?"

I shrugged, "It was never going to be easy. However, it's not necessarily game over. We would both be carrying guns. We would have to kill whoever was in the room even if it weren't Riddle. Does that bother you?"

She spat, "Deatheaters are vermin just as much as Riddle. No! It doesn't bother me. But won't all that shooting make a lot of noise?"

"Not necessarily. There are devices called 'silencers'. They make . . ."

She almost spat again. "I get it. No one outside the room would hear the guns. OK. So, if we just keep finding Deatheaters, we just keep going until we find Riddle. Chancy, but as you say, it was always chancy from the get-go."

I had found a couple of gun shops where I wanted to go. I used the hotel stationary and pen to write down the phone #'s and addresses. I was careful to write on a magazine that I'd brought along so that there was no impression of what I wrote for future investigators to find.

Ginevra said, "OK. Are we ready to go?"

I shook my head. "First we need to review what's going to happen when we talk to people in the gun shops."

She shrugged. "We just say that we want to buy guns—lots of guns."

I actually laughed. "No we don't. We have to have a back story ready. We go in and say that we want to buy some guns for self-protection."

Now Ginevra laughed at that. "You're sure right! We want to protect ourselves from Riddle and Deatheaters."

"We'll play that down. We'll say that we want to buy two handguns and silencers."

She asked, "Isn't that illegal—buying silencers."

"Sadly, not in the States. Anyway, we'll also buy some larger clips. I'll save you time asking." I opened my purse and got the Glock out. I released the clip and ejected it. "This is a clip. Every gun comes with one. Typically, they hold around a half dozen bullets." I shook the bullets out. "Now, larger clips can hold up to several dozen bullets. I'll be looking for several that hold around twenty bullets."

She asked, "Why several?"

"Well, if the clip is too large, it becomes unwieldy and gets in the way of accurate aiming. A couple of clips per gun is about right."

"Do you think we'll need that many bullets?"

"If there are a lot of Deatheaters around, maybe."

She sighed. "That's not all, is it?"

"No. I'll have to have a background check before I can actually complete the purchase. That will probably take a couple of days."

She commented, "Not so bad."

"No. We'll have to get concealed carry permits too. That won't be bad for me. I'm a US citizen. I have a passport. For you, I think we'll just say that you're not going to carry the weapon with you. You may have to use the confundus charm to get the salesperson to accept that. They'll require that I take a gun safety course. That's fine. You'll take it as well. It's got a lot of good information."

She asked, "What about sniper rifles?"

"Oh, we'll buy those too."

She put her hand on my arm to get me to stop talking while she thought. "Why do I need handguns? I've got my wand."

I nodded. "Well, if we land in a room with several Deatheaters, we'll need to kill them quickly. I've seen people killed by *avada kedavra*. It takes time even if you do the curse silently."

She nodded. "You're right. You really have to mean it when you use the forbidden curses. For ordinary people it takes time to work up that intensity. It's not that hard with guns, right?"

I agreed. "It's just point and shoot."

Another big sigh. She reached into her handbag and got her wand out. She held it in her hand almost lovingly. She whispered something like, "I'm sorry. I have to go Muggle with this." Then she seemed to make a decision. She looked up at me decisively and said sharply, "Keep going."

"Back to sniper rifles. Whatever you do, don't use that term. Always say 'long rifles' or just 'rifles'."

She asked, "Will those have clips too?"

"I'm not sure. I'll try to get ones that do. We may have to shoot more than one round. Without a clip and semi-automatic, it takes time that we don't have to get the next round in the chamber, aim, and fire. We'll have to see."

"Are we ready to go?"

"No. One more point. What is our relationship?"

She stared at me, "Will that be important?"

"I hope not, but we want to be as inconspicuous as we can be. We need a well-oiled back story to help with that. As I see it, these are our possibilities:

"One: You're my girlfriend and want to go in for my hobbies to help our relationship.

44

"Two: We're married. To do that, of course, we both should have wedding rings. That's not a big deal to get. We could be newly-weds, and you want to be part of my hobbies.

"Three: We know each other through work. You want to learn to defend yourself. You've asked me to help. Maybe I hope this will turn into a relationship. Maybe you do too."

She nodded. "I guess the first option. I don't really like any of them. That's the least objectionable."

"That's why I named it first. I think it's at least as plausible as the rest."

I finished by saying, "A couple of minor things. I don't want us to be traced, so we're going to do all our gun transactions with cash. We'll stop at a bank to get cash—lots of cash."

She shrugged. I stood to go, and then I said, "Oh, one last thing. I'm going to ask about shooting ranges so that we can both get practice—lots of practice."

She shook her head and said, "How could there not be one last thing?"

I handed her the list of four gun shops that I had. "Do you think you can disapparate us to those addresses?"

She thought. "I've never been here before. I don't think so. It would help—a lot—if I could see a map."

"That shouldn't be a problem. We'll go down and use the Business Office of the hotel to find maps on the web."

She shook her head and said, "I'm not going to ask. You know what you're doing. Let's just get started."

We took the elevator down to the Lobby. I found where the Business Office was. Fortunately, they let you use it without revealing your identity. I opened a web browser on the computer. I brought up Google maps and entered the first address. It brought a map up with our current location and the target address.

Ginevra looked at it and said, "I suppose there's no chance we could see a view from the air?"

I smiled. "Sure." I switched to the satellite view.

Ginevra gasped. "Oh, my. I feel like I'm flying a broom. Yes. This is wonderful. Show me the other addresses."

I entered them one at a time. The locations showed. A couple of times, the view had to expand to keep them all in. After the last had been displayed, she stared at the map for a while. Then she said, "I've got them. We can go now."

□

The first place we went was a bank that I found on the Google map. It was a branch of Barclay's. We entered. When it was our turn for a teller, I told her, "I'm a Barclay's customer."

The teller didn't seem particularly impressed—at first. I said, "I'd like to make a rather large cash withdrawal using my credit card." I opened my purse to get the credit card.

The teller nonchalanted it. "How much." She had a withdrawal slip out.

"Twenty thousand US dollars."

That caused a reaction. She inhaled sharply and said, "I'm sure that your account will not allow that large a withdrawal."

I smiled. "I think it will."

She frowned and said, "Please take a seat over there. I'll have to call a bank officer."

Ginevra giggled as we sat. "Now, you're in for it. Do you want me to be ready to confund him?"

I grimaced. "No. It won't be necessary."

After a while, a bank officer joined us, "Please come to my desk." We did. I handed him my credit card and said, "Twenty thousand, please."

He smiled, took the card, and worked the terminal on his desk. After several minutes of working it, he said in hushed tones, "I see that I can give you that much. Please excuse me for my doubts. It'll take a little while to get that much money together. Uh, what denominations would you like?"

I had had plenty of time to consider it. I promptly said, "Ten thousand in hundreds, nine thousand in fifties, and the rest in a mixture of twenties, tens, and fives."

All he said was, "Yes, sir." He left Ginevra and me alone.

I said, "I'm thinking of giving you five thousand. Is that enough, do you think?"

Her eyes had remained wide for a while. Then she said, "That's probably too much."

I shook my head.

After a while, the bank officer returned with a canvas bag. It had the money in it. He said, "It's all there. Please count it. I'm sorry that I don't having anything to give you to carry it. I wouldn't just put it in your lady friend's handbag. I wouldn't want to risk it."

I smiled. "Believe me, it would be at least as safe as any alternative."

His face alternated between open incredulity and doubt. I said, "Would you please give us a little time in your cubicle to count it and put it away?"

"Oh, oh, yes. Of course. Take your time." He left the cubicle.

The money was a banded stack of one hundred hundreds, a banded stack of one hundred fifties, a rubber banded stack of fifties and rubber banded stacks of the other denominations. I broke the band of hundreds and counted out ten for Ginevra. I just handed her the rubber banded fifties. Then I pealed off a few of the other denominations for her. The rest I put in my purse. She put hers in her handbag. Then I asked her, "Ready to go?"

She nodded. Outside, she said, "You really are rich." No comment was necessary.

I led her back to the elevator level of the office building the bank was in. She took my hand, and we disapparated. We landed in an alley that was a mess. There was garbage all around. I had a bad feeling, but we walked out to the street. A quick glance was enough. I said, "Let's go to the next."

She said, "This isn't awful compared with . . ."

I just said, "I don't want to hear what it's not bad compared to. Just go." We did. The next location looked a good bit better.

We walked to the entrance. It was locked. I wasn't particularly surprised. Ginevra got out her wand and started to say a spell. I took her hand and shook my head. She asked, "Why?"

I said, "Watch." I pressed the doorbell. It buzzed almost instantly, and I opened the door for Ginevra. She preceded me in. A salesperson was with us almost immediately. "What can I help you with?"

I said, "My girlfriend and I are looking to buy some guns. Actually, I'll be buying the guns."

The salesperson smiled at the mention of the plural of "gun". He said, "Well, we have a good selection of guns. What specifically are you looking for."

This was the Rubicon. So far, we might just have been hobbyists. Shortly, our requirements would have identified us as something more serious. I said, "We're looking for his/hers handguns. We also want a pair of long range target rifles."

He nodded. Then he said, "Do you have specific brands in mind?"

"I am kind of partial to Glocks, but I am very open to other brands."

He nodded again. "Good. What specific requirements do you have?"

"In handguns, I'd like guns that can accommodate larger clips. Oh, also, I would like ones that are compatible with silencers."

The salesperson smiled again. "So, then you want, two handguns, two larger clips, two silencers right now or do you want to just buy guns now?"

"Yes, I want the complete package."

His smile grew. "Well, then. I can suggest several very fine weapons. Will the lady want something smaller and easier to handle?"

Ginevra answered for herself. "The lady can handle anything the gentleman can." She was pointedly looking at him, not me, when she said that.

"Very well. Then, let's go to the display case and look. By the way, what caliber are you thinking of?"

I said, "I want lots of stopping power."

He said, "Self-defense?"

"Certainly."

"Very good. Then please follow me."

I interrupted him. "First, I want to talk about rifles. I'd like to make all the purchases at one establishment. Let's talk about rifles first."

He shrugged. "OK. Let me guess. You want something that will be accurate at . . . oh, a thousand meters and have good stopping power?"

"That's it."

He frowned. "I don't currently have much in that category. As a matter of fact, I have only one, the M40. It's a fine weapon—maybe not quite got the range that you're looking for."

I asked, "Is it bold action?"

He seemed embarrassed to say, "I'm afraid so."

I shook my head.

He sighed. "Well, surely we can supply your handgun requirements."

I shook my head again. "I really want to buy everything at one store. Could you suggest a store that meets our requirements?"

He rubbed his chin contemplatively. "Well, the best would be . . ." He named a store that I recognized.

I asked Ginevra. "Isn't that on our list?"

She nodded.

I said, "In that case, we'll be going."

He made one more attempt. "After you've bought your pieces, you might want to consider us for ammo. We have very competitive prices."

"Thanks. We'll definitely keep you in mind. Thanks for the recommendation."

When we were outside, Ginevra asked, "What's 'bold action' and what's bad about it? It sounds good."

I managed not to smile. "It means that every time you fire the rifle, you have to remove the spent round from the chamber by working a mechanical ejector that is called a 'bolt' spelled with a 'T'."

"Oh." She took my hand and led me into the alley. Then we disappeared. We landed in a rural area next to a large building. It was the gun store. Inside, we had a very similar conversation to the one that we'd just had in the other store. Ginevra had apt comments, particularly about bolt action rifles.

The salesperson appreciated that. He said, "Well, since your tougher requirements are around the rifle, let's look at some first." He took us back to a separate room. The walls were mounted with gun racks. He pointed at one

48

and said, "That's the venerable M40." He glanced at the glare on Ginevra's face and said, "I know. It's bolt action." Then he unlocked another rack. He took a massive rifle out of it.

"This is the Armalite AR50. It's a beauty. It is accurate with punch at over two kilometers. The scope we have mounted on it is extra. That means if you've got a different scope that you prefer, we can probably supply it, and you won't pay for the scope that we've got on it now." He handed it to me. I hefted it. It was massive.

I said, "I want something that both Gin and I can use with ease. This is kind of heavy." This time, I got the glare from Ginevra. I handed it her and said, "What do you think?"

She actually handled it rather well, but she said, "I'm afraid you're right, dear. It's kind of cumbersome."

The salesperson was not daunted. He took the Armalite back and took another from the rack. He said, "This may be exactly what you want. It's not got the range of the Armalite, but it's lighter and semi-auto. It's still got decent punch at almost a mile. It's the SR-25 Match Rifle." He handed it to me. I nodded. I handed it to Ginevra. She took it and balanced it on a hand.

She said, "I like it."

I said, "That's good enough for me."

The salesperson said, "Now, you have to realize that some people say that it has a certain tendency to jam, but you run into that with all semi-auto's."

I thought about it. Then I said, "We'll take two."

He smiled. "His and hers, eh?"

She said, "Definitely." That brought a smile.

I asked, "We both need to train and practice with these. Can you recommend a target range?"

He smiled again. "We're a full-service establishment. We have a two mile target range out back. We can train you, and you can practice as much as you like."

"Good."

"Now, let's look at sidearms."

We went to the front of the store, and the salesperson showed us a few handguns that he recommended. After hefting them and getting a feel, we picked a model. Then he said, "Well, now we come to the government bullshit. We've got a raft of forms for you to fill out. Of course, I'll help and keep you from committing the big boners."

"Thanks."

"Now, do either of you need a concealed carry permit?"

Of course, I was ready for that. "Just me. My girlfriend's gun will just be kept at home for protection."

He nodded understandingly. Then he asked, "Well, are you buying all the guns?"

I nodded.

"Fine. Then we need to do a background check on you alone." He got out several pages of forms. When he asked for identification, I got out my passport. That made him lift his eyebrows. "Don't you drive?"

"I live in England. I have a license there, but I came here because it would be a lot easier to get the guns that I want."

That made him shake his head. "You don't think you're going to get any of those through customs do you? You'll be filling out paperwork that will make your head spin."

I said, "I won't be taking them through customs."

He frowned but said, "OK. Are you going to be spending a lot of time here? You mentioned using the firing ranges."

I nodded. "Yes, I do. We'll need classes and lots of practice time on the range."

"Well, your guns should be ready in a couple of days. I'll give you a call when they are. You can get around OK without a car?"

I said, "Sure. We've got that covered."

Then he said, "Well, all that's left is the damages for the guns, accessories, ammo, permits, lessons, and so forth." He toted them up. Then he said, "You don't have to pay for all this right now. I'm happy to wait until the paperwork comes through and just get a deposit right now."

I said, "Don't worry. I'll pay the entire amount right now."

That definitely made him smile. He presented the bill which came to over three thousand. I opened my purse under the table where we were sitting. I pulled out a wad of hundreds and counted out thirty-three of them. I handed them to him and said, "I know there's a little change. Why don't you keep it for all your trouble?"

He took one of the hundreds and returned it to me, saying, "I depend on repeat business. Let's just round down to the nearest hundred. I'm sure that with all the practice you'll be doing, I'll make plenty on ammo sales."

I agreed.

He said, "We've got a gun safety class tomorrow. It includes a little firing range experience—with our guns. Why don't you come back tomorrow at seven and go with that class?"

We agreed and left. I had the receipt for all the things we'd bought. Ginevra led me around a corner of the building, and we disappeared. We reappeared near our hotel in the park across the street. She said, "Well, we've got the rest of the day and night. Have you got any ideas for what to do?"

I asked her, "Have you ever seen a movie?"

"A what? Oh, wait. I've heard of movies."

"Let's find one to go to tonight." She agreed.

There were still a couple of copies of the *Dallas Morning News* in the coffee shop. We had an early leisurely dinner. As we dawdled over tea, I opened the paper to the movie section and read. I asked her, "Do you want to see a comedy, a drama, an action, an animated film, or a romance?"

She said, "Let me get this straight. These movies are like plays except that it's recorded in advance, right."

"You've got it."

"And like plays, there are a variety of types?"

"Yup."

She thought a moment. Then she said, "Action."

"OK. Here's what's showing now in Action: *The Dark Knight, Iron Man, and Quantum of Solace.*"

She chuckled. "OK. *The Dark Night* must be about a cat burglar, right?"

"Not really. It's based on a comic book character who thwarts criminals."

She shook her head. "Comics? No. Then *Iron Man* must be about somebody who walks across Europe with nothing more than a knapsack?"

"Sorry. It's science fiction. It's about an irrational genius who invents a mechanical suit of armor and goes around fighting criminals in it."

She shook her head. "Oh. It sounds like comics. No. Then *Quantum of Solace* must be about Physics. That's it right? I read somewhere about Quantum Mechanicals or something like that."

"No. It's about a criminal organization that takes over countries. You might like *Twilight*. It's about . . ."

"Don't tell me. It's like that Dark Night but it's not a comic book."

I shook my head. It's a romance, sort of. It's about Vampires and Werewolves. You might like it."

She rolled her eyes. "Just because you're a witch, it doesn't mean that you want to talk shop all the time, and let me tell you, there's nothing romantic about vampires or werewolves."

She said, "Let's go with *Quantum of Physics.*"

I rolled my eyes. "It's *Quantum of Solace*. I agree."

I gave her the address of the theatre, and we disapparated nearby. We got there shortly before the movie started. The theatre was pretty full, but we found two isolated seats near the edge. The good thing about James Bond movies is that they start fast and speed up as you go along. It was an engrossing movie. Ginevra laughed at some inappropriate moments, but on the whole she seemed to like it.

As we left the theatre, she surprised me by saying, "Let's go to a coffee shop and get a tea." I agreed. Fortunately, there was a Starbucks in the mall where the theatre was located. We could actually walk there.

She ordered a plain vanilla black tea. I ordered Earl Grey. When we were seated, she said, "I've not had so much fun in a long, long time. That was so funny when Bond shot that spy at the end of the movie."

"Yeh. He's always good for some laughs."

She asked, "He's a Brit, isn't he? How is it that I've never heard of him?"

I shrugged. "You've lived a deprived life."

She shook all over. "You can say that again. Can we see another movie tomorrow?"

I growled and said, "Maybe." Then we returned to my room by disapparation. Ginevra went through the connecting door and said, "Good night" without looking back.

<br>

Genevra is smart if she is anything. The next day, gun safety class was a breeze for her. We went to the shooting range for some practice with handguns. She didn't want to wear the safety goggles and ear protection, but after she'd shot a couple of rounds, she had to admit that it was a good idea to have those safety devices.

The day after my background check came back fine. We went to the gun store to pick up the guns. The handguns came in boxes. I didn't need any help setting them up. The rifles were a different matter completely. The salesperson helped us assemble them. He said, "You can keep them here while you're learning and practicing. When you're ready to go, we'll see about cases for them."

We agreed. The next marksman class didn't start for a couple of days, but we could go to the gun range and practice with the handguns. They required a lot of getting used to. I'd forgotten about all the time that I'd practiced with the Glock before I was any good with it. We ended up hiring someone to give us pointers with the handguns. He was with us once every day when we were on the range practicing.

Early on, Ginevra and I had an argument. She thought that we could get good in practically no time. I insisted that we had to practice an hour in the morning and the afternoon every day. She wasn't awful after a few days, but she just wasn't good enough to reliably hit someone within seconds of disapparation. I wasn't much better, but I recognized how awful I was.

It didn't come home to her until we had been practicing rifle marksmanship for a few days. We were lined up next to each other. We were starting at 150 meters. One day, she got up from the prone position that we were firing in, ripped off her goggles, and shouted, "I'm shooting blanks. I haven't hit anything all day!"

I stood and took off my ear protection. She did, too. Then I said, "Look. I've maybe hit the target three times today. It's time to call it quits for the day. Why don't we go see a movie?"

She said, "You're just babying me."

"You bet I am. I'm babying myself, too. How about seeing *Iron Man*?" She agreed. We went to a matinée.

Her first reaction was, "They let people go to afternoon movies?"

"Sure."

She was slapping the seat throughout the movie. When it was over, we went to dinner. As we were finishing, she admitted, "I'm almost as awful at handguns as I am at rifles, right?"

I chuckled. "We're both pretty bad at both. Let's take it easy for a couple of days. Only one hour a day on handguns and an hour on rifles." She agreed. After that our marksmanship improved noticeably.

After a couple of weeks, we had progressed to five hundred meters on the rifle range. We both could hit the body of the targets about half the time. One time, after a session, Ginevra came to me and said, "We're not going to get any better, are we?"

I shrugged, "I don't know."

She went on. "This is good enough isn't it? If we're both shooting from five hundred, one of us should hit the first time, right?"

I shook my head. "Not good enough. We both have to hit 90%. Oh, one more thing. We maybe don't need to hit from a mile. Let's go for a kilometer."

She just said, "Oh, shit." I could tell though that she was agreed. She just didn't want to admit it—yet.

I said, "We need to take a vacation. We're stale. Let's go someplace for a week. When we come back, we'll see where we are."

"That's crazy. We'll lose our edge. We'll lose half of what we've gained." That was just a sample of what she had to say. I stayed at it and in a couple of days, she agreed. Then we had to decide where to go. We spent all of a long lunch discussing destinations.

Her first words were, "You know this country. I don't. Suggest something."

I said, "Let's talk categories first."

She scoffed, "You and your categories." However, she went along with the idea.

I said, "OK. This country has lots of options. There's seaside. There's mountains. There's rolling country. There's desert. There are small towns. There are big cities. What do you think?"

She started to say something, but I interrupted her, "Oh. Oh. I forgot rivers. We've got some great rivers that we could take a cruise on."

She said, "This is too much! How can you pick just one?"

I said, "Then start with the ones that you definitely wouldn't like. Pick a card, any card."

She laughed at that and said, "OK. Small towns. I've seen all the small towns that I want to for the rest of my life."

"Duly noted. Name another."

She scratched her head. "Let's . . . say . . . seaside. I've been to Brighton Beach. That set me up for a lifetime."

"Another?"

She leaped up. "I've got it—the desert."

"Good. Another off the list."

"No. No. I mean I want to go to the desert."

"Great! The States have lots and lots of deserts. As a matter of fact, a lot of people would say that Dallas is a desert."

She almost laughed. "Don't be silly. Dallas isn't a desert, and I've seen plenty of Dallas. I'm trying to think of anything that is really unique to Dallas. About the only thing that I can think of is the Sixth Floor Museum. It's a good museum, but really—a museum dedicated to one man's death."

"OK. I was just kidding. I actually have a place in mind."

"So, what is it?"

I hesitated for effect and said, "The Gage Hotel."

Genevra said, "I like the name, but I've never heard of it. What's it famous for?"

"It's on the edge of Big Bend National Park."

"Again. I like the name, but I've never heard of it."

I stopped a minute to marshal my rhetorical forces. "Here's the thing. Big Bend is named after a very large bend in the Rio Grande River. That river marks the border between the States and Mexico."

"Interesting. Anything else to distinguish it?"

"Well, it's extremely remote. It's hundreds of miles from the nearest freeway and dozens of miles from the nearest highway of any size. The only people who go there are outdoors fanatics who love deserts."

Ginevra frowned. "Well, if we want to avoid anyone recognizing us, it sounds like a good spot. It also sounds like it's unpleasant."

I smiled, "That's the thing. The Gage Hotel is beautiful, historic, and comfortable. With disapparation, we can visit Big Bend, but begin and end the day in comfort."

"Sounding better all the time."

I started to enthuse about it. "This is the ideal time of year to visit Big Bend. During the summer and late fall, parts of the park are closed because it's so hot. February is the peak season."

"How do you know so much about it?"

I shrugged. "I have a cousin who visited there a couple of years ago with his wife. He was enthusiastic about it. I think that his enthusiasm was mainly based on the fact that it is remote and hard to get to. That sort of works into our needs. The other desert parks are all extremely popular. There are people at them from all over the world. You know, places like the Grand Canyon, Yosemite, Carlsbad Caverns, and so on. We might easily run into someone who would recognize us at them."

"OK. let's go there. I suppose we can get there in a single hop by disapparation?"

I smiled. "Once again, think very remote. I think it would take us at least two hops to get there."

Ginevra shook her head. "I keep forgetting how huge your country is. Well, good for us. Get us some good maps so that I can do the disapparation and we can be on our way."

We packed, but before we left, I suggested some additions. "We need sunscreen, sunglasses, hats, and durable walking shoes to go down to the southern tip of Texas."

Ginevra sighed. "I suppose you know what you're talking about."

"You bet I do. That's not all, of course. We will need bottled water and some energy bars as well, but we'd be better off getting them when we're there."

"Where to, then?"

"We can get most of that at a drug store."

She looked puzzled. "You have stores that sell drugs?"

"Well, among other things. Nowadays, it's mostly other things. Let me look up a drugstore near us." I did. It turned out to be on our street and within six blocks. I suggested walking. Ginevra agreed. Along the way, we talked about supplies. She asked why we needed sunscreen.

"Well, there is this thing called skin cancer. I know that you think you're immortal and can't be harmed by things like cancer, but . . ."

She grabbed my arm and stopped our walk. "I know I'm not immortal. That's the point. I want to enjoy life for the little time I've got until Riddle or a Deatheater kills me. In England, you just don't get that much sun. I want a good tan before I leave."

I nodded. "I get that. I have an uncle who had skin cancer. It was treated and he survived that, but later he developed another form of cancer and died in a couple of years. Maybe the two cancers weren't related. Maybe. I just don't want you to die of cancer."

She smiled. "Right. You want me to die at the wand of Riddle."

We reached the CVS then. Inside, we quickly collected the supplies that I wanted. Ginevra commented, "You can buy sunscreen, but you can't make me use it."

I mumbled, "Is everyone in your universe as stubborn as you?"

She said, "No. A lot are more pig-headed."

I said, "We'll look at the *Yellow Pages* to find an REI."

She shook her head, "You know that I don't know what that is."

"Oh, it's an outdoor sporting supply store. They'll have good footwear and good hats/caps."

I found an address. Ginevra disapparated us there. Inside, we found the selection of footwear to be narrow, but we found good options for both of us. The hats were not to Ginevra's taste, but I bought one for her anyway. Back at the hotel we finished packing. We took our scant luggage down to the Business Office where I printed off maps of Marathon, TX where the Gage Hotel is; Big Bend National Park; and Texas. The last map we would use for guidance in choosing a disapparation middle point. We were too far to disapparate directly to the Gage Hotel.

She looked at the map and said, "I suppose San Angelo is a good mid-point. Are you ready?"

I admitted it. She held out her hand. I took it. Our first stop dropped us onto a park-like campus of a university. She smiled and said, "Don't you wish this were our final destination?"

"Oh, yes. This would be great. Prepare for a change." She took my hand again and we were off.

We reappeared on a dry, dusty side street. Ginevra looked around and asked, "Are you sure this is it?"

I saw a larger street at the end of the short street we were on. "Let's walk down that way." At the end was a broad street that might have been part of the main street of any small American town. Standing out like a rose in a field of dandelions was the Gage Hotel. Ginevra looked at it and said, "Maybe you do have a winner here."

We entered the lobby. It was empty other than the desk clerk. I greeted her. She welcomed us but started to apologize because she didn't have any open rooms.

Ginevra reached into her handbag and asked, "Are you sure that you didn't just have a last minute cancellation."

The clerk glanced down briefly at her computer screen and said, "Why, you know, you're right. We do have an open room. How long do you want it?"

I stepped up. "Can we have it for four nights?"

She glanced down to the computer screen for about a tenth of a second and said, "Oh, yes! That wouldn't be a problem at all. Can you fill out this guest information card?"

I nodded and started to fill out the card. I saw Ginevra start to reach for her bag again. I took her arm and said, "I can finish this without help. Why don't you take a seat? We'll be in our rooms shortly."

The oh-so-helpful clerk added, "Yes, ma'am. This won't take a second." I finished the brief card. The clerk asked, "How will you be paying for this?"

"Credit card."

"Excellent. May I have the card and your ID?"

I handed her the card and my passport. She glanced at both and ran the card. She said, "We'll put a hold for one thousand dollars on the card, which covers the four days." I thanked her and accepted the two keys. We went up to our room quickly.

When we arrived, Ginevra fixed me with a baleful glare. "One room! One bed!"

I tried to smile. I said, "It's your bed. I'll sleep on the floor. I'll sleep in the WC if you want me to."

She continued to glare but relented and said, "I think this hotel has a restaurant. Let's have dinner."

We went down to the lobby. Sure enough there was a restaurant off the lobby. We were seated quickly and perused the menu. I commented. "This is typical western fare. There's a lot of Tex-Mex. They have salads if you don't want to take your luck with fish tacos or stuffed pepper. I don't say that I think you'll not like it. The thing is that every chief has a different idea about spices."

Ginevra smiled and said, "I like to be adventurous with food."

I smirked. "Just remember that when the food arrives."

I ordered the fish tacos. Ginevra ordered a chimichunga. They came out quickly. Ginevra's comment was, "Well, Hogwarts, it isn't. As a matter of fact, it isn't even my Hogwarts, which is not anything like your Hogwarts."

I objected, "This isn't bad. It's not spectacular, but it's decent."

Ginevra just nodded. "Right. Not spectacular."

We decided to take a walk around town after dinner. The sun was close to setting, but there wasn't a lot of town to see. The main street had several touristy stores and a restaurant. When you got off the main street, the town was pretty dismal. There was a store that had just closed that looked like it must be a small grocery. I noted it for the next day when we'd want to buy water bottles and fixings for sandwiches for lunch.

At the end of our short walk when it was beginning to get seriously dark, I was running out of things to do. Back at the hotel, I bought the local paper, *The Alpine Gazette*. I suggested that we could read it until it was time for bed.

# Whose Bed is it Anyway?

When Ginevra had finished reading the front page, she declared, "Well, if I were excited by news from Alpine, Texas, I might just read the rest of the paper. However, I kind of lost interest below the fold with the article on the start of the winter semester at Sul Ross University."

I countered, "You haven't seen the crossword puzzle."

She glanced at the grandfather clock in the Lobby and noted the time, 8:15 PM. Then she asked, "Are you good at crosswords?"

"I always work the crossword in *The Times of London.*"

She scoffed. "Work or finish?" However, she had a smile on her face. She asked, "Group effort?"

I answered, "No other way."

So we worked the *Alpine Gazette* crossword puzzle. It took us about fifteen minutes. That includes my going to the bar of the restaurant to get two coca-cola's. When we finished the cokes, we were back to the problem. So, we went up to our room. When we got there, a really strange conversation ensued.

Ginevra said, "OK. You get the bed."

I said, "What? I thought I said that you could have the bed."

"Yes, but you deserve the bed."

"How in the world do I deserve the bed?"

"Well, you paid for the hotel room. The bed is yours."

"Look. You have to put up with me because we have to share a room. You deserve to have the bed."

She looked down to the floor and said softly, "The room was so very expensive that you deserve the bed."

"That was nothing."

"Nothing? A thousand dollars is a lot, isn't it? What is that in galleons?"

"Oh, I guess around four hundred galleons."

She gasped, "Four hundred galleons! That is half of my dad's monthly salary. How can you say that's nothing? Besides. If I have the bed, don't you expect . . . oh something in return?"

Then it dawned on me. I said, "No. I don't know what the standards in your universe are, but if I offer you the bed, it's an unconditional offer with no strings attached not to be repeated. Do you still not want the bed?"

She said, "No. It's yours."

I said, "Thanks. If you get changed in the bathroom, I'll find blankets and a pillow for you for the floor."

She sort of stared at me, but she took her handbag to the bathroom. I found the blankets and pillow in the closet and made a makeshift bed on the floor. When she came out of the WC, she looked at the little bed rather glumly, but rolled up in the blankets.

I went into the WC and changed. When I got out, she seemed to be asleep. I slipped into bed as silently as I could. Then she asked, "You really meant that about me having the bed."

"Sure."

"And it's too late to change my mind?"

"I told you. You get one chance. I'm a man of my word."

"So, I'm down here for the rest of the stay?"

"No. Just tonight. The offer is open tomorrow."

That was all that I heard from her until the bedside alarm clock went off. I groggily lifted my head off the pillow and asked the only intelligent question in that situation, "Whut?"

Ginevra said, "I want the bed?"

"Yeh. Tomorrow night."

"Right. You said I could ask tomorrow."

"So." Then I looked at the alarm clock. It was 12:02 AM. I said, "Yes. You have it this evening—and the rest if you want them."

"Yes, I do. Thanks." Then she added. "I don't have to pay for the privilege with any favors?"

"Of course not."

"Good night, Wendt."

"Good night, Weasley."

☐

The next morning, Ginevra was up before I was. She had already showered and dressed. She was wearing very serviceable clothes for hiking in the desert. I kidded her a little. "Very stylish shoes."

She grimaced and said, "Charming of you to notice. Did you also notice that I've applied sunscreen liberally? Do we breakfast in the hotel?"

"No. I think there is a small restaurant down the street. Why don't we try it?"

She had no objection, so we went down to the lobby and proceeded down the street to the Paradise Cafe. It was a small storefront, but there were several people already seated and enjoying breakfast. Inside, we were seated and looked over the menu. As we read, Ginevra was looking at the other customers. The menu was not lengthy, so we quickly chose our breakfasts. As we waited for our food, she leaned over and asked, "What's with the strange outfits of those men over at that table?"

I shrugged. "They appear to be cowboys with typical wear: hats, chaps, boots. I see that a few have spurs."

Her mouth dropped open. "You're kidding, right?"

"No, those are real spurs. I think there are real working ranches around here."

The food was quite good. I'd just ordered eggs sunny side up and biscuits. She'd ordered pancakes and sausage. We both agreed that it was the best we'd had so far in the States.

When we finished, I suggested that we do some shopping for lunch at the grocery that we'd seen the night before. It doesn't take more than a few minutes to get anywhere in Marathon, so we were quickly shopping at the grocery. We bought a couple of cold cut sandwiches, an apple, a banana, a couple of large cookies, and several bottles of water. Outside the grocery, she slipped it into her capacious handbag, and we were ready for a day of fun in the sun.

She asked, "Where do we disapparate?"

I had a map of Big Bend from the hotel. I opened it, pointed out where we were and where the main visitor center was. I said, "Let's go there first."

The visitor center had its own general store. I kicked myself for not waiting until we were there to purchase lunch. There were also camp sites and some cabins. Ginevra was already grousing. "Why didn't we stay here?"

I sighed. "First, these locations are probably reserved six months in advance. There would be a row that we don't need if you'd confunded park personnel to get us in."

She pouted but said nothing. I went on, "Second, the Gage has air conditioning and other amenities that are nicer than these."

She sort of grunted and said, "I suppose you're right about that."

We spent enough time in the visitor center to look at exhibits and attend a half-hour lecture about the park and what you could do at this location. It turned out that there was a good deal. There were several trails of varying difficulty that led up into the hills. We decided to try one in the morning and one in the afternoon. The morning trail was more difficult than either of us expected. When we'd gotten back we'd nearly exhausted our water and were more than ready for lunch.

In the afternoon, we reconsidered the longer, harder trail that we had originally decided to take. Instead, we got a recommendation to visit another visitor center. We did. It had another set of exhibits. The most interesting was a cactus garden that included a wide variety of cacti and explanatory signs. We were not in a great hurry, so we spent a good bit of the afternoon slowly walking the trail and reading signs. By mid-afternoon, we were hot, tired and had sunburn.

Ginevra complained, "I thought the sunscreen was supposed to prevent this"

"Well. You have to apply it every couple of hours for it to be effective."

She added, "I'm absolutely bushed. Why don't we go back to the Gage?"

I was completely in agreement. When we got back to our room, Ginevra asked, "How can I be so tired? We did some walking, sure, but I shouldn't be so pooped."

"Intense sun, sunburn, partial dehydration will take its toll. We need to remember that for tomorrow. For the time being, let's take a nap and have dinner."

She said, "Agreed. I get the bed, right?"

"Sure. Enjoy." The maid had put away the makeshift sleeping bag on the floor. I almost just lay down on the floor and slept.

Instead, Ginevra said, "I'm not a troll. Just nap up here on the bed with me. It's the most gigantic bed I've ever seen. I won't even know you're on it."

I was too tired to argue, so I gave up on the floor, slipped off my shoes, and collapsed on my side of the bed. After what seemed like ten minutes, it was dark and someone was shaking me. "Get up you sluggard. We've got to get down and have supper."

I groggily got up and mumbled something in agreement. I put on my shoes, and we were off to supper. This time we ordered quickly because we already knew the menu. We both ordered water and something stronger to drink. I tried to talk Ginevra into ordering Jameson's, but she was dead set against anything Irish. She ordered Dewars.

We talked about the day and the exhaustion that we were still suffering. She said, "I'm in no hurry for dinner to arrive."

I agreed. "No argument from me. I think this is the best part of the day."

She seemed to be looking off into the distance and said, "Oh, yes. Right. What are we doing tomorrow?"

I asked, "Aren't the troubles of the day sufficient for the day?"

She laughed. "Right. Let it be a surprise, but I swear that if it involves hiking through this desert, I might just disapparate us to someplace where there's snow on the ground."

"I certainly am not going to tell you then."

We spent the rest of the evening waiting for dinner and slowly enjoying it when it did arrive. Back in our room, we worked the crossword in the San Antonio paper. If I'd know it was available, we'd have done it the previous night. When we thought it was time for bed, Ginevra invited me to share the bed.

"Nope. I promised you'd have exclusive use of the bed. That is final. I'll enjoy the floor."

She whined, "Oh, don't be silly. I know that my virtue is safe. Why not get a good night's sleep?"

"I will—on the floor."

She knew me well enough to know that I would not be dissuaded, so she shut up. We prepared for bed and turned out the light. She said, "Night, Wendt."

"Night, Weasley."

⊓

The next morning, we were both rested and ready for another challenging day, relaxing in the sun.

Breakfast was at the Paradise, which we shared with the same cowboys as before. Ginevra wanted to know where we were going today. I was cagey. "Well, I'm reserving that as a little surprise."

"It's hard to see it as a surprise. The desert is all the same."

All I would say was, "We'll see."

When we left the cafe, I got out my area map and said, "Can you take us to San Antonio?"

Ginevra asked, "That name is vaguely familiar. Where is it?"

I pointed on the map and added, "If you could put us in the Alamo, it would be just peachy." The Alamo was marked on the map.

She said, "I think we can manage that." With that she held out her hand. We both glanced around to be sure no one was watching and we disappeared. We appeared across from the Alamo in a little alley. She asked, "Is that the Alamo?" She pointed at a wall. "And what is it?"

"The Alamo is an old Catholic mission that dates back to the time the Spanish owned this part of the States. It was a place where Texans, who were revolting from the Mexicans who owned the area at the time, made a stand. All the Texan soldiers were killed, but their families were spared.

63

Anyway, although it's an interesting place from the history of the States, it's not what we're here to see."

She said, "Good. Looks boring, but the weather is more pleasant than back at Big Bend. What are we here to see?"

"There's a bend of a river that runs through this part of the city. It's been developed commercially and is pretty interesting. Let's go."

She laughed. "What is it about you people and bends in rivers? I hope it's more interesting than where we were yesterday." She then held out her hand.

"We're going to walk there. It's only a few blocks away."

She shrugged and said, "I suppose the old-fashioned way is OK."

I was none too sure about how to get there, but I knew that if we kept walking in the general direction, we'd cross the river. As a matter of fact, it was almost a quarter hour before we crossed it. Ginevra looked around and asked, "What's the big deal? It's just another big city."

I said, "Follow me." I led her across a bridge and then down a set of inconspicuous stairs that led to the river proper. When we got to the bottom, the river stretched out with broad walks on both sides lined with restaurants and shops."

She hit me on the shoulder and said, "I guess you know what you're talking about. Which way?"

I said, "It doesn't matter. Just start walking and try not to walk into the river."

She asked, "Is it deep?"

"No. I think you could wade through a lot of it." As we walked, we passed a restaurant that had seating next to the river. Ginevra asked if we could order a tea and sit by the river. I was satisfied with that. We went to the *maître'd* and asked to be seated by the river. There were not a lot of people sitting outside. It was a cool day, after all, so he seated us. As we sat, there was foot traffic walking past, river traffic, and birds.

Ginevra asked, "Why didn't we come here to start with?"

"It's still pretty busy. We'd be a lot more likely to be noticed."

We ordered and were served. We silently watched the traffic around us. I was beginning to think that we'd stay there for the entire day, but Ginevra suggested that we move on. She said, "I suppose we'll not find another nice location like this."

"Don't be so sure." We paid our bill and proceeded to walk along the river.

After a while we reached a place where there was a small amphitheater on one side and a small array of seats on the other. Ginevra grabbed my arm to stop me. "Is this a for-real theatre or what?"

"Sure it is. I think that there are plays here some evenings. If you're on a riverboat, you can catch parts of the play as you drift past or you can buy a ticket and watch from here."

She grit her teeth for some reason. We continued our walk. After a while we reached a spot where you could buy tickets to ride one of the river boats. I asked her if she wanted to go boating. She grit her teeth again and said, "Maybe later."

I nodded. "We should do that after the sun sets. I hear that the lights along the river are beautiful."

We just kept walking. We reached a little bay off the river that was surrounded by a building. It had a dense collection of shops and food establishments. I suggested that we have a late lunch. She agreed. We picked a place that had a view of the river. While we were waiting to be served, a small Mariachi band went to the little island in the center of the bay and began playing.

She asked, "What kind of band is that?"

"Oh, it's a Mexican band. They call them Mariachi's. I'm afraid that I'm not much of a fan of accordions, but a little of their music is nice to listen to. Also, a little goes a long way."

After we'd finished the late lunch, we walked through the mall at the upper level. We'd not gone far when Ginevra grabbed my arm and said, "Stop!"

"Ok. Did you see something that interests you?"

"Oh. I just can't stand any more of this. Let's go back to our hotel."

I said, "Yeh, a little of this commercialism goes a long way too. Please, let's just go back and walk through the Alamo before we leave. You shouldn't come to San Antonio and not visit the Alamo."

She was not totally sold on the idea, but she agreed to at least see the interior. I said, "Let's take the quickest way out." We went through a dark hall that took us past a movie theatre and out of the mall. I could see that we were very close to the Alamo. I pointed at an entrance to a building and said, "I think that if we go through it, we can have a short-cut to the Alamo entrance."

Ginevra was unsure, but I took her hand and led her in. It turned out to be a hotel. There was one long corridor that led to the lobby. About half way there, I noticed a small pub off to the right. I thought it might bring a whiff of her home to her, so I dragged her into it. "Let's have a drink before we go to the Alamo."

She agreed. I ordered two Jamesons on ice. She selected a quiet booth in a corner. When we were seated, I asked, "What's going on with you? I thought you were having a good time?"

She was almost at the point of tears. She took a gulp of her drink and almost sobbed, "That's the problem! I found myself wishing that we wouldn't have to go back and take Riddle on. This is way too nice."

"Well, I admit that San Antonio is a place that's designed for vacations, but . . ."

"No! It's all too nice. Everywhere we've been is wonderful—even Big Bend. Where I come from, Wizards have it a lot better than Muggles, but even Wizards don't live as well as you all do here."

I frowned. "Oh, there are plenty of poor people and downtrodden. You've just not seen them much."

She pounded her fist on the tabletop. "Well, I don't want to see lots more people having a good time." She took another big gulp.

I said, "OK. OK. Let's just walk through the Alamo. I think it's just outside the main entrance of this hotel. We should be able to disapparate from inside." She agreed to that. I decided that it would be better not to walk through the lobby. It would just depress Ginevra more. So, we took the street exit of the small pub. Across the street was the Alamo and just around the corner was the entrance. We walked through the main entrance and walked around the grounds a little without going into any of the buildings. The garden was pleasant without being flashy. I was thankful for that.

Shortly, Ginevra held her hand out to me. There was no one in sight. I knew that this was the end of our stay in San Antonio. I took her hand and we were in a dusty alley in Marathon. We rounded a corner and passed through the pleasant entrance of the Gage. I hoped that wouldn't set off more sadness. She just said, "I'll go up to the room. I want to get a nap in before dinner."

That was fine with me. I said that I'd stay in the lobby and do some reading. We had a late dinner as usual and after dinner went to our room. There was the usual little discussion about whose bed it was tonight. I convinced her that it really was hers. She had accepted gracefully and changed for bed while I waited for the WC. After I got out of the WC and into my home-made bed on the floor, Ginevra said, "'Night, Wendt."

"'Night, Weasley."

We had established a pattern. So the next day was breakfast at the Paradise —no menus necessary. Then we walked out to the sidewalk and around the corner. Ginevra asked where we were going. I had my map out. I pointed to the main visitor center. She nodded, extended her hand, and we were gone.

At the visitor center, we visited the little grocery, bought some things for lunch, and walked outside. Then she asked, "Are we doing a trail?"

"No." I had the map out again and pointed at the very tip of the river. "We're going there."

She shrugged and we disappeared only to reappear in a parking lot. It had been warm at the Gage. Here it was becoming positively hot. We walked on a trail that passed through some reeds on the bank of The Big River. It led up a hillside on a gentle slope. As we climbed, we could see more and more of the river. As we neared the top, the trail became tougher to climb. We reached the top of a ridge and walked out along it. At the end, we had a panoramic view of the river. Directly below us the river executed an almost 360 degree bend. As we looked down, I commented, "I think this is the 'Big Bend'."

Ginevra took a long drink of water from her bottle. She asked, "This is what we came here to see?"

I hadn't thought about it, but I decided that she was right. "I think it is."

She sighed. "I think I'm ready to go back and keep sharp-shooter training going."

"Good."

She looked at me and said, "You know, you needn't be such a task master."

I said, "I thought that was my role. But seriously, I thought we might visit one other place before we were done."

"What's that?"

"Sul Ross University in Alpine." That brought real mirth to Ginevra. "You don't mean to say that someone had the nerve to name a place around here after the cool mountains of central Europe."

"I'm afraid so."

"Then lead on. Get your map out."

I did. Ginevra studied it a minute, and then she held out a hand, which I took. "We materialized on a green campus beside a tree that was obviously well-watered. The grass was green too. In the shade, the air was cool and pleasant."

Ginevra commented, "Well, we might be in England. Of course, the blue skies are rather too blue for this time of year."

We walked around the campus and stuck our heads into the Museum of the Big Bend. It was not the British Museum by a long shot. They did have a nice collection of maps. There was Christian art. It was getting to be time for dinner, so we found a secluded spot and disapparated back to the Gage.

That night over a leisurely dinner, we discussed the next day. Ginevra said, "I suppose that it's your turn for the bed." I agreed. "Tomorrow, why don't we have breakfast here. We've not done that before." I agreed again.

67

There was a long pause. Then she said, "Despite what I said yesterday, I'm not anxious for this . . . uh . . . interlude to be done."

I smiled. I was happy that she had enjoyed it. We could get back to work. Maybe not tomorrow, but certainly the day after. After we were ready for bed that evening, and the lights were out, she said, "I wish I'd come from this world and met you here."

I nodded. Of course, she couldn't see me, but I said, "'Night, Weasley."

She said, "'Night, James."

The next morning, we did have breakfast in the hotel. It was good. They offered some options that the Paradise Cafe didn't. They had crepes, for example. However, we stuck with our usual choices.

After breakfast, we went back up to our room, checked that we had everything packed, and brought our keys down to the lobby where we checked out. The clerk asked if we would review the Gage on Yelp. Ginevra's mouth hung open. I wasn't sure what Yelp was, but I was pretty sure that it must be an online review site. So I said that I certainly would when I got in front of my computer. That was a rather empty promise since I didn't have a computer.

Ginevra and I walked around to a side street. We stood there for a moment. I asked, "Well, are we going?"

She said, "I wish we could have a picture of us in front of the Gage."

"Sure. I don't have a camera nor do you."

She still stalled. "I wonder if anyone at the hotel has a camera."

I was beginning to get worried. Even in a sleepy town like this, we'd begin to attract attention. "Come on. Let's go."

She sighed. "OK." Then she held out her hand. I took it and we materialized in San Antonio outside the Alamo. She gazed wistfully at the hotel across the street that we'd walked through two days before. We were still holding hands. I sort of jiggled her hand to get her moving. She nodded and we were outside the hotel we'd stayed in when we were in Dallas before.

# How Long Before You Give Up?

When Ginevra released my hand, I led her back into our old hotel. They were still able to give us two rooms with a connecting door. We moped up to our room where we agreed to take a nap and then meet for dinner.

Over dinner we were both restless. We were ready to get down to work the next day, but we wanted to do something more like a vacation before to-morrow. I suggested a movie. Ginevra agreed.

We got the *Dallas Morning News* movie section. I scanned through what was currently available. I decided that we'd see *Star Trek*. I found a theatre in Plano, TX that was showing it. We talked before the movie during commercials. She wanted to know what kind of movie this was. I thought for a few minutes and then said, "Well. Do you know what science fiction is?"

She shrugged, "Unreal science?"

I replied, "Well, in good science fiction, only some of it is. Most is real science. The theory is that only a few features are extensions of real science. The rest is supposed to be the real deal."

She smiled. "But I guess this movie has more extensions to science than real science fiction."

I chuckled. "You're right. Let's just say that this is more like fantasy than science fiction."

At that point the movie started. She interrupted at various points, whispering in my ear about the preposterous things that were happening. At the end, as we left, she suggested stopping for a tea at the bar area in the lobby of the movie theatre. We ordered tea.

When we were seated with our teas, I said, "Well, however implausible, you must admit that it was exciting."

She glanced down toward her feet as she said, "Well, yes. It was excit-ing, but it's embarrassing just how much I felt that I was being manipulated by the movie's script. I just wish that the motivations of characters were better." She thought a moment and said, "I can't believe that the things that happened on the screen were all real."

"Oh, you're right. There's this thing that has been present in movies since the very beginning—special effects. Nowadays, almost all movies have some special effects. They can make it seem like things are happening that can't possibly happen or that you're someplace or sometime that can't be reached."

She smiled again. "Well, you're right. I did enjoy the movie. I can see why you thought I'd like it. It was so very different from *Quantum of Physics*."

I almost tried to correct her, but the twinkle in her eye warned me that she was just trying to kid me. I said, "You're right about *Quantum*. You have to be in the right mood for it."

"What kind of mood do you have to be in so that *Quantum of Physics* seems good?"

"You have to be in a mood to punish impudent witches who just want to make fun of you." She laughed at that. Then she said, "I guess we'd better get back to our hotel. Tomorrow comes early in the morning." I agreed.

□

The next morning we were up early and had breakfast in the hotel before proceeding to the practice range. We were the first ones to the range that day. We spent an hour each practicing with our handguns. We'd lost some ground while we'd been on a "vacation". It wasn't a lot, and we assured each other that we'd be back in form before long.

After lunch we switched to the rifle range. We had lost a lot more ground with the rifles than we had with the handguns. At the end of an hour of practice each, we didn't seem to have improved a lot.

At dinner that night, we talked about the day. Ginevra said, despair heavy in her voice, "We're never going to get to the point that we can kill Riddle from a distance."

I said, "Well, let's give ourselves a week of practice. At the end of that time, we can seek professional help."

She laughed. "You mean like your 'Doctors'?"

I laughed, too. "No. I mean." I hesitated, "I mean like a professional trainer."

She turned serious. "Won't that blow our undercover or whatever you call it?"

70

"Everyone we talk with is a risk. Sometimes, you just have to take a risk to get where you want to be."

She grimaced but said nothing.

During the next couple of days, we regained our handgun proficiency and even improved it, but the rifles were coming along only slowly. On Friday, I asked the owner of the range for suggestions for someone serious to help us.

He nodded and said, "I know an old Army Ranger who sometimes will do a little tutoring. I'll get in touch with him and see if he'll talk with you."

Ginevra was still depressed but was still soldiering on.

⊓⊔

The next Tuesday, I had a call on my cell phone from someone who said that he'd been referred to me for a little training.

I agreed to meet him. We were to meet at the rifle range at one in the afternoon. When we arrived after lunch, there was a neat, short-haired, muscular man wearing jeans and an underarmor T-shirt waiting for someone. We were the someones. He introduced himself. We introduced ourselves.

The first thing he said was to ask us, "You're not from around here, are you?"

I said, "No. I'm originally from Ohio, but Ms. Weasley is from England."

He nodded and said, "I'd have guessed England for the little lady, but you have a bit of the Brit about you. I could see you as mid-east. So, I hear you want help with your marksmanship. Just how good do you want to be?"

Ginevra smiled and asked me, "Yeh. Just how good do we want to be?"

I said, "I'd like to be able to hit a cantaloupe at about a kilometer. It would be nice if Ginevra could do the same, but I don't think she needs quite that much accuracy."

He frowned. "Who is the cantaloupe?"

I shrugged.

He nodded. "Not anybody that I'd know, right?"

I said, "Maybe you're not the right man for this job."

He said, "I'll decide if I'm the right man for the job. Now, let me see how good you are."

I took the first turn. I set up my SR-25 and prepared to fire." He said nothing. I lined up the scope on my target and fired twice. The second one caught the edge of the outer ring of the target.

He hummed. Then he asked, "How long have you been practicing?"

71

"We took most of a week off last week. Before that it was over two weeks."

He said, "Not awful for a couple of weeks self-taught."

I corrected him. "We had a couple of days of training before that."

"Like I said, not awful for a couple of weeks. Let's see the little lady's style."

She gritted her teeth. I watched carefully for signs that she would reach into her handbag. She didn't. She did say, "I'm not that good. No need to see me."

He said, "I don't want to know how good you are. I want to know what bad habits you've gotten into that I'll have to train you out of. So, down on the ground and let's see you shoot."

Her mouth relaxed. She got on the ground with her rifle, set up, and fired twice. Neither hit the target.

He said, "I'll help you. Now, to start with, I've got a question. Why the automatic rifles?"

I said, "We might have to get several rounds off in a short period of time."

He nodded. "Yup. I'll get you inside the target before we're done."

That was the beginning of a week on the range. We each did an hour in the morning and the evening. Our trainer taught us how to adjust the scope for distance and windage. He had us take all the time that we wanted between shots. He rushed us through shots as quickly as we could pull the trigger. He lectured us on how to set up for the shot.

The last day that he agreed to help us, I was hitting inside the ring 75% of the time. Ginevra was hitting 25% of the time. His final advice was, "OK. Keep practicing. Ginevra, I think you can reach 50%. Wendt, I think you can hit 90% or more. Keep working until you hit that level.

"Now, you're traveling to somewhere else that you'll actually use these pieces." It was a simple statement of fact. "Now, it's on you getting your weapons into the country you're going to. I don't want to hear that you were stopped in an airport."

I smiled. "I think I can guarantee that."

"Pretty sure of yourself, aren't you?" He looked from one to the other of us. Eventually, he said, "OK. I'll buy that. When you get to wherever you're going, you need to sight the guns in and make sure you're at your peak."

Ginevra said, "Good advice. We'll sure do that."

He sighed deeply, "I sure hope so." He turned and walked off without looking back.

I turned to Ginevra and said, "We're really on our own now. Let's take the rest of the day off and start fresh tomorrow."

She was completely agreed. At dinner, I browsed the entertainment section of the *Dallas Morning News*. Ginevra noticed and asked, "Another movie?"

"No. I thought we could go see a play."

She brightened. "What play?"

I could see a battle coming. "Oh, nothing that you've heard of. There's a local theatre group that does minor authors and original works. They're pretty well reviewed. What do you think?"

"Oh, it's got to be better than *Quantum of Physics*."

"Oh, give me a break. It's *Quantum of . . ."*

She said, "I know it's *Quantum of Solace*."

We went to the play and enjoyed it.

Three weeks later, we were on the range doing our practice. At the end of the afternoon session, I toted up our score. "Ninety point seven percent for me. You're in the sixties. I've been the weak link for the last week. We're ready."

Ginevra's eyes wouldn't meet mine as she said, "We really need more practice. This is the first time that you've been over 90%."

I shook my head. "I've been within a point or two all week. How long before you give up? I'm not going to get any better before doomsday—which might be coming along pretty quickly considering how much time we've given Riddle."

She still wouldn't raise her head. She said, "How do we get back to England with the guns?"

I said, "Let's go have dinner and talk that one over."

Back at the hotel, we ordered and started talking it through. Ginevra asked, "What about Muggle means to get back to England?"

"Well, there are two ways—by airplane and by boat. Airplane is theoretically possible."

She supplied the implied word, "But."

"Yes, but the security is really tight when you travel by plane. We'd have to . . . that is, you'd have to confund people right and left. We might not get everyone. We'd almost certainly attract a lot of attention."

"Then by boat."

"Well, the security situation is basically the same but security is not quite so stringent. After all, you can't take over an ocean liner and drive it into Parliament."

She laughed at the idea. That was a good sign. I went on, "So, I think we really need to go by magic. What have you got?"

She concentrated. "Well, almost everything is possible. Almost all are very hard. For example, the easiest would be to get a port key to take us to Edinburgh. The problem is that I can't just walk into the Department of Magic and ask for a port key."

I said, "I've got lots of money if bribery is required."

"Oh, forget the magic of galleons. We'd probably get picked up and sent to whatever corresponds to Azkaban here in the States."

"I've seen people do it. They don't seem to require anything in the way of identification when you ask to buy a port key."

She looked frustrated. "Well, you've not paid much attention, then. You do need to identify yourself. You submit your wand. There's an international registry of wands. What would happen if I submitted my wand?"

"Well, you are Ginevra Weasley. They'd identify you as her, wouldn't they?"

"They might. They might also not identify me as anyone. Then we'd be in trouble. I might do it as a last resort, but not the first thing I'd do."

She went on, "In theory, you could go by broomstick. At a little over a hundred miles per hour, you could do it in thirty or so hours. How does that sound to you?"

"Not so great."

"Of course, disapparation is right out. If you could find the right pair of vanishing cabinets, it would work. My bet is that there isn't a 'right pair' of vanishing cabinets in existence."

I frowned and closed my eyes. I kept them closed and pursed my lips. Then I opened my eyes and smiled. Ginevra made a low keening sound that turned into, "I don't know what you're thinking of, but I don't like it on principle."

I smiled at that. "No. No. It's not so bad. I think it might just work. Let's take another look at disapparation."

She shook her head and chuckled. "Well, the furthest that you can disapparate—on a good day—is four hundred miles. It's a lot farther than that across the Atlantic the last time I looked."

My smile broadened. "Yes. And then again, maybe no."

She shook her head again. "Just how would that work?"

"Well, I haven't checked the mileage, but you could do it in eight or ten steps. First, you get to Newfoundland. That's easy."

Ginevra mumbled, "Easy for you to say."

I went on undeterred. "From Newfoundland, Greenland's a short hop—probably only two or three hundred miles."

"OK. Go on."

"We'd have to jump to the right point near the Eastern coast of Green-land, but from there to Iceland is probably less than four hundred miles."

She scoffed, "Then what?"

"Well, we'd probably have to jump to the eastern edge of Iceland, but from there we could probably reach some set of islands north of Scotland."

Her frown had disappeared. "And?"

"And from there, we could probably jump directly to Scotland. Once we're in Scotland, the rest is easy as pie."

She tapped a finger on the table. Our meal had arrived, but was getting cold at our places. She asked, "How can you check those distances?"

I smiled. "Oh, there are some great mapping apps that can calculate those distances."

"Well, why don't you get on that? As much as I would like to take a boat cruise to Europe, I just can't resist the temptation to disapparate across the Atlantic."

We finally turned our attention to our cooling meals.

It took two days to collect the information, but I came back from the nearest library with a list of coordinates for jump points and printed maps of each of them. We met in her room. It turned out that there were more than a dozen points. Ginevra looked at the sheaf of maps and waypoints in dismay. She said, "God, how I wish you had gotten a two-way port key from your Ginny."

"She isn't my Ginny, and we were lucky to get what we did get."

"OK. So, we've got a route. It looks like we'll need coats for a lot of it."

"Right. OK. So, we need a duffel bag with an expandable interior for all the guns and ammo and accessories."

She had less problem with that than I had with the maps. We visited a luggage store. We found a relatively small bag that had a wide mouth. Back in her room, she performed a spell on it to make the interior variable in size. Then we went back to REI where we bought some cold weather gear. The sales clerk in the store was rather surprised that we wanted parkas and lined boots in the spring, so far from fall let alone winter. Ginevra reached into her handbag. I suppose she was intent on confunding him. However, I took her wand arm and restrained it. I said to her, "It will be alright."

Indeed it was. The clerk had to go into the back room to see if there was left-over inventory from the winter. He found two parkas that would serve. He asked how we were going to use them. I provided an answer. "We're going to help some people open a hunting/fishing lodge in northern Ontario. It's still pretty cold up there.

The clerk smiled knowingly. "I went on a fishing trip up there a few years ago myself. It was a beautiful lodge on a crystal lake. I'm trying to remember the name."

While he was recollecting, I remembered a name. "Could it have been the Ludlow resort."

"No way! You are going to work for the Ludlow resort?"

I said, "I can't tell you if we are going to work for Ludlow or not."

He winked and said, "Sure, sure. I get it. Wink. Wink. Nod. Nod."

Ginevra's eye winked surreptitiously. We paid for the gear and left. Back at our hotel, Ginevra asked, "Was that an incredibly lucky guess about the Ludlow resort?"

"A bit of luck, but the Dursleys worked for a resort in northern Canada when they lived there while running away from Riddle and the Deatheaters. There must be several resorts up there, but it wasn't that surprising that it was the same one."

"OK. What is your plan once we get back to England?"

I had to laugh. "I might ask the same question of you. I'll tell you what. I'll start making a broomstick level view of what we should do. Add to it. Correct parts as you feel necessary.

"First, we need to make preparations to go to your universe. So what are our major objectives there?"

She shrugged. "Well, we have to get Ron to help us get into the Chamber of Secrets so that we can find some basilisk fangs. First, we need to get into Hogwarts to get those fangs. Then, assuming that you're right about the final horcrux being in the Room of Requirement, we search for it and destroy it. I think that's everything."

"That's a good start. Questions: Will it be easy for us to get into Hogwarts? How long will it take us to find the horcrux?"

Ginevra's answers were, "Getting into Hogwarts has gotten harder. Of course, we can't disapparate in. I think all the floo connections are password protected. The place is guarded. I don't think they work hard at it, but we can't just walk up to the front gate and come in without a good reason.

"You said that Harry found the horcrux pretty quickly. So, I don't know. Maybe give us a day or two. Say a couple of days—worst case."

I thought about that. "Well, I heard that there was a direct tunnel into Hogwarts Room of Requirement from the Hoggshead. Does Abeforth still run it?"

That made Ginevra run a hand through her hair. "I'm not sure. I can't imagine that anyone else would run it."

"Well, then, we'll have to do some research into that. It would be really convenient if that were still going. But we've got to assume that Murphy's Law is still working."

"Murphy's Law?"

"Oh, it's a Muggle aphorism. 'Anything that can go wrong will go wrong.'"

"Great! You Muggles are real worry-warts."

"You bet. It keeps us alive. Anyway, I think you may be too optimistic about finding the Horcrux."

"Why? You say that Harry found it in a few hours."

I said, "Like calls to like."

Ginevra grumbled, "Another Muggle aphorism, I suppose."

"As a matter of fact, yes. In this case, it means that since Potter was a horcrux himself, he had an affinity for other horcruxes. He just kept finding them—and pretty easily, too."

Ginevra frowned, "Do you mean that he was evil. I admit that he had a temper at times, but . . ."

"No, I don't mean that exactly. I mean . . . well, think about it. He started off knowing where absolutely none of them were. They could have been almost any object located almost anywhere. He had virtually no help. He found all of them—ALL—in what? Nine months? Almost miraculous without some form of help."

She was still not happy, but said, "I get it. The horcruxes helped him find them."

"Right. And we won't have that help."

She was truly glum now. "The horcrux may actually keep us from finding it."

I said, "We might have one advantage."

She scoffed. "What would that be?"

"You."

She exclaimed, "Me!"

"Yes, you. After all, you had the first horcrux that was found. You found it even before Dumbledore or anyone had a hint that there was even such a thing as horcruxes. Do you really think that it was totally luck that Malfoy dropped it in your book bag?"

"You mean that it had an affinity for me in some way?"

I shrugged, "Could be. The bottom line though is that we may take a long time finding it."

"So?"

"So, how do we eat while we're in the Room of Requirement? Do we go out and get the house elves to provide food for us?"

Ginevra laughed. "No. House elves are loyal to their masters, in this case the Deatheaters who are running Hogwarts. They'd report us in a Ministry minute. If we get in via the Hoggshead, maybe we get Abeforth to supply us with food."

I sighed and shook my head. "I think it's chancy just getting him to let us in through the secret passage. We've got to have a better source of food."

She said, "It sounds like you have an idea."

I nodded.

"Well?"

"I need to do some research first. But there's another issue that I think we need to deal with while we're in your universe."

She leaned her head over to one side and gave me a quizzical look, "What?"

"Well, let me review our plan. The dragon's-eye view is that we destroy the last horcrux and then return here to kill Riddle."

"Yes."

"I think he's likely holed up either at the Malfoy residence or the Riddle estate."

She seemed to be getting impatient. "I'll stipulate that. Come to the point."

"OK. I will. If we don't pick him off by being snipers from a distance, we'll have to go inside and find him. We'll disapparate from room to room. That will take inside information about the layout of the hideout. The best way to get that is to practice in those places in your universe."

She was still grimacing, but said, "OK. I don't know if the Malfoy place is occupied, but probably the Riddle estate isn't. I guess you've got a point. That will take more time and require more supplies."

"Right. I'm going down to the Business Office to make some more maps for you."

"I'm coming too. I want to see what you've got in mind."

We went down. I got on the Mapquest site and printed some maps of northwest Europe."

Ginevra watched and said, "What would we be doing in Europe?"

"Scavenging for food."

She frowned. "What's wrong with London?"

"Let's finish packing and get on our way."

Ginevra reminded me that we had to pick up our rifles. I agreed. "Right. Let's go pick them up."

After arriving at the gun shop, we requested our rifles. The owner asked, "Does this mean that you're moving on?"

I said, "I'm afraid so. We've learned everything that we can."

Always ready for a sale, he suggested, "You'll really need a carrying case for your rifles."

I agreed. It would be incredible to just walk out of the store with our rifles held in our hands. He tried to sell us on fancy leather carrying cases. I insisted on the least expensive.

"Surely, after spending all that money on these beauties, you don't want them to be damaged accidentally while carrying them in cheap cases."

My patience was wearing thin, but I stuck to my guns—so to speak. I said, "Just get the cases." He reminded me that I should stock up on ammunition. He was partly right. I didn't expect to get in a gun battle with the rifles the way I might with the handguns. I bought a couple of boxes of cartridges for each rifle. I decided to buy a lot of ammo for the handguns. That pleased him.

He commented, "I see why you're going cheap on the carrying cases. You're arming up for a . . . Well, you're pretty well-armed for the handguns." As we walked out of the store, he called after us, "Hope you return some time. You're among the best customers that I have."

I turned back and said, "Well, we're really pretty unlikely to come back to Dallas, but who knows? Good luck."

So we went back to our room. We loaded the rifles into the extensible case along with most of the ammunition. I insisted that we carry at least some ammunition for the guns with each of us as well as the gun bag.

We patrolled our rooms to make sure that we'd not left anything behind. I went down to the lobby to check out while Ginevra moved our things into the hall. When I got back, I said, "Let's put the parkas on so we'll be ready when we leave."

She grumbled, but we did. We both had a bag or two in hand. I named our next destination, "Springfield, Missouri." I had the map out that showed both Dallas and Springfield. Ginevra was studying it when a maid came out of a room. She stared at us. I just smiled.

Ginevra said, "I've got it. What's the food we're scrounging for?"

I said, "MRE's."

She shrugged, and we disapparated.

# MRE's

When Ginevra and I landed, we were in an alley. I asked, "Do you want to be sure that we've landed where we wanted to?"

She sneered, "When I disapparate you somewhere, you stay disapparated and you're in the right place."

"OK. OK. So, our next destination is Springfield, Illinois."

"Are you sure? We're in Springfield right now."

"Look, when I give you a destination, I give it to you right. Here's the map."

She studied and said, "You ready?"

"Always." Then we spun through the universe and landed in an alley that was so similar to the one that we'd left that I opened my mouth to ask if she were sure we were in the right place, but a warning look from Ginevra made it clear that we were where we wanted to be.

She asked, "Next?"

"Ann Arbor, Michigan." I had the map out. There was the hesitation as she got herself oriented. She held out her hand, and we were gone. We landed in an alley that was at least different from the previous two.

I handed her the next map and said, "Ottawa, Canada." She took a look at it and held her hand out to me. I took it, but she hesitated. I asked, "What?"

She took a deep breath and said, "This is a long haul, near the limits of my range. I want to be really sure that we can make it."

"Take your time. Safety first."

She continued to stare at the map and then she said, "Ready."

"Are you sure? We can pick an intermediate spot."

She shook her head.

"Then go."

We did.

We were in another alley, but it was definitely cooler than Michigan had been. I handed her the next map and said, "Sept-ille, Quebec."

She looked and said, "Another tough one, but we'll make it." We did. We were standing near a rail yard.

I handed her the next map. "Hopedale, Newfoundland." She looked and shrugged. She held out her hand, and we landed on a gravel road with nothing in sight. It was cool enough that we were glad that we had parkas.

In a bored voice, she asked, "Next?"

"Nouk, Greenland."

She took the map, studied it a minute and said, "Easy-peasee." She took my hand, and we were there. It was desolate and cold. She said, "We're going to need our parkas for sure from here on."

"Right. Our next destination is Kulusuk, Greenland. Here's the map."

She glanced at it, took my hand, and we were there. "Where to next?"

"Reykjavik, Iceland." She little more than glanced at the map. She didn't release my hand, but suddenly we were back in an alley. It was a cold alley. I got out the next map and said, "I can't pronounce this place. Just read it off the map." It was Neskaupstadur, Iceland. She glanced and disapparated. We were in another cold alley. I handed her the next map and said, "Torshavn, Faroe Island."

She nodded. Her comment was, "Kind of long, but we'll make it, no sweat." We did. It was not as cold as the last couple of destinations, but I was still happy about wearing a parka.

I quoted, "Home again, home again, Jiggedy-jig."

She was not up for humor. She asked, "Where to next?"

I handed her the map and said, "The Isle of Skye. That name has always fascinated me. It might be a little long. I've got an alternative, if it is."

She studied the map. "It's not the worst so far. Shouldn't be a problem." She held out her hand, and we were on the rocky, barren island.

I said, "You probably need some rest. I've got a place that can be our safe-house. We can leave the guns there and trust that they'll be safe. It's in London. Let's get there and hole up for a day or two."

She shrugged. "I'll need to do an intermediate. Let's say the Isle of Man since you're fascinated by islands. Then on to your hidey-hole. Where is it anyway?"

It was my original rooming house. Before we'd left, I'd phoned to reserve my old garret, and since there was another room available, I'd reserved that as well. We flashed through the Isle of Man so fast that I barely noticed. We landed in an alley in London that I'd been in many times before. It brought a tear of recognition to my eye.

Ginevra noticed and said, "After all these awful disapparations, you have a hard time with the last, easy one?"

I shook my head. "I just realized that this landing spot was the exact one that Minerva had taken me to many times."

She seemed to resent that even more. She said, "Well, we've hardly begun visiting old haunts. Get a grip on."

We walked around the corner and found the entrance to the old place. I knocked on the door. No one answered. Ginevra reached into her handbag for her wand. I took the arm to stop her. "Just wait a minute. I'll show you a bit of Muggle magic." I opened my purse, got out a credit card, and slid it along the lock bolt. It released, and the door opened. "See."

She shook her head in disgust. I let her in. We went to the kitchen. On the bulletin board, there was an envelope with my name on it. I removed the tack and the envelope. Inside it were four keys—two house keys and two room keys. There was also a note. I started to read it, but Ginevra snatched it out of my hand.

She commented, "It's obviously for me as much as for you." Then she read aloud, "Mr. Wendt. You friend's room is 3D. Yours is the garret. The keys are labeled." There was some sticky tape on each key. Each had one of the following letters on it: G, H, 3D. She said, "Well, we really didn't need two rooms."

I said, "You've not seen my garret. Besides, remember, I'm rich."

She smirked.

We went up the stairs and dropped her bags off in her room. She insisted on coming up to see my garret. The stairs up to it were as narrow as ever. Ginevra insisted on taking my key and going up first. Near the top, she slipped and sort of fell back on me. She said, "See, it's good that you let me go up first."

"Right."

She opened the door. The interior had hardly changed. There were the one narrow bed, the armoire, the two chairs and table. There was the one window. The sloping roof was only slightly taller than I on the edges of the room. Ginevra took it all in while pirouetting once. "Well, I can see why you prefer this to my room."

"Yeh. There's nothing so cozy as this room. Let's look for dinner."

□

We found the small Italian restaurant that I'd visited many times. We arrived just after they technically began dinner service. Technically, but not actually. That was OK with me. We had a lot to talk over.

"OK. Ginevra, you wanted to know about MRE's."

"Yeh. What are they?"

"The name is an acronym for 'Meals Ready to East'. They were designed for the US Army. They are prepackaged complete meals with all the nutrition that you need to go indefinitely."

Ginevra sneered, "But none of the flavor."

"Probably not. They keep forever. They're compact and pretty light weight. They have everything you need in them. You don't need water or a fire to prepare them. They're ideal for keeping us alive in the Room of Requirement while we search it."

Ginevra smiled. "You seem to have thought of everything. That's lucky. You can't create food magically. So, what do we do? Walk up to a US Army base and ask for some?"

"Well, sort of."

"Oh, come on."

I took a deep breath. This was going to require some explaining. "In your universe, the Muggles lost, right?"

"Sure."

"Military disbanded?"

"Right. Pretty darn early on."

"Military bases abandoned?"

She stared at me hard and long. "So, you think there's an Army base somewhere that we can go and loot."

"Yes, but not in this universe. They're still guarded and we'd have to do some fancy confunding to succeed. I was thinking in your universe."

She smiled. "Well, I can't guarantee that they'd not have been looted already, but its worth a try."

I said, "Good. Then that's settled."

Ginevra smiled, "Not so fast, partner. You want to practice disapparating in the Riddle estate over there."

"Right."

"Well, I want to practice disapparating to this base here before we go. Where is it?"

"It's Darmstadt Air Force Base in Germany."

"You've got maps?"

"Sure."

"Well, let's go first thing tomorrow."

"If you feel up to it?"

She laughed. "After today, I could disapparate across Europe in my sleep."

I grimaced. "Good, just don't do it."

"What?"

"Disapparate across Europe in your sleep."

She slapped my back playfully and said, "I'm tired enough to hit the sheets as soon as we get back to the safe-house."

□□

The next morning we didn't disapparate across Europe as soon as we got up. We had breakfast in the kitchen, sharing the table with a couple of other residents. When they had finished and were off to work, I said, "There's something else that we need that I hadn't thought of."

Ginevra asked in a bored voice, "What now? Nothing big, I'm sure. Only a nuclear submarine."

"Oh, this is easy. We should get a couple of pair of good binoculars."\

That actually excited her. "Let's make it omni-occulars!"

I saw just one little problem. "Where are we going to get them?"

The smile subsided off Ginevra's face. "In Diagon Alley. OK. I see the problem. We'll go to one of your REV shops."

"That's REI."

"Whatever."

By this time, Ginevra knew her way around REI's. We gravitated to the binocular display. She smiled at the salesperson who managed to reach us in record time. He asked, "What can I do for the young lady?"

I wanted to disabuse him of any misapprehension that the young lady was unaccompanied. I said, "We're looking for two," I emphasized the word. "Pair of good binoculars. They should have variable magnification, good optics, and be light."

He sized us up and asked, "Is there a price point you're looking for?"

It's always dangerous to say this, but I did anyway, "Price isn't a very important criteria."

He became all business and showed us two pair of binoculars. One was considerably smaller and lighter than the other. That one was almost a pair of opera glasses, but when I looked through them, their quality was apparent. The other larger one had a much brighter field of view. I told him that we'd take those. Ginevra objected, so I compromised. "We'll take one of each."

The salesperson said, "Very good. His and hers."

After we left the REI, Ginevra asked, "Are we finally ready to go?"

"Sure." I handed her a map showing our first destination, Amsterdam.

She smiled, "Piece of cake." We were standing in an alley as usual. "Darmstadt next?"

"You bet. Make it close to the Air Base."

She said nothing, but we were standing on an access road that surrounded the base. I took her arm and said, "We'd better go up on top of that hill. We'll have a good view, but base security won't have as good a view of us." She did it.

We used our binoculars to scan the base. It was huge, sprawling. There were long runways, large hangars, and what I recognized as warehouses. I sighed at the memory from long ago. "Ginevra, do you remember when your dad and I got together shortly after your third year at Hogwarts?"

She nodded slowly. "Sure. I don't remember much about it. You and he went off to do something about Muggle artifacts."

"Right. We came here. I think we stood at this very point, looking at the base. He helped me break into one of those warehouses over there. I found the Muggle artifacts that I wanted. I stole some."

She stared at me. "Somehow, I can't quite picture you as living a life of crime."

"Well, I did. That was one of the darkest days of my life. Riddle had just had Peter Petigrew kill my chessmaster, Cedric Diggory. I was full of hate and determination to kill Riddle."

I was silent for a while. Ginevra broke in on my thoughts, asking, "What did you steal?"

"Hand grenades. I intended to use them to kill Riddle and me."

"It didn't work."

"No. I told you a little about it before. Ironic. I'm back here again, preparing to kill Riddle. Maybe it will stick this time."

She squeezed my hand and after a while asked, "You ready to go?"

"Sure. I've had far too long here."

This time, the return was very fast. We flashed through Amsterdam and were back in my garret. I asked Ginevra, "Isn't it a little dangerous disapparating directly into our safe-house?"

"Oh. I just wanted to drop off our binoculars and then go directly to someplace for lunch."

We stood there a while. I asked, "How about Indian?"

"Sure. I know a good one." She squeezed my hand, and we were in another alley.

The next day we were trying to come up with reasons that we weren't ready to go to Ginevra's universe. I thought that I'd found a good one. I pointed out that we wanted to avoid people in our Hogwarts just as much as we wanted to avoid them in her Hogwarts. She agreed.

Then we looked at the calendar in the kitchen of our rooming house. The date was March 20. The calendar declared that the next day was Good Friday. Hogwarts would be on spring break here and maybe in her universe as well. That sort of clinched it. We went upstairs and packed what we were going to take. Besides clothes there were the handguns. I didn't want to lug around rifles, but handguns—even Ginevra's—could turn out to be handy. So we left the rifles in my garret.

By noon we had everything packed, and we were really committed to go. I asked Ginevra how we would get there. She said, "We'll disapparate to the Isle of Man. Then we'll disapparate to the Forbidden Forest." When I began to object, she said, "Not deep in, just on the inner edge. It will be less than a half-hour walk from there to the main gate of Hogwarts."

I agreed.

Then she took my arm and pulled me to a chair. "Sit."

"Sure. What did we forget?"

"Nothing. There are a few points that we need to cover before we go."

"Go ahead."

She took a deep breath, released it and began. "In my universe Muggles are all, ALL slaves. Most live on agricultural plantations where they grow food for the wizarding population. The few that don't, are the personal slaves of wizards and witches.

"Whenever we're in public, our cover story is that you are my personal slave. As such, you must walk behind me at all times, except to open doors and such. You must never talk to anyone except when asked a direct question. Then you must give the minimum answer required by the question. At all times, your head must be lowered.

"When you are in public with me, you will be subject to abuse of all sorts. You will be verbally assaulted. You will be physically assaulted. I have seen wizards throw stones and excrement at Muggle slaves. You must not EVER show any reaction to these assaults. Is that clear?"

I lowered my head and nodded mutely. That made her laugh. "This is serious!" She was still chuckling. "Oh, you will be the death of me. Literally.

"Now, they will quite likely ask you things like what kind of service you provide for me. They will imply or state outright that you provide me with sex. There must be no reaction. Whatsoever!"

"I understand."

She shook her head. "I wonder if you do." She hesitated. "Are you sure that you want to come with me? I think I can do this by myself."

"Maybe you can. Probably you can. I still want to go. This is my world. It's being invaded. What happened to your world can happen to mine. I want to prevent that."

"You do my world nor yours any good if you screw up and finish our plan before it's fairly started. You get that? Yes?"

"I get it."

She said, "Then pick up the bags. You might as well get used to being my slave."

"Yes, suh, ma'am."

She shook her head. "Oh, shut up. You'd joke while climbing the gallows." Then she held out her hand, and we landed on the Isle of Man. We were there, and then we weren't. We were in a forest. There was a trail that led into a clearing. The clearing opened into a wide open field. In the distance a lake was visible.

I said, "It's good to be home."

Ginevra shook her head. "I still can't believe you teach at Hogwarts. Nowadays in my universe, you can't teach at Hogwarts unless you're a Deatheater or at least approved by a Deatheater."

"Well, let's go. We're burning sunshine." We did. We went through the clearing and then into the open ground and then onto the path that led to the main gate of Hogwarts. We were quickly through the main gate and then through the main entrance. Our goal was the Room of Requirement of course. We had just reached the third floor when Filch appeared around a corner. He got a glance of us and ran toward us. Well, he shuffled very rapidly. There was no point in pretending that we hadn't seen him, so we waited.

He reached us and actually threw his arms around me. "Where in the world have you been? And why haven't you sent an owl or something? What have you been doing?" Then he seemed to notice Ginevra. He said, "It's good to see you, miss Ginny. What brings you here with Wendt?"

I said, "I'm sorry that I've not been able to be in touch with you." I hesitated and noticed Ginevra reaching into her handbag. I took her arm and whispered to her, "Give me a minute here."

I went on. "Here's the deal. Miss Ginny and I are on a very important, secret mission. It's so secret that I can't share anything about it, even with the OBC."

He looked puzzled for a minute and then said, "Sure. The Oldbay Oybay Lubcay."

"Right. I can't even share it with you."

His face fell at that. Then I said, "It would be a great help if you would not let anyone know that we were here."

Filch nodded vigorously and said, "You can count on my discretionism on this conferential mission."

I smiled and said, "You don't know how happy that makes me." His smile widened even further. Then I said, "If you were to go down to your office for about a half-hour, it would be great."

Filch smiled still wider. "You bet. It was about time for a break for me anyway. Good luck. You too, Ms. Ginny."

He disappeared down the stairs. When he was out of sight, we went on to the location of the Room of Requirement. Ginevra took her wand out and said, "I need a place where I hid Snape's Potions book." A door appeared in the wall. It had a rose carved into the center of one panel. I opened the door, and we entered.

It took a few minutes to find the vanishing cabinet. Ginevra opened its glass door and motioned me in. I said, "It might as well have the motto, 'Abandon all hope, ye who enter here.'"

She grimaced and said, "Just go in."

I entered, and she followed after. It was not quite snug for the two of us, but there wasn't much room to spare. Ginevra brought her wand out and pronounced a spell barely audibly. It was a rather lengthy one. I supposed that to get to the right parallel universe, you would require more than a simple spell. Immediately after she finished, the view through the glass walls of the cabinet changed. She took my hand, and we were suddenly standing in the open in an alley. However, the alley was completely different from any other that I'd been in. At its end was a sidewalk. Beside that there was not a street, but a canal. I commented, "Amsterdam?"

Ginevra nodded, and without letting go of my hand, we were on the hill where we'd stood with binoculars looking over the Darmstadt Air Force Base. It was worlds away from the scene that I'd seen the day before. The long airstrips were still there, but through the binoculars you could see plants growing in the seams of the runways. More than one hangar had a partially collapsed roof. The warehouses seemed pretty much intact, but even with binoculars, it was hard to be sure.

I looked in other directions. Streets seemed to be in not much better shape than the airstrips. There might have been a few people walking on the sidewalks. I turned to Ginevra and said, "Gruesome."

She shook her head. "This is the 'pretty' face of Muggle territory."

The sun was close to setting. I said, "Let's start on the warehouses." In response, she nodded and held her hand out. She didn't ask which one to begin with, but I guessed that it didn't really matter. We were inside one of them. It was evidently not the one we wanted. It contained tanks, Hum-Vees, armored vehicles of various sorts.

She said, "Not it, right?"

I nodded.

"We'll try another." I took her hand and we were in a different warehouse. It was dark in this warehouse. She lit her wand. By its light we could read labels on packing crates. The closest ones were labeled M-15. She asked, "What are M-15's."

"Rifles."

Her eyes shone. "We could have come here for rifles."

"No. Keep looking."

We moved around the warehouse and found a variety of items, but no MRE's. We moved on to another warehouse. This time, Ginevra said, "I've got an idea. Stand back."

When she said that I had an idea of what she was going to do. I was right. She said, "Accio MRE." Immediately, we heard something moving in the back of the warehouse. Suddenly, a packing crate flew through the air and landed at our feet. Stenciled on the crate were the words, "Meals Ready to Eat." I congratulated her. Then she said, "Accio pry bar." That really scared me. I had no desire to see a cold steel pry bar flying through the air to me. However, when we saw it flying toward us, she used the "Arresto Momentum" spell to stop it before it landed a blow on one of us.

I used the pry bar to open the packing crate. It was full of MRE's. Ginevra asked me how many we needed. I said, "I think we should have three months worth. Let's say two meals a day for each of us."

She stared at me. "Only two meals?"

"Those meals are intended for young men burning 3000 calories or more a day. Two will be plenty for us." We stuffed the duffel bag that had contained the rifles with them.

Ginevra asked if we should collect other things. I said, "No. I think we've got everything we need. Let's just find your brother and try to get into the Room of Requirement."

She was reluctant, but agreed. So, we sat down, opened an MRE apiece and discussed it over dinner. I asked, "Where's Ron? How do we find him?"

She answered, "When I left he was working for George in the family business."

"You mean the joke shop in Diagon Alley?"

"Right."

"So where does he live? With your parents?"

"Oh, no. He lives in the apartment over the joke shop. Most of the time he's in the building."

"Then we could go there and find him right now?"

She shrugged, "Probably. But there's a difficulty."

I slumped. "What is it?"

"Well, security at all wizarding places has tightened up. The only way into Diagon Alley these days is through the Cauldron."

I could see there were problems coming, but I asked anyway. "So, we have to disapparate to the Cauldron. Then we go through the wall to Diagon Alley. We have to walk down the street and finally enter the store."

Ginevra smiled and said, "Yup. That's it."

"Great! So, I have to practice my shuffle."

She said, "It won't be bad. We'll go early tomorrow morning. Practically no one will be around. We might not even run into anyone other than Tom in the Cauldron."

I thought to myself, "Fat chance of that." What I said was, "Let's stay here tonight, that is, unless you have a better spot?"

She considered and finally said, "My parents would probably let us stay with them." A brief vision of Mrs. Weasley's cooking and a warm bed danced in my head. Meanwhile, Ginevra was going on. "Dad would love to see you, but you know, I just don't want to take a chance with their lives." She finished decidedly, "No!" She thought some more. "There's nowhere else that we could stay that would be better than here. As a matter of fact, no one has been here for years. We're probably as safe here as anywhere in the world."

That was fine. The only little problem was that it had been nearly a decade since the warehouse was heated, and it was looking like a cold night. I said, "I guess we'll need those parkas to stay warm through the night."

Ginevra agreed. "Yeh. I'll put my parka down as a mattress. You cover us with yours."

That wasn't the solution I was expecting, but I didn't have any better ideas. I sure wasn't going to suggest a wizarding inn, and there weren't any Muggle ones anywhere. We sort of ended up huddling for warmth in our clothes. I was still sort of cold, but managed to get a good bit of sleep.

# Basilisk Fangs

When we got up the next morning, we weren't particularly hungry. We decided to hold off eating until closer to lunch. We got organized and were ready for disapparation back to the Cauldron. She took a deep breath and asked, "You're ready to be my slave?"

I nodded.

She took my hand and we were back in Amsterdam briefly followed by the street outside Diagon Alley. It was a dark day. Ginevra led me to the door. I kept my head down both figuratively and literally. She opened the door and entered. I followed closely so the door wouldn't close before I entered. I couldn't tell how many people were in the Common Room of the Cauldron. From the sounds, there were at least a few.

I heard Tom call to Ginevra, "I see you finally got yourself a Muggle." He chuckled and asked, "Anyone I know?"

Ginevra said nothing and walked toward the back door. As she opened it, someone called out. "Does he give good service?" She said nothing. Outside, she used her wand to open the way into Diagon Alley. I couldn't see much, but it seemed dingy and dark.

We were about half-way to the joke shop when someone approached Ginevra and stopped her. Ginevra said, "Well, Lecto, what can I do for you?"

Lecto said, "Well, I see you have a likely-looking Muggle here. I thought you didn't want a slave."

Ginevra said, "Everyone changes. I just thought it would be nice to have someone to do the heavy lifting."

She almost cackled, "Ho! Ho! You noticed someone who appealed to your feminine instincts, eh?"

Ginevra chuckled. "Well, he has his uses."

Lecto walked around Ginevra and squeezed my arm. "Yes. He could do some lifting." Then she pinched my rear—hard. "I reckon he might be fun in milady's boudoir, eh?"

I could hear the smile in Ginevra's voice. "He does have his uses."

She squeezed a thigh and said, "Would you consider loaning him out sometime?"

Ginevra said, "Could be. I'm not tired of him yet."

Lecto walked away. "You be sure to let me know first, you hear?"

Ginevra said, "You can bet I won't forget you."

We resumed walking. We reached the joke shop without further incident. There were a few customers inside. We didn't see either of the brothers Weasley right away. We walked a couple of aisles before encountering George who was working with a customer. He glanced up and noticed Ginevra. He seemed surprised, but he recovered quickly. He said, "Hi, Sis. Ron's back doing inventory. Why don't you go back there. I'll be by in a bit."

She led me to the back room. Inside, we both relaxed. Ron was out of sight, but he heard us enter. "Is that you George?"

Ginevra said, "It's me."

Ron ran around a shelf that was stacked high with boxes. His mouth dropped open, and he said, "You two are the last two people in the world that I would have guessed would come here this day. What happened to you, Ginny? You dropped off the face of the Earth." Then he approached and stared at me. "And who are you?" Almost immediately, he said, "You look an awful lot like a Muggle I once knew." He turned to Ginevra and asked, "You've not taken a slave, have you? I thought you were completely opposed to that vile business." Then he swung around and asked me, "I know you, don't I? You're that Muggle professor at Hogwarts. I thought that you were dead."

I couldn't help laughing. "The rumors of my death are greatly exaggerated." Then I realized that I might just be dead in this version of reality. I added. "Maybe I am."

He threw the clipboard down to the floor and said, "You are no ghost!" Then he looked suspiciously at me. "Are you using Polyjuice Potion?"

I shook my head. "Professor Wendt at your service."

Ginevra grabbed my arm roughly and said, "Don't you dare joke about that!"

Ron laughed, "You don't want to get on the wrong side of Ginny, do you, Sis?"

Ginevra still seemed angry. She said, "We've got to talk seriously. Can you and George close the store early?"

Ron shook his head. "This store is the last thing that George is holding on to after Fred's death and the Deatheater takeover. I'll see if I can talk him into it."

Ron went out front. We overheard parts of a conversation. George had raised his voice. "Well, that's one more reason to close the store early. You've run off the few customers who were here!"

Ron said, "Good. We've got to talk—in the back."

They came into the back room. George's mouth fell open. He ran to me and put his arms around me. "What are you doing here? I was sure that you were dead. Where are you from? How did Ginny get you? Why aren't you dead?"

I said, "That's a lot of questions. Unfortunately, I can't answer any of them."

George laughed. "Typical Wendt. Force the student to work the answers out on his own. Well, I've heard that there was a Muggle hideaway where they were plotting a revolt. You're from there, aren't you?"

"No comment."

Ron asked, "Why are you here? I don't know what you're up to, but you've always been on the thin edge of illegal."

I deferred to Ginevra. "I think you'd better do the talking."

She said, "I need something from each of you. First, George, I need to get into Hogwarts undetected. You were always the expert at getting out and in undetected. What's your idea?"

He just stared at me and said, "Sis, you don't have any idea what this bloke did with us. I couldn't say anything before the final battle because it was all hush-hush. You wouldn't believe what we did." He sighed. "Then after we lost that battle, we didn't dare say anything."

Ron asked, "How do we get in?"

George said, "You know what it is. Go through the Hoggshead. Ginny, you know there was a passage from there directly into the Room of Requirement."

I asked, "Abeforth still runs the Hoggshead?"

"Yes. He is the one fixed point in this crazy spinning world."

Ginevra said, "We've got to get going. Ron, I'm going to ask you to do something for us, but I'm not going to tell you what until we get into the Room of Requirement.

George exclaimed, "Why can't I do it?"

I shook my head. "Sorry, we can't tell you, and we can't tell you why we can't tell you."

George put a hand to his head and said dramatically, "Oh, how will I go on without knowing what Ron can do, but I can't?"

Ron scratched his head and asked, "Yeh. What CAN I do that George can't."

George had a quick answer. "You can make a fool of yourself."

I sighed. "It takes us back to the old school days. We've got to be on our way. I suppose that we have to walk the gauntlet back through the Cauldron to get out of Diagon Alley."

George laughed. "No, it's the opposite of Hotel California. You can hardly get in, but you can always, always leave. You could disapparate directly from here."

Ginny hugged both Ron and George. George wouldn't let go. He asked, "Aren't you going to tell us where you've been these last few months?"

She smiled. "Dear brother, it's strictly need to know."

He immediately followed up, "Yeh. I know. I don't need to know."

He released her and turned to me. "Be careful with our baby sister. She's the only one we've got."

She pulled her wand out of her handbag and said, "I'll show you 'care'." Then she held her hand out to me. I took it. She then asked Ron, "You're going to join us at Abeforth's right away?"

Ron shrugged. "Sure. When haven't I gone off on a dangerous mission without knowing anything about it?"

With that we disapparated. We appeared in a back street of Hogsmeade. I actually recognized it. The Hoggshead was right around the corner. Ginevra tried the door. It was locked. She pounded on it, but there was no answer. She shouted, "You open up Abeforth if you know what's good for you."

There was an answering shout, "I've already called last round, my paying customers have left, and I locked up for the night."

I said, "Come on Abeforth. It's all old friends. Tell you what. We won't pay for drinks if it makes you feel better."

There was indistinct grumbling for a couple of minutes, and we heard the door latch open. Then the door opened, and out of the shadows someone motioned us in. After we entered, he said, "Follow me back to the kitchen. I don't like having the light on in the Common Room after hours." We did follow him.

Once inside the kitchen, he asked, "What would you like to drink?"

Ginevra immediately said, "Butter beer." That was a safe drink. It came in bottles and you didn't have to trust to the cleanliness of the glassware. Everyone else followed suit.

Abeforth looked from one to the other of us as we drank. "Well, you didn't come here for a butter beer. What do you want?"

I said, "We want to get into Hogwarts."

He laughed. "Since you could walk up to the front gate and present yourselves for entry, I'm pretty sure there's more than that. I suppose you want to enter unobserved."

Ron said, "Well, yes. You see . . ."

Abeforth hastened to hold up a warning hand and said, "Don't tell me! What I don't know, I can't reveal under *Veritas*."

I said, "We don't want you to know."

Then he said, "Then it's the tunnel for you. Follow me." He led us down the stairs into a cool basement where food was stored along with a variety of other things. He led us to a painting of a young lady. He spoke a few words that I didn't catch to her. Her image turned from us, and the painting swung away from the wall revealing a tunnel that was lined with masonry close to the opening, but the walls turned in stages from fine masonry to rough cut stones and finally to soil.

We entered. As we did Abeforth said a few parting words. "I in truth don't know if this tunnel still leads to the Room of Requirement. If you return this way to go somewhere else, please disapparate directly from this room." We agreed to his terms of use. Then we turned our heads down the tunnel, which was dark except for Ginevra's and Ron's lit wands. The door closed behind us.

We walked for quite a distance before a blank wall appeared before us. As we approached, it was apparent that it was not quite blank but had an edge around which a little light leaked. When we reached the door, which it was, I took a deep breath and pushed on it. It swung on invisible hinges. The light of a vast warehouse opened before us. I said, "I've never been in the Room of Requirement until yesterday. Is this really it?"

Ron said, "Bloody right, it is." I set our duffels and bags down, noting carefully where I put them.

Ginevra closed the door behind us and said, "We can now tell you, Ron, what we need from you."

He gave a nervous laugh. "I don't know whether to look forward to it or not."

I said, "Let me remind you of some ancient history. You went into the Chamber of Secrets with Potter."

He nodded and said, "Bloody spooky it was."

"Yes. There is a dead basilisk down there."

He shuddered. "Glad I don't have to go down there. I was never in the deepest part of the chamber."

I asked, "Didn't you and Hermione go down there to get basilisk fangs?"

Ron said, "What are you talking about? Hermione and I fought in that last battle, but we never thought of going into the Chamber of Secrets.

Wouldn't that have been sort of . . . you know, cowardly?" He made a face at that idea.

I was faced with a dilemma. Should I tell him about being from a different universe, one in which, he and Hermione had gone down there to find basilisk fangs to use to kill horcruxes? I decided that that would have been against my agreement with Ginevra.

Ginevra said, "I'd like you to take us down there to retrieve some basilisk fangs."

He said, "I just knew you were going to say something like that."

She drilled him with her eyes. Finally, he said, "I suppose there's no time like the present."

She nodded and then said, "I wish we had Harry's cloak of invisibility."

I said, "Now that you're both adults, I doubt that the two of you would fit under the cloak."

She agreed. "It doesn't matter to you."

Meanwhile Ron was scrounging around for something. The something that he was looking for was a pair of broomsticks. I asked, "What are those for?"

He answered, "Better that you don't know until we need them."

"Right. I'll be here waiting for you with bated breath."

Ginevra shook her head. "You will be coming with us."

I stared at her. "What can I possibly contribute to the endeavor?"

She smiled. "Nothing. But . . ."

I answered, "But what?"

"But if something happens to us, you can always walk out of the castle on your own. If you were here, you'd need magic to get you out."

I thought about that a moment. She was right, but what good would it do me to be out without anywhere to go. Maybe Abeforth would hide me—for a while. What then?

I weighed slowly starving to death against having freedom of action. I chose freedom. "You're right. Let's go."

By this time, it was totally dark outside and inside the castle. Nearly everyone must have been gone for the spring holiday. Maybe Filch was patrolling around somewhere. I hoped we wouldn't meet him. We were fairly close to the girl's WC where the entrance to the Chamber was located. Ron led us to a washbasin. He then made a strange sound that I wouldn't have guessed that he was capable of producing. The basin moved and revealed a hole leading into an even darker dark than the dark where we were. Ron said, "Jump." He pushed me. I landed fairly hard on my rear end and slid down a very slippery slope. We reached the bottom. Ginevra knocked me down just as I was regaining my feet. Then Ron knocked her down.

96

Their lit wands revealed a heap of stones that was apparently a collapsed ceiling. Ron commented, "Looks like nobody ever cleaned this up. We can climb over it." We did. On the other side was a circular door on hinges that looked like snakes. Ron made the same strange sound that he had above. The snakes wriggled and settled. Then the door swung open. We went in. There was a long hall surrounded by pools of water. We walked to the end where there was a pile of bones, including a nearly complete skull. There were a number of fangs.

Ron asked, "Well, here we are. What do we do now?"

Ginevra answered, "Break several fangs off." Ron bent down and was about to do so when Ginevra exclaimed, "Be careful. They've still got venom on them." She added in a voice that only I heard, "I hope." She had a small bag where Ron dropped them.

I said, "Well, that's it. Let's go."

Ron agreed and said, "Here you go, Ginny. Take a broom."

She did and turned to me. "Hop on. We'll fly out of here."

I exclaimed, "What? This is your exit strategy? Fly up the tunnel?"

"Right. Don't be shy. You've flown on a broom before haven't you?"

I grimaced. "Yes, once. We were dodging nuclear weapons at the time. It was about the worst experience of my life."

She shook her head, "Minerva was right about you. You are such a wuss!"

I grumbled, "Better a live wuss than a dead hero."

Ron had already taken off. Ginevra just said, "Accio Wendt." I found myself flying the few feet between her and me. I was deposited against her side on the broom." She kicked the ground, and we were into the air. The gap above the collapsed ceiling was small. As we approached it, she said, "Mind your head." I ducked, and we cleared the pile. Then we were flying up the tunnel toward the girl's WC. We arrived. Ron was already there, standing beside the washbasin. When we arrived, he shoved it closed, and we walked out of the WC. We jogged to the entrance to the Room of Requirement.

Ginevra said, "I need a place to put discarded things." She added under her breath, "Like Wendt."

We were inside. I thanked Ron for his help. Ginevra said, "Ron, Nothing that happens in Hogwarts leaves Hogwarts, right?"

He nodded. "Sure. Nobody knows we've been here except Abeforth, and no one pays any attention to him."

She nodded uncertainly. "I guess you're right." Then she hugged him and said, "Get on your way."

Ron extended a hand and said, "I don't know why you're here, and that's probably a good thing." I shook his hand.

Then I said, "I've got a feeling we will never see each other again. Good luck." Ron stared at me as though he wanted to ask a question, but didn't know what to ask. Finally, he waved, opened the door to the secret passage, turned back to say, "Good luck", and then he disappeared into the dark passage.

Ginny turned back to me and asked, "Just what are we looking for? Some kind of diadem?"

"Yeh. It's like a crown, I guess. It's not fake. I'm pretty sure the jewels are real. We wouldn't want to confuse it with part of somebody's Halloween costume." Then I asked a question. "How do you want to organize the search?"

"What do you mean, organize?"

"You know. How will we know where we've searched already?"

Ginevra looked around the vast interior of the Room of Requirement and sighed. "OK. How do we know?"

I shrugged. "I don't know. But I do know that we'd better have a plan before we begin searching."

She agreed and then said, "It's pretty late. Why don't we have something to eat and then go to bed."

We decided to split one MRE, since it had a lot of calories and neither of us were especially hungry. We improvised beds by using our parkas. Just before Ginevra put out her wand, I said, "Maybe we'll find a couple of mattresses tomorrow while we search."

She said, "'Night, Jim."

"'Night, Weasley."

# The Long Dark of the Room

When we awoke the next day, we were both hungry. This time, we each ate a whole MRE. The first question from Ginevra was, "How do we mark what we've searched?"

I asked, "Can you mark the floor with your wand in some way that's permanent?"

"Yes and no."

"Perfectly clear."

She growled at me. "As long as we remain in the Room of Requirement, any changes that we make to the room are permanent. Once we leave, they disappear."

I sighed sadly, "Well, that means that we stay until we're done—one way or another." Then I had an idea. "Everything placed in the Room of Requirement stays regardless whether people leave the room or not, right?"

She laughed and motioned around the room, "Well, obviously."

"Then we could use parchment and pens to write labels that we could attach to the piles of junk as we finish them. They would stay, right?"

She pondered and then said, "I think so."

"We'll do it. You don't happen to have parchment and pens in your handbag?"

She smiled, "Always."

I tore off a piece of parchment and wrote on it "1A". She glanced at it and said, "Give that to me." When she had it, she scratched out "1A" and wrote something in characters that I'd never seen before.

"That's a rune, isn't it?"

"Yes. Very good. I thought that it might be mistaken for something that came with the thing it was attached to rather than something recent if it had a rune rather than an English character."

"Ok. No problem."

We picked a pile of *detritus* and began to investigate it. It quickly became obvious that we would have the take the pile completely apart to know for sure if a small diadem was hidden somewhere within. After a little discussion, we decided that we'd have to re-assemble the pile or we'd soon run out of space to disassemble piles into. So we had twice as much work in front of us as we thought. The results of the search of that first pile was not surprising—we didn't find a diadem. However, it was only a little discouraging. After all, we hadn't really expected to find it on the first go.

We re-assembled the pile and marked it with a parchment label. As we finished, there was something that struck me as very funny. Ginevra began to be angry with me. She asked, "What in the world can possibly be funny in this situation. Answer me and answer me quick or . . . or . . ."

Still chuckling, I asked her, "Do you know the game, Jenga?"

This moderated her anger a little, but she quickly asked, "What in the world does a child's game have to do with us, and what is Jenga anyway?"

I calmed down and said, "Jenga is a game. You start by building a stack of 54 wooden blocks. The stack has three blocks on each level. After it's been built the players take turns removing a block from any level below the top two and adding it to the top level. If the top level is complete, they start a new top level. Anyway, it's a game that has one winner—the last person to place a block without causing any blocks to fall. Elegant in its simplicity."

Ginevra smiled in spite of herself. "Ok. I get it. That's what we're dong —playing Jenga in reverse."

I couldn't help smiling, "Actually playing it both ways."

"Great! Well, let's keep playing. What stack next?"

I looked around. There were lots of fairly short stacks, but there were several in view that were more than twice as tall as the height that I could reach. "We should tackle a high stack. We'll have to sooner or later."

Ginevra grimaced. "I suppose you're right. I just hate the idea of having to take that on so soon."

"I'm not excited about it either, but we've got to."

She had an idea. "Maybe the horcrux is in a short stack. That way we wouldn't have to even touch a tall stack."

"It's a reasonable hope. I'll tell you what. Here's a deal. We tackle one of the tall ones now, and after that, we work exclusively on short ones until we find the horcrux or have to move to the tall ones."

She bought that idea. She asked, "OK. What ideas do we have for dealing with the tall stacks?"

My first thought was that it would be easy with a scaffold. I named that idea. Ginevra thought about it and asked, "Do we have materials to build a scaffolding?"

"There's so much junk around, I'd think so."

She said, "I've got an idea. *Levicorpus*."

The word was so far out in left field that I didn't recognize it at first. "What?"

"*Levicorpus*—a spell that can lift someone into the air. I could use it on you. Then you could take things off a couple at a time."

I was suspicious of that. "I'm not so sure, but I'm willing to give it a try —IF we try to build a scaffold first."

Ginevra agreed reluctantly to that proposal. So, we went off looking for materials. We found a number of boards that looked strong. The trouble was that we didn't have nails or a way of fastening the boards together to make a sturdy structure. We managed to find some ropes. I tried assembling a short scaffold that would let us reach some of the taller stacks. The first time that I tried ascending it, after about one minute, it started swaying and was quickly lying on the ground. Ginevra looked at me haughtily and asked, "Well?"

I had to give in. "OK. We'll try *Levicorpus*."

The first attempt was hilarious—for Ginevra. I was upside down. I said, "Very funny. I don't think I can do all that much like this."

She let me down and said, "I think I've got the proper spell. Let me try it again."

I frowned and said, "Sure, go ahead." This time, I rose a little unsteadily. I took a couple of items off the tall stack beside me. Ginevra let me down. They were just a couple of shoe-boxes. Inside were ancient running shoes. I commented, "Well, it works. Let's keep going."

Ginevra wanted to move on to a different stack then and there. I said, "No. I don't think that's a good idea. Something that works OK with a couple of items might not work so well to completely demolish a stack. I think we need to bring this one down to the floor. Then we need to rebuild it— probably not so tall—to prove the concept."

Ginevra wasn't happy, but she reluctantly agreed. I was up in the air again. This time I brought down several items—just to see how many I could handle. On the way down, I lost control and a couple dropped. They almost hit Ginevra. She shouted, "Be careful. Not so many at one time."

I agreed. By the early afternoon we had completely brought the stack down to the level where we could both work on it. We stopped at that point for lunch. We finished by mid-afternoon. We re-constructed the stack— wider and not so tall. Then we moved on to the next stack. We stayed at it for a while.

We stopped—not because we were tired—but because it was getting too dark. We tried working for a while with wand light, but there were too many shadows. There were no windows in the Room of Requirement, but the light seemed to be coming from the outside. It started getting light in the morning about the same time the sun rose and it started getting dark in the evening about when the sun set. That was a happy piece of luck. I had a watch, but Ginevra didn't use one. I suppose we could have had an alarm clock, but we didn't need one. It was strange. Sometimes in the afternoon it got dimmer. I wondered if the light in the Room of Requirement depended on how light it was outside Hogwarts.

□

The next week or so went according to the standard routine. We got up at first light. We de-constructed stacks, carefully. We searched the stack for any signs of the horcrux. We re-constructed the stack and labeled it.

One day, at the bottom of the stack, there was a large mahogany desk. As usual, we opened draws and pulled them out. Then we began searching each drawer. In the second drawer that I examined, there was something that made me gasp.

Ginevra was at my side immediately. She breathed, "What is it?"

I picked the object up to get a better look at it. It was an old tattered book. The binding was delicate. You had to catch the title in just the right light to read it. It said, "*Advanced Potionmaking*." I carefully turned the cover. I read the inscription on the flyleaf.

Ginevra was more insistent this time. "What in the world have you got there?"

I simply said, "The Half-blood Prince."

She hadn't been expecting that. She repeated her question.

I repeated more firmly and carefully, "The Half-blood Prince."

This time, she gasped. She started to say, "It's not possible." But half-way through she realized that it was possible. Instead she said, "I suppose it was almost inevitable that we'd find it sooner or later." Then she reached out a hand, "May I see it?"

I handed it over. "Be careful with it. The binding is . . ."

She finished the sentence for me, "Fragile."

"Yes."

She was careful. She looked through a few pages and laid it down. She asked, "What do you know about this?"

I said, "I'll tell you that I know a lot more about it than you do."

"Oh, come on. Your specialty was never potion-making." Then she was silent a moment and asked, "Do you really?"

I nodded my head. "Oh, I know that Potter used that to make a reputation for himself as a potion-maker. I know that someone was disgusted with his use of this book and got rid of it in the Room of Requirement."

She asked, "How can you possibly know that?"

I said, "We were not the first ones to find this book."

"You mean someone back at your Hogwarts found it. Who was it?"

I sighed, "Dudley Dursley."

She laughed. "How could someone like Dursley possibly find it?"

I suggested that we stop for an early lunch while we discussed it.

She was beginning to show some anger in her eyes. "Well, you've got to try to explain to me how it was possible that he wasn't found by the Ministry when he was a kid."

"Oh, it wasn't so strange. Both his parents were Muggles. Who was it who lived with the Dursleys when Dudley was a kid?"

She scoffed, "Well, of course, Harry . . ." She was silent for a while mulling over the possibilities. "So, you're saying that everyone at the Ministry assumed that all the magic going on in the Dursley house was due to Harry, and they missed Dudley?"

"Exactly."

She was still unconvinced. "What about when Harry was off to Hogwarts? If Dursley were a wizard, there'd still be magic in the house, right. How did the Ministry miss that?"

"Oh, you forget that there were magic spells on the house that protected Harry when he was there. They were in operation all the time."

Ginevra's shoulder dropped. "Hummm. So, Dursley went to Hogwarts as a student?"

"No. He went as an apprentice to Filch."

Ginevra almost split her side laughing. "Apprentice . . . to . . . that Squib?"

"Yes."

"Did he sit in on classes? How did he learn magic?"

I took a deep breath trying to remember how it happened. "Well, it was observing students do magic and working with Slughorn on their revisions to this book."

"How did that ever happen?"

"Well, Dursley found this book in this room."

Ginevra interposed, "In your universe."

"Right. Anyway, he was curious and started trying to decipher the margin notes that Snape had written. The first potion he tried, he made mostly on his own. He ran across a student who was trying to brew a love potion. Dursley offered to help him in exchange for some magic lessons.

"The potion that they brewed was pretty amazing. It seemed to be permanent."

Ginevra gagged. "Really?"

"Yes. The girl they used it on—really, she was an adult—a seventh year who was seventeen, fell in love with Dursley."

Ginevra laughed at that. "How unlucky!"

"The girl didn't think so. Quite the opposite. Anyway, brewing the antidote put Slughorn's attention on to Dursley. They came to an agreement to publish a new version of *Advanced Potionmaking*. They both worked on it. Dursley did the interpretation of Snape's notes, and they brewed the potions together as a test of the interpretation."

Ginevra began to be suspicious, "How do you know all this anyway?"

"Oh, that's not strange. Minerva punished Dursley by sending him to Coventry—that is, living in my office."

She nodded knowingly. "Yes. Was Minerva punishing you too?"

"I guess so."

She commented, "Publishing makes strange bed-fellows and all that. Why are you so protective of Snape's book?"

"Snape and I were friends, I guess."

She stared incredulously and asked, "You and the number one Deatheater were buddies?"

"Well, he really wasn't a Deatheater."

She scoffed. "He sure fooled a lot of people, including You-Know-Who."

"Right. He did fool a lot of people. The only way that we learned was through the death of Riddle."

Ginevra shook her head in amazement. "I keep discovering the most amazing things here. Dursley whom I would have been willing to use the *avada kedavra* curse on." I frowned at her. "Well, I probably wouldn't, but the *Cruciatus* curse was a real possibility. So, he was actually not a stupid Muggle. He was a stupid wizard?"

I said, "Actually not so stupid as you'll see."

"Then there was Snape. He killed Dumbledore! But you say that he wasn't really a Deatheater! What was he? One of those double down agents?"

I sighed. "Yes, he was actually an agent of Dumbledore."

She shook her head. "Well, I guess that explains why You-Know-Who killed him at the end."

I said, "No. He had Riddle fooled up to the end. Riddle had this crazy theory about why he couldn't kill Potter with the ultimate wand that he had. His theory was that the wand was actually 'owned' by Snape. He figured that he had to kill Snape to make it truly his."

Ginevra scoffed. "Well, in this universe it seemed to work."

"I don't know why he was able to kill Potter, but I'm pretty sure that it wasn't because the loyalty of that wand had switched to him. Part of it surely had to do with the fact that that last horcrux wasn't destroyed. Maybe, it was that Potter gave up when he couldn't find that horcrux."

She shook her head sending her hair flying—information overload, I suppose. "OK. I'll accept that Snape was actually a good guy. So, you two were buds. What about the book? You could just buy a copy of the revised *Advanced Potionmaking,* right?"

"I did, but the original got destroyed."

She shook her head. "Bad luck."

"Not bad luck. There was somebody who really hated Snape."

She scoffed. "Just about everyone who knew Dumbledore hated Snape."

I asked her, "Do you remember the Muggle Studies professor, who died before your sixth year?"

"Sure. By the way, she was the last Muggle Studies professor period. Just like you were the first, last, and only English literature professor."

"Well, there was evidence that Snape had killed her. Her brother set out to obliterate the memory of Snape. When it looked like the *Revised* was to be publish, he blackmailed us into destroying it."

She gasped. "Someday, you'll have to tell me how that ever worked. For now, I think lunch is over. Let's get back to work.

☐☐

The work continued—the rest of that day, the rest of that week and into the next week.

At the end of one day, I said, "While it's still light, let's take a little walk. I want to know how much more we have to get through before we've got a good chance of finding the diadem."

Ginevra agreed. We walked down the corridors and talked. She asked, "Do you really think we'll find that horcrux one day?"

"I don't know. I'll calculate a guess of how much time it will take when we finish surveying the Room of Requirement."

She looked up at me and was about to say something when she slipped on some piece of junk that someone from the twelfth century or maybe the twentieth had tossed there. I caught her and righted her. She stood there next to me, looking up into my eyes. She stuttered, "Th-thanks." Her mouth was hanging open. I suddenly realized how much I wanted to close it with a kiss. It happened.

She opened her mouth slightly and then drew back. "Oh. Oh. Sorry, I didn't mean to . . ."

That surprised me. It was I who had done something. I said, "I did mean it."

Her uncertain expression opened up into a happy smile. "I . . . I'm glad you did."

Then, she drew me close and we kissed again. By this time, it was getting rather dark. Neither of us said anything until it was totally dark. She said, "I've got a wand. I could . . ."

"Light it?"

"Oh, yes. Yes." She did.

We found our way back to our campsite despite tripping over all sorts of things in the dim wand light. Back there, we sat in each other's arms. I said, "You know, I wouldn't mind it if we never found the diadem."

She squirmed a bit in my arms and said, "You mustn't say things like that."

I asked, "Why not?"

"You might convince me."

That was as much as I wanted to know right at that moment, and come to think of it, maybe forever.

The following days were frequently joyful. We never stopped looking for the diadem, but we never stopped looking at each other either. At times, it took an act of will to pay attention to the stacks of *detritus* through which we were combing, but we could always muster that will.

The second night, we made love on our parkas that we'd been using as mattresses. After that, many nights included love-making. Many didn't. One wonderful night after, we were spooning. Ginevra asked me. "Did you like your Ginny?"

I started to ask, "My Ginny?" Then I realized what she meant.

"You know. The Ginny in your world."

"Yes, I did."

She asked, "A lot?"

"Yes, a lot."

She seemed on the point of asking something. I anticipated her. "The Ginny from my world married Harry."

She asked a different question, "Did you love her?"

There was no time for thought. I answered truthfully, "Yes."

That didn't seem to bother Ginevra. She then asked, "Do you still love her?"

I answered so quickly that it was obviously from my heart. "I love you more than anyone else."

That seemed to satisfy her. Her body relaxed. I'd not the slightest idea that it had been tense, but it was now obviously at total rest in my arms.

Another day, we were lying in the half-light of the early evening, basking in the light of our love when a thought occurred to me that made me gasp. Ginevra picked up on it immediately, "What is it?"

I said, "Nothing."

Her temper flared immediately. "Nothing bloody hell! It's something. What is it?"

You can't hide things from Ginevra. Sometimes I swear she's a legilimans. I said, "OK. It's a long story."

Her mercurial moods could change in an instant from fiery to warm to sizzling. I wasn't sure where she was now. I could almost see the smile in her voice as she said, "You mean we have something else to do tonight?"

I couldn't help chuckling. It would be the last semblance of good humor for quite some time. I nodded. "Well, here it goes.

"You remember about Dursley's version of *Advanced Potionmaking*?"

"Of course." Then, she said, "Yeh. I remember that he had some sort of super love potion. Someone gave it to you, didn't they?"

I hesitated. Ginevra took it as affirmation of the assertion. She was starting to spin a story of my being in love with Jaimie because of it.

I said, "That's a different story. You're right. Someone did give me a dose of that potion."

She laughed. "I knew it!"

"You're still in love with her, aren't you."

"No. Someday, I'll tell you that story. Since it involves Ginny from my universe . . ."

She shook her head and said, "I can't believe that I would—in any universe—use a love potion."

"Oh, you didn't. Look. I'm not telling that story today. Just let me tell my story, will you!"

Ginevra seemed a bit abashed and let me tell my story without many interruptions. I went on, "This is serious. Listen carefully." She did.

I went on. "This happened five years ago. Let me establish the back story. Did Aurora and I go to the Halloween parties in your world?"

She laughed. "Sure, She did. You two were always good for an entertaining performance at those parties. It's amazing that Dumbledore let you do all those crazy masquerades that you two did."

I scoffed. "I hope you don't think that they were voluntary—at least on my part."

"Well, you always did seem to get the short end of the stick, but who knew? Maybe you enjoyed them."

"Think again."

"Well, why did you put up with them all those years?"

"It's a long story. You had to be there in my office to understand how it worked out that way."

She scoffed. "Do you have anything other than long stories?"

"Probably not. Anyway, one day she decided to use Dursley's super Polyjuice Potion rather than the normal kind. It was strictly experimental. As a matter of fact, Dursley and Slughorn were afraid to experiment with it. Aurora got a sample of it. She had the brilliant idea that it would be a good joke if she put a lock of her hair in my Polyjuice Potion."

Ginevra chuckled, "What happened? Was it the usual hilarious evening?"

"I suppose so. You have to understand that I hardly ever had a good time at those things. The thing that usually happened was that the potion would wear off in a few hours. If I were lucky, what happened afterwards in the morning was not as bad as your average hangover.

"However, this time was different. When I woke up, the potion hadn't worn off."

Ginevra's mouth gaped open. "You mean you still looked like a woman?"

"More than that."

Her face fell. "You mean you were . . . what DO you mean?"

"I mean that I was still a woman in every way. It was as if I were a twin sister of Aurora."

Ginevra asked, "How long did that last?"

I took a centering breath. Ginevra was more insistent in her question, "How long?"

"It was permanent."

Ginevra stared at me, "That's not possible. Here you are! I know you're not a woman, let alone the twin of Aurora."

"Well, just let me tell the story. Minerva took me down to Madame Pomfrey's. She declared that if I'd taken enough Polyjuice Potion that it lasted that long, then I'd be dead. Of course, that would have been true for normal Polyjuice Potion. This super Polyjuice Potion was permanent. I was a woman and a witch. Ordinary Polyjuice Potion never made a Muggle into a witch or wizard. This did.

"By that time, a strange thing happened. My personality sort of faded away, and a different one was born. That personality was a witch in every sense. She was someone completely different. I was gone—completely."

Ginevra was incensed, "That's not possible. You're here."

"Yes. Hear me out. My memories were still in her brain. This new witch, who decided to call herself Jaimie Sinistra, was determined not to let me return. She fled Hogwarts and set about a program of training herself to be a witch. I have to admit that she was brilliant at it.

"She hired a tutor to teach her to disapparate. She went to a beautician and had a crash course in cosmetics and hair care. She had all my memories of what witches could do to guide her. In less than a month, she could pass herself off as a normal witch and an English literature teacher. She went to Hogwarts and applied for my job."

Ginevra laughed at that. "She didn't."

"Not only did she, but she got herself hired."

She asked, "How did you ever come back? Did your personality begin to leak back in to her?"

I shook my head. "No. The longer she was around, the more confident in her persona she became. She dated."

Ginevra was struck dumb for a moment. Then she asked, "Surely she didn't sleep with anyone?"

I said, "More than that. She became engaged to the widowed father of a Hogwarts student."

Ginevra's voice had become grim. "She married him, didn't she?"

"Yes, she did."

She exclaimed, "That isn't the end of the story—obviously. What happened. How did you come back?"

"Well, I was saved by the aliens that we both know as the Souls."

She felt around for something. She found an MRE. She threw it across the Room of Requirements "You are lying. Why in the world would the Souls want to save you!"

"Oh, that wasn't their intention. They were under attack by another race of aliens. They just didn't know it. What they knew was that their colonies were starting to be affected by a strange sickness that they couldn't diagnose. They came to the Earth for help. They were that desperate. They knew that I had been instrumental in their being defeated. They wanted me to lead a mission to help them."

Ginevra's eyes widened and she said, "Oh, yeh. You weren't available. You were as good as dead. What happened?"

"Well, the Ministry of Magic put lots of pressure on Hogwarts and Minerva, who was then the Headmistress, to find me. Of course, she had no idea where I was or how to reach me."

Ginevra nodded. She said in flat tones, "Jaimie gave herself up for the aliens. God damn! I can't believe that I would have in her place. How did they bring you back?"

"Oh, it wasn't as hard as you might think. There was some of my hair left in my razor. It was enough. I was back. I'm sure she never would have let me come back if it weren't for the Souls."

Ginevra said, "So that was it." She gave a satisfied sigh.

"No. That wasn't it. I wouldn't be telling you this right now if that were it."

She said, "Oh shit!"

"Yeh. I wouldn't have let her come back either. However, something happened. There was that second alien race—the PAK. The disease that was affecting the Souls wasn't a disease. It was the PAK, poisoning the Soul's food. The team that I was on learned about the poisoning and stopped it."

"The PAK came looking for help in finding the home world of the Souls. That had been their goal all along. They knew that we had stopped their first attempt to beat the Souls. They figured that what we'd done for the Souls we could do for them. They threatened the world with destruction. We put together a team to help them."

She said, "You were on it surely."

"No, the PAK wanted the original team that had gone with the Souls. The Ministry of Magic wanted to have as many witches on the team as possible. They wanted Jaimie to replace me. They really, really wanted that."

Ginevra said, "They forced you to convert yourself to Jaimie?"

"Not exactly. I cut a deal with Jaimie's husband. She could have a body for three years if and only if I could have it for the next three years."

Ginevra asked, "Her husband agreed to that deal and you gave up your body for three years. Then they kept their end of the bargain?"

"That's right. He had Jaimie for three years. Then they brought me back."

She shook her head in confusion. "Wait a minute. I can't believe that you were gone completely and some other person was in your body."

"It wasn't Jaimie in my body. It was Jaimie in her body."

Ginevra was still unconvinced. "But she had your brain, your memories. You said so yourself!"

I shook my head in negation. "It wasn't my brain. My brain wasn't immersed in a bath of female hormones. It's actually not that strange. There's a recognized disorder—multiple personality disorder. You don't even have to have different genes and hormones. There are people with several personalities. Some can be male and some female. Some can share memories."

Ginevra stared at her feet. "So, how long have you got left with a body before you have to give Jaimie her 'turn'?"

"I've had the body for a little over a year and a half."

She lifted her eyes to mine and gazed searchingly in mine. "Are you going to honor your half of the bargain?"

I nodded. She asked, "Then we've got less than a year and a half before . . ."

I said, "Yes. But, I'm going to ask for us to alternate—a year on and then a year off."

She was silent for a long time. By this time it was pitch dark. I finally said, "Not something you exactly look forward to, is it?"

She said in a small voice, "Would you consider cheating?" Almost immediately she followed up by saying in a firm voice, "I didn't say that." And then she said in a rock solid voice, "Forget I said that—please."

"Sure. Maybe we should just get a good night's sleep. It's been a hard day."

She said, "Yeh."

We didn't talk about that again for a long time. Nor did she ask for stories from before we met for a long time either. I suppose that she was afraid of what troubling incident might come out of my past.

This incident set me to thinking about my history and what other things that I ought to talk about with her. That night, I wondered long into the night if we'd ever make love again or if she'd even want to be with me at all after this quest was finished. I didn't get a lot of sleep that night.

One day toward time for dinner, Ginevra turned toward me from stacking up junk from the latest Jenga pile. She looked me in the eye and asked, "Would you like me to let my hair down?"

The question came from nowhere. I returned her gaze and said, "Yes. Why do you ask?"

She reached up on top of her head and began removing hairpins. "Well, we're going to find out for sure." She quickly finished. Then she uncoiled her hair and let it fall around her shoulders down close to her hips. She was so close that she was instantly in my arms. I'm not sure whose initiative it was. I didn't care. After some serious snogging. I repeated my question, "Why do you ask?"

She looked down toward her left foot and said, "I remember that your girl friend back at Hogwarts always wore her hair down. I wondered if that were what you preferred."

I chuckled. "It's whom I prefer not what. And, I prefer you." I pushed her back a little, waited a tick, and said, "Oh, one last thing. I do like your hair down."

She gave me a wicked smile and said, "As your highness requests."

Most days after that, she wore her hair down. Frequently, she had braided it in a long ponytail that reached her midriff. Every morning was a fresh day in a wonderful world. Then one day . . .

# Whom Do You Really Love

When that day dawned, I was ready for another day in Paradise. That's the way that I had begun thinking of the Room of Requirement. It had the one person in the world who meant more to me than any other.

Ginevra's smile was glorious. We had breakfast. We fed each other from the same MRE. I could happily have spent the rest of my life in that beautiful room with that most beautiful woman in the world.

We went off to find the diadem as we always did, hand-in-hand. We'd both taken to wearing gloves lately, but not until we got to the work site. This day, we began with one of the taller stacks. Ginevra levitated me close to the top of the stack. I couldn't quite see what was on the very top. I fumbled around trying to feel it. Suddenly, I felt a pinch as though something had bitten me. I drew back reflexively. Below, Ginevra asked, "Anything wrong, love?"

I answered, "I don't think so. Hang in there." I reached up again and this time got a good hold on something. It must have had a hundred sharp edges, but I held on long enough to pull it over the edge so that I could get a good look at it. It was a tiara. It seemed to bite me fiercely. I dropped it. It fell to the floor. Ginevra stared at it and partially released her concentration that held me up. I seemed to slip down to the floor and landed partially on her. She seemed not to notice. The impact did bring her back to the present.

She gasped. "That's it!" It seemed to have a life of its own. It didn't move, really, but it seemed about to run off. I pulled my shirt off and threw it over the thing. I held the edges of my shirt down, trapping it.

She exclaimed, "Good. Hold it. I left the fangs back at the camp." She ran off, muttering to herself. I suppose she was castigating herself for leaving them behind. She returned. When she did, she said, "OK. Hold the thing for dear life. Try to get it partially uncovered so that I can use a fang."

"Right." I muscled it around so that I could turn it over and reveal what was inside the shirt." Then I said, "Say when."

She took a deep breath. Then she said, "When." I flipped the damn thing over and exposed it. A cloud seemed to rise around it. I could hear it say something, but I couldn't tell what. Then, Ginevra struck. I felt a tiny prick on my hand and I fell unconscious.

□

I had a terrible headache. Someone was pressing a cold cloth to my head. It obscured my vision. She wiped my head and cleared my vision. At first, I had a hard time focusing. When I did, I realized it was Ginevra. I asked, "Don't laugh, Ginevra. Where am I?"

She did laugh.

I tried to shake my head. Then I said, "I thought I told you not to laugh."

That really set her off. The strange thing was that there were tears some-how mixed with the laughs. I could tell. Her kisses were wet with her tears. She asked, "I suppose you want to know what happened."

Somehow I was totally exhausted. I struggled to say, "Yes, but I'm afraid I'm going to pass out. Save it."

She nodded and forced some MRE dreck down my throat. Then I did fall asleep. Later when I woke up, she said, "I'm going to tell you what hap-pened. Don't interrupt. You've still got recovery in front of you.

I nodded feebly.

⊟

You had just uncovered the horcrux. It knew that I intended to kill it and that I had something that I could kill it with. Its scream was terrible. The next thing it did was to fill the air with a dark cloud. In it I seemed to see an image of myself and you, but it wasn't me. It was some other me. A voice in my head was saying, "You think he loves you. But he doesn't. He loves the real Ginny. The Ginny in his world. He only is with you because you remind him of HER. She is more beautiful than you. She desires him, and he desires her. He was lying to you when he told you that he liked you. He just wanted for you to do the dangerous work. When you have done it, he will leave you and fly to his real love. He is laughing at you right now. She is ready to throw herself into his arms the moment he returns. She is laughing at you. Your brothers laugh at you. Abeforth laughs at you!

113

"You must kill him now while he is near. Then you will laugh at him and at the other Ginny and your brothers. Do it now! Do it before he can escape!"

Somehow, what that voice said seemed so very true that I stared at the fang that I was going to use to kill it, and I realized that I'd really been planning all along to kill you with it. It would be so very, very easy. I just would raise my arm as though to strike it, but at the last instant, I'd twist and strike you with it.

Something in my head hurt like I'd never hurt before. I couldn't understand what it could possibly be. All I needed to do was to strike you. It would be so very easy. I would have outsmarted you, all of you. I did it. I swung my arm down. I didn't even pretend to strike the beautiful diadem. How could I ever have wanted to mar its perfect beauty? I stared at it fascinated. It seemed to whisper seductively in my ear, "Now. Now is the perfect time. Strike." My arm arched down with all the force that I could put into it. It struck your hand. Only it didn't cut. I realized that you were wearing gloves. In that moment, a terrible scream seemed to shatter my calm. I saw how terrible what I'd done was. I swung my arm around, and the point of the fang grazed the horcrux. It screamed. That truly woke me up. I swung the fang again. This time, my aim was true. I hit it dead center. The scream split my head, but I struck again and again until the scream died.

Then I was truly aware. I saw that you had fainted. I examined the glove. I couldn't see a mark. I pulled the glove off your hand. Then I saw the small pinprick that was colored red.

I knew that I had nothing that could be used as anti-venom. I thought first of going to the infirmary to get help. Then I realized that Madame Pomfrey was no longer there. Whoever was there would not lift a finger to save a Muggle.

I realized that I needed to get out. I didn't know what to expect if I left you alone in the Room of Requirement, but I knew that dragging you around outside would mean death for you. So, I made you a bed and laid you on it. I then worked my way back through the tunnel to Abeforth's. He was upstairs minding the bar. I found my way up there and called him aside.

He was not happy. He took me back to the kitchen and said, "I guess I didn't make it clear not to show up when other people are around. Don't!"

I took his arm. "I need help. Wendt has been nicked by a basilisk fang. He's unconscious. I don't know how much time he has."

He drilled me with his eyes. Then he sighed, "Of course, Slughorn probably has anti-venom. Do you know where to find him?"

I shook my head. He paced back and forth. "All right. I'm going to write an address for you. That's where he should be. You're not to reveal where you got this address."

"Of course not." I took the parchment scrap and managed to get out of the Hoggshead without drawing much attention. I disapparated to the address. What I found was an old Muggle neighborhood. It had rows of houses that at some point were well-kept, even pretty. The gardens were no longer recognizable as places where beautiful plants thrived. The gates of the wrought-iron fences were mostly off their hinges and were badly in need of attention. The paint on doors was badly worn. I could barely read the street number on the house that was my goal.

I knocked on the door. There was no answer. I repeated several times. Then I took a deep breath, brought my wand out of my handbag, and disapparated. I appeared in a dingy sitting room. I swung my wand around, ready to curse at the slightest provocation. I didn't see anything other than dilapidated furniture such as an old overstuffed armchair. So, I shouted. "Slughorn, I know you live here. Show yourself."

There was no response. My patience was evaporating as fast as water in the Sahara. I was so angry and frightened that I didn't even try to channel Mum. I spoke in a deadly quiet voice, "I swear to you, Slughorn, if you don't show up right now, before I'm done, you'll wish Riddle had gotten his hands on you."

I heard a squeak of a voice that I couldn't locate say, "What did you say?"

In that same serious-as-death voice, I said, "I'm not repeating."

Then, the overstuffed armchair seemed to blur and shake. It slowly transformed into the familiar form of Horace Slughorn. He stepped forward toward me. I swung my wand around and pointed it at him. He said, "OK. OK. You've made your point. I'm here. What do you want?"

The tension released, I broke into tears that I quickly suppressed and said, "It's Wendt. He's been wounded and has basilisk venom in him. Please, please help us."

Slughorn's head shook as though he hadn't been hearing right. "Wendt? Basilisk? What's going on?"

"You shut up. Listen. I'd better not have to repeat."

He nodded rapidly. Then I said, "I don't care what you think you know. Here's the deal. Wendt has been poisoned with basilisk venom. It doesn't matter how. I need to get anti-venom or a potion or something to cure him."

Slughorn concentrated on me and said, "How long ago?"

I had to think hard. "I'm not sure. Maybe forty-five minutes or an hour."

He glared at me and then his face fell. "I'm sorry. He's dead. If you got anti-venom or some potion to him in five, at most ten minutes, he could be saved. No. He's dead." He hesitated and added, "I thought he was already dead. Has he died a second time?"

115

I didn't break down this time. I said, "I don't care. If there's no chance he survived, I want to find something. I'm going to force it down his throat or whatever whether he's dead or not. So, get thinking—fast."

Slughorn frowned deeply. He was clearly concentrating. I was raising my wand out for serious work. Just as I was about to decide on a good curse that wouldn't kill him, incapacitate him, or keep him from thinking, he looked up and said, "Well, let me get a reference book. It won't take more than a minute." I doubted that, but what else could I do but let him work? I nodded.

He went through a back door. I followed. We went through the connecting corridor to a room at the back of the house which had a large window. There was a desk, a sofa, a variety of chairs, and many bookshelves built into the wall. He walked to a shelf that was just above his eye level. He removed a book and quickly thumbed through the pages. He stopped. I saw his eyes scanning the right page. He turned it and read more slowly. Then he snapped it shut and said, "We have to find Hagrid."

I couldn't believe my ears. "What in the world could he do for us?"

He opened the door that went from that room onto a courtyard. I followed him. Outside, he said, "Would you disapparate us or should I?"

I shook my head. "Where would I disapparate us?"

Slughorn slapped his head. "Of course, you don't know where." He held out his hand and I took it. We appeared in a forest. He walked determinedly down a narrow, but definite trail. In a few minutes we were surrounded by forms that I didn't recognize immediately, but one stepped out from the shadows of the close-packed trees. It was a Centaur. We were in the Forbidden Forest, the home of the last clan of Centaurs. He said, "You are trespassing! You will leave immediately or we will kill you."

I quickly said, "Do you want to throw away the last chance to kill Riddle?"

He said, "That is impossible."

My blood boiled, but I kept my face calm. "Only if you send us away."

"Why?"

I said quickly, "There's no time. You either trust me or not."

He grimaced. "I hate all you self-important wizards. What do you want?"

Slughorn sighed a breath that I supposed he'd been holding for the last minute. "We want to find Haggid. I know he's somewhere in the forest."

He turned and said, "Forensee, you keep contact with Hagrid, right?"

A Centaur came forward and nodded. "Please lead these people to Hagrid."

Forensee came to us and said, "You will have to climb rocky hills. Are you up to it?"

I said, "We can disapparate over the obstacles."

Forensee said, "You won't always be able to."

I shook my head in confusion. We just didn't have time, so I didn't object. We started off. As it turned out, we had to occasionally disapparate to keep up with him. There were way too many exposed roots for us to run to keep up. I decided that it was good that we were following a Centaur who could make very good time in this environment. We came to the hills that border the forest. We started to climb them. We still disapparated to keep up. We began having to disapparate around large boulders—still no problem. Before long we reached a cave. I almost didn't notice it. Forensee went directly to it. I called out for Hagrid.

Hagrid asked, "Who is it?"

I said, "Why don't you recognize my voice?"

A giant head appeared in the dark cave. Beside it was a somewhat smaller head. I recognized both. I said, "It's good to see you, Hagrid—and Grawp."

Hagrid said, "Come inside. I don't want anyone to see you here." We followed him. Almost immediately, he lit some lamps and we saw that the cave was really, fairly comfortable. It had a couple of large couches (both large enough for Grawp). There were also a couple of smaller chairs. There were tables. He then asked, "How can I help you?"

I said, "Wendt is sick. He has been poisoned with basilisk venom. We need an anti-venom. Slughorn thought you could help."

At that point, Slughorn said, "The blood of unicorns can save anyone from death, regardless how close death is. You have unicorns in this forest. Can you help me?"

Hagrid shook his head, "Wendt? Really?"

I finally lost my temper. I almost screamed, "We don't have time! Can you help or not!"

Hagrid took a deep breath. "Yes and no."

I had finally lost all patience. I jumped up and drew my wand out of my handbag. "You start making sense, or I'll . . ."

He raised hands and said, "I'll help. It's just that the blood of unicorns would work . . . but only if the unicorn dies in the taking of the blood. Do you really want a unicorn's blood on your hands?"

I threw my wand down, dropped into a chair, and wept into my hands. "What good is this damned wand? I can't force anyone to do anything."

Hagrid came to my chair, bent down and took my hands. "Ms. Ginny. There's another way."

Slughorn exclaimed, "Really!"

"Yes. The tears of the phoenix can cure such wounds."

My heart fell again. "Where can I possibly find a phoenix quickly?"

Hagrid said, "Well, do you not know that Dumbledore's phoenix left Hogwarts and now lives in the Highlands above us."

I raised my eyes to Hagrid. "Thank you, thank you, thank you! I can disapparate there immediately."

Hagrid shook his head vigorously. "Sorry."

"What!" I grabbed Hagrid by his lapels and tried to shake him. That would have been funny if I hadn't been so desperate.

He said, "Phoenixes don't like people to surprise them at their nests. Disapparating is definitely surprising. She would just fly off."

"So, you're saying that I have to . . . what? Climb up there?"

"I'm afraid so. A plus is that the Phoenix will be very impressed that you would climb up there."

I dropped back into the chair. "So, let's see, I need to climb up to the Phoenix nest. I have to convince it to give me some tears." A little problem occurred to me. "Hagrid, you don't happen to have a vial?"

He answered, "No. We don't have much use for any of those up here, Grawpy and me."

Slughorn entered the conversation to tell us that he always kept a few vials about his person. You never knew when a rare sample collecting opportunity would arise.

I kissed Slughorn and accepted a couple of vials from him. I turned to Hagrid and asked, "Would you come with me?"

"Sure, young lady, but I can't go all the way. Phoenixes might not see more than one person at a time at their nests. Very particular birds they are. I can help you get close to the nest, though."

I thanked Hagrid from the bottom of my heart. At first, I thought that he really deserved my gratitude. That was only until we got to the point when he could point up to a mountain peak about a mile away and say, "There it is Ms. Ginny. Now all you have to do is climb the rest of the way."

I glared at him and said, "You expect me to climb up there? It's a good thousand yards of jumbled rock and then it gets even easier. There's a sheer rock face that must be two thousand feet high."

He looked up and then back at me, "Err, yeah. That would be a little harder for you than for me."

I practically screamed, "A little harder for me than you!"

"Sorry, Ms. Ginny, this is the best I can do for you. The rest of the way has to be up to you."

I frowned and then managed a smile, as I thanked him. "Really, Hagrid, you've been a great help. I wouldn't have a hope to save Wendt without you. I'm on my way."

Hagrid waved to me, I turned, and I started the climb.

You can't imagine what that afternoon climb was like. The first couple of hundred feet was not awful. There was a rough trail between the boulders. It wasn't that the "trail" was smooth and gravel-covered. Rather, the "trail" had only medium size rocks with the occasional small boulder. You could always either step around or over the boulder and didn't have to actually step on it to get past it. I made pretty good time navigating that part of the path.

Next came a disorganized boulder field. I began to think that there had been a landslide long ago that had dumped all these bigger boulders around willy-nilly. They varied in size from small boulders to giant-size ones about the size of houses. The going there was much rougher. I pretty much gave up walking around boulders. I just had to climb them somehow. On one of the smaller ones where I relaxed my vigilance, I didn't assure my foot-hold and ended up slipping down to the bottom of the boulder.

I suppose I was lucky. I could have sprained an ankle or even broken a bone and that might have been the end of this quest. Instead, I sort of rolled with the fall, and it was my left knee that stopped my slide. It didn't even hurt that much. There was a small amount of moisture on the knee of my jeans. That was blood, although I didn't think much of it at the time.

Later I was getting close to the face of the cliff. That proximity seduced me into relaxing my vigilance. I didn't get a really secure hand-hold. I fell and again was lucky. This time, I was stopped by that left knee. This time, the blood was flowing for real. I pulled up my jeans to check how bad it was. I could have risked disapparating away to put a dressing on it if it were bad. Of course, then I'd have to start over again from the base. Fortunately, the scrape (for that was all it really was) had mostly clotted and the worst thing was that the jeans looked bad.

Again, I resumed the climb—with more care. I reached the base of the cliff. Fortunately, the cliff face was not perfectly vertical and there were a number of ledges that weren't apparent from a distance. I stopped for a few minutes to gather my strength and found a small bottle in my handbag. I filled it with water using the *Auguamente* spell. That kept me hydrated.

Then the serious climb began. Reaching the first ledge was not awful. I stopped and rested there. I also had some more water. Then I resumed the climb. There were slips and near falls, but somehow I kept my balance and my feet under me. Then there was a long near vertical section with nothing but little hand-holds that scared me every time I took one. I almost had reached the next ledge when the strength of my right hand failed me. I couldn't support my weight on the three fingers that was holding me up. I fell.

I had no choice. I used magic again. I breathed, "*Arresto Momentum.*" I landed easily back at the base of the cliff. I dropped to my rump with my back against the wall, and I cried. I couldn't have cared less who heard me. Riddle could have shown up at that moment, and I wouldn't have cared.

I got up and walked it off. I dried my face and had some water. Then I was ready to try it again. This time I learned a little from my last attempt. When I reached that final ledge, I looked harder for good hand-holds. I cried some on the way up as I passed points where I'd been before. This time, at that final point, I gathered my strength and seized that final hand-hold. This time I went over the lip of the ledge. It was wide enough to stop and really rest. I had water. I turned back to the rock face. Now, the slope was fairly gentle. It was still difficult, but the hand-holds were all better than on that last slope.

I reached another ledge that was fairly wide. I rested there and noticed something that I'd not paid much attention to before. The last rays of the sun were shining on the last length of the climb. It was a fairly gentle slope, but it must have been another couple of hundred feet. I supposed that I could survive on this ledge through the night, but would Wendt survive the night? I couldn't chance it. I got up before I was truly rested and without more water. I started working my way up the final climb.

It was certainly the easiest part of the climb, but with the failing light I was never sure of the footing where I put my feet or the rock that I grabbed for support. I reached the top. By great good fortune the moon was nearly full and illuminated the nest of the Phoenix pretty well.

I suddenly realized that I didn't really know what I was going to do when I arrived other than look pitiable and stupid. I just got onto my knees before the creature, wept, and said, "Please, help."

The bird seemed to understand. Or maybe, it was just sorry for this miserable fellow-creature who was prostrate before her. I noticed a tear form in one of its eyes. I was dumbfounded for a moment, but I managed to find a vial in my handbag. I opened it and extended it toward the bird's head. It moved a little closer and I was able to catch three small teardrops that fell from its eye. I stoppered the vial.

Then the Phoenix rose, spread its wings, and took off. That was it. I either had enough or not. I put the vial back in my handbag. I grasped my wand and disapparated back to Hagrid's cave. Slughorn and he were waiting for me. Slughorn said one word, "Yes?"

My radiant smile surely told the tale, "Yes! I'm going directly to the Hoggshead."

Slughorn said, "I'll go with you. I don't know how much help I can be, but I want to do whatever I can." He held out his hand. We joined hands and were off. We arrived outside Hoggsmeade and walked into town, avoiding people. I was afraid that the Hoggshead would be closed again, but it really wasn't that late. The door was unlocked. We entered.

Abeforth noticed us immediately and came to greet the new customers. I whispered to Slughorn, "Let him take your order. I'll go to the WC. I won't return." Abeforth nodded. Slughorn asked for a fire whiskey.

When I left the WC, I went directly down the back stairs. I found the portrait. Dumbledore's sister must have known what I wanted, because her portrait swung open. I climbed in, lit my wand, and closed the door behind me. I ran down the passage not caring how much noise I made. I flung the door to the Room of Requirement open, leaped down, and ran to where you were lying. You'd not moved in the least. I took your hand that had been wounded.

I lifted it and gasped. The hand was shriveled and blackened. My tears flowed, but I found the original pinprick wound. I opened the vial and poured the contents on the wound and massaged it in. Then I dropped beside you. You were burning with fever. I wondered that you were still alive. I found some old towels, soaked them with water, rung them out, and applied them to your feverish head.

By this time, Slughorn had arrived. He was standing over me evaluating the situation. He said, "I have some medicine that will help with the fever." He had the audacity to chuckle. "It's actually Muggle medicine. It's called astin or aspin or something like that. I'll crush the tablets and mix them with water. Then we'll try to get him to swallow a little."

I exclaimed, "You have something to crush them in/with?"

He chuckled again, "You don't think that I did nothing all that time you were taking your little hike?"

I let a lot of the pent-up emotion go in the next few minutes. "Little hike! Little hike? I ought to force you to take that little hike and you'll see how you feel about it." Of course, that mild reproof followed some rather strict words that were the first out of my mouth. Slughorn took it rather well. He was working the mortar and pestle furiously all the time. Then he took the result which was almost more like a paste than a liquid. He added a little water and the result could be swallowed—if you didn't gag on it.

He then brought it in a spoon to your mouth. He raised your head a little and tried to get it down your throat. More dribbled out on your chin than got in, but some did. He then turned to me and asked, "Do you think you can do that three times a day?"

I was still testy. I said, "God damn you, I'll do a whole lot more than that if it's necessary."

Slughorn smiled. "Good. I think with a little practice, you can. Now, let's see you try it."

I picked up the mortar and pestle. Slughorn took three of the pills out of the bottle that seemed to have hundreds of pills. He placed them in the mortar and smiled. "Your turn." I conjured a little water into the mortar and started grinding. Of course, I didn't have a good technique at first, but I managed to grind the pills to powder and add water to make something that could be swallowed.

Slughorn said, "OK. Now get him to take it."

"But, you've already given him a dose. Won't this be too much?"

He shook his head. "Oh, girl, there's almost no way that you could give him too much. Now, that doesn't mean that you can grind up fifty pills and try to give it to him. It's just that you don't have to be too fine in your judgment."

I asked, "What about food? He's not eaten in almost two days."

Again, Slughorn was dismissive. "People can go for more than a week without food. Water is a different thing. If he isn't well enough to take some water soon, we may have to consult a healer."

My immediate reaction was sharp, "NO!! NO!! They'll just send him to a labor camp. That is IF they even care to save him."

Slughorn sighed, "I suppose you're right. I'll do a little very, very cautious feeling around to see if I can find some healer who has the milk of human kindness in her. But we'll wait for a couple of days to see if he comes around."

The possibility of his leaving to look for a healer troubled me for another reason. "Do you have to go? You know so much more about this than I do."

He smiled and said, "You will do fine."

"Should I start to try to get him to drink or eat?"

"Don't do either until he actually asks for it. Even then, don't give him much of either food or water for the next couple of days after he comes around. I'll be back before then." He smiled and said, "Don't worry. If he survived this long, he's got a real will to live. He's probably past the worst. Look at his hand."

I did. The swelling and discoloration were noticeably less.

Slughorn went on. "He'll be OK. Just don't try to rush it." He turned to leave, but then stopped and added, "With a devoted healer like you, he's got what he really needs—someone who cares about him. Take good care of him, as I'm sure you will."

I leaped up and ran to him. I took his hand and wrung it. "I can't thank you enough for risking your own life to rescue him."

He said, "You know, when I was younger, I thought that I could buy friends by doing little favors and having influential friends. Now I know better. The friends you have are friends because of the big favors you let them do for you."

I've still been trying to puzzle that out. Anyway, he left, and I was here with you. Most of the time, I just sat next to you and held your hand that was fast healing. You were still unconscious. I kept feeding you the "astin" or whatever it was. After the second dose, your temperature was clearly less. By the second day, you were as close to fever-free as I could tell, but you were still unconscious.

At one point, I was so afraid that you'd never wake up that I just swore. "God-damn you to hell, Riddle. You fucking coward, just come here and face YOUR medicine."

Even though you were getting better, that was the low point of our life together. Then, the next day, something happened—you fluttered your beautiful eyes and said something about being embarrassed.

# The Battle of Riddle Place

The next thing that happened was that I opened my eyes. I found Ginevra hovering over me. She had a spoon of noxious stuff that she was trying to force down my throat. I said, "OK. OK. I'll take it, but it had better be followed hard on by some food and drink."

The way she carried on, you'd think that I'd returned from the grave or something. She seemed stunned. Then she threw her arms around me and kissed me. Then she held up a finger and said, "Food and water coming up." I had to admit that she did move quickly. She was back with an MRE and a small glass of water. She gave me the water first. The only problem was that she would only let me drink a little of it. But she did follow it with some beef stew—a spoonful or two—and mushed-up carrots. I said, "I see that you've decided to starve me slowly rather than all at one time."

Her face didn't change its beatific smile in the slightest, but she did cry a lot of tears as she fumbled out. "You have to take your time. You don't want to . . ."

I sighed, "I know, throw it up all at once. Fine. Fine. Just give me as much as I can have."

That day was slow. She mostly just sat next to me and talked a little. She wouldn't let go of my hand. I didn't complain. I just hoped that we'd get to share the bed that night. I had another tiny meal that evening. Shortly after than, I found that I could hardly keep my eyes open. I fell asleep without knowing if we'd shared the bed.

□

I awakened to find Ginevra at my elbow, ready to feed me some MRE. She started to push a spoon at me. I was strong enough to take it from her hand and put it in my mouth. I said, "How about handing the MRE to me?"

She actually cried as she shakily handed it to me. She just said, "Don't eat too much. Leave some for me."

I laughed. "Have I been out so long that we've eaten all the MRE's we had?"

She laughed and cried at the same time. "No. You should just eat slowly and not too much."

I asked, "Do we have anything more to do here?"

She stared at me as though I were crazy. Then she said, "Are you up to doing some things?"

"Sure. We've got to get on our way. What's our next step?"

She stared at me and asked, "You always seemed to have the answer to that. What do we do next?"

I stared for a minute while I ate. Then I said, "OK. The next thing is to familiarize ourselves with the possible places where Riddle could be hiding in my universe. Those would be the Malfoy and the Riddle mansions. Can we get into those in this universe?"

Ginevra answered, "I don't know. You stay here, and I'll investigate them. I'll find out."

I was frustrated. I wanted to help. I said, "Look. I hate to think of you out there by yourself taking risks."

She looked frustrated as well. "You aren't well enough to walk by yourself. You drive me crazy. Why do you want to put yourself and me at risk by insisting to come along."

I said, "Watch. I'll get up and show you who's able to travel." I stood and I grimaced in pain. I lowered myself back to the makeshift mattress where I had been sleeping. "OK. You go and find what we can do. Just be damn careful."

She smiled and bent to me. "I will. You get better." Then she kissed me. That was wonderful. She headed for the exit to the tunnel to the Hoggshead. She opened the door, turned and smiled at me.

□□

I took time every couple of hours to stand and walk. I took a tour of the Room of Requirement. It was a strange place. I'd already seen a lot of it, but now I could actually take time and appreciate what was around me. Sure, it was mostly junk—broken flying brooms, broken furniture, and things that I couldn't identify other than to say that they were broken. It was hard to believe that students would pile objects as high as they did.

The next day, I decided to see if I could find the wall opposite the entrance to the tunnel that led to the Hoggshead. I walked and walked. The one good thing that I was accomplishing was improving my endurance. I eventually came to a stack of *detritus* that stretched to the ceiling. It might have just been a wall of the stuff, but I was pretty sure that on the other side was the wall of the Room of Requirement.

When I returned from that last walk, I found Ginevra waiting for me. She had two MRE's out. I asked, "Dinner time?"

"Yes, sir. Let's eat and then talk."

The meal was as it always was with MRE's: nutritious, varied, warm, and boring. I joked, "It's sad to think that we are just feet away from the best food in the world, but we have to eat this . . ."

We finished and she said, "All right. Here's the story. The Malfoys still own and frequently occupy their mansion in the country. Now, they mostly live in the city in an abandoned home. I think that I heard that it had belonged to the PM, whoever that was."

I considered that. Then I said, "It sounds like you don't want to try to explore it."

She said, "I didn't say that. I just suggest that we spend a limited amount of time there. We should watch it a while to determine for sure if the family is at home. When they are not, we disapparate in and do a quick reconnoiter. We draw a map. We leave."

I commented, "That sounds good to me."

She said, "You're not completely well yet."

"How do you figure?"

"If you were, you'd have additional ideas." With that she snuggled close and we did some necking.

The next morning, we packed for an extended stretch of camping outdoors. The parkas and several weeks of MRE's went into the one large extensible bag that we had. I discovered that Ginevra had also bought some additional supplies—a pair of omni-occulars, a small tent, some nondescript robes for the both of us.

I asked her how she'd got the galleons for that. I had plenty of my world galleons, of course, but they were no good here. She said, "Your name apparently carries some weight at Gringotts. I mentioned your name. I had to wait a while for someone to show up. Toward the end of the wait, I was fairly afraid of the possibility that Deatheaters would march through the main entrance and try to haul me away."

I asked, "OK. What actually happened?"

"A goblin came out to the waiting area and invited me back to a back office. In the back office, there was a female goblin waiting. She queried me closely about you. It appears that you must have worked with her to a good extent. She asked me all sorts of questions about you such as where you came from, what you did at Hogwarts, and so forth.

"Frankly, I think she was more hoping that you were alive than believing that I knew you. Anyway, at the end, she had me wait while she went down to your vault. She came back with two thousand galleons that she said was from your vault. They were new style galleons, so I guess she must have converted your old galleons to new style."

I nodded. "Her name was Javeen, right?"

Ginevra's eyes bulged out. "You mean that you really worked with her?"

I grimaced and admitted the truth. "Well, it was more like she worked for me as a little side job, but yes."

She shook her head. "Well, we've got to get going if we're going to get to the Malfoy place before nightfall and set up our camp."

We walked out the tunnel. At the end, after we got into the basement of the Hoggshead, she said, "We're going to disapparate directly from here. Abeforth agreed to that after I pointed out that the more that we were seen in the common part of the inn, the more danger there was for him."

I scoffed. "I'm surprised that he didn't just throw you out at that point."

She smiled. "He's a cagey old cuss. I think he's more on our side than you might think. Anyway, that makes things really sweet for us. We can come in and out totally unobserved and go anywhere we like." Then she held out her hand and we disappeared. We landed in a clearing near the edge of a forest. I breathed in sharply when I saw where we were.

Ginevra asked, "What was that about?"

I shook my head. "I've been here before. It must be the ideal place to observe the mansion."

Ginevra nodded. "Right. We can see the main entrance. The Malfoys still subscribe to the old code of customs. You disapparate outside the gate to an estate and then walk in. That works for leaving as well."

"Will everyone go when the family does, including all house elves?"

Ginevra shrugged. "That's the custom. These Deatheaters hold by customs pretty rigorously when it's other wizards they're dealing with." She added with a smile. "Of course, we're not going to abide by those traditions."

I smiled at that. Then she set up the small tent on the other side of a hill from the mansion. It was about the size of a pup tent. I commented that it reminded me of a tent that I'd once shared with a canoing buddy with whom I'd once canoed the boundary waters between Minnesota and Ontario. It was just large enough for two.

Then, Ginevra took my hand while we entered it. Like all wizarding tents it was larger than it looked from the outside. In this case, there was just one large area that included a kitchenette, a folding table and four folding chairs, and a queen-size inflatable mattress. She said, "Modest, I know, but I wanted something that would look unpretentious." Then she smiled. "Sorry about there being only one bed."

"I think that we can muddle through." With that I wrapped an arm around her and began to lead her toward the bed.

She easily twisted free and said, "We can manage that later. For now, let's set up to watch and plan next steps."

We went back outside and laid down a blanket so that we could lie on the ground with only our heads extending over the hill where we were. The omni-occulars were impressive. We watched over the next couple of days, including nights. We could see at night almost as well as during the day with them.

Our plan was to watch for a mass exodus from the house that would signal the end of the occupation for a while. We had two watches during the night. One was from sunset to after midnight. The other was the rest of the night to sunrise. We always had a watch on the house, so the only joint use of the bed didn't happen while we were at the Malfoy residence.

One day while one of us was watching, and the other was fixing breakfast, the entire household assembled outside the house. There were the three Malfoys and several house elves.

We had occasionally seen other people arrive and leave. Some were probably Deatheaters. At least one was a young woman. Ginevra commented, "I think that must be Draco's girlfriend. She reminds me of that girl that he was dating at Hogwarts."

I asked, "You mean Astoria?"

Ginevra agreed. Then she said, "I'm not sure it's her though."

"No matter. If this is it, I think we should wait until afternoon just to make sure that nobody comes back for anything."

"Agreed."

They all disapparated. We waited until the afternoon by my watch. Ginevra never wore one. When the time elapsed, I said, "OK. Let's walk down. I want to allow a little extra time, and I want us to use as little magic as possible on their property."

She just nodded. Then we walked. The hillside down was gentle and had only a few trees before it broke into grass. It was a quarter mile walk to the gate and then a good long walk from the gate to the front door. We approached it slowly. When we arrived, I asked, "Let's try the door. First, can you detect any defensive spells?"

She shook her head and started to reach forward. I took her arm and said, "Let me. If something's going to happen, I want it to happen to me." Ginevra didn't argue.

I grasped the doorknob and turned gently. Nothing happened. I swung the door wide, and we entered. Inside the layout was what I remembered from the only other time that I'd been in the house. The main floor had a grand staircase that led up. On the right and left were doors. Ginevra got out a piece of parchment and drew a rough diagram of the first floor. We entered the room on the right.

Ginevra asked what this room was.

It looked to me like a waiting room where guests would wait while their card was taken up to the family to decide whether the visitor would be taken up to see family members. I said so.

Ginevra laughed. "You're kidding, right?"

I shook my head in agreement. As we walked through the other rooms on the main floor I commented. Across from the waiting room was a simply furnished dining room. "This is where the servants would dine below stairs. Behind it is a kitchen, where meals are prepared." We kept walking. Behind it was a dormitory. I said, "I suppose this is for part of the house elves." Next to it was another similar dormitory. "This is for the other half of the house elves."

We went up to the next floor. There was a parlor where guests were entertained. Behind it was a library. Behind that was a small room with flatware and china. Next to it was a large dining room where the family and guests dined. Next to it was a large room that connected with the dining room by a sliding door. I guessed that it was a ballroom. We proceeded to the third floor. There were a number of bedrooms there. One was obviously the master bedroom. As we walked, Ginevra was extending the map of the Malfoy Mansion. At the end, I said, "Ok. Let's practice disapparating into each room. Give me the map. I'll name rooms at random. You'll disapparate us to them.

We did that for a while. I repeated rooms occasionally. Every now and then we went to a different room than the one that I'd named. I expected that. By the end, we'd visited every room at least twice and had gotten every single room right on the first try at least once. We'd ended in the waiting room on the first floor. Ginevra asked if we couldn't finally leave. I agreed.

I stepped out into the entry hall. Ginevra stayed in the waiting room looking around.

As I was about to call Ginevra out, the doorknob rattled and turned. The door opened. I spun around. Framed in the door was a figure that I didn't recognize at first. He was back-lit, but as my eyes adjusted, I recognized Draco Malfoy. He didn't recognize me at first. He raised a wand and pointed it at me. He demanded, "Who are you and what are you do . . ." He stopped and his voice changed. He asked THE question, "Who are you?" He hesitated and said, "You're Professor Wendt, aren't you?"

"Yes, I'm Professor Wendt." I quickly added, "I'm not here to steal or cause any harm to your house or property." I lied by telling the truth (partial). I wasn't there to steal or pillage. I was strictly there for information.

He just stared at me with his wand up. I asked, "What brought you back?"

He said, "I felt a strange thrill go through me, like someone stepping on my grave."

Ginevra appeared behind him with her wand pointed. I shook my head slightly, hoping that she would notice. I said, "Draco, we used to be friends, almost."

He said, "What were you here for if not to steal?"

"I came to see your home. I live 'rough' now. I wanted to see how people lived who don't have to struggle every day wondering what they'll eat that night."

He said, "How do you find something to eat?"

"I am a mendicant."

He laughed, "A fancy name for beggar. Whom do you beg from?"

"There are wizard families who take pity on the remaining Muggles."

He was silent. This was it. What way would he come down? Then I said, "Why don't we just walk out the front door together? You know, like the friends we used to be."

He sighed. Then he nodded. He turned toward the door. I walked quickly to join him. He opened the door and extended his hand as though I were a guest who was on his way and might return again soon. I exited. He followed me. We walked a few steps away from the door. He raised his wand and disapparated. I stood for a minute or two and then proceeded to the main gate. I started to walk in a random direction generally away from our camp. Ginevra quickly followed me, shouting, "Wait up. I'll be with you in a few ticks and we can disapparate to our tent." I did.

Back at the camp, it was now late afternoon. We decided to have a meal and take it easy for the rest of the day. That night we had a special meal that consisted of fresh food that she had purchased along with the tent. That night we slept together. It was a time of catharsis. Somehow, meeting Draco had brought back a lot of good things, and frankly, some bad memories too. We didn't make love. It would have been too hard, but holding each other was necessary.

The next day, we broke camp. Almost everything went back in the expandable duffel. As we packed, I talked about our next destination, Riddle Manor.

"When we get there, I want to handle things a little differently than here. When Draco showed up, it was lucky that I could truthfully say that I only wanted to look. I was being completely honest. At Riddle Manor, things will be different. No one is likely to walk in on us. We need to do a full exercise of how we'll attack Riddle. I think he'll be at Riddle Manor, but I can't be sure that he won't be at Malfoy Manor.

"So, we're going to be packing handguns with full clips of bullets and be ready to use them."

She looked at me hard. "This means we're almost ready to really do it." She paused. "I didn't realize that I might be killing people I knew. It could have been Draco. It still could be."

"Right. This is the time to do the practice—everything included except actual human victims."

She said softly, "It'll only be Riddle, right?" She added, "And Deatheaters in the room."

I shook my head. "You know better than that. We'll disapparate into the room that we think is the most likely for him to be. If he's not there, but there are people there, we have no choice."

She gulped. "I thought I could just kill all the faceless Deatheaters with no compunction. I thought, 'It's for the greater good'." She made a sound that might have been an attempt at laughter. "I'm not so sure, now."

I said, "The way you do it, is to practice and practice and practice until it's automatic. Until the only thought is that you kill with your mind. You've already decided and practiced killing."

She nodded.

We were ready to disapparate then. I took her hand and we landed in a cemetery. I didn't immediately recognize it, but a quick look around reminded me of the one time in the past that I'd been there. Ginevra was already setting up the tent in a hollow in the ground that was surrounded by low hills. The terrain kept it from being used for graves. We ate a humble meal of MRE's and then held each other again that night. We tried a little foreplay but we just weren't up for sex.

The next morning, we set up a place where we could watch the house and not be observed ourselves. During the day, I preferred the binoculars that we'd brought. Ginevra used omni-occulars. Our goal was to assure ourselves that no one was using the house, including squatters.

We watched long after sunset, but then a little foreplay got the better of us. We retreated to the tent where we had long-overdue sex. Then I watched for four hours followed by Ginevra. The next day, we began watching the house seriously. We agreed that if no one had arrived by the evening, no one was going to be there that night. I insisted that we watch the house for a solid week before entering it and doing our practice. In the mean time, I sent her off to find fluffy pillows. I wanted at least fifty. Ginevra was puzzled, but didn't press to have answers.

On the first day, she had found a store and bought about a dozen. They easily fit in the expandable duffel bag. On that day, an idea occurred to me. "Ginevra, we don't need perfect new pillows. Old dirty ones will do just fine for our purposes. Just find some Muggle houses and loot them."

She agreed. By that evening, we had more than the fifty that I wanted. The next days were boring. We sat and watched the mansion through binoculars and conversed softly. As the days went by, we both became anxious to DO something, as Ginevra would say.

One evening, as the sun was setting, I asked Ginevra, "When the Souls invaded, what was it like? What happened?"

She took a deep breathe and began to speak.

The first story that appeared in the *Prophet* was probably not a description of the real first incident—you know how the *Prophet* is. I've never heard another story, so it's probably as good as you'll get.

It started on a plantation in the States. I think it was in Alabama. It was a cotton plantation. In any case, raising cotton is very labor intense work. The ratio of slaves to Deatheaters was well over one hundred to one. At the time, there were far more slaves than could be profitably used, so no one particular tried to make the work any easier or more pleasant than they had to.

The overseer of the plantation was surprised as the summer wore on that year that the slaves seemed to work harder and with less "encouragement"-- that is the *Cruciatus* Curse—than usual. He was becoming rather famous among the Alabama plantation owners for the amount of output and profit that he was achieving. However, that success was short-lived.

The overseer had become so confident of the docility and reliability of the Muggle slaves that the guards had been given the night off. Then one night, the slaves overwhelmed the locking spell that kept their dormitory closed. There was no one to observe this escape. The slaves approached the overseer house with stealth. There were half a dozen wizards and witches sleeping in the mansion. One wizard, Rupert Goss, was up. He was having a butter beer when there was a knock on the front door. Puzzled, he went to the door and asked who was there. He says that the person who knocked on the door said, "Master, there's a man who's really sick."

Goss said, "Come in the morning. No, don't come in the morning, we'll see you then. Now get back to your dorm." Meanwhile, there was a crash at the back of the mansion. Goss had his wand out and ran to the back. This was the critical moment for the invasion. Goss was the smartest Deatheater on the plantation. Rather than assume that he would handle whatever the slaves could do, he disapparated to the bedroom level two floors above. He blasted the bedroom doors down and raised the alarm.

Goss's hardest challenge was convincing the rest of the wizards that they needed to mount a defense. Meanwhile the slaves were struggling up the one flight of stairs to the main living floor. They split into two groups— one to search the second floor, the other to proceed to the bedrooms.

Meanwhile Goss had put together a rough line of defense at the top of the stairs to the third floor. The slaves swarmed up the stairs. They were met by a ragged line of wizards. One or two tried petrificus spells, but as the rest of the swarm ran over the fallen slaves, they all immediately switched to *avada kedavra*. There were perhaps eight or ten killed but the rest of the swarm was now over them and there were only a few feet separating the swarm and the wizards.

Goss again proved his mettle by immediately shouting out, "Disapparate to the Auror Office!"

They arrived at an office in Vancouver, Washington that was crowded with wizards from plantations all over the West of the States. It was pandemonium. Goss struggled to find his way to the Chief of Aurors. He ended up having to mill around with all the other Deatheaters.

The East Coast Auror Office was also swamped with Deatheaters fleeing mobs of formerly cowed slaves. No one had an idea of what was happening. The Secretary of Magic called an emergency meeting of his staff. They did two things. First, they called in the Wizard Radio executives. As a result Wizard Radio broadcast emergency instructions for all wizards to gather at the larger wizard towns. Aurors were sent to all of them to organize defenses of the towns.

The second meeting that the Secretary of Magic called was a deeper strategy session. During all of this time, Goss had stayed at the West Auror

Office continually. When everyone had left for the enclaves, Goss stayed and waited. When the crowd thinned out, he had migrated up to the Secretary's office. No one paid attention to him. When the second meeting happened, Goss mildly joined a small crowd that went into the Conference Room. There was a lengthy period of introductions. He was next to last. He simply said, "Rupert Goss, Supervisor." He spoke it softly. In the excitement, no one was paying a lot of attention.

The only agenda item was how to deal with the insurrection. All of the invited wizards were mystified by the uprising. The Head of Aurors was asked to give a status. He turned to an assistant, Edward Jones.

He stood, walked to the whiteboard and drew a rough outline of the United States. He then took a green marker and made a dozen green circles on the map. He then took a yellow marker and drew two circles. He said, "The green circles are wizard enclaves that seem to be safe for the moment. The yellow are ones that are under attack at this moment. Everything else is enemy territory."

The Secretary of Magic exclaimed, "That's impossible! How can mere Muggles have taken control of the country?"

The Auror, Josh Greenbaum, said, "They outnumber us almost a thousand to one. If they are determined, they can simply overrun us."

Goss raised a hand. "That requires coordination. I can see how a single plantation could be overrun, but how could all the plantations be overrun at the same time?"

Greenbaum said, "The Muggles had means of communicating across the world instantly. We've never been able to duplicate that power. Maybe there is an underground resistance that has never been captured."

The Secretary interrupted the conversation and said, "Why does it matter how they coordinated? All we have to do is defeat them. How do we do it?"

The Secretary of Food Production was recognized and said, "First, we need to secure food supplies. There are some critical warehouses that are in enemy territory that we need to capture. Then we can distribute food from them to our enclaves. Once our food supplies are ensured, we can mount a counter-offensive."

That was so obviously true that no one argued against it. The Secretary of Magic said, "Goss, you got into this meeting under false pretenses. You are going to pay for that. You are to lead a team of Aurors to conquer and secure the most important of the food warehouses. You will work with Greenbaum to achieve that."

Greenbaum was about to object, but noting the expression on the Secretary's face decided not to. The Secretary was continuing, "The Secretary of Food Production will be in charge of distributing it to all our enclaves."

Just then, a messenger entered the Conference Room and placed a small parchment in the hand of Greenbaum. He glanced at it and hung his head. The Secretary asked him what had happened. Greenbaum rose, walked to the whiteboard, picked up a red pen and drew an "X" through one of the two yellow circles. No one had to ask what that meant.

The next week, Goss was meeting with a team of wizards consisting of Aurors and volunteer Deatheaters.

He began, "As you know, we are dealing with a suicidal revolution of the Muggles. I was on a plantation when the slaves revolted. We killed until they were stacked like cordwood." There were appreciative laughs and incoherent words of approval at that statement. Goss went on, "We are now cowering in small enclaves. One has been attacked successfully. It was overwhelmed by sheer numbers. Supplies of food are becoming scarce in those enclaves. Our mission is to attack a complex of warehouses in Denver, Colorado."

He signaled the projectionist at the back of the room. A slide was projected on the wall that showed a photograph that included several warehouses and surrounding streets. "We will disapparate onto the sides of this area." He used his wand to draw a red line around the area. "Everyone will set a Muggle-repelling spell. Then, we will locate any Muggles inside this area with a *revellio* spell. I want them stunned, not killed. I'll select a couple of them for interrogation. Then the rest of them may be disposed of.

"In the next phase of the operation, experts in creating port keys will disapparate into the warehouses. They will make pallets into port keys with destinations in the enclaves. The rest of the force will load the pallets with food from the warehouses. The port key experts will direct loading the pallets so that all of their cargo can go directly to the enclaves. Each port key wizard has a list of destinations for the food. Usually it is one or two per wizard. At the end of the operation when we've sent a couple of month's food supplies to the enclaves, we will evacuate the facility. What questions are there?"

One Deatheater in the back of the room asked, "What's a pallet?" Goss looked over at Greenbaum who just shrugged.

Goss went on. "We leave immediately. Prepare to land in enemy territory. In truth, I don't know what we will face. You should be prepared to enter a fight the moment you land. Is anyone not ready to leave?"

No one would admit it. Goss waited a moment and then said, "On the count of three: one, two, three." With that, the room emptied. The moment that Goss disapparated on the street there was a rush of Muggles toward him and the other wizards. They placed a Muggle-repelling spell around the blocks where they landed. The Muggles approached the barrier, slowed, and then stopped. Goss released a sigh of relief. He'd been rushed by a horde of Muggles once before. He didn't want the experience repeated. This was not a horde. There were not enough to form a continuous line around the blocks that were protected, but that did not make him feel any better. He ordered the wizards to stay in place. He disapparated around the perimeter to make sure that all was well. When he'd completed the circuit, he left a token guard on all sides to watch for trouble and brought the rest of the wizards into a warehouse.

Inside, the light provided by grimy windows into the warehouse was sparse, but wizard wand-light provided an acceptable level of lighting. He sent a wizard back to headquarters to bring the port key wizards. He then sent wizards to inventory what was in the warehouse.

The port key wizards arrived quickly. Goss sent them off to find pallets. In a short while the inventory wizards returned with their survey results. The items that they had found were: breakfast cereals, canned vegetables, canned fruits, canned beans, canned meats, and some kind of deserts that were called "Hostess". There were Hostess Twinkies, Hostess HO-HO's, and Hostess Cupcakes. At least, he knew what cupcakes were. He hoped they were what he thought they were.

Goss gave instructions. "Put together equal numbers of cans of vegetables, fruits, beans, and meats. Throw in a case or two of one of the Hostess products and send them to each of the enclaves. After we've gotten enough of the basics to them, we can circle back and start sending breakfast cereal and deserts. Someone should go with each pallet to make sure that distribution happens fairly."

One of the Deatheaters said, "Deatheaters first." He sighed. That was the sort of idea that would get everyone killed. He said, "There will be enough for all." He left it at that.

The first few pallets transported were overloaded and shaky. When one landed, it smashed, but the cans were mostly intact. After that, the port key wizards had a better idea of how to load the pallets. Shipments went easily. They worked through the day and into the night. He finally let the wizards rest for the night.

He had left a watch through the night. In the early hours of the morning, there was an alarm. Goss was awake instantly. He ran out to find a huge crowd of Muggles illuminated by wand light. They were pressing against the Muggle repelling charm. The guard who set off the alarm ran up to Goss, who asked, "Why did you get me up for this? They'll never get through."

The guard shook his head and said, "I'd swear that that line of Muggles is slowly working its way in."

Goss didn't want to start a panic, but he could see that it was a spooky scene in the wand light. He wasn't so sure that the line was advancing slowly. He asked his guard how much time there was until he was relieved.

"A little less than an hour."

Goss decided that it would be a good idea to get fresh eyes on that line of humans. He sent the wizard for his replacement. He added, "Don't say anything about your suspicions."

The replacement was none too happy, but Goss gave him permission to get his replacement an hour early. He added, "Stay sharp. I might just come out and check on you later."

After breakfast, the line was still holding, but Goss could swear that it was closer to the warehouse. He set his team to work. He told his second in command that he was going to get more help.

He returned to the Department of Magic and found Greenbaum. Greenbaum was hoping not to see Goss before the mission was completed successfully. His appearance couldn't be good. So, he asked with real trepidation, "What can I do for you?"

Goss was not shy. "We're in some trouble at the warehouse. The Muggles are . . ." He wasn't sure how to finish the sentence.

Greenbaum asked, "What in the world could the Muggles be doing?"

Goss sighed and said, "I don't understand it. They seem to be on the verge of breaking though our Muggle-repelling spells."

Greenbaum asked, "What do you want?"

"I want more wizards so we can finish up as fast as possible."

Greenbaum seemed relieved. He said, "Is that all? I was afraid. Well, I'm not sure what I was afraid of, but I can tell you that what you just said was a relief. How many do you want?"

Goss was relieved too. He didn't think it would be that easy. He thought a moment and decided, "If you can double my numbers, it would be great."

"Is that all?"

Goss chuckled. "Sure. I don't think I could use more if I had them. They'd just be tripping over each other if I had more. Thanks."

Greenbaum hesitated. "I'll send them, but, before you go, stay for a meeting that's about to happen."

Now was Goss's turn to shudder. He nodded. Greenbaum took him by the elbow and said, "We only have a few minutes before the meeting starts. Come." They went to the same conference room as before. Many of the same participants were there. However, there was one new one. Her name was LeStrange, Bellatrix Lestrange. She quickly took over the meeting as soon as the Secretary of Magic introduced her. "Bellatrix is the Minister of Muggle Affairs in the Ministry of Magic."

The words were hardly out of his mouth when she stood and said, "I report directly to Lord Valdemort. He has sent me out to inform all the major Ministries that Lord Valdemort has decided how to deal this insurrection.

"First, we don't know what caused this sudden uprising. Even worse, it seems to be worldwide. We have no idea how the uprising was coordinated worldwide.

"Second, Lord Valdemort has decided that the only way to deal with this uprising is to kill all Muggles that we can until it stops.

"Finally, I've been sent to get ideas on how to kill Muggles en mass. We will evaluate them and suggest the best idea, but you should not hesitate to use your best idea immediately. So, what ideas do you have?"

It's a funny thing about people who work for Riddle. They hate to stick their heads above broom level. No one had anything to say. That is, except Goss. He thought for a few minutes and said, "The problem is not how to kill Muggles, there are dozens of ways. The problem is how to kill them in large numbers quickly. I have a modest proposal. What would happen if a wizard flying, maybe a thousand or two thousand feet above ground level used the spell, *accio* Muggles? Then, released the spell?"

Lestrange smiled and said, "How quickly can you test that?"

Goss said, "I've got at team on site with many Muggles nearby."

"Then let's go right now." Then she hesitated and added, "I want to do it myself. I'll need a broom."

The Head of Aurors said, "I'll have one brought here immediately."

She cackled, "Make it quick."

A broom was brought up by a flunky in the Auror Office. She handed it to LeStrange. Goss motioned her to accompany him to the Atrium of the Secretariat. When they arrived, he held out his hand to her. She took it haughtily and they disappeared.

They reappeared at the warehouse. One of the Aurors ran up to Goss and said, "The Muggles! They've almost broken through. We've still got a lot of food to transport."

LeStrange interrupted him, "What are you saying about Muggles."

He turned to her and said, "The Muggles have been inching through the Muggle repelling spell. It seems like there are so many Muggles pushing at the barrier that they are just being forced through somehow. We don't know what to do."

LeStrange said, "I do." She walked out of the warehouse and was struck dumb by the sight of so many Muggles pressing against an invisible barrier that was slowly giving away. She mounted the broom and flew high into the air. Suddenly, she leveled off, and the Muggles flew up into the air. They went hundreds of feet up. Then suddenly, as though they were puppets on strings that had broken, they fell. They formed a pile a little distance from the warehouse. No one moved on the pile. Then LeStrange flew down and landed next to Goss.

She said, "Now that's the way to deal with Muggles! You're a smart wizard. So far no one has had a suggestion as good as yours. When you're finished here, I just might ask you to come back to London."

Goss shrugged and said, "I am at your disposal."

The meeting in the Minister of Magic's Office was two months later. Goss had been put in charge of the Muggle Eradication project. There was a weekly progress report meeting. Goss had authored the report. He had a difficult message to deliver. It wasn't any easier due to the fact that Valdemort himself was to be present.

The meeting was called to order by LeStrange in advance of Valdemort's appearance. Everyone in the room immediately became as silent as the tomb, and only then Valdemort would appear. This time Valdemort stormed into the room ready to use the *Cruciatus*.

He faced Goss and said, "Mr. Goss, I've just finished reading this progress report. It says in the executive summary that the Muggle rebellion is effectively over. That's true even though we have killed somewhere between five and ten percent of the Muggle population by your own reports. Would you please explain that?"

Goss stood and breathed a calming breath. Then he said, "Your numbers are correct. However, I have been approached by a representative of the Muggles who gave me convincing evidence that the rebellion can be over without wizard loss of life. IF—and this is the critical point—you agree to a cease fire for a month."

Valdemort laughed. "Are you a simpleton? They just want time to regroup and resume the battle."

Goss said, "I don't think so. The message came to my home by a mechanical device. The message said that if we didn't agree to it, they would incinerate the surface of the Earth."

Valdemort's laugh resumed but was subdued. "And you believed that?"

Goss said, "I didn't at first, however, the message invited me to witness a small demonstration. It happened on the northernmost point of the State of Alaska—a place called Point Barrow. It happened last Friday. I had a port key made that would take me there. I arrived an hour before the appointed time. When the hour arrived, the sky was filled with light and after two or three minutes I was knocked down by a wind that was like a wall. I returned and wrote my report for this Monday morning meeting."

Valdemort was silent for long moments. Then he turned to the Head of Aurors and said, "Bring *Veritas Serum*. We will learn the truth of this." It was twenty minutes before an aurorflunky appeared with the *Veritas Serum*. She gave it to Goss who drank it down readily.

There were questions that verified the truth of what Goss said. Then, Valdemort asked the important question. "How much time do we have?"

Goss said in a flat voice, "Just one week. Then the cease fire either begins or 'bang'."

Valdemort turned without a word and left the meeting room.

The next day, there was an emergency meeting with Valdemort, the Head of Aurors, LeStrange, and Goss. It was the shortest meeting in the history of the reign of Valdemort. He called the meeting to order himself and said, "Stop all action against Muggles immediately. Contact all Ministries around the world. Inform them that if they don't end all actions against Muggles, I will personally deal with them. The meeting is adjourned."

I asked Ginnevra how many died in that awful incident. She replied, "We never knew for sure. I think the five percent figure for deaths from Valdemort's war against them is close to the truth, but there were more than thirty percent of Muggles who died. We never knew how they died."

I said, "I think I can explain a lot of what you don't understand.

"The aliens inserted Ghosts into Muggles. Once inserted, they could control the 'host' Muggle. When they attacked our world, we eventually had the upper hand over them and forced them to remove the Ghosts from Muggles in such a way that the Muggle didn't die. Ordinarily, the removal resulted in the death of the 'host.' That happened in well over ninety percent of the cases.

"I think that the Ghosts had been inserted in no more than thirty percent of the Muggles. The rest were just ordinary Muggles."

That night we were both wrung out by the terrible story. Our love-making was much more intense. It was the only thing that gave us release from the seeming endless *ennui* followed by the hour of terror of that story. Finally, the seventh day arrived. Ginevra rejoiced, "At last. We can go in now!"

"Not quite. I wanted seven full days. We've not had that yet. Besides, I want a little more time. Let's enter early morning on the ninth day."

Ginevra shook her head and muttered something under her breath. There was no love-making that night, but we did spoon. The next day was tense. We were both counting the hours until we could go to bed and get some sleep. That time finally arrived.

The next morning, we were both up at first light. We ate a quick breakfast and walked to the main entrance. We were constantly watchful for observers.

We reached the main entrance and hesitated. Ginevra said, "Me first, this time."

I accepted her decision. The door opened. We went in. It was dark—darker than the Malfoy Manor had been. We did the same reconnoiter that we had there, mapping every major room in the house. The layout was similar, but there were differences. The lower level was actually mostly below ground level. There were servants quarters down below. They were furnished for pairs of people. They were small and utilitarian, but afforded some privacy. The first level above ground had all the features of the Malfoy Manor except that there was a combined waiting room/parlor rather than separate rooms. The second level above ground had the master bedroom at the head of the stairs and lesser bedrooms along both sides. There was an attic, which seemed to have some storage rooms and a couple of servants' rooms.

Then we mapped this house more carefully. We finished about lunch time, so we had lunch in the servant's hall—still MRE's. During lunch we discussed the plans for the next couple of days. I suggested, "Why don't we do a simple, one pass disapparation practice today. Once per room. Then we can set up for the exercises the next couple of days."

Ginevra asked, "What setup do we need to do?"

"I want the pillows that we have to be used as targets. Each time we disapparate into a room, we'll face four, five, or six pieces of furniture with pillows on them. The pillows represent Deatheaters or Riddle. We'll have five seconds to kill everyone in the room. After we disapparate into a room, I'll do a slow five count. If we don't kill all the pillows by then, we're dead."

She scoffed. "Why five seconds? Hummm? What's the magic about that?"

I smiled. "No magic, just neural science."

She scoffed again. "What kind of science?"

"The science of the nervous system. Military studies have shown that when something unexpected happens on a battlefield, it takes a minimum of five seconds for someone to react effectively. Disapparating into a room unannounced surely counts as unexpected."

She smiled and squeezed my forearm. "You've got an answer for everything, don't you?"

I replied, "What would your life be, if I didn't?"

She mumbled, "A lot more enjoyable."

So we disapparated into every room. As we went, I distributed pillows as randomly as I could manage. At the end, I declared that we were taking the rest of the day off so that we could "forget" where the pillows were in each room. We then talked about the live fire exercise that was coming up. I outlined how we would prepare.

"First, every time we disapparate, we'll do it back to back so that we can visually cover the entire room. Before we begin, we'll make sure all our magazines are full. We'll mount the silencers on our guns. We'll disapparate with safeties off and guns in hand.

"When we land, we'll kill the pillows in the room. Then we'll check our magazines. If they're less than half full, we'll change magazines before disapparating again. I sure hope that we'll not encounter enough Deatheaters before reaching Riddle that we'll need to reload when we're doing this for real, but we definitely will need to tomorrow."

Ginevra asked, "How many times will we do this exercise?"

"Until we can enter every room and kill all the pillows in five seconds."

She shook her head. "God! We'll be at this forever."

I sighed. "I guess if we plateau and can't improve, we'll just stop."

That night was one marked by the desperate affection of the last night before the deluge. We sat facing each other and avoiding thinking about the next day. That day could be the day that we were perfect, and we'd be forced to move on to the next stage—moving back to my universe and attacking Riddle. We held each other in our arms and snogged long into that night. Then we made love with abandon. The next morning, we loaded and checked our magazines, the guns, the silencers. Everything was in place. I picked up the map of the mansion. Then I named a destination—the master bedroom.

We landed back to back. I had two pillows in sight. I was so concentrated on shooting them that I forgot to count. I did get two good shots off. One was dead center. Another was a near miss. I hit the next target on the next shot. By this time, Ginevra had gotten off two shots—both found their marks. The third was a near miss. I'd got my third off by then. It hit. Unfortunately, no one knew how long it had taken. We shook our heads and swore we'd do better at the next chance.

I picked up the map and said, "Bedroom 2." We were not at each other's back, but we arrived. I did count up to five. I identified three pillows and began firing. The soft explosions of the bullets firing filled the time up until four. We looked around and did a high five that all pillows were killed in five seconds. She said, "It was great, but we didn't disapparate back to back."

The next target was another bedroom. It had six pillows. We disapparated in back to back and counted up. The sixth pillow died at the five second mark. Then we went on. We had shot over one hundred rounds. Seventy were hits. That finished the morning for us. I thought that we had done well. Ginevra was unhappy. We took a long break and returned to live fire practice in the afternoon.

This time, things were different. Almost the instant we arrived, we were firing. The silencer reduced the sound of the gunfire to quiet whistling. Almost all of the rooms were finished in less than five seconds. There were just two rooms that went over five seconds. They were large rooms with targets spaced at substantial distances.

We decided to try a night-time exercise that night. It went pretty well. It was harder to find good marks, of course. We had gone into each room with Ginevra's wand lit. The light was much like fluorescent. We still were pretty accurate despite the fact that it was harder to identify objects in that kind of light. When we were doing an attack for business, I didn't want to go night-time unless we had to. However, we decided to practice again the next night as well as during the day.

We were exhausted that night and just spooned our way to sleep.

The next morning, we loaded up and headed for the mansion. Inside we started the exercise with a string of successes. We entered a room and we hit all the targets in two or three shots each. We used fewer than four seconds to compete the job. However, by the last few rooms it took us more than five seconds.

We took a rest. My take was that we were really close to total success. Ginevra was practically in tears. "We can't do a night-time attack with lit wand. We have to use the light that's naturally there. We'd be a perfect target otherwise!" She wanted to be able to attack at night confidently in ambient light. So, we scheduled a session for that night.

We wore dark clothes. We counted the shots fired rather than the seconds expended. I thought that at night there would be more time because it would be harder to identify that an attack was happening—especially with silencers being used. The rooms were only illuminated by moonlight from a quarter phase moon coming in through unshuttered windows. It was a surreal experience. The dark rooms seemed filled with the ghosts of Riddle's victims.

Our eyes had become dark-adapted, but we frequently mis-identified objects. Flashes of gunfire lit the rooms briefly. We were trying for accuracy over speed. Our accuracy of identifying targets and hitting them was well below fifty percent. At the end, Ginevra was not happy, but doing the exercise seemed to fill a need that she had.

I flippantly commented, "We would be so much more effective if we had Muggle night vision goggles."

She whirled on me, "Shut up about your damn useless Muggle things. You know we can't use electronics around magic!"

That night we fell into bed in a flood of exhaustion.

The morning was slow and lazy.

We woke up half-awake. We spoke softly in each other's ears about the future. We would leave for my world. We would prepare for Riddle. Ginevra had an additional plan. She realized that we might not come back— so she wanted to say good-bye to friends and relatives.

She wanted to visit her parents. I couldn't deny the desire. As a matter of fact, I wanted to visit them too. Ginevra took my hand and we re-appeared in the Weasley front yard. It was about lunch time. We walked up to the front door and knocked. Mr. Weasley answered the door. The first person he saw was me. His mouth dropped open. I said, "Maybe we should come in right away."

He nodded. "Sure. Come in." As I passed through the door, he noticed Ginevra. He said, "OH."

Molly was as hospitable as ever. She invited us to lunch. We accepted eagerly. I said, "I don't know how long it's been since I've eaten a home-cooked meal!"

Molly asked, "What have you been eating then?"

Ginevra just shook her head and said, "Don't ask."

Arthur asked the obvious questions. "How did you get here, Professor Wendt? Why aren't you in one of the concentration camps? I hope you won't take offense at my openness."

I said, "No. No. I don't take offense at simple prudence. We are here because your daughter and I are about to take a trip from which we are unlikely to return. She and I want to say our final good-bye before we leave the country."

Mr. Weasley hung his head in sorrow. Then he said, "I'm sorry to hear that. Can you safely tell us what you are going to do?"

Molly Weasley convulsively took her daughter's hand. "Please, Ginny."

I knew there was no hope to be given, so I just looked on at the scene. Ginnevra said, "Professor Wendt and I are going on a quest. We very much doubt that we will see you again."

Mr. Weasley asked, "So, you're not going to tell us what you're going to do?"

Ginevra nodded. There were long moments of silence. Then Arthur was about to turn to me when Molly Weasley interrupted to invite us to lunch. She said, "You'll have plenty of time after lunch to fill us in on this terrible thing that is coming up for you, but for now, let's talk of old, happier times."

I agreed. I reminded them of the times that I'd come to the house looking for Muggle artifacts, and when Mr. Weasley and I had spent time out in the shed naming unknown Muggle things.

We had almost completed the lunch when Mr. Weasley brought the topic of the day up. "Can't you tell us anything of what you two are going to do that will get you sent to Azkaban or worse?"

Ginevra glanced at me, seeming to ask me to explain. I did. "Mr. Weasley, Mrs. Weasley, Ginevra and I . . ."

At this point, Molly interrupted. "Why are you so formal. Why don't you use Ginny's nickname."

I said, "Well, we are doing something very serious. It will be dangerous. Since it's serious, I want to stick with formal names."

Mr. Weasley asked if we would at least stay the night.

I immediately answered that I could not in good conscience do so. However, I offered to visit his collection of Muggle artifacts one last time. He agreed. The two of us went out to the shed.

When we got there, Weasley opened the door proudly. There was the amazing collection that I'd visited across the years. I nodded in appreciation. "Wonderful."

Weasley gave me a tour of his most recent acquisitions. He picked one up, a black device with a small qwerty keyboard. He asked, "What in the world is this. I can't make heads or tails of it. It's a little like a typewriter, but who cold read the pages typed with this?"

I smiled. "It's called a blackberry."

He puzzled over it. "How in the world could this be a blackberry. It's not a fruit of any sort. Why would anyone want a keyboard on a piece of fruit?"

I pondered how to explain. "I think it's called a blackberry only because of the color, which vaguely resembles that of a real blackberry. It's a communication device that let's you send typed messages rapidly over great distances."

Weasley scratched his head in puzzlement. Finally, he said, "It's just a mystery to me."

I asked, "With all the Muggles gone from their homes, I'd think that you'd find it easy to find all sorts of strange Muggle artifacts."

He grimaced. "Breaking into someone else's home to collect things just seems wrong. In the old days, I'd go to junk yards and trash dumps to look for things."

I nodded agreement. Then, I went on to a more important question—one that concerned him even more closely than this Muggle curiosity. "Mr. Weasley, I have a question for you."

"Fire away, lad, as the Muggles say, but first I have a question. Why do you call Ginny, Ginevra? I can't believe it's really about this formal, serious business excuse."

I smiled, "For the obvious reason."

Weasley shook his head, "And that would be?"

"I know another Ginny whom I don't want to confuse with your Ginevra."

"OK."

I said, "Please sit down."

"So, your question is serious."

"Very. Here's my dilemma. As I told you and Molly over lunch, there's a mission that Ginevra and I are going on. We really don't expect to return from it. I also wanted to see you for another reason.

"I've not said anything to Ginevra about this, but it is very important to me. I hardly know where to begin. Let me just say that before this mission is over, I may ask your daughter for her hand in marriage. I want your approval for that before we leave."

He stood, staring at me wide-eyed in shock. Finally, he collected his wits and said, "I'm glad we're sitting. There's hardly anyone Muggle or wizard that I like more than I like you. It would be a great honor to have you as a son. . ."

I finished for him, "But."

He nodded, "But, you're a slave. How did you ever escape and meet up with Ginny?"

I chuckled. "Well, the truth be told, she met up with me. It's going to be really hard to explain this, but there is a scientific theory that there are a large number of universes. They all have their own unique histories. Your Ginny found me in my universe. In my universe, Riddle lost. Potter lives. Muggles are free. I decided I had to help her with a goal that she has. I can't tell you what that goal is."

He shook his head. "This is terrible. The two of you would have nothing but serious trouble here. In your world, I don't know what you'll face, but the best would be that we will not see you often. What can I say?"

146

I started to answer him. He interrupted me, "I don't really have a choice, do I? Ginny is an adult and deserves to make her own decisions. But for me, I want you to know . . ." He paused and seemed to be wrestling with something that was terrible and irresistible. Then, he said, "I totally support you. If she wants to marry you, God help anyone who wants to keep her from you."

I nodded slowly. "Thanks. I don't know what will happen. I'm not entirely sure whether I want to marry Ginevra. I will tell you something that I am completely sure of—I love her with all my heart."

Weasley said, "That doesn't surprise me in the least. My Ginny deserves that love. Well, we'd better get back before we are severely missed." He had risen and walked toward the door. He turned as he reached it and said, "Oh, one more thing. If you really love her, I think you're crazy not to ask her to marry you as soon as possible."

We returned to the house. Ginevra and Molly were cleaning up lunch and talking heatedly. We entered, and they immediately shut up. The rest of the day was quiet. Everyone knew that this might be the last time we would be together. We hugged at the end. I heard Molly tell Ginevra, "Don't wait. It may be the last chance." Then Ginevra and I disapparated back to our camp.

# The Road Forks

That last night, we slept snuggled together in fear. We feared the fact that we had to face our worst enemy. So far we had fought pillows in the dark and faux Deatheaters unseen in the gloom. The next day, we were going to the opposite extreme. We were to beard the lion in his very den.

We woke that morning and ate a sparse breakfast. We began breaking camp. Our plan was to go to Diagon Alley and then into Knockturn Alley and then into Borgan and Bourke's and then into the vanishing cabinet and then into the vanishing cabinet in the Room of Requirement.

We had almost completed the packing our campsite when I noticed a man walking across the graveyard directly toward us. I was the first to notice him. I took Ginevra's arm and said, "Look here."

She looked up and said, "Oh, my God! He is a Muggle."

I said, "Oh, God! I know him."

She swung around to me and asked, "YOU know him? How?"

I said, "His name is Lieutenant Philip Minns."

She scoffed, "Well, that explains a lot."

"If you knew him, it would." By this time, he was within earshot. I took a step forward and said, "It must be something very important for you to show up here at this point."

He nodded and said, "You're right. You've not yet finished packing. Perhaps we could enter you tent and discuss the state of things."

I agreed. Ginevra wasn't so sure, but Minns and I were going in. What choice had she?

I invited him to sit at the folding table. He invited Ginevra by name to join us. We sat and he said, "I have a very important request for you both. Since you know me, Mr. Wendt, I'll depend on you to fill in details that Ms. Ginevra may need."

I shrugged. "Sure. It's only logical."

Minns smiled at that. Then he turned to Ginevra. "Please listen carefully. What I have to say would strike many as preposterous, but then, so would magic a quarter century ago to many a Muggle."

He returned his attention to me and said, "Perhaps you could give Ms. Weasley some background on me."

I took the cue, and I began. "Ginevra, this gentleman is a human being who has some very extraordinary capabilities. In my universe . . ." I paused and looked to him to ask the question, "Are you from this universe or mine or somewhere else?"

He smiled, "Oh, this universe, definitely."

"Good. Well, this person in my universe received something as a sort of inheritance. I think it would be safe to call it a gift. He is able to do a lot of amazing things. One that is far from the most amazing was to build a spaceship that could travel between the stars."

She started to laugh and then decided that it might not be a good idea. Then she drew her wand from her handbag. She pointed it at Minns. He smiled the gentle smile that I had come to think of his own patented expression. He said, "Ms. Ginevra, I think you'll find that you can use that wand only on yourself."

Her mouth opened and closed. Then she started to say a spell. As she spoke, her hand lowered and then raised itself so that the business end of the wand pointed at the base of her throat. She croaked, "OK. I don't know what you're doing, but I'm going to put it away in my handbag if you'll permit."

"Certainly, Ms. Weasley."

He turned to me and said, "Would you mind explaining more fully?"

"Of course, but there's really not much more for me to say. The Lieutenant here can do amazing things without magic, as I'm sure you can realize now. His intentions always turned out to be benign. I'd at least hear him out if I were you."

"Well put, Professor Wendt."

"Why don't you explain what you want? I've reached the end of my knowledge."

He smiled. "Actually, you aren't at the end of you knowledge, but I'll proceed a little further. You'll see where I'm going and then you can go forward."

I doubted that, but I nodded. I was anxious to see where he'd go with this. He began, "Something of which even you wizards are aware is that there are  interstellar civilizations that have visited Earth."

Ginevra said a cautious, "Yes. The Souls."

Minns agreed. "Yes. They are barely capable of interstellar travel at sub-light speeds. Recently, another race achieved a much higher capability of interstellar travel. In Professor Wendt's universe, he called them 'The

PAK'. I think it is a rather clever title, using the name given to a similar fictional race by the science fiction writer, Larry Niven. In any case, they are much smarter than the Souls. They were on the point of committing genocide against the Souls when a third interstellar race dropped on the scene. They are not smarter than the PAK but they are more advanced than the PAK due to their longer history." He paused at this point. I'd never known Minns to hesitate in his life, so I was a bit concerned about what would come next.

Well, I should have been. Minns proceeded, "Here's the problem. This third race has a madman who has decided to destroy the universe."

Ginevra gasped and then laughed. I didn't. I knew roughly what was coming. She said, "How is that conceivably possible?"

Minns turned to me and gestured. I guess I was supposed to tell that story. I began, "Remember that we talked about multiple universes?"

Ginevra nodded a little uncertainly.

"Well, those universes all started in what physicists in my world call a Big Bang. The Big Bang is an explosive expansion of space itself. It is caused by a force called Inflation. Like all forces, it is communicated by a particle, the inflaton. All particles have an anti-particle, that is a particle that is its opposite. In this case, the anti-inflaton."

Ginevra stopped me. "OK. So this anti-inflaton thing causes space to contract on itself, right?"

"Good going. Now, in my universe, small amounts of anti-inflatons and inflatons can be used to propel spaceships."

Ginevra nodded and asked, "So, what's the problem?"

Minns said, "In large quantities, they can cause the universe to explode or implode. Someone of the third level aliens can create large quantities and cause this universe to end in a Big Crunch—the opposite of the Big Bang."

Ginevra was catching on quickly. "There's someone who wants to do that, don't they?"

Minns said, "Right. They will do it in the near future if Wendt, you, and I don't stop them."

Ginevra looked at me and asked, "This sounds like a clever plot to stop us from getting in Riddle's way."

I shook my head. "I'm sorry. I kind of wish it were. In my universe. Minns was around, and things went exactly like this, except it happened a couple of years ago."

Minns smiled that irritating smile, "Well, every universe has its own events and timetables. It came up a little sooner in your universe. That's not strange."

I asked, "So, you're saying that you want us to drop everything and go with you just like Aurora, Nicholas, Ginny, you, and I went in my universe?"

"Yes."

I asked, "And if we don't, this universe is going to collapse?"

He nodded.

I closed my eyes. I guess I was half hoping that when I opened them, Minns and this threat he brought with him would be gone. Of course, that was a short-lived hope. I then pursed my lips in thought. There were problems with Minns statement. I worked through the problems for a while. At some point Ginevra became concerned that I might have had a stroke or something. She shook me gently at first and then harder.

I nodded and said, "Give me a couple of minutes." At the end of those minutes I opened my eyes and said, "Minns, I know that there was a group of intellectually advanced children who traveled to an enclave for such. It is my belief that there must be similar, but more mature people, at that enclave. In my universe when you recruited Ginny, me, and others, you told me that we could save the universe without their assistance. Why can't they help now?"

Minns didn't smile when I'd finished my question. He looked at me and asked, "Do you know much about this universe?"

I shrugged. "The very small part of it that I've experienced has not been particularly pleasant, just, or happy."

He nodded. "That is the problem. Our people have a council." Then he began his narrative:

□

I received the realization that I was to be summoned to the council of delegates to testify on an important matter. My presence at the central system was never anticipated when I sent our delegates there. Those youths along with all other delegates were thought to be adequate to decide all issues that might arise.

As a result it was with great surprise that I found myself summoned while my associates—Connover, Hadley, Rinaldo—remained here on Earth. A ship was being sent to bring me to the conference that was even then in progress.

The ship slipped without detection onto the surface of the earth in the Cotswold Plantation where I was a slave. Of course, no one—either Muggle or wizard overseer of the plantation noticed its arrival. I was aware of its arrival, of course. I was also aware of the reason for its arrival—to take me to the conference. At the time, I wasn't aware of the reason for the conference, but I knew that it was unprecedented for any of us who were left behind to come to the central system.

I approached the ship. It had landed in the center of a Quidditch field next to a lower form school. The ship was perfectly visible with no cloaking device. However, no one noticed it except for me. I walked from the field where I was working. No overseer thought that anything was unusual. As I approached the school, a Deatheater who was overseeing a physical education class did notice me. He raised his wand and approached me.

He began to say, "What are you doing here, slave?" As he started to say that, he raised his wand toward me. Before it was level with me, it swung away and around so that it was pointed at his own head. He dropped to his knees and tried to say something. He finally settled for, "Who are you!"

I simply said, "I am a slave."

He almost screamed, "What is happening to me?"

"You are learning what it is to live in fear." With that I walked past him and on to the Quidditch field where my ship was waiting. It was much like the ship we built for the delegates from Earth. There was no crew. I was the crew. I sat at the control console. I touched the key area. The ship woke up, and I keyed in my destination and arrival time. I knew that I had to arrive within two days. I requested thirty hours.

The thirty hours passed with meditations on the cause of this unique summons. After meditation, I prepared a report on the state of the human race on Tellus. At the end of that time, I entered the solar system that was my destination. As that happened, I received a message of welcome and instructions for final approach and landing.

That approach was designed to give me a complete view of the world as I approached. I saw the continents, the oceans, the polar caps, the deserts, the boreal forests and mountain ranges. The planet might have been Earth—an Earth that was far more beautiful than ours. On the way, I passed two other planets that were very different from Earth. One was cold and remote from the G4 star that was the heart of the solar system. The other was closer to the star and much warmer. I would later discover the significance of those two other planets.

I landed on the planet in the midst of a large plain. There were clear signs of farms. However, the landing site was beside a small structure that turned out to be the entrance to an underground complex. There were no other ships on that landing area. I never saw much of that complex. I instinctively followed a path through the complex that led me to a large conference room. The conference room was circular with tiers of seats completely surrounding the central stage. I went to a seat that was apparently saved for me. It had a holographic projector set in a continuous desk that circled the room. I sat and the projector activated, giving me a closeup view of the figure at the center of the stage.

That figure was slowly, slowly circling the stage, apparently waiting for some event. That event happened shortly after my arrival. It was a person taking a seat on the opposite side of the hall. The central figure then made a short speech in a language that I had never heard before, but which had enough similarity to human languages that I knew how to quickly pick it up. He said, "You all have been summoned here from your various worlds to report on the state of intelligent life on those planets. You have all submitted your reports, which are available to you at all times on any device that supports our network.

"The purpose of this convocation is making a decision on the fate of the Universe. There is an entity who wishes to force the universe to enter a Big Crunch so as to remake it by the subsequent Big Bang. He will shortly have the capability to carry out that purpose. Our purpose is to decide whether we will prevent it or not.

"His contention is that the universe is so perverse that it should be destroyed and remade. The purpose of those reports to which you have access is informing our judgment on that belief.

"Our procedure will consist of three parts: You will review the reports. There will be debate of various actions that we could take. You will vote on the fate of the universe. We will carry out the decision that you collectively make. What questions are there?"

It seemed such an elementary and obvious program that no one rose with questions. We dismissed ourselves by rising and leaving at our own will. I instinctively knew where my quarters were in the complex. I took an elevator down several levels, exited it, and quickly found my place. It was not especially unlike any hotel room in your world.

In the next month, I read reports, exercised, ate in one of the cafeterias of the complex, and debated with fellow delegates. The debates tended to have advocates for various proposals. I will report a conversation synthesized from a number of conversations. I will use names that will be familiar to people, such as Professor Wendt, who knows some of my associates on Earth.

◻◻

We were slowly having dinner one evening—Reynaldo, Connover, and I. The subject that was on everyone's mind was the topic of the evening.

Connover said, "I'll be damned if I can find a single civilization that I could argue deserves protection. Won't someone suggest an example?"

Reynaldo said, "That isn't the point! The point is this: Can you point out a civilization that is so devoid of deserving individuals that you would be comfortable with destroying it?"

Connover responded, "I don't propose destroying anything. I just say that I can't find a civilization that makes me feel obligated to exert the effort of a single finger to protect it. What about you, Minns?"

I thought about the question and answered, "I think the question really is how much effort should we exert to save a civilization."

Connover said, "You are splitting hairs. Does it matter whether we devote one person for one hour to save this universe or all our resources for all eternity to save it?"

I replied, "Does a civilization that would not lift a finger to save itself, justly deserve to be saved?"

Connover answered, "Think of all the unborn octillians of people who will suffer in this universe if we prevent the Big Crunch."

Reynaldo replied, "Do we have any reason to think that what follows the Big Crunch and Big Bang will be a better universe than the one we inhabit at the moment? Suppose I could point out a dozen worlds with worthy societies? Would that be enough to convince you?"

Connover said, "Certainly. Do you know a dozen?"

Reynaldo answered, "No, but suppose you found a half dozen civilizations?"

Connover said, "Probably. Do you know half a dozen that you would recommend?"

Reynaldo replied, "No, but suppose that you found three civilizations worthy of saving?"

Connover said, "Maybe. Point out the three."

Reynaldo answered softly, "No. What about one civilization?"

Connover said determinedly, "No."

I asked, "Have you read the statistical study of integrity of civilizations of similar universes?"

There were grumbled "Yeses."

I went on. "If these statistics are typical, there's a good chance that the octillions who would be born in a new universe would lead far better lives than the ones in this one."

Reynaldo was not pleased with the fact that he could not deny that, but he said, "There are many people in this universe who live decent, even happy lives. Would you take that away from them?"

We were reconvened weeks later in the same conference room as before. The moderator from before announced that the meeting was being done by conference holograph with similar meetings on the other two planets that were hosts to people of very different physiology from those in this meeting room.

He opened the meeting with a call for proposed actions. The following proposals were quickly made:

- Do nothing and abandon this universe to its fate.
- Provide the opportunity for one civilization to defeat the bad actor, who called himself Kali. We would use minimum effort necessary to end his threat to the universe. However, the bulk of the effort must be provided by the civilizations of the universe.
- Directly intervene to end Kali's threat by any means necessary. That means would be rather small in any case.

There was a vote. The second option was chosen. Then, there was the selection of the actor to lead the effort and carry it out. At this point I was happy that the chances that I would be the chosen one was vanishingly small.

There was a nomination process. It worked like this. On each of the three planets, the meeting room would be divided into eight sections. Each section would nominate one of their number. There was a "black ball" process where any member of the meeting could veto a candidate. The candidates who were left from that process would be presented to the entire meeting. Anyone from the entire meeting could blackball a nominee. When only one was left, he was the chosen one.

Each nominee was given time for a brief speech. My speech consisted of a description of how I succeeded in building an interstellar ship and collecting children to travel here. Of course, my speech didn't describe you, Wendt, or your magical associates who attempted to stymie The Project in another universe.

My description went like this:

I collected financial resources for The Project. To explain my method, I must explain the way that resources are allocated in my world, Tellus. The quickest means is by shrewdly manipulating the free market of financial resources. At root, it is a game of chance in which guessing the motivations of the other players allows one to anticipate their purchases and sales. The transactions happen in millionths of seconds—far faster than even our reflexes work. So, deducing the actions of others is critical to winning.

I quickly accumulated enough working capital to fund The Project. My largest problem was preventing my detection by the officials who enforce a semblance of fairness on the capital market that I used. The other beneficiaries of the Legacy carried out the other components of The Project with the resources that I had acquired. In all cases, there was no one who deduced the implications of what we did:

- Not the military officials who allowed The Team to walk off without permission to work on The Project.
- Not the metallurgist who provided us with the casting of parts that we used to assemble the spaceship,
- Not the parents of the children whom I identified and rescued for The Project,
- Not the owner of the warehouse where we assembled the ship,
- Not the officials in the Amazon River basin where we collected rare organic chemicals which were the basis for the atmosphere that we synthesized to be used in the spaceship during its voyage.
- Not the electronics firm where the control and defensive systems of the ship were built.

I met no opposition worth the name during the entire Project. I have not demonstrated any particular worth in this project. I do not deserve to lead this effort to save the universe.

I was completely surprised when I was the last man standing who had not been blackballed. I even reached for the controls to blackball myself. I had no belief that I would survive the vote without receiving at least one veto. I decided that it must be because the real intention of the delegates was that the universe should be reborn. I was just a sop to their collective consciences, proving that they were not without empathy for the universe.

The chairperson congratulated me and gave me this charge. "You must go alone without assistance other than the use of a ship to travel to a planet of your choice. There you will recruit a team to help you thwart Kali's intention.

"If they succeed . . . and mark our intention . . . if they succeed on their own, this universe will be worthy of continuing. If not, then you have permission to retreat to another universe of your choosing as will the rest of us. Godspeed in your Endeavor."

Those were almost the last words that I heard on that planet. I had brought nothing to that planet and I was leaving with nothing other than the charge of the delegates.

The ship that I had come in was waiting for me on the landing area. I entered it and set my return course for this planet. I specified a trip of four hours. When I arrived, I landed on the same Quidditch field that I left from. I walked from there to here. I selected you because some of you are magical, and in another universe, I worked against your team, Wendt. You assembled a team that was a worthy opponent.

I was shocked by the narrative that Minns had provided us. It was a view of the universe that took one's breath out of one's lungs. I literally didn't have the air to speak for a moment.

Then, I turned to Ginevra. "I know you're not going to like this, but we've got to go help out with this."

Ginevra turned away from me. She held her breath and seemed deep in thought. Then she gulped and turned back toward us—Minns and me. She almost wailed, "Why not other people? I know that Aurora is still around. I don't know about Nicholas. There must be other wizards that you can use."

Minns shook his head. "No. It's either you two plus me or its no one."

I asked, "We rendezvoused with the American Trident sub and a PAK ship to do this. Are they all available?"

Minns nodded, "My ship is available. That is all we need."

I said, "OK. It's your parents too, Ginevra. Come to save them."

She was resolute. "No. If we don't stop Riddle, he'll conquer all the universes. That's more important than one—even if Mum and Dad are in it." She gasped the last out with a flood of tears that she'd been holding back.

I almost shouted, "You just want revenge!" She said nothing.

I leaped up and said, "I'm going with you Minns. We can get another witch. It won't be easy, but it can work."

He shook his head. "No. It's you, Ginevra, and me or its nobody."

I exclaimed, "Great! Come on Ginevra. We can go with Minns and do our duty. Then we can go get Riddle."

She shook her head. She screamed, "You're self-deluded. That crazy trip never happened!"

Minns just said quietly, "You know that's not true."

She sobbed as she said, "I know what I say. I feel it. If we don't keep to our plan, nothing will work."

I dropped my head to my chest. Then I went to my knees before her and said, "Please. I'm begging you. Go with us. You'll never go to space if you don't now."

She again shook her head. I looked into her eyes and saw her determination. I turned to Minns and said, "I'm sorry. We're not going with you. Maybe if there's time after we get Riddle, we'll go with you."

Minns shook his head. "I think it will be too late by then."

I sighed. "You know, it's ironic. We were on opposite sides back when you were building a spaceship."

Minns said, "I will be around as long as it is possible to stop the Big Crunch. Help will always be given to those who choose it."

He turned and walked away.

I said to Ginevra, "I guess it's time to go. How are we getting into Borgan & Burke?"

She said, "We're going to walk. Let's go. Don't forget that you're from this point on, an abject slave."

I laughed and said, "When was I never that to you."

We arrived outside the Cauldron. I got in line behind Ginevra. We walked to the door that I couldn't see. She opened it for me. Then we both walked through. This time, there were more people present—an early lunch crowd. Amazingly, no one seemed to pay attention to me this time. We crossed the Common Room and left it. I released a sigh of relief. The brick wall opened at a touch of Ginevra's wand.

Inside Diagon Alley, there was a good bit of foot traffic, but not much over toward Knockturn Alley. I was really afraid of it. Even when Riddle wasn't in charge, it was dicey down there for ordinary wizards—for Muggles?

Ginevra was good though. She could be pretty scary when she had to or even just wanted to kid around. One lowlife started to put a foot out to trip me. He ended up on his back with a leg that seemed to be folded in a way that nature never intended. I'd been here once before. I was walking with two Deatheaters from Borgan & Burke to Diagon Alley. The route went a lot easier this time.

We reached Borgan & Burke, entered, and found the vanishing cabinet. The shop was nearly empty. We took a quick look around. When no one was watching, Ginevra sent us back to my universe. We came out in the Room of Requirement. I can't describe how happy I was to be back in my universe. Ginevra and I kissed, and we left for the nearest floo connection, which happened to be in the Great Hall.

# The Riddle Hunt

We took the floo network to an obscure inn called the Roan Festral. A quick drink there, and we disapparated to a wooded hillside overlooking the Malfoy Mansion.

We arrived, and both of us gasped for a moment. I think it was a panic attack. I thought, "God, we're almost a stone's throw away from Riddle."

Ginevra disagreed about panic attacks. She claimed it was just the effect of disapparation. That knocked me out of my panic. I laughed. "You don't like disapparation! What is coming of this world if you, who constantly accuse me of wussery, can't take a simple disapparation." She chuckled at that but refused to admit that she was panicked at being so close to Riddle.

We chose a relatively level spot on the far side of the hill from the Malfoy Mansion. The setup of the tent went quickly. We'd had a lot of practice. Then there was the very careful process of setting up a surveillance post complete with binoculars, omnioculars, and rifles with barrels barely protruding above the hill. We then went back into the tent to plan. Ginevra used the muffliato spell so that no one outside the tent could overhear. We divided the day up into watches. The night watches were solitary with one person always resting or sleeping. The day watches were mostly joint except when one of us was preparing meals or doing something else like cleaning our weapons.

Before we started, we shared a meal in the tent. It was a rare luxury that we could eat and talk at the same time. Ginevra was hesitant to use any spell outside the tent. So, we rarely could eat and talk outside the tent. That didn't keep us from holding hands occasionally. We couldn't do it a lot and keep a good watch on the house. The Malfoys maintained the same habits that they had in the other world. However, they didn't have a "town" home in London, so they spent a lot of time as a family away from any place that they could call home.

After a couple of days we decided to have a conference over lunch in the tent. Once inside, we quickly prepared an MRE and spoke as we worked and ate. Ginevra said, "We've not seen any sign of Riddle or Deatheaters since we've been here. How long are we going to keep watching?"

I asked, "Suppose, Riddle and Deatheaters have been entering and leaving by direct disapparation, so no one would observe them?"

Ginevra grimaced. "I can't prove they're not. I can't think of a way that we could verify whether they are or not."

I said, "I think it's unlikely that we'd see no sign of Riddle or Deatheaters after . . . oh, say two weeks if they were actually spending time with the Malfoys. What do you think?"

She grimaced again. She seemed to be concentrating on something. She didn't make eye contact. I took her hand and said, "Honey. I support you in your decisions. If you really want to move on now, we will."

A smile cracked the grimace, and she said, "You're right. We should stay longer—maybe two full weeks, let's see." I agreed and we shared the MRE. She made a loud complaint about the MRE. "If I have to look at one of these god-awful things again, I'm going to curse my head!"

I patted her back and said, "Look on the bright side. If you keep yelling like that, a Deatheater is going to show up and put us out of our misery."

She released a held breath and nodded. "Right. Things could be worse, couldn't they?"

I held her and said, "Tonight, let's take a break and make love." She agreed. I wanted to breathe a sigh of relief, but I was afraid to. We then quickly completed lunch and returned outside to watch the house through binoculars and whisper the occasional word of encouragement.

□

That night we did take an hour to make love. It was difficult. We hadn't done it in a while and under the "battlefield" conditions, it took a little time to relax. It also took a while for me to work my foreplay magic, but we did end with a satisfying result. I took it as a good sign that Ginevra was disappointed that there was no time for spooning. Honestly, I was disappointed as well.

The rest of the night and the rest of the week were totally uneventful. One day when I brought lunch out, Ginevra shook her head and said, "It's time to go." I couldn't argue.

The next day, we packed, cleaned up the camp area, and prepared to disapparate.

160

# The Riddle Mansion

We quickly set up the pup tent. We'd had a lot of practice with that. Then we had a hearty MRE dinner, and we were able to have the first really good night's sleep in a long time. That was strange because Riddle might well have been within a mile of us, but the relative relief of being away from that terrible Malfoy Manor gave us a new lease on life.

The next day, we set up camp properly. We had both rifles set on the ground and focused on the main entrance to the Riddle Mansion. We had blankets set on the ground to lay on as we observed with either binoculars or rifle sights. For now, we took turns observing the house from a distance. Our plan was that if we discovered that Riddle ever came outside, we would start determining if he had a pattern which we could use to our advantage.

As it turned out, we never saw him come out. He would occasionally appear at a window as clear to see as day with the omni-occulars or the scopes on our rifles. He never stayed there long enough to get a reliable shot.

Once when Ginevra had him in the scope of her rifle, she said, "I've got him. He's standing still."

I said, "Count to five. If he stays still for that long, you've got a chance to hit him."

"What! Why so long?"

"We're almost a mile away from him. The bullet will take at least five seconds to reach him. So, you first have to be sure that he's standing still and you need a sure five seconds more."

She almost shouted, "Then why are we trying to shoot him with one of these bloody rifles? Why did we spend all that time training to use these things?"

I was a little exasperated myself, but I tried to keep my temper. "Here's the deal. When people go outside, they often stand in place for long periods of time—like when they're talking to someone. Inside, you stand near a window to see something outside. You may not stand there very long. Besides that, standing next to a window, the bullet has to break the window, too. That decreases the energy that it can deliver."

She hissed, "Which means?"

"Which means that it's less likely to kill."

We started to argue about how long we would wait for him to establish a *modus operandi*. It turned out there wasn't one. However, we caught glimpses of him at the main entrance and occasionally at windows. He never developed a pattern there either. It was becoming progressively apparent that we were going to have to go in after him so that we could win our goal.

Then we began to discuss to what room to disapparate first and when to begin the search for Riddle in the mansion. My idea was to disapparate to the master bedroom in the late evening. It seemed the best place. There was one problem. It would be hard to prove that we'd gotten him. We might attract attention before we knew for sure.

My second approach was the same room when there was a light on in it. Ginevra's preference was the dining room in the morning. We'd catch everyone there. That was my argument against it. There would be too many people.

In any case, we decided to keep up the vigil to see if a pattern of movement developed over time. It didn't.

Finally, we decided that there was nothing for it, but to pick a time, date, and location and simply do it. So, we picked Monday early evening. We picked a bedroom where we'd seen lights most nights.

□

The couple of days before, we abstained from sex and even from intense displays of affection. A last minute thing occurred to me. I had Ginevra take me to a hardware store, where we bought two tool belts. The tools that we would wear were magazines and boxes of cartridges for our handguns.

The day of the attack, we ate an early light dinner. We dressed in dark clothes. We unloaded our guns, cleaned them, and reloaded them. We reloaded all our magazines. We each held a gun in our right hand. In addition, I held my dependable old Glock in my left hand. The first bullet in the chamber was my old bullet from Mr. Weasley. I intended to save that for Riddle, but if I ran out in my right hand gun, I sure wasn't going to hesitate to use it. We had laid out the sequence of rooms that we'd disapparate to. We'd both memorized it. If we were lucky, it would turn out to be exactly one.

162

We lined up in the tent back to back. Ginevra's free left hand held my right forearm. We stood that way waiting for the chosen hour. As we waited, I said, "Just in case, Ginevra, I love you."

She said, "Same here. I'll see you back here."

I added, "Or in the clearing at the end of the path." I could feel her nod. She'd braided her hair and pinned it securely to the back of her head. I could feel it at the back of my neck.

We had an alarm clock that we'd been using. It was compact and reasonably loud. We'd decided on 7:30. The big hand had just moved to the six. She whispered, "Now." I echoed her.

We appeared in the master bedroom. There was a table set up with places for four. Three were sitting at the table. One was standing next to a dresser. I could see the three out of the corner of my eye, the other was directly in front of me. I brought my right hand around, aimed, and squeezed the trigger twice. I didn't even hear my silenced gun. I did hear Ginevra's gun's soft susurrations. I had swung around and shot another. He was the last. No one had made a sound.

I released my breath. We looked at each other. I whispered, "Four shots."

She said, "Five."

I asked, "Ready."

She nodded. We aligned back to back. She squeezed my forearm, and we appeared in another bedroom. It was empty. We aligned and went again. This was another bedroom. It was empty. We kept going.

After we'd finished most of the bedrooms without finding anyone else, I said, "I say we go out of sequence and go to the dining room. There's a good chance that they're having a meeting." We had been saving that room for last.

She nodded. "It's really likely that Riddle will be at one end. I say, the one next to the china room. I'll try to put us close there."

I said, "This is probably it." I held her head and turned it to me. I kissed her.

She broke the kiss and said, "Let's get this bastard once and for all." I nodded. We turned back-to-back. She caressed my forearm briefly and squeezed it. Then we were squeezed through the ether and landed in the dining room. There was a meeting.

I was facing Riddle, Ginevra was facing everyone else. My left hand rose, aimed, and I squeezed the trigger. I fired again. The first time, I'd hit his right eye. I wasn't sure that I'd hit him, though. The second shot was dead center in his forehead. I could hear Ginevra's gun talking. My right hand sought targets. The man sitting next to Riddle was next in line. I fired. His face was surprised. I fired again. Then I swung down to fire into the

163

back of the head in front of me. The woman next to him was raising a wand and turning. Ginevra shot her above her temple and another shot a bit below.

I had no idea what Ginevra had done. I could hear her shots, but I hadn't been counting. A couple of wizards had disapparated. All the rest were dead. Ginevra walked close to the body of Riddle. She fired into his head twice. Then the hammer of her gun hit nothing. She kept squeezing the trigger. Finally, she ejected the empty clip and expertly inserted another. Then she fired into his body three times.

I said, "It's time for us to go. There may be more Deatheaters on the way here. A couple got away."

She said nothing. She just stared at what was left of Riddle. I walked around and took her free hand. I'd turned the safeties of my guns on and returned my Glock to my purse. I shook her and said, "Come on! It's time to go."

She looked up at me with a twisted face. I said, "It's never good enough. Let's go!" She finally gave a ragged sort of nod.

I pulled her close and whispered in her ear, "It's enough." We disappeared. We arrived in the tent. I said, "Come on. Let's pack and get out of here. I don't trust those Deatheaters not to come looking for us."

She moved mechanically, putting things away. Then she ran out of the tent. I followed her. She was on her knees, her head down, wretching. I took her by the shoulders from behind. I squeezed gently and said, "It's all right. It's over." Of course, that sort of experience is never over. I knew that she'd have dreams far into the future about it just as I had nightmares about killing Ghosts with my Glock during the invasion.

After a while she nodded and got up shakily. She stumbled to the tent and entered. She still had said nothing.

We resumed packing. As we did that, I talked. "It's never going to bring them back. It's never going to make it feel OK that they're gone. It's just something that we had to do."

We tossed our utility belts in with everything else, but kept our guns out. I finished the packing and realized that we'd not decided where we would go next. I guess it just seemed to be bad Karma to plan for what would follow our success.

She looked up at me and said, "Where?"

I made a decision. "The Shrieking Shack."

That seemed to snap something in her. She laughed hilariously. "The Shrieking Shack! Why in the world would we go there?"

"I know someone who works there."

She stared. "You know someone who *works* there? Doing what?"

I had to stare in my turn. I said, "I could tell you what he does, but that wouldn't really tell you what he does."

She shook her head and said, "Whatever you want."

I took the expandable duffel in one hand and her in the other. I mean really took her. I put my arm around her waist. Then we appeared next to the Shrieking Shack. We set up the tent. Then I took her by the hand and walked around to the entrance to the shack.

Ginevra asked what I was doing. I said, "Just be patient and see." I punched the old code on the keypad, hoping that the Boy Genius hadn't changed it. Apparently, he hadn't because the door unlocked. I opened it and led Ginevra in. I closed the door behind me and shouted up the stairs to the main workroom, "B. G. You'll never guess what the cat drug in."

We started to climb the stairs when the B. G. appeared running down the stairs. "Where in creation have you been?" He added, "And what's Ginny doing with you?"

I said, "It's a long story. Could you please go find Slughorn, Sally, your wife, Dursley, and . . . oh what the hell . . . Filch. Bring them here so that we don't have to tell this story a half dozen times."

He'd been staring and seemed to wake up. "Oh, sure. But Mrs. Potter. She doesn't look right. She looks like death warmed over."

Ginevra said, "There's a good reason for that. I'm not Mrs. Potter. Also, I'm not the Ginny Weasley that you apparently know."

He said, "Right. I'll be back as quickly as I can. Go on up to the main work room. Get something to drink out of the refer. Also, food if you're hungry."

He ran down the stairs. We walked up. When we got to the top and entered the workroom, she said, "This isn't the Shrieking Shack."

I smiled, "Well, not the one that you know, anyway."

⊓⊔

It took the B. G. a good hour to assemble everyone and get them over to the Shack. We sat around the main workstation. I generously offered the B. G.'s drinks. When we were all settled, I began.

"I'll settle your frequently asked questions and then we go into details if there are any left.

"Question: Where have you been these last months?

"Answer: There is another universe that is very similar to ours. It has differences, though. One of them was that Riddle won the war. I have spent a lot of time there with THIS Ms. Weasley from that universe.

"Q: What have you been doing there?

"A: Finding and destroying the last horcrux that the Riddle from that universe had created. Also, we spent some time in this universe killing that Riddle.

"Q: What are you going to do next?

"A: I can't answer for Ms. Weasley, but I plan to ask her a very important question."

At that point Ginevra jumped up and shouted, "The answer is 'YES!'"

I said, "You haven't heard the question yet."

She pounded a fist on the table and said, "I don't care what it is, the answer is 'YES.'"

Slughorn asked, "Here's a FAQ that you missed out: Are you planning on giving up on teaching?"

"A: No. I know that I've not been very dependable lately, but I'd like to continue teaching."

Filch asked, "Are you trying to say that Ms. Ginny is two persons?"

"No. I mean that most wizards and witches have people in other universes that are very like them."

He asked, "Then I have a doppelgrazer just like me somewhere else?"

"You've got it."

There were a lot of questions that I don't mention because I didn't answer them—like where was Riddle when you killed him? There were other questions, of course, that I simply didn't know the answer to—like, how many other Riddles are out there wandering around?

Finally, Dursley asked the question that I had been avoiding like the plague. "What are you going to tell your Jaimie?"

Everyone looked at me intently. "Well, there isn't all that much to tell her, is there? I mean: Sure, we were an item for a while. We were very close. However, the truth is that it was mostly that we got together on the rebound. I had been dropped by someone with whom I was in love." At this point, Ginevra kicked me in the shins. No one seemed to notice. "And, uh, I fell into the first arms that happened to be around. They belonged to Jaimie. It's too bad that things like that have to happen."

Filch asked, "Is that it? Is that all you have to say?"

"Yup. I'm going to go up and tell that to Jaimie after this little get-together is over."

Everyone got up and evacuated other than the B. G., Aurora, Ginevra, and I. Aurora asked, "Can I have a ringside seat for that discussion?"

Ginevra fastened a stare on her that made me think that she'd mastered the evil eye.

The B. G. simply said, "I'm going to be up here the whole time working."

I said, "I'm leaving." I leaned over to where Ginevra was sitting. I said to her, "Just in case." I then kissed her, and she kissed me back seriously.

It seemed a really long walk up to the castle and from the castle entrance up to my office floor and then to the door on which I knocked .

An answer came, "Come." I did.

I opened the door. Jaimie was sitting at my desk in my chair. I said, "It's ironic my knocking on the door. I always used to sit where you are now and listened and dreaded that knock on the door."

Jaimie looked up. Her face was inscrutable. She said, "I think I know what you've come to say. I've been too clingy and something happened that gave you a shock. It forced you to look at our relationship from a fresh perspective. So, you've come to tell me that we are splitting up."

I started to answer, but she quickly said, "Why don't you take the red leather chair. Have you ever before? This would be a unique, perhaps never to be repeated, opportunity."

She was being amazingly kind. I did take the red leather chair. "Thanks."

She added, "Would you like some of your Blue Label. This is a big event, isn't it?"

I licked my lips. "Yes, it is a big deal. However, may I suggest our sharing a glass of Jameson whiskey instead. I think I had some in the desk drawer before I left."

That made her smile. "You know, I do like that. I think there might be just enough for two glasses—with ice."

"Sounds perfect."

She conjured two glasses and ice. She poured out the last of the Jameson. Then she said, "To the future."

I thought that toast was a little too ambiguous for me, but I didn't hesitate to take a sip. She said, "Well, anything you want to add?"

I said, "Well, there is more to talk about than just what you've mentioned. I want to tell you what's happened in a good bit more detail and then we do need to do some planning of the future."

She perked up at that. "Please talk."

As I started to talk, she pulled the braid of her hair over her left shoulder and slowly unbraided her bright platinum tresses. I said, "I should tell you that I didn't completely abandon you without good reason. The day that I disappeared, another traveler from another universe came through the vanishing cabinet. She was not from your universe. She was from a terrible universe where Riddle had beaten Potter and the Deatheaters ruled. Many Muggles died in the invasion of the Ghosts and to Deatheaters. It was a bleak world. The person who came through was Ginevra Weasley."

Jaimie had finished undoing her hair that spread over her left breast and most of her body that was visible behind her desk. She interrupted me, "Don't you mean, Ginny Potter?"

"No. Potter had died in her universe. I call her Ginevra—her real given name in both universes—just so that I can keep the two of them straight in my head."

Jaimie said, "Extremely important. You wouldn't want to make the mistake of thinking that our Ginny was available."

"Right. Anyway, she had come here because the Riddle from her universe had traveled to ours. His plan was to take over ours the way that he'd taken over his own. I ran into Ginevra during Christmas Holiday outside the Great Hall. She was looking for Riddle. I offered to help her."

Jaimie stood and began pacing behind her desk the way I often had. She forgot about her hair, which was flowing around willy-nilly. She said, "Had all of that Riddle's horcruxes been destroyed?"

"No. The only one that survived was the one in Hogwarts—the diadem. She and I devised a plan to return to her universe, find and destroy that horcrux, and then return here to kill Riddle."

She stopped pacing instantly, turned toward me, and asked, "Why didn't you recruit help? You could have taken a dozen top-notch Aurors back with you."

I looked her directly in the eye. "Ginevra didn't even want my help. She was morbidly afraid that including anyone else would be to jeopardize her mission. I forced the issue by not telling her the location of the horcrux unless she included me."

Jaimie shook her head sadly. "You silly boy. Don't you see that she could have forced you to reveal that information by using the *Imperious* curse or *Veritas Serum*. She wanted you along."

I replied, "I know that. I implied that I would be useful in ways that she couldn't anticipate, so she agreed to let me come. And . . ."

Jaimie had been running a hand through her unbound hair absent-mindedly. She walked around the desk and went to one of the guest chairs near the sofa as I continued. "you have no idea how hideous that world she came from is. You can only trust people to whom you are related. It was a terrible risk that she was taking by including me."

I had to almost look over my shoulder to talk to Jaimie. She leaned back in the chair and seemed to be permanently settled there.

She asked, "So, what did you contribute to the effort—besides information that most wizards here have?"

I was tired of looking over my shoulder, so I walked to the sofa and sat at the far end of it from Jaimie's guest chair. "I provided the plan for killing Riddle."

She leaned toward me and asked, "Just what was that plan?"

"Well, something that she didn't know was that Riddle had spent most of his time in the last year or so before his defeat in one of two places."

She languidly supplied, "Yes. The Riddle Mansion and the Malfoy Mansion. So, how did you think you two would kill him when so many Aurors had failed?"

"In the first place, he had horcruxes when the Aurors were trying to capture or kill him. The first major step was to destroy his last horcrux. Since we would be in a different universe, he probably wouldn't be aware that it had happened. So, he'd be less cautious about being seen.

"In the second place, we had no intention of capturing him. We were simply out to kill him." That seemed to excite her. She leaned further in toward me and said, "God, I wish I could have been with you. How were you going to kill him?"

I was feeling rather proud of myself. I said, "Well, it struck me that spells, though powerful, frequently take time—even if you're saying them silently in your head. On the other hand, a bullet can take less than a second or two to be aimed, fired, and strike its target. I convinced Ginevra that we should first train to use firearms. Second, we would practice disapparating into a room that might have Riddle in it, so that we could kill him with a well-placed bullet after he had become vulnerable."

Jaimie's eyes widened, and she slipped over onto the sofa as she leaned toward me, and her silky hair splayed over the sofa like a comforter. She asked breathily, "So, you killed him with one shot?" She reached out and took my forearm in her hand.

I hadn't realized how really close she had become as we were talking. My heart skipped a beat, and I felt an urge to take her shoulder with my free hand to pull her to me. In that moment, I realized how much more powerful sexual desire was than almost any magic.

I leaned back, which just resulted in my pulling her closer to me. Her shimmering, silvery hair slipped silkily over my free arm. I gulped and was sure that our lips would meet. At that moment, my glass of Jameson was knocked off the arm of the sofa. It fell to the floor and shattered into a shower of sharp fragments.

I rose and apologized rapidly as I backed away from the mess on the floor. Jaimie quickly used the *repairo* spell to reassemble the shards of the glass into a whole.

I quickly apologized again, saying that I had promised Ginevra that I had a very important question for her that I'd not asked yet. I backed out of the office and sprinted down the hall. Ginevra must have sensed that there was a problem. She came up the stairs and met me at the top of the flight of stairs.

We ran into each others' arms. She said, "I can smell that vixen on you. I hope you didn't give away the store."

"No. It was a close thing, but no. That brings me," I said, "to one more thing from me."

She shook her head and said, "What now?"

"We'd better go to our tent to discuss it."

"That bad, eh?"

I honestly replied, "I don't know. We'll find out." We went to our tent. We sat at the camp table facing each other. I took both her hands in mine and said, "You know that I'm going to be away. It's not even going to be out of this universe. It's going to be out of all universes for years on end if we're married. Can you really . . ."

She interrupted me right then and there. "I'm disappointed in you."

I started to say, "We're just facing reality." I didn't get to finish.

She said, "Even I know that in your universe, the typical military wife or husband has to be apart from their spouse for months and months on end. It's not unusual for them to be apart for a year at a time, is it?"

I had to admit it, "You're right. But it's different."

She stuck her nose up and said, "Tell me how?"

"Well," I took a deep breath and went on, "They can talk on the phone. Of course, that's only been recently. But they can write to each other. That wouldn't be possible for me."

She asked, "What about navy people on submarines?"

I growled, "Well."

She said, "I'm disappointed that you don't think that I'm as good as the average military wife!"

I had to hang my head in shame. "You're right, but the military only have to do that a year or less at a time. I signed up for three years at a time."

She snapped back, "Didn't you say that you could get the Brewsters to agree to a year at a time."

"I thought that was possible. I didn't guarantee it."

She got up and walked around the table to me. "You need to get in touch with Brewster and get him to agree to our proposal. And, it's time for you to admit that you need to accept me."

I nodded and asked her, "Will you marry me?"

She pinched my rump. "How many times do I have to tell you 'yes'?"

I laughed. "There are never enough times for me. I have a different question for you. Where do we get married? And one last thing."

"Yes?"

"Will you marry me?"

"In my home, of course." She turned, and we began walking down toward the lake, arm in arm. She stopped midway and said, "Oh, one more thing. 'Yes'."

Ginevra started planning the wedding by going back across to the other universe. Before she left, I gave her my power of attorney. It was our first real argument. Well, OK, it was our first real argument after getting engaged. She didn't want to have it until we were married. I said, "Look, I know this wedding is going to be a low-key thing, but I don't want our parents to be burdened by it. With this power of attorney, you won't have to wheedle with the goblins to get money out of my vault."

She replied, "Will you let my Mum and Dad not have the pleasure of paying for the wedding for their only daughter?"

"OK. But you could pay for the little incidentals that people don't plan for in a wedding. That could add up to a lot."

She growled but gave in, saying, "Just because I've got it doesn't mean that I have to use it."

We left it at that. I turned to a related topic. "OK. Now, when we get married in your world, I suppose we'll have a marriage certificate."

"Probably not. In my world, it's illegal for Muggles and witches to marry. This ceremony will strictly be under the table."

I said, "Well, then, it makes what I have to say all the more important. I want to have a regular ceremony here as well. That way, we'll have a marriage certificate and everything. Now, if you want to do it on the QT, in an informal way, I wouldn't . . ."

She laughed. "Are you crazy! What woman wouldn't want to have two weddings? Of course, it can be a big deal. You can have your chance to pay for a wedding after all."

I couldn't help taking a deep breath in preparation for what I was about to say, "One other thing."

Ginevra went back into growl mode. "What is it now?"

"Oh, I would just like your Mum and Dad and as much of the family as could come to be here for that ceremony as well." I quickly added, "Who would give you away here?"

She sort of rocked her head back and forth in thought and finally said, "I suppose that wouldn't be awful. What made you think of that?"

"Well, we're talking about weddings . . ."

She narrowed her eyes and stared into mine. "You aren't going on about this 'end of the world' craziness are you?"

It looked like we were up for our second argument of our life together. "Look, I'm not trying to convince you that it's real. I'm just saying that it would be great to have your family here for our wedding. If it turns out that Minns was right . . . well, it would be really, really nice to have them here when it happens."

Ginevra was digging in her heals, "Well, if that's the way you feel, I'm surprised that you want to have our first wedding in my world."

"I would go anywhere to have our wedding together whether it's into the Big Crunch or it's the world where Riddle won."

She couldn't stay mad at me after I made that declaration. While we were talking, an owl showed up. It was from Slughorn. I was invited to a meeting. We had set up the tent behind the Shrieking Shack. So, I didn't have any trouble getting to Hogwarts for the meeting.

The B. G. and Aurora had tried to talk me into staying in the Shack. They would convert a little-used storeroom into a bedroom. I insisted that I was more comfortable in the pup-tent. The truth is that I was.

The meeting was for just after lunch. Ginevra and I walked over to Hogwarts for lunch. School was still in session, although final exams were less than a month away. Ginevra and I ate in our tent, of course. Slughorn had wanted me to sit at the head table, but since I wasn't really a teacher in the current term, I insisted that I would sit with Filch if anywhere.

All of the students who knew or even had seen Ginny were graduated and gone, so there weren't any inconvenient questions about why Potter wasn't with her. As a matter of fact, the only questions that we got while we walked inside Hogwarts were from the many students who'd had me in class and wondered if I were coming back. I told them that I had a meeting with the Headmaster about that very question. We would see.

After lunch, Ginevra told me in no uncertain terms that she was not going to be at the meeting. As a matter of fact, she was going straight to the Room of Requirement to head back to her parents. Her plan was to get in touch with the few close relatives who could be trusted to keep quiet about the wedding. They would pick a day for it and make the few preparations necessary. One preparation that she would not miss was buying a wedding dress. I made a brief plea for her to buy it on this side, but she was determined to do it where she'd always lived. She'd come back for me the day before the wedding.

So, we walked up the stairs—I toward the Headmaster's Officeand she toward the Room of Requirement. There were students changing classes as we parted ways at the second floor. I pulled her off to the side and broke the general school rule against public displays of affection by kissing her passionately. I then begged her to be careful.

She had a mischievous smile as she warned me, "You be careful in that meeting. I don't trust that Jaimie as far as I can throw a dragon."

She went further up the stairs. I went down the hall to the meeting. At the office, I found that the other people at the meeting were waiting in the outer office—Jaimie and the B. G. We were all sitting silently. I would have talked with the B. G., but I couldn't with Jaimie there. If I had spoken, I'd have felt required to talk with her as well. That was a dangerous path to tread, so we were all silent. I didn't even say anything more than a hello to Sally.

A light flashed on Sally's desk. She rose and said, "The Headmaster is ready for you." Then she opened the door. We trudged in like students about to face the Headmaster to atone for our sins.

He invited us to sit. I waited for the others to sit so that I could place myself with the B. G. between me and Jaimie. Slughorn turned to Sally and asked, "Would anyone like something to drink? Pumpkin juice, tea, coffee." Then he added, "Or much harder. I think I'll have a glass of Dewars, Sally."

Jaimie started to object that it was during the school day, but Slughorn said, "This is an exceptional day." The B. G. asked for a bottled water. I asked for a cup of tea. Jaimie also asked for tea.

As Sally was organizing drinks, Slughorn began. "Let me say at the beginning that I expect this meeting to be conducted on the part of all at the highest professional level. Also, I want to assure everyone that I have always been pleased with the performance of both of my English literature Professors. I realize that Professor Wendt has a spotty attendance record, but I am totally satisfied that all breaches of attendance were explained. Not only that, it's also quite likely that none of us would be here alive if he had been in attendance on those occasions."

I started to make an objection that I wasn't absolutely sure that that was true, but Slughorn raised a hand to stop me from speaking. He went on, "The purpose of this meeting is to determine if both our professors wish to continue as professors of this school. If one or the other of you don't wish to continue, then we really don't need to prolong this meeting."

Jaimie's answer was almost instantaneous, "Yes, I do want to continue. Although, I could understand if Professor Wendt didn't want to continue if I were still here."

My answer was almost as quick. "Yes, I do want to continue. I am willing to work with Professor Sinistra. That assumes that our relationship both at school and away from school will be conducted on the highest professional level that the Headmaster has requested for this meeting."

173

Slughorn gave a sigh of relief and said, "Good. I was afraid that I would have to hire another professor or even two professors. I never understood how one person could handle all the English lit classes that you have, professors. So, now we come to the difficult questions."

Jaimie said, "I know. How do we divide up the classes between us?"

Slughorn emphatically said, "NO. As a basis for next year, I suggest that you use the division with which we started this year. As a matter of fact, I insist on it. The school year after, we can deal with changes. What I'm talking about is who gets the office that has been used by the English literature Department for more than twenty years."

Jaimie mumbled, "If we were married, that wouldn't be an issue."

Slughorn gave her a sharp look that would have withered a banshee. Jaimie quickly said, "Nothing."

Slughorn said, "That had better be the last 'nothing'!"

I said, "I have to admit that I have a deep sentimental attachment to that office." I quickly added, "I completely understand how Professor Sinistra feels that way as well."

She said, "You had priority. You have more seniority than I do. Please have it."

I replied, "My situation is unsettled. I suggest that Professor Sinistra keep the office and quarters for the summer. I probably will be traveling a lot during the summer. After my fiancée and I are married, we'll discuss living arrangements. Maybe we'll buy a house somewhere, and I'll commute to Hogwarts. Of course, I'll still need an office where I can meet students. We don't have to settle that for a couple of months, at least."

Jaimie reached across the B. G. to put her hand on mine as she said, "That's so generous of you, James. I'm sure we can work out some arrangement."

"Right," I thought. Then I decided that I had to give her some lee-way to adjust to the big changes that were happening with our relationship.

Apparently, Slughorn agreed. He didn't object to this unprofessional familiarity. Jaimie released my hand almost immediately. He went on, "Professors, I think this completes our business."

The B. G. interrupted. "Why am I here?"

Slughorn waved a hand as if to brush away a fly, "Oh, I thought we might have to discuss living arrangements in the Shrieking Shack. That discussion may be required later, but for now, we all seem to be good, right?"

Everyone nodded.

Slughorn amplified, "Then all conduct will be totally professional from here on out?"

I said, "Yes."

Jaime nodded but added, "Yes. I will conduct myself professionally."

Slughorn thanked us and we left. On the way out, Sally asked me, "Will you stay for a few minutes?"

I pulled up a chair to her desk. As soon as everyone was gone, she asked, "You're getting married, right?"

"Yes, ma'am."

"You're doing it here?"

"Well, I'm hoping to. I've not had a chance to discuss that with Ginevra yet."

Her head dropped, apparently to consider a non-existent paper on her desk. She asked, "Would you talk to Ginny about my being a bridesmaid?"

I had to smile at that. "Of course, I will. Also, I'll insist on it."

She smiled. "That would be swell."

"I think so too."

She said, "I'll talk with Slughorn about using the castle for a wedding. Do you know when it will happen?"

I laughed. "God, I hope it's before the end of the summer, but who knows?"

She gave me a condescending look. "Do you have any idea how much has to be done before a wedding. Why sorting out a wedding dress by itself is . . ."

I said, "I'm glad to say that that will be sorted out by the bride—without bridesmaids—in a week or two."

She shook her head but let me go.

# The OBC Steps Up

The next day at breakfast, Filch whispered, "OBC today."

I nodded and continued my breakfast. I didn't really have anything to do, so I went to the Shrieking Shack and let the B. G. treat me to some internet access. I read the news and checked my email, which rarely had anything other than junk mail.

As noon approached, the B. G. and I walked over to the Three Broomsticks. We arrived and found Slughorn, Filch, Dursley, and Hagrid waiting. Filch had the first word, as we sat. He said, "Finally, it's about time that the whole band is back together again."

I agreed. We ordered drinks and our usual dishes. I was one of the few who actually looked at the menu and picked a different dish most days. That business completed, Slughorn announced, "We have an important piece of business to consider."

Filch suggested, "The return of hanging students from their feet as a mild discipline!"

We all sighed. Slughorn clarified. "It perhaps is not my place to make the announcement. Perhaps, Professor Wendt ought to."

Everyone turned to me. I said, "OK. It's really official now. Ginevra and I are engaged to get married. I'm not sure just when it's gong to happen, but I think it will be sometime this summer."

Some jaws dropped. Some nodded wisely. Filch asked, "Who is this Ginevra? Is she some relative of Ginny Potter? The two look like evil twins."

I prepared for the worst and dug in for a lengthy discussion. "OK. Ginevra is almost a twin of Ginny. They come from a world where things are very different, but they have a lot in common. She and I have grown very close in our war against the Riddle from her world. I have to admit that she had a great head start with me because I already loved the Ginny from this world."

Filch's jaw dropped, "You mean that Ginny dropped you for Potter?"

I said, "She married the man she loves. That is good. I'm going to marry the woman I love. It's win-win."

Filch muttered incoherently.

Slughorn broke in. "We need to help Wendt with this. Wendt wants to get married at Hogwarts. We can all help. My wedding present to him is that I am providing the Great Hall and food for the reception from the house elves."

The B. G. said, "I'm providing Wendt with a place to stay until the wedding and maybe after."

Hagrid said, "My wedding gift to the two of you lovely people is that Madame Maxine and I will let you spend your honeymoon in her summer home in Monaco, Monaco. Oh, I don't understand it, but I guess it's sort of a city-state."

I asked, "You can make that offer for her?"

"Well, we're really close these days. Maybe I was a little over the top with that offer, but I'm sure that I can talk her into it."

Dursley said, "I have an idea how Filch and I can help. You are going to need an office for office hours and maybe someplace to do lesson planning between classes. How about if Filch and I let you use our office?"

Filch's mouth opened wide and then it changed to a smile. "Yes. Professor. It would be our honorability to let you use our official office to provide your students accessibiliness to your personalness."

I bowed to him and said, "You're a scholar and a gentleman, Mr. Filch."

He waved my thanks off as though it were the smallest trifle to him.

Our meals came, and we enjoyed a get-together that hadn't happened since the previous year.

□

I asked the B. G. to ask Aurora if she would take me to Diagon Alley. That way I could drop in at Gringotts to get some galleons out of my account. I anticipated spending a lot on the wedding. All weddings are expensive if you can afford it, or at least, if your friends think you can afford it.

She dropped me off in front of Gringotts on the next Saturday morning. I went in, trying to fly under the radar. The fact was that most employees: first, knew that the only Muggle that had any business in Gringotts was me and second, actually knew my face.

So, I really wasn't surprised when an employee, whom I couldn't remember having met, ran up to me and said, "Ah, Professor Wendt, it is so good seeing you. Please come with me. There is much business that we need to have with you. The Executive Vice President for Paper Galleons desperately needs to consult with you."

I sighed. "Sure. Let's go."

The goblin led me back into the interior of Gringotts. We took a turn that I'd never taken before. We arrived at the EVP's office. Of course, there was an outer office. It had a secretary whom I'd never seen before. At our arrival she looked up from papers on her desk. She wore her hair up in something like the old beehive hairdo.

She asked my guide, "Belknap, why did you bring a Muggle here?"

He hissed and whispered, "This is The Wendt."

Her frown dissolved into a smile as she said, "I'm sure that Helheimr will see the Professor immediately." She rose, walked to the door of the inner office, opened it and said something in Gobbledy-Gook to Mr. Helheimr. I couldn't hear the response, but I didn't need to because she opened the door wide and he said, "Please come in Professor."

My guide stuck his head in just long enough to introduce me. Helheimr stood, walked around his desk and raised his hand to mine to shake. He said, "You can't imagine how happy I am to see you." He invited me to sit and asked what I would like to drink.

Just to show him who was running the show, I told him. "Oh, just my usual."

He didn't want to admit that he didn't know what my usual was. His response was clever. He rose, walked to the door saying, "I'll just have Ms. Munpny get it for you." He walked out, closed the door, and then in a moment returned. He said, "I'm sure Ms. Munpny will have it shortly. We don't have much call for it in this office."

I didn't laugh. He apparently was having enough grief as it was. So, I gave him an easy out. I asked him, "What can I do for you, Mr. Helheimr?"

Helheimr released a sigh and said, "Well, you are aware that the former liquidity crisis—as you termed it—was caused by our inability to mint enough galleons to keep up with demand. Your solution was inspired." He said that with obvious admiration.

"It worked remarkably well. We borrowed money to buy gold from Muggle sources. We began printing money for the government to finance public works. They were well-received. The paper money has gotten into circulation and after a couple of years became very well accepted."

I asked, "It sounds like a roaring success. What went wrong?"

"Oh, well. We really somehow got into a strange situation. The paper money became very popular, in a way."

I said, "I'm still not getting it."

He looked down at the floor as though he expected a crack to open up and swallow him. Finally, he said, "Here's the problem. Paper money completely dominated the markets. No one will use gold galleons anymore."

I prompted him. "And?"

"And, people have all hoarded the gold galleons away—many in our very own vaults."

I nodded. "Gresham's law."

Helheimr nodded wisely and then said, "I know most of the famous laws of magic, such as Gopeloz's law concerning antidotes for poisons, but I'm not familiar with this Gretham's law."

"It's not surprising. First, it's Gresham's law. It was proposed by a Muggle financier."

Helheimr said, "I really should make a study of Muggle economics. You seem to have it all over us when it comes to money. But what does it say?"

"It says that if you have two kinds of money and one of them is more intrinsically valuable than the other, the less intrinsically valuable one will dominate the more valuable one. For example, if you have paper galleons, the paper, or in this case the paper plus gold threads in it, is much less intrinsically valuable than pure gold galleons. So, people will hoard the gold galleons and use the paper galleons whenever they can. It would be my guess that if you went into a store in Diagon Alley, you would hardly ever see a gold galleon in circulation."

Helheimr hung his head again. "Right. It's easy to see why, although nobody thought of the consequences of that fairly obvious law."

At that moment, we were interrupted by Ms. Munpny who came in with two glasses. One was clearly pumpkin juice. The other was a tan liquid with ice that I surmised was some form of whiskey. I sipped it and was gratified that it seemed to be Jameson whiskey. I thanked Ms. Munpny and turned back to Helheimr. I asked, "What then was the bad consequence of Gresham's law? It seems to me that other than turning gold galleons into collector's items there isn't much of a problem."

Helheimr took a sip of his pumpkin juice and said, "Well, strictly speaking it's not a problem for Gringotts. However, it is a problem for the Ministry of Magic. It's coming to a head, and no one is quite sure how to deal with it. The Ministry is putting pressure on us to deal with it, but I don't see how we can."

"OK. What is the Ministry's problem?"

Helheimr leaned over his desk and whispered as though he were afraid that someone would overhear. "Here's the deal. The Ministry borrowed Muggle money to buy Muggle gold so that we could mint gold galleons."

I began to see the problem. "OK. I get it. Those loans are starting to come due. The Ministry doesn't really have much money that they can use to repay those loans. Muggle governments won't accept paper galleons. They will accept gold galleons. The Ministry has plenty of paper galleons, but not much in gold galleons. They are putting pressure on you to sell them gold galleons for paper galleons."

Helheimr practically wailed. "We don't have big reserves of gold galleons. We've been selling them to the Ministry, but we can hardly do that any longer. We can't dip into our clients' vaults to get gold galleons. It would be unethical to replace gold galleons with paper galleons without their permission."

I nodded. "And nobody wants to give you that permission."

He agreed. I said, "Well, I can give you a suggestion that will help some. You may already have thought of it, but here it is for what it's worth."

Helheimr brightened visibly. "How much do you want for this suggestion?"

I smiled. I really wanted to give it to him for free, but if I did, goblins would think that I was losing my grip. I said, "You might not be aware that the Bank and I have long standing commercial agreements on remuneration for leasing ideas."

He smiled. "Oh, yes. Those agreements are almost legend. I certainly do."

"Good, then, I will lease you this idea for the standard percentage that I get for all my ideas."

Helheimr practically fell to his knees thanking me. He asked, "Do you want a contract drawn up?"

I acted offended. "Why, no! The Bank and I have for years worked on the honor of our word. As a senior officer of the bank, you are worthy of complete trust. I will give you my consultation for the standard rate, which I fully expect you to honor."

"Oh, yes, indeedy!"

I began. "Very well. You are familiar with the virtual vault concept?"

He was almost offended that I thought there might be some question on that score, but he wanted my help more than he wanted his reputation. "Oh, of course."

"Mind you. This idea will not dig you out of your hole, but it may provide you with some breathing space. Don't get your hopes up too high."

"No, sir."

"Whenever any one requests money from their virtual vault, you provide it in paper galleons. However, you take from their real vault, of course, whatever galleons are actually there. That would almost always be gold galleons. You state that you have a new policy that only paper galleons will

180

be dispensed from virtual vaults. Perhaps a full page add in the *Prophet* and other publications."

Helheimr thought that over. He said, "That sounds good, but won't people stop using their virtual vaults?"

"Some people will, but the virtual vault is such a useful convenience that most people will continue to use them as they always have."

He asked, "What about when people put gold galleons into their virtual vaults?"

I replied, "You have to move those galleons into their real vaults as soon as possible. You see, that will help keep up the use of virtual vaults."

He nodded.

Then I said, "I must really be going. However, this solution is only a stopgap. I will try to come up with a better one as soon as possible." With that I rose, we shook hands, and I exited the inner office.

□□

I thanked Ms. Munpny for the Jameson. She smiled and said, "Your preferences are known among the Personal Assistants rather well."

I opened the door to the hall and walked out. When I closed the door behind me, I discovered a person who surprised me, though she shouldn't have. It was Javeen. We both stood for a moment trying to come up with something to say.

She spoke first. "Surprising to see you here."

I had an intuition. I said, "Would you have lunch with me today. I know it may be a little early . . ."

"Absolutely. Of course, I have a flexible lunch hour."

"Good. Why don't you pick a good place, and we'll go right now."

Her face lit up. She led me to a meeting room that turned out to have a floo connection. We were standing next to it. She turned to me and asked, "Would you prefer a primarily wizard pub or a goblin?"

I smiled. "I meant it when I said that you should choose. Believe me, I say what I mean and I mean what I say."

Her smile was radiant. "That's what I like about you. You are a true goblin. You speak your heart." With that, her smile didn't dim but her face turned an interesting shade of red."

She found that I already had my hand extended. She took it in hers without the slightest hesitation. We stepped into the floo and found ourselves in a dimly lit pub. It was mostly occupied by goblins, although there were some wizards. She kept my hand in hers and led me to an empty table, saying as we went, "This is a very informal pub. You seat yourself."

I selected instead a booth closer to the center of the Common Room. I still held her hand as she lowered herself to the bench and slid in. Then I went to my side of the booth. A waiter joined us almost immediately and took our drink order. I said, "I suppose that you can't order anything alcoholic since this is your lunch hour."

She said, "Oh, no. I will have a Jameson whiskey."

I said, "The same." As the waiter turned to go, I signaled him. He turned his attention to me. I said, "It's my check regardless what she says." He nodded and left.

I asked, "Do you have a recommendation?"

She only glanced at the menu. Then she said, "The portions here are so large, and I really hate to have to bring a 'to go' bag back to the office."

I said, "We can share an entrée. What do you fancy?"

She hesitated not at all. She said, "I really like the grilled salmon pasta primavera."

I nodded. I didn't want to start a serious conversation only to be interrupted by having to place an order for food. Fortunately, the waiter was back quickly with our drinks. He assumed that we needed more time, but I corrected that misapprehension. "We're ready to order. We would like one order to share. We want the grilled salmon pasta primavera." He left promptly.

I said, "Javeen, we know each other way too well to need to have small talk before we cover serious matters."

She colored a bit and said, "I'm not sure whether to take that as a compliment or not."

"I'll clear that up. It was a heart-felt compliment." Her smile positively glowed. I went on. "As you know, I've been away nearly all year. I've been out of the country, and to be honest, I've been out of the universe much of the time."

Her puzzlement showed even before she asked, "What do you mean?"

I said, "I'll not pretend that I understand it very much. It turns out that there are multiple universes. All of them have different histories from ours. Many of them are practically indistinguishable from ours. Others are desperately different. One way of getting between them is to use a vanishing cabinet."

She wanted to know how that worked. I tried to explain. "Vanishing cabinets are usually one-offs. You enter it. You vanish for a while and then you reappear. A small percentage are paired. You enter one and you might exit its twin. Now, I'm really going out on the limb with what I'm about to say."

I took a deep breath. "It seems when one cabinet of a pair is destroyed, the other can pair with any unpaired cabinet in a different universe. In this case, the cabinet in Borgen and Burke's was paired with a vanishing cabinet in Hogwarts. The one in our Borgen and Burke's was destroyed after it had been used to allow Deatheaters to enter Hogwarts."

She said, "So, the vanishing cabinet in some other universe connected to the one in Hogwarts. Someone came through that pair, didn't they?" She gasped, "And you went back through it didn't you?"

"True. I'm not going to tell you the full details of that incident, but I will tell you things that you will be very interested in. Before I start that, there's some background information that you need."

At that point our waiter returned with our order. He had failed to bring a second plate. I started to ask him for one. However, Javeen took my arm to keep me from speaking. She said, "Don't. I'll just move around next to you and we can share the plate." She did. I had no intention of objecting.

Once we were both seated and had begun our meal I continued. "The person who came across the vanishing cabinet connection was someone whom I knew in this world. As a matter of fact, you might know her."

Javeen's face fell. "You're talking about Minerva, aren't you?"

I almost cried. The possibility had never occurred to me. I said, "No. It was Ginevra Weasley."

Javeen asked, "Who?"

"Ginevra Weasley is the true given name of the woman whom you may know as Ginny Potter."

"She isn't married to Potter in that other universe?"

"No. She isn't. In that other universe . . ." My throat caught.

Javeen said, "Potter is dead there."

I nodded.

"That means that He-Who-Must-Not-Be-Named is alive there."

I shook my head. "No. It's complicated, and I don't want to go into it right now. I'll just say that he did survive for a while, but he's dead now."

Javeen whispered, "Completely? Not like he was before when young Potter defeated him?"

"He's completely dead forever."

Her face lit up again. "You had something to do with it, didn't you?"

I wished for a moment that she wasn't so intuitive. I couldn't lie. "Yes, I had a certain role in his death."

"That wasn't what you wanted to talk about, was it?"

"No. What I want to talk about has to do with Ginevra. I think you knew or at least guessed that I loved Ginny Weasley—the one who is married to Potter."

"Yes, I thought so." She seemed about to say something else, but had cut it off.

I went ahead to name the dragon in the room. "In working with her to kill Riddle, we fell in love. It wasn't much of a stretch for me. After all, I had already loved her in this world. I thought I was over her, but no."

Javeen sighed. "Well, I suppose she loved you in that other world too."

"No. She only loved Potter. We hardly knew each other. She was pretty different from Ginny here. I don't think she'd have fallen in love with me, just because we saw each other for the first time. She's tougher than this world's Ginny. That's why I call her Ginevra. I have to distinguish her from Potter's Ginny. Anyway, we're in love, and we're going to get married soon. I'm not sure when. I hope to God it's before the summer is over."

Javeen nodded. I went on. "Do you want to come to the wedding? I suppose I have to invite your dad because of our business involvement. I don't have to invite you if it would be painful for you."

She didn't hesitate. "Yes, yes. I want to come. Oh, yes. I won't make a scene either. You deserve to be happy, and I suppose after all that Ginevra's been through she deserves to as well."

We finished the meal quietly—a pleasant quiet. When we finished, she asked me where I wanted to go. I answered, "Well, really back to the Bank. For one thing, I need to get some cash out of my vault."

She said, "Oh, good. I'd be happy to take you down to your vault. We'd be talking about getting you a larger vault if it weren't that most of your money is now in print Galleons."

"Good to hear, I guess." I signaled the waiter who came by with the check. I glanced at it and gave him a generous tip—generous even if we'd ordered two entrees rather than one. We went to the floo. I held out my hand. She took it and said, "We should do this more often."

"I think we probably will be. You know how business is." She squeezed my hand, and we flowed through the ether. We returned in the meeting room where we left. Javeen quickly led me down to my vault. I found stacks of hundred galleon bills banded together by rubber bands. I picked one up and put it in my purse. I thanked Javeen for her help.

She led me back up to the front of the bank. She asked, "Can I drop you off somewhere?"

I shook my head. She touched my arm briefly and said goodbye.

I left Gringotts. It was a little after noon. Aurora had arranged that I could find her at Madame Malkins. I did find her there. We went to the Cauldron. I'd promised her lunch in payment for giving me a lift.

She ordered both drink and entree. Then, I ordered just a drink. Aurora wondered why. I said, "They insisted at Gringotts that I join them for lunch. So, I'm just having a drink. I'll be happy to drink and talk with you while you eat."

She just nodded and went with the flow. She wanted to give me advice on wedding plans. I sat and listened as she went on and on about colors and suggestions for groomsmen and so on.

When she dropped me off at Hogwarts, I walked down to the Shrieking Shack. I needed to make a couple of phone calls. That was the place to do it.

I called my contact at Barclay's, Quinn. I was impressed that she recognized my voice when I called. Her first words were, "Have you dug yourself a hole and pulled the dirt in over you? I haven't heard a peep from you in almost four years."

"That's not quite accurate, but it's not far wrong. I've been out of the country a good bit over the last four years. Can I have a lunch meeting with you soon to pick your brains?"

She asked, "You know, lately, I've been giving the store away to you a lot. I need to get something good in return. What is it?"

"Well, first of all, you'll get the greatest lunch of your life. No wait, let me offer you something better. We'll leave London Saturday afternoon, go by Eurostar to Paris. We'll have dinner on the Eiffel Tower. Then we'll return and be back to London before midnight."

There was silence on the line. I almost asked if our connection had dropped, but she came back on and said, "OK. That's a nice start. But I've got to have more than that."

Now it was my turn to drop back and think. I made a decision. "I'll be honest with you. As you know I'm a consultant, and I'm working on behalf of my principal. I don't know what will come out of it, but I promise you that if there were any way that I could give you something, I will. As a matter of fact, I'll give you absolutely everything that I possibly can. I can't offer more than that."

Another silence on the phone. Then, there was a laugh. She said, "You've got me. I've never been to Paris, let alone on the Eiffel Tower, let alone had dinner on it. It's crazy. I could do it any time I wanted to. But I don't. Why?"

"We could talk about that too." I said.

"No, let's stick with your problem. We can deal with my problem the next time."

"I'll meet you at St. Pancras at 2 PM this Saturday. Don't forget your passport."

"It's a date."

I got Dursley to drop me off at St. Pancras at 1:45 PM. I had purchased tickets and was ready for Quinn when she showed up ten minutes later. She looked me up and down. "How have you been doing? What have you been doing?"

"I had some assignments away from England, and I don't mean France. I suggest that we limit ourselves to light banter until we get to the Tower."

She sighed. "Sometime you've got to tell me about some of these out-of-country experiences, but I'll agree to talk about trivial topics—sports, the weather, politics."

The trip to Paris was actually pretty exciting visually even without any commentary. Every now and then, one of us would point to something out the window. We arrived at the gare in Paris. A cab ride took us to the Tower. I had a reservation for us, so we were up to the restaurant level quickly and seated. After ordering drinks, I took a moment to look around. The only time that I'd been there had been as Jaimie. That was a very different experience. Quinn seemed to be enjoying the view as well as I was. It was a pleasant summer day. We said nothing until we'd ordered. I'd insisted that she not even glance at prices.

She laughed, "I'd given up looking at prices when the day began."

I said, "You ready?"

She shrugged. "Any time."

"OK. Here's the story. Let me tell you a fairy tale."

She scoffed. "Why not. Half the time when we talk I wonder if it wasn't all a fairy tale."

"Just listen. There's a country that has currency consisting of paper money and gold coins."

She laughed. "Everyone hordes the gold coins and uses the paper. Gresham's Law. I hope that's not a mystery to you."

"That's not the problem. The problem is that they have a balance of payments problem. They are also in debt to some big players."

She asked, "IMF?"

"No. Individual countries. Just to make it clear, I can't name names—to protect the guilty."

I went on. "OK. Your unnamed countries that have initials UK and US have lent them money that can't be repaid in the paper currency of the country."

She shrugged. "Classic problem. You want a solution. Is there enough gold currency in the country to cover the debt?"

"Yes, easily—I think."

186

"Raise taxes. Oh, of course, everyone pays in paper currency. That's not a solution."

Our meals arrived. We ate for a while. She said, "Can your government declare that the only valid money after some date is paper money."

I thought a moment. "Hmm. Theoretically yes, but wouldn't that make them very unpopular?"

"No doubt there would be resistance, but the government could agree to redeem your coins at more than the official rate of exchange. That would pull some gold coins out. Eventually, more would be redeemed as people needed to use their coins. The exchange premium could be a limited time offer. After the time limit the price for gold drops down again."

"Interesting. I suppose that happened at some time in most countries' history when gold coins no longer were legal tender."

"Yes. But I'm concerned about the long term financial health of this mythical kingdom. If they have a balance of payments problem, do they not produce enough to satisfy most of their needs?"

"Oh, they do. It's a long story. That's really not their problem."

Quinn said, "Now, you owe me something."

I said, "You're right. Let me suggest something. Someone who could loan this mythical kingdom some hard currency could probably work a good deal. They'd be sure of eventually being re-paid, so it would be a pretty sure bet."

She considered all through the rest of the meal and even into the coffee after. Finally she said, "Would you put me in touch with your mythical government representatives who could negotiate?"

"Yes."

She said, "How do I get in touch with you. Your phone seems to be off most of the time."

"I'll give you my email. I only look at it once a day, but it's dependable."

She finished her coffee and I my tea. "I guess we've got to get on our way?"

"Yes, we need to make the train station by seven thirty."

"Do your clothes turn to tatters if we wait for the sun to set before leaving?"

"No. The problem is that by that time it's way too late for the return train. We might have to stay the night in Paris."

She leaned in and asked, "Would that be awful?"

I said, "My fiancee might think it was not that great an idea."

She nodded her head.

We got back to London well before midnight. She found her way home without my help.

The following Monday, I talked Dursley into sending an owl for me. It was addressed to the Minister of Magic, although it might better have been addressed to the Minister of Finance. I asked for a meeting to discuss fiscal policy.

The answer came back in two days. It showed up in my morning sunny-side up eggs. It didn't directly materialize there. Rather, the owl who delivered it, seemed to be a dive bomber, depositing it as a direct hit in my eggs. It read,

Dear Professor Wendt,

We are anxious to hear your views on the fiscal current situation vis-a-vis loan repayments. We understand that you are currently not teaching, so we've taken the liberty to schedule the meeting for tomorrow afternoon. A Ministry representative will join you for lunch at Hogwarts and bring you here.

Best regards,
Pamela Moertl, Minister of Magic

PM/jp

When the next day arrived, I took my time getting up to the castle from the Shrieking Shack where I'd been reading the latest *Times of London*. I arrived shortly before noon. It turned out to be just in time to watch Ginny Potter step out of the floo connection. I knew it was her by the way she wore her hair. It was shorter and worn down. That was very different from the way that Ginevra wore it.

I stepped up to her and asked, "Are you the Ministry Representative that I'm looking for?"

She chuckled. "Yes. Why don't we sit at the Gryffindor table."

We found an empty spot on the bench and sat. There was a sixth year boy sitting across the table. He asked, "Who is your friend, Professor?"

Ginny answered for herself. "I'm a former Gryffindor. I'm also an Auror." That pretty much shut down conversation with him and the rest of the people around us. That was good because I wasn't interested in an extended conversation with students. You might think that we could have switched to the head table. That would actually have been worse. A lot of the professors at that table would remember Ginny and not be so intimidated by her being an Auror. So, we talked about her recent wedding and honeymoon.

She smiled, "Oh, we went to the French Riviera. It was beautiful. The only problem was that the beaches had some thieves. After we discovered that, it was rather easy to put a Muggle repelling spell on our stuff." She paused to laugh. "It was actually rather entertaining watching the thieves trying to approach our things. They'd get within three or four feet and suddenly not be able to go further. After a while, we started to place little bets as to how close each thief could get to our stuff before he was stymied. There was one who made it to about a foot away. He stood there gazing at it. His arms sort of moved aimlessly. After a while I almost felt sorry for him."

She asked me what I'd been doing this term, since I wasn't teaching. I said, "Oh, you know. It seems like I can't get through a year without some world being in danger and needing saving."

She laughed. "Isn't that the truth. Which one was it?"

"Oh, I can't tell you."

She bent close and whispered, "Considering all the things we've been through, it's really not that you can't trust me. It's that you don't want to tell me. This must be something that you did outside the Ministry."

All I would say to that was, "You're very smart."

We finished the meal and went to the floo to leave for the ministry. We stepped out into the Minister's Office. She rose immediately and said, "Let's go, the others will be here shortly." She came up to me and poked me with an index finger. "You, Weasley, and I are going to have a meeting here after this meeting."

I shrugged. We went to the Minister's Conference Room. There was the usual tray of snacks and drinks on the side. The Minister sat at the head of the table. Ginny and I sat near her. Shortly, others dribbled in. I recognized none of them. Altogether there were three others. The minister had us introduce ourselves, starting with Ginny who was sitting next to her.

"I'm Ginny Weasley, uh, that is Potter. I'm recently married to Harry Potter. I'm from the Auror Office."

I said, "I'm Professor James Wendt. I'm on leave from Hogwarts. I'm also a consultant for Gringotts."

Next was a man who had a mustache and was wearing a dark grey suit. He was short and slightly on the paunchy side. He said, "I'm Ponsonby Brix. I'm the Finance Minister of Magic." I reflected that there'd been a change in minister.

Across the table from him was another Brit. He was tall and thin. He didn't have a mustache. His introduction was, "I'm Edward Smithe, the First Assistant Undersecretary of the Exchequer, UK."

Next to him and Pamela was Joshua Weedon. He was the Finance Attaché of the US embassy in London. Pamela introduced herself and her personal assistant, Joyce Poynter. Pamela introduced the topic. "As you all know, both the UK and the US are pressuring us to speed up repayment of the loans that we made to buy gold to mint more of our currency. Frankly, we are in something of a bind here. We're paying back as quickly as we can. The problem is that we can't buy back enough gold galleons with our paper money." She then looked at me directly and said, "Gringotts could be much more helpful in this matter."

Brix was staring at me as well. He asked, "You represent Gringotts, don't you?" I hardly had time to answer when he went on. "Why isn't Gringotts being more helpful? You have lots of galleons in your vaults. Why don't you sell us them?"

I sighed and thought, "So, it's going to be like this, then." What I said was, "Well, first, Gringotts doesn't have lots of gold in ITS vaults." Brix looked like he was ready to retort, but I went on quickly. "As a matter of fact, Gringotts has sold you almost all the galleons that it actually owns. Now, we've come up with a scheme that will free up some gold and permit Gringotts to sell you some more galleons, but that is at best a stopgap measure. There are lots of gold galleons in Gringotts vaults that are owned by Gringotts clients. It would be a serious breach of contract for Gringotts to steal those galleons and replace them with paper ones."

So far, the UK and US representatives were smiling, apparently enjoying this little internecine battle. Brix was close to shouting when he demanded, "Can't the bloody goblins do something?"

Pamela stepped in at this point. "I believe that Professor Wendt has a proposal that might help us in this matter. Would you mind explaining, Professor?"

I said, "Certainly. In consultation with other experts, I've proposed that the Ministry begin a phase-out of gold galleons as official currency. That would turn most wizards' gold galleon holdings from cash to collectibles. Undoubtedly, many would hold on to some as investments and collectibles. However, most would trade their gold galleons for paper ones, especially if there were a limited time offer that would provide a small enhancement of the redemption value of gold galleons."

Everyone around the table chewed on that idea for a few minutes. Then, the Finance Minister of Magic raised objections. "We've always had gold galleons as legal tender. This would cause a revolt."

I said mildly, "What about the Ministry defaulting on a loan, hmmm?"

He harumphed.

The Minister of Magic said, "You said phase-out. How would that work?"

"I'd suggest that there be a period of time, maybe a fiscal quarter, during which both gold galleons and paper would continue to be legal tender for all purposes other than paying taxes. Taxes could only be paid by gold galleons. During that period, there would be an enhanced exchange rate for galleons for paper."

Brix nodded. "That might work. However, I think that you ought to allow taxes to be paid in paper currency as well. Some people might not have gold galleons."

Pamela asked Smithe and Weedon, "If we implement this procedure, would you give us a little leeway to make repayments. I can't promise anything, but I think we might be able to make substantial progress repaying you by the end of the quarter when the phase-in occurs."

Wheedon said, "I think that we can work with that. What do you think, Smithe?"

Smithe pursed his lips and said judiciously, "If everything works as you propose, and you start the phase-in promptly, and these additional payments that Wendt hinted at happen soon, I will definitely recommend holding back on legal action." That was a ringing success from the staid British Exchequer.

Pamela closed the meeting. "My PA will forward to you all minutes of this meeting and the statement of intent from the US and UK representatives. Now, if there is no other business for this meeting, I have other commitments. Thank you all for attending." With that, she rose and marched out of the meeting, leaving Poynter to clean up the loose ends. When Pamela reached the door, she turned and shook her head at Ginny and me. We got up and followed her to her office.

When we arrived, she ordered us to sit. When we were, she said, "I invited Ms. Potter to this meeting because there are things that need Auror involvement. Is there truth in the report that I've heard that you're engaged and will marry soon?"

I shrugged. "Yes, the report is true."

"Is that all you can say?"

"Well, I can tell you that the young lady is sort of a distant relative of Ms. Potter. Her name, coincidentally, is Ginevra Weasley."

Ginny's eyebrows shot up. Also, she started to rise but restrained herself. She asked, "You're joking surely. That is too much of a coincidence to be true."

I said, "It is true. She is truly a different person from you. You will easily see that if you meet her."

She replied, "IF I meet her! If I'm invited to the wedding, how could I avoid the acquaintance?"

"Well, we've not planned just how large a wedding it's going to be." My voice trailed off. Ginny's didn't.

She said, "Of course, I'm coming to your wedding! I invited you to mine. You owe me." Her chin had jutted out just a bit as she finished the statement of intent.

Pamela broke in. "Settle you differences elsewhere. There's a more important issue here. I happen to have heard from a very reliable source that you, Professor, were involved with the death of someone claiming to be Thomas Riddle. What do you say about that?"

I asked, "Who was that reliable source?"

Pamela laughed. "You surely don't expect that something shared at Hogwarts doesn't travel at the speed of a broom?"

I gritted my teeth but realized that it was inevitable. This was probably the most favorable official audience I'd be likely to have. I determined that I'd better make a good impression now. I began.

"Ms. Potter is aware that there is a way that people can travel between independent universes."

I was immediately interrupted by Pamela. "What are you talking about?"

"Well, there are serious Muggle scientists who have believed for quite some time that there exist multiple universes. They are separated and never interact—until now. Ms. Potter is aware that a witch traveled from one of these universes to ours using the vanishing cabinet at Hogwarts." I turned to Ginny for confirmation.

Ginny said, "I'm afraid that is true. I've never written a report on it, but I met such a person who actually teaches at Hogwarts right now."

I went on. "In the past year, there were at least two other people who have traveled from another universe. They are Thom Riddle and Ginevra Weasley."

Pamela interjected, "How is that possible? Riddle was killed by Potter almost ten years ago."

I said, "In this universe. Unfortunately, not in every universe. In Ginevra's universe, he survived, killed Potter, and came to this one in order to establish his rule here as well as in his native universe."

Pamela dropped her head to her desk and said, "Why is it always me?"

I said, "However, Ginevra and I found the last remaining horcrux that he had, destroyed it, and came back to this universe to kill him. We succeeded a couple of weeks ago."

Ginny asked, "And now you're marrying this Ginevra?"

I nodded.

Pamela asked, "What happened to his body?"

I looked down now, "Well, after verifying that he was actually dead, we left it where we found him."

"And where would that be?"

"In his ancestral home, Riddle Mansion." I grimaced. "Oh, one more thing. We actually had to kill a few Deatheaters at the same time."

Pamela groaned, "All at Riddle Mansion, I suppose."

I agreed.

She leaned back and closed her eyes—for quite some time. She seemed to be talking to herself. Eventually, she sat up and said, "Just how many Deatheaters are we talking about?"

I said, "There were at least a dozen. A couple of them escaped."

Pamela asked, "Were they from that other universe?"

"I've talked with Ginevra some about it. If they were from that other universe, they were lower echelon people. She didn't recognize any of the heads of departments."

Pamela rose from her chair and began pacing. She signaled us to remain seated. "I suppose that would be good. I'd hate to think that there are experienced rebels running around primed to overthrow the Ministry." She kept pacing behind her desk. Then she said, "But how can we be sure?" Now she was wringing her hands as well as pacing.

I said, "Think about it. See it from Riddle's perspective. He's always been very cautious. He wouldn't want to risk his base of power by taking the key heads of government away.

"Another thing is that he really needed local talent. The political climate here is very different from his universe. He needed to have people who knew who likely recruits would be, who knew the key players in government here. That was the way that he developed his network of Deatheaters when he worked here before. He developed his team slowly, carefully. It's what he knew."

Pamela shook her head as though dispelling a cloud of gnats. "I suppose you're right. I just hope he didn't get far in developing a new network."

Then she sat again. She turned her full attention to Ginny. She seemed to be seeing her for the first time. She bit her lower lip and then cleared her throat. When she spoke, she spoke with confidence and authority. "Ms. Potter, would you consider it a dereliction of your duty as an aurorif you paid a visit to Riddle Mansion, checked on the death of Riddle and others, and . . . uh . . . disposed of all evidence that another Riddle has been roaming about England, possibly with a group of Deatheaters. I think this legitimately falls under the Magical Secrecy act, wouldn't you agree?"

Ginny frowned, but said, "I think you're right. If that is a direct order from the Minister of Magic based on that understanding of the Magical Secrecy Act, I will."

Pamela said, "It is a direct order. Now, get out of here and sort this out right away. Oh, one other thing, since you're acting directly for me, your superiors don't have to know about this."

We all rose. Ginny asked, "Can I drop you anywhere on the way?"

I was about to say no. Then it occurred to me that there was somewhere that she could drop me. "Yes. Would you drop me off in Diagon Alley?"

She smiled, the first in a while. "Certainly. Do you have a preference?"

"Oh, Flourish and Blotts would be good."

"Right away." We walked to the floo connection. I held out my hand, and we were off.

I was greeted at Flourish and Blotts as a long lost relative. Considering the amount of business that I directed their way, it wasn't surprising. Unfortunately, I had to limit myself to buying a copy of *The Times of London* and running out.

I made my way to Gringotts. Inside, I was greeted cordially as always. When I announced that I needed to see Glorblaz, I was led back to his outer office without delay or comment. Inside, I found Javeen. She greeted me very cordially with a hug. She said, "I just knew you couldn't stay away for long. Do you want to see Dad?"

I agreed. She opened the door to the inner office and announced me. She asked me, "Should I stay to take notes?"

I agreed. I took the large red leather guest chair. She took a yellow guest chair. Gorblaz asked, "What can I do for you today?"

"Oh, it's about the Ministry loan repayment issue."

Gorblaz said, "You've got a solution, don't you."

Javeen said enthusiastically, "A real genius!"

"You may not think so, when you hear the solution that I proposed and that the Ministry accepted in principle."

Gorblaz asked, "What's our part of the deal?"

"Well, actually nothing. If it works, you don't have to do anything and the pressure to sell gold will drop dramatically."

Gorbalz enthused, "You are a genius." Javeen's eyes welled up with tears.

I said, "You haven't heard it all. Save your praise for later. The deal is that the Ministry is about to start a three month program in which they will phase out the use of gold galleons as money and replace it completely with paper money. People will be encouraged to sell the gold galleons to the Ministry at a small premium to value."

Gorblaz's mouth dropped, "That means we don't have the coin minting business any more."

I said, "Right, but you will still be printing paper money."

Gorblaz sighed. "I guess that is good news for us. All the pressure from the Ministry is a bloody nuisance. We'll probably still print as much total money as we always have. I was just hoping we might be able to make a little extra out of the deal."

I said, "I know. It is disappointing, but considering the amount of effort you have to expend, the result is pretty good."

He nodded. Then he asked, "Is that all?"

I said, "I suppose that Javeen has told you that I'm getting married."

He sighed again. "I guess when troubles come they come not as single spies but in battalions."

"I won't argue. So, I'll be on my way."

Gorblaz waved good-bye. After the door closed, Javeen asked, "Can I drop you anywhere?"

"It would be nice if you could drop me off at Hogwarts."

She looked down at her watch and said, "Oh, my. It's almost close of business. Would you be interested in dining with me?"

I looked at her. "Sure. Why not? Only if it's my treat, though."

"Are you sure your sweet-heart won't object?"

"Let's just go."

She popped her head into her Dad's office and said, "I'm going to dinner. See you later." She took me to the same pub that we'd been to before. We actually had the same waiter.

I asked Javeen, "I know I'm boring. What about the same deal as the last time?"

She said, "I'd love it." So, I placed the identical order down to drinks as before.

As we waited for our food, she asked me, "Couldn't you have cut a deal that would be better for us?"

"Oh, I got the best deal for everyone. You can't always be a genius."

She laughed and impulsively took my hand for an instant while saying, "You'll always be my genius."

# Something Borrowed

Things were boring for a while. That didn't bother me in the least. However, on July 24, there was a visitor who entered my tent unannounced. When I saw her, I leaped to my feet and swept her into my arms. I asked, "How did things go?"

She said excitedly, "Better than I expected. It appears that with Riddle dead, along with a few of his Deatheaters, the ones remaining in my universe are not so bold. But, you want to know about the wedding. It's all set. It will happen a week from tomorrow. You should get a new set of dress robes for the wedding. It will be a little bigger wedding that we thought at first. Besides my family, I've invited Slughorn, Filch, and a few others who can be trusted. It's still not like Bill's wedding, but it will still be so very, very nice!"

I agreed. "OK. We can go to Madame Malkins today if you like."

She fairly bubbled, "I like!"

So we did. Negotiating something that we both liked was a challenge. While we did that, she filled me in on other details. She'd recruited her surviving brothers to be my groomsmen. Conveniently, that made four: Bill, Percy, George, and Ron. I could pick which would be the best man. Her bridesmaids were to be Fleur, Luna Lovegood, and two other of her friends from Hogwarts whose names didn't ring a bell for me.

We talked about our wedding at Hogwarts. She said, "Well, we can invite loads of people in your universe. We don't have to be in a real hurry."

"That sounds nice, but school is starting. I'm going to be buried in the beginning of the new term. Please, can we make it in August, anyway?"

She pouted, "What about the students? Surely, there will be some of your older students who would like to attend?"

I sighed. It wasn't looking good for a quick marriage. She was certainly bubbly today. "Oh. Oh. I know. We can get married at Halloween. It's a Saturday this year. It's perfect!"

There are times when you have to cut your losses and accept the inevitable with as much grace as you can muster. This was such a time. I said, "Sounds good. Halloween it is. It will give us enough time to marshal our forces for the event, but it's not too late. It will only be three months after our first wedding."

She was delighted. We decided that we'd leave for her universe on the following Monday. I'd stay in Ron's room at the Weasley's. We'd have a small family rehearsal dinner. The only extra people would be Ginevra's two friends who weren't married to other Weasleys.

□

Traveling to her universe was even easier than the last time. We landed in the vanishing cabinet in Borgan & Burke's. We disapparated directly from it into the family room of the Weasleys. It was a small surprise for Mrs. Weasley, but compared to all the unpleasant surprises that they'd had over recent years, it was not a bad one.

We arrived in the mid-afternoon. I tried to get Mrs. Weasley to let me help with dinner. She insisted, "Now, your beautiful fiancée and I will fix dinner. Just you sit down like Mr. Weasley does and read the paper." I looked to see what papers were there. The only one was the *Daily Prophet*. I gagged and opened it to the Sports page, trying not to see any headlines from the front page. I almost succeeded. Unfortunately, I noticed a headline, "Muggles Caught in Raid of Chicken Processing Plant."

The sports page featured articles about the upcoming CONCAQ tournament. Apparently, Latin America was a major Quidditch power in this world.

It turned out that most of the Weasleys were coming for this meal. Ron arrived first, followed by Mr. Weasley and then George last.

Fleur wanted to know how Muggles had fared in my world. I answered, "Really about the same as always. We're pretty much separate from the wizarding world."

She hemmed and hawed and finally asked, "Do you know what happened to you in this world?"

"I'm afraid not. My bet would be that I'm dead, but I really don't know."

After that exchange, Mrs. Weasley steered conversation to more bland topics, like the Wizard Chess tournament that was about to start. She asked me if I were still interested in Chess. She had a slip of the tongue, though. Her pronunciation of Chess sounded suspiciously like "Sex".

I answered with a face that I managed to keep under control, "I'm just as interested as I always have been, as Ginevra can testify."

Ginevra lost it when I said that. She had to cover her mouth and bend over to keep from spraying the room with spittle. Ron saved the evening by asking me why I used Ginny's given name. My answer was simple, "Well, you see, in my world, there's also a Ginny. In order to keep them straight, I use your Ginevra's real name for her, although if you'd like, I can go back to her nickname."

Ginevra said, "You're the only person who uses my real name other than Mum when she's angry at me. I like it." With that she squeezed my thigh. I almost lost it myself at that point. Thankfully, the rest of the meal was uneventful.

The rest of the week waiting for the wedding day was also uneventful. I was deeply thankful for that.

⊓⊓

The wedding rehearsal was very much like the first meal that I'd had at the Weasleys at the beginning of the week. The only difference was that there were a few more faces. Ginevra had found a Christian minister who agreed to perform the wedding. He was a wizard. He was also a Catholic. His name was Father Brown. He tried to convert us to Catholicism.

He said, "You know that the only true faith is the Catholic."

I said, "I agree. If you mean by catholic, the common meaning—universal."

He laughed at that. I asked him, "Do you believe in the priesthood of all believers?"

He grimaced. "You are really trying my faith." He sighed and said, "Yes, I do. But . . ."

I said, "But?"

"Oh, you'd have to spend a year in seminary to understand why the 'priesthood of all believers' doesn't mean . . ."

I interrupted. "The Priesthood of All Believers."

He laughed. "Yes. Well, there's still time while there's still breath. For the moment, I'm going to agree to marry you, IF you promise me that you will be true to your vows and seriously consider The Faith."

I agreed as did Ginevra. He then admitted, "In truth, with the current state of Muggles, all priests have become like chaplains, having to do the

198

sacraments for all of every faith. This is not the first marriage of non-Catholics which I've officiated."

That hurdle passed, he gave us good advice on patience and love in marriage. He led us through a practice of the wedding ceremony. That night—to honor the beliefs of Father Brown—we slept in separate rooms.

The next morning after breakfast, I took Mr. Weasley aside. I asked his wife to excuse us because I wanted to see Mr. Wesley's collection. Mrs. Weasley said, "His Muggle collection, you mean. He'll be the death of us yet! Go ahead, get us all arrested on the day of your daughter's wedding!"

We beat a hasty retreat to the outbuilding where his collection was. Before we entered, he said, "I have a little magic trick to show you."

I laughed. "A little magic trick? All I've seen here are large and small magic tricks."

He shook his head and said, "This is special." With that he opened the door to his shed. We stepped inside. There wasn't much to see other than some normal farm implements—hoes, rakes, shovels, and so on.

I smiled and said, "Yep. I don't think I've seen a farm building like this more than a few dozen times."

He laughed at that and led me out. He did something with the wand and then invited me to open the door. We entered. This time all his collection of Muggle things were proudly displayed. I said, "Impressive. I like your magic trick. Anything new since the last time I was here?"

He sighed, "Not really. Now, I know that you didn't bring me out here just to look at my collection, lad. What is it?"

"OK. We'd better sit down. This may take a few minutes."

He frowned, "This is not like you. This is serious, isn't it?"

"I'm afraid so. Here's the deal. As soon as possible after the wedding, I want to take you and as many of your relatives as you can manage on my honeymoon—in my world."

He asked, "Why in the world would you want to do that? I've heard of generosity, but that's ridiculous!"

"Here's the deal. Let me finish before you respond."

I took a deep breath for the plunge into the incredible. "I've learned from a very, very reliable source that the universe that we are living in now is about to undergo a radical change. As a matter of fact, It's about to collapse into a very small point. I desperately want you and everyone you care about to come into our universe before it happens. I don't know how soon it will happen, but I'm pretty darn sure it will be soon—very soon."

Mr. Weasley stared at me as though I'd gone crazy. "How in the world can anyone know that!"

I said, "Look, the way I know is that it almost happened in my world. This same person or at least my world's version of that person showed up in

199

my world. He didn't tell me that story. He just asked for help. I was part of a team sent by the Ministry to go with him. We discovered this plot to restart the universe from scratch. We traveled around a fair amount of the galaxy tracking it down. We fought in a battle that ended in the bad actor and his spaceship falling into a black hole. It's real!"

Mr. Weasley sighed. "I know you fairly well—at least this world's version of you. You always seemed sensible to me except that little excursion to kill Riddle. I guess this time, it really worked. OK. You're not the typical 'chicken little'. Still, I just can't believe that what you say is actually going to happen."

I said, "OK. I understand that. Can you at least come along and get as many of your kids to, as well. And, this is really, really important to me. Stay until our wedding in October."

"You mean, Halloween."

"Yes."

He sat for a long time. Then he said, "I'll try to talk Molly into it. It won't be easy."

I actually dropped to my knees. "Please, please do it. I don't want your Ginny to live the rest of her life without family other than in-laws."

He stared at me, and it finally hit him that I was totally serious. He said, "I'll do my best." We left the shed then.

The rest of the day was a joy for me, but only because Ginevra was radiant. Her wedding dress, which I didn't see until she walked down the stairs from her bedroom, was as white as could be without blemish or ornamentation of any sort. It was not a very traditional cut. It could have been worn to any event.

Her red hair that fell down mostly over her back stood out like lava on a field of snow. I also thought of blood on snow when I saw it. She was stunningly beautiful. Whatever happened next, I swore to myself that I would never forget her standing there on the staircase.

The ceremony itself was totally normal but full of meaning for me. At the end when I kissed Ginevra, I whispered to her, "You're everything to me."

The reception was pleasant. The toasts had many fine phrases, all quite forgettable. When I rose to offer a toast, I didn't. Instead, I said, "There is nothing that I can say that would be as elegant as the beauty of my bride beside me. Instead, I make an offer. I doubt that my wife . . . By the way, that is a phrase that I have the greatest pleasure in saying. I doubt that my wife has informed any of you just how rich I am in my world. I say this not to brag, but to make an absolutely genuine offer. I would like everyone here— all dear friends of both MY WIFE and me—to join her and me in celebrating our honeymoon. Believe me," Here I had to fight back tears. "Believe me, I can't imagine anything I would enjoy more than for all of you to come with us this night to our honeymoon in Monaco. The expense would not scratch the outermost edge of my wealth. That wealth is nothing compared to having my wife, my new in-laws, and my dear friends with us."

There was a strange silence. Then, there was applause.

Ginevra kicked me under the table and whispered in my ear, "You are totally insane. I want you exclusively to myself. What are you doing?" Then she gasped. "I know what you're doing. You are really serious about this Big Crunch, aren't you?"

I said only one word, "Absolutely."

She stood and said, "I won't offer a toast either. I'll just say that I feel exactly as MY HUSBAND does. You are all as welcome as anyone could possibly be to join us in our honeymoon." There was a standing ovation after her offer.

During the dinner afterwards, almost all our guests approached us, thanked us from the bottom of their hearts, and gave us their sincere apologies for not being able to accept our offer. I decided not to beg.

Finally, Bill and Fleur leaned across the table and he said, "God, I wish I could come. I just can't get away from Gringotts."

I tried one last ploy, "I'm sure I can get you your same job at Gringotts in my world."

Fleur stared at me and said, "You're deadly serious, aren't you." Her emphasis was on the word, "deadly."

"Yes, I am deathly serious."

She pulled him aside and said, "Bill, I believe him."

He took a deep breath and said, "Come outside. Let's talk."

In the end, Bill, Fleur, Mr. and Mrs Weasley accepted our offer. George seemed on the verge of it but didn't.

At one point while we were dancing, I told Ginevra, "There are two other people that I'd like to invite on our honeymoon."

"Who's that?"

I took a deep breath and said, "Minerva's sister and her aunt Beryl. What do you think?"

She broke off our dance and led me over to where her Dad was enjoying watching the dance. She asked him, "Do you know what happened to Minerva's sister or their aunt Beryl?"

Arthur shook his head sadly and said, "I'm not sure about Beryl, but I know that Minerva's sister died while resisting Deatheaters. I only met her once, but she seemed like a decent sort of person. I'm sorry."

We went the next morning to the Cauldron via the floo. I had asked Ginevra to give me most of the gold that was left from what she'd gotten from my vault. When we arrived, I took Tom aside and said, "Here. This isn't adequate for all the hospitality that I've had at the Cauldron. It just is a token." He was shocked into silence.

Then we went into Diagon Alley. Without pre-planning, the five of my companions formed around me as we walked to the entrance to Knockturn Alley. As we entered it, there were several fellows loitering. They started to make sport of me. One look from Bill and his half-Vela wife laid most of them low. We reached Borgun and Burke unmolested. Inside, we were not challenged as we all walked to the vanishing cabinet, entered, and disappeared.

We walked out in the Room of Requirement. It was a quick, unmolested walk to the Great Hall hearth. We exited in the Cauldron. When Tom saw us, he said, "Bless my soul, if it isn't the Weasley clan! What can I get you?"

I approached him, pulled a few bills off my sheath from my recent visit to Gringotts. I handed them to him and said, "Drinks for the house as long as this lasts."

He stared at me and said, "Surely, you've not noticed that these are hundred galleon bills?"

I smiled at him. "Sure I have."

We then left by the front entrance. Outside, we disapparated to LeHavre. From there we disapparated to Monaco. I hailed a taxi and asked for a good four-star hotel. When we arrived, I had to do a little haggling with the staff to get us a suite with three bedrooms. When they saw that price was really no object, they managed to get a suite opened up.

That evening there was nothing new that Ginevra and I had left to explore. However, we enjoyed sharing a bed but not as before. Before, we were always living under threat, frequently in a tent. Don't misunderstand. I wouldn't go back to that life voluntarily, but it added an urgency to everything we did, not least of all sex.

After our week-long stay, we returned to the Cauldron where we had three rooms reserved. I called a meeting of the three families. We had it in the Common Room at a quiet period of the morning. We sat in a dark corner. After ordering drinks, I began my talk. "Each of the three families has someone with whom I've been open about my desire for you all to migrate permanently to this world.

"I'll now discuss my reasons in more detail for all of you. I convinced one of each pair that my reason was good. The other should consider that before prejudging what I have to say.

"This is a fairly long story, but I'll try to stick with dragon's-eye view as much as I can. Feel free to ask questions as we go.

"This story starts at least four years ago. Its roots go even further back." I reflected a moment and added, "Much, much further back. No one else at this table knows that more than a half a dozen years ago a group of four American soldiers were wounded in Iraq. Their wounds were such that shrapnel from an improvised bomb entered their brains. That shrapnel was actually fragments of a device constructed more than thirteen billion years ago by a race that wanted to preserve its knowledge by encoding it in RNA and protecting it in meteors. The lucky (or maybe unlucky) people who might have a fragment of those meteors penetrate their brains would become the inheritors of that knowledge and intellectual power.

"Minerva, Aurora, and several others were recruited to capture the four people who had become the inheritors of this knowledge and power. The four had a project that they moved relentlessly to achieve. The combined resources of the United States military and civilian police along with the wizards and witches that we assembled couldn't stop them from completing their project."

Fleur asked, "What was that project?"

I nodded. "It was the construction of a faster than light interstellar, perhaps intergalactic, spaceship. That was only part of their project. They wanted to recruit a small group of humans to go to a distant planet to restart the civilization that the builders of the meteors had had."

Fleur again asked, "What was the name of this race?"

I shrugged. "There was no name. We didn't even have a nickname for them. As I said, they achieved their goal. We didn't hear from them again or expect to until the leader of the project, a Muggle nicknamed The Lieutenant, walked into Hogwarts over four years ago. He said that there was a tragedy that we needed to help prevent. He didn't tell us what it was, but he had already earned a reputation that kept us from ignoring him. Just being able to walk into Hogwarts uninvited all by itself convinced us that we needed to listen to him.

"We consulted with the Ministry of Magic and the US Navy. The decision was made to make him the lead of a project to prevent whatever tragedy was coming. He would never tell us what it was, but as I said, our trust was so solid that we followed him unquestioned."

Bill asked, "Did he use the *Imperious* Curse."

"No."

He asked, "How do you know?"

I asked in turn, "Has anyone ever used the *Imperious* Curse on you?"

He shook his head warily, "No."

"I have had the *Imperious* Curse used on me. I know what it's like. That never happened. Also, remember that he is a Muggle."

I went on. "He had contacted an alien civilization that has interstellar travel. We already had a name for them—the PAK. They got back to us and arranged a rendezvous so that we could fly with them back to their home world.

"We flew there and found a planet that was nearly shattered. Perhaps a sixth of their population was dead. They were murdered to coerce them to aid another civilization build a device that would reverse the Big Bang and compress the entire universe to a point."

Fleur asked, "Does this race whom you were helping have a name?"

"We don't know it. We just called them the PAK."

She followed up, "Why did you call them the PAK?"

I laughed. "There is a series of novels written that involve a race that is far, far superior physically and mentally to us. The author called them the PAK."

She laughed at that. I went on, "Anyway, we followed the ship of the race that wanted to restart the universe. He had a name for himself that he adopted from Earth Indian mythology, Kali. Kali was supposed to remake the universe."

Arthur Weasley said, "Shit" softly.

I agreed. I went on. "We caught up with him. We were able to defeat him only with the help of The Lieutenant and a fleet of the PAK.

Bill asked, "You really believe that this Kali could destroy the universe?"

"My belief is immaterial. The key point for me is that the PAK believed it. You could maybe doubt The Lieutenant, but the PAK are way too down to earth—forgive the pun—and real to ignore."

Molly said, "You didn't tell us this fairy tale just for fun. What's the point?"

I turned to her. "The Lieutenant found us in your world and told us, Ginevra and me, that the same thing was happening in your world."

She went on. "He didn't do that just to warn you. What was his real goal?"

"He wanted Ginevra and me to help him prevent the Big Crunch in your universe. He said that we were the only ones who could prevent it."

Arthur said quietly, "And you didn't."

Ginevra looked her Dad directly in the eye and said, "I made the decision."

Bill asked, "So, you want us to find a place in this world of yours."

"Yes. I'm more than willing to help you do that. I can rent extended stay apartments for you for a few weeks as you get jobs and get back on your feet."

Then Fleur stood and her eyes filled with tears. "Gabrielle! I must go back for her."

Bill stood and took his wife by the arm. "I'm going with you." He turned to his sister and asked, "What spell do you use to return through the vanishing cabinet?"

She said, "I'll go with you and work it."

Molly jumped up and said, "Ginny. Talk to your brothers. Get them to come with you."

Ginevra nodded. I got up to go with them. The four of us stepped out and disapparated to the outside of Hogwarts. We practically ran up to the main entrance. Inside, we ran up the stairs and entered the Room of Requirement. When we reached the vanishing cabinet, we all entered. Ginevra kissed me and said, "You can't come. You will only slow us down."

I realized that she was right. I stepped back out of the vanishing cabinet. The three of them then vanished. Almost immediately, they reappeared and stepped out of the cabinet. Their faces were grief-stricken.

I didn't have to ask. I said, "You couldn't get back."

Ginevra shook her head. I said, "That doesn't mean that your universe is gone. It might just have been that someone broke the vanishing cabinet on that end."

Fleur looked up. She said, "Non. Tu as tort." It was easy to hear the pain in what she said. She went on in English. "Even before we reached the Salle de Besoin, . . . Room of Requirement, I knew. I knew Gabrielle was gone!" She dropped to her knees and hid her tears.

# Something Blue

There were far too many gone to do anything truly meaningful for each. We gathered at the island in the lake where Dumbledore's grave was. It was before school began. We each brought a black ribbon for someone. We wrote words of farewell in blue ink on parchments and tied them with the ribbons around a sapling on the island. My ribbon was for Madame Pomfrey.

The plans for our marriage moved on slowly. The groomsmen were chosen: Dursley, Filch, Brahms, and my Ohio cousin. The bridesmaids were harder to choose. Ginevra knew hardly anyone in my world. I respectfully suggested Sally, Slughorn's personal asssistant. She chose Dursley's Pamela, with whom she developed a friendship. Aurora became another selection. Finally, she picked a friend whom she'd known in the other world, Pavarti. Which would be the maid of honor? Ginevra was puzzling over that one. Once she had her bridesmaids chosen, they began working on things like the colors for the wedding, whom to invite, what would be on the menu for the reception dinner, etc.

Meanwhile, I was working on getting jobs for Bill and Arthur Weasley. Bill was pretty easy. He and I went to Gringotts one day. I stepped in the door and was instantly greeted. I asked to see the hiring manager. That was pretty fast. He was in a meeting when we arrived. We had to wait about a half hour. When we were summoned, the goblin was very apologetic. Bill laughed and said, "I don't remember them ever being this accommodating."

We were introduced by the manager's secretary. He seemed rather puzzled by the visit. He said, "I know that you, Professor Wendt don't need a job." He then turned to Weasley and shook his hand. He said, "It's good to see you again. Who needs to be hired?"

I explained. "You see, Mr. Shlagbutt, Mr. Weasley here of course is very similar to Bill Weasley, but they are indeed different people. Mr. William Weasley is a distant relative of Bill Weasley. The similarity in appearance and name make it difficult to tell them apart. However, let me assure you that Mr. William Weasley is every bit as hardworking and talented as Mr. Bill Weasley."

Schlagbutt stared at Bill and said, "Yes, I see that you don't really look very much like Bill. You have the general same stature and coloring, but your hair is completely different and your voice would be hard to mistake for Bill's."

I nodded wisely. Then Schlagbutt went on, "If you have Professor Weasley's approval, I don't see how we can afford to be without your services. Now, you'll have to start near the bottom. We have an opening in a branch in Sunderland. It's only for a wizard to be a personal assistant to the vice-manager of that branch, but you can advance as fast as you prove your metal."

Bill said, "I would be honored to prove my metal in your organization." While we were discussing details, Schlagbutt's PA knocked on the door and stuck her head in. She said, "I have a message for Professor Wendt if I may speak with him for a moment."

Schlagbutt waved me out. "I don't think you need to stay for the rest of the details and parchment-work."

I got up and left the office. In the outer office, I discovered Javeen. She said, "Come with me." Outside the office she leaned toward me conspiratorially and said, "My Dad wants to see you as soon as you're done here. As a matter of fact, if you could come now, it would be even better."

"I don't think it would be a problem for me to go with you now. Mr. Weasley and Schlagbutt have said that I'm not really needed further."

She said, "Excellent, let's go."

I said, "I just want to let his secretary know that I'm going to see Gorblaz and that I don't need transportation back to Hogwarts. That is right, Ms. Javeen?"

She smiled broadly and said, "You can always depend on me for transportation, Jim."

I then followed her to Glazblaz's outer office. Once inside, she said, "Dad's really happy about how the problem with gold has turned out. So, if there were anything you wanted to ask him for, this would be an especially good time to do it."

I said, "I'll bear that in mind."

We were inside momentarily. Javeen asked if she were needed for any note-taking. Her Dad said, "No. You may go." She was somewhat sulky as she left.

I asked him what I could do for him. He leaned back in his chair. He said, "I was rather quick in my assessment of your help in the golden problem. I have to say that you continually under-promise and over-deliver. We found that the Ministry is particularly happy about how your ideas have worked out. I have to agree."

He sighed and closed his eyes for a moment. Then he said, "I know that you are engaged to be married soon. I understand your passion to move on that front, but I'd like to urge you to reconsider your headlong plunge into matrimony.

"Like all good businessmen you should consider carefully the alternatives that are available to you before making a rapid commitment. I've hinted before that a firmer liaison with Gringotts might be greatly to your advantage. There is literally no limit to the heights that you can reach with your talents and . . . your relationship with other bank employees."

I nodded. "First, I want you to know that I respect all the employees of Gringotts highly and that there are some whose qualities have struck me highly favorably.

"Second, if I didn't already have the very firmest commitment to my current path in life, I would consider what you are hinting at as the greatest honor. As a matter of fact, I do consider it to be a very great honor." Gorblaz smiled at that benevolently.

"The fact of the matter is that I'm already fully committed to my current liaison both by honor and by legal sanction. The marriage that you referred to earlier has already happened in a different locale, and I am bound totally to it."

He said, "I see. I respect your honesty and your commitment to honor. I hope this will not prejudice our future dealings?"

"Certainly not. I look forward to future dealings with Gringotts that will be profitable to both sides."

He nodded. I rose and approached the door, which opened as I reached for the handle. Javeen was on the other side with a very red face. I walked through the door. She closed it behind us. She faced the floor as though it were covered with galleons. I asked, "Could I trouble you to take me to Hogwarts—perhaps via a pub for lunch?"

She brightened a bit and said, "Certainly."

We entered the floo in the outer office and emerged in our favorite pub. The waiter now considered us regulars. He took us to our usual booth and merely asked, "The usual?"

I nodded and then said, "Wait." I turned to Javeen and asked, "You never know what the future will bring. Would you like something different this time?"

Her smile was genuine. "No, not at all. I definitely want our regular. If that's all right with you Jim?"

I nodded, "Certainly, J'een."

After the waiter left, she asked me what that word was. I said, "well, you have a nickname for me. I thought I'd give you one as well. It's just a contraction of your name dropping the second and third letters." She smiled at that.

□

Looking for a position at the Ministry for Mr. Weasley was a bit harder. I didn't quite have all the personal relationships at the Ministry that I had with Gringotts. I had Mr. Weasley aka "Art" to make an application in his favorite department in the usual way. Then we'd see if we could get some help from my connections.

He did. It took over a week before he heard anything back. Even then, it was just a form letter stating that his application had been received and would be considered in due course. When he read the reply, he laughed and said, "File 13."

I smiled. "We'll see. I think I might have a little pull where it counts. Let me see what I can do."

I got the other Arthur Weasley to send a little note by owl to the Minister of Magic. It said,

> Madame Minister,
>
> I respectfully request a meeting with you at your earliest convenience to discuss a matter of some importance to the Department of the Misuse of Muggle Artifacts.
>
> Respectfully yours,
> Professor James Wendt, Hogwarts

I hoped that I'd not have to wait too long for her "earliest convenience." As it turns out, she requested a meeting with me two days later. The note said that I should go directly to her office floo connection at 2 PM. Of course, I chose Art Weasley aka Arthur Weasley to take me there. I thought that it would be good to have a different name to distinguish the two Weasleys.

When the day came, Art joined me in the Great Hall. We arrived in the Officeof the Minister of Magic at five minutes to 2 PM. She greeted us with some surprise. "I expected you, of course, Professor. However, I didn't expect Mr. Weasley to bring you."

I smiled. "You don't know who this is. He is a distant relative of Arthur Weasley. Please meet Art Weasley."

She nodded. "We'll, I've got the Head of the Misuse Department arriving in a few minutes. We'll see what he says."

He did arrive. Introductions were made. The Department Head was named Tolkine. He said, "I've read this Art Weasley's resume. I have two things that trouble me. First, he doesn't seem to have much in the way of prior experience. The other is that he looks way too much like Arthur Weasley. There's even the similarity of name."

I said, "Minister, you are quite aware of my reputation for honesty and accuracy of assessment. Let me assure you that Art Weasley is well qualified for this position."

She looked at the resume. "I don't see how he could be. However, I do take your point that if you say that he is an accomplished wizard, then he is. Also, I agree that it could become confusing in the Misuse Department with two employees so similar."

She said, "Tolkine, would you mind leaving. I'm not going to override your decision for your department. Oh, yes, send my PA in as you leave." Then she turned to me and said, "The two of you stay, please."

When Ms. Poynter arrived, the Minister said, "Ms. Poynter, I have a dilemma here. I owe Professor Wendt more than one favor. So, I very much want to pay him a favor by getting Mr. Weasley here a position. Unfortunately, the one that he would be best suited for is in a department where the Head is opposed to giving him a job. Have you got any suggestions for me?"

Poynter nodded slowly and closed her eyes. "I seem to recall hearing a secretary in the Department of Sport Regulation saying that there was a position that had long gone unfilled. It's really not much more than an entry level position, but if Mr. Weasley here feels that he has some knowledge of sports, particularly Quidditch, he might be a decent fit for that position."

The Minister pursed her lips, "Yes. Would you please summon the Head of that Department to my office right now?"

She said, "Certainly. I'll see how quickly she can come."

The Minister said, "Would you two mind waiting in the Reception Area?"

We didn't, so we followed Ms. Poynter to her desk where she was sending a short interoffice memo to the Sports Regulation Department. Shortly, a return memo arrived. She read it out to us. It said, "Be there after my three o'clock. It should be short." She then went into the Minister's Office to report the return memo.

As a matter of fact, it wasn't until after 3:30 that the Head of Sports arrived in Poynter's office. She was immediately ushered into the Minister's Office. We had waited for more than a half hour. I was beginning to think that we would be sent home when Poynter was summoned into the Minister's Office, and then we were.

We were introduced to the Sports Head, Roberta Peeler. She was not petite. Instead she seemed built along lines that a Beater might like to have. She further introduced herself by announcing that she had, in another life, played Quidditch professionally.

That inspired Weasley to say, "Wait a sec. Didn't you used to be a Chaser for the Holyhead Harpies. Yes, back in '97 and '98."

Her somewhat dour expression turned to a smile. "Why yes, I was. That's been a long time. Do you really remember me from then?"

"Certainly. You were the top scorer for the Harpies for the early part of '98, weren't you?"

She actually blushed. "You know, I was the lead scorer for almost the whole of that season." She frowned then.

Weasley said, "You were at the peak of your career. Why did you ever leave Quidditch?"

She said, "My Mum was struck ill. I was the only daughter in the family. My Dad had died in the battle against Riddle. There was no one else to care for Mum. I never made it back to Quidditch."

Weasley said, "Shame. I only saw you play once, but it was an exciting game. You were playing the Cannons. It was one of the rare years when they had a half-way decent team." His mouth dropped open. "Why, you scored the winning goal, didn't you? You'd gotten way ahead of the Cannons and then their Seeker got the Snitch, but the last goal that you scored shortly before that made the difference."

She actually smirked. Then she said, "You are really familiar with the game. We need someone to train referees and test candidates. You'd also have to update the rule book. Occasionally, you'd have to travel to international conferences to help represent England in rule book revision meetings and planning World Cup events that happen in England. Now, this is an entry level position, so you'd not be in a lead in any of those efforts, but we really could use some help to carry water for the team. What do you think? Are ye game?" She was so excited that her Scotch roots appeared in her accent.

Weasley's eyes widened. "Well, I would certainly like to. You know, all my kids are . . ." I was afraid that he'd break down. He finished by saying, "Out of the house, so it's not much of a problem to travel occasionally."

Peeler asked, "When can you start?"

You could have flown a dragon through Weasley's wide-open mouth. "Well, I'd love to come down right now to have a look around if it's all right with everyone."

Pamela shrugged and looked over at Peeler. She said, "Sounds great!" So they were off.

Pamela asked, "How are you getting home?"

I had forgotten for a moment that Weasley was my way home. I smiled a crooked smile and said, "I can probably find another Weasley somewhere who could take me home."

Poynter, who had stayed during the interview said, "It's almost end of day. I wouldn't mind giving the Professor a lift back to Hogwarts, if that's where you're going."

I said, "That would be fine, if it's not a trouble."

She said, "Of course not. I've got a memo or two to get out. If you don't mind waiting ten or fifteen, I could drop you off on my way home."

"That's fine with me."

We went out to her desk. I looked at the newspapers and magazines in the reception area. Let's see, there was the *Prophet, Witch Weekly, Transfiguration Today,* and a few others. None were worth the paper they were printed on. I had a glance at *Transfiguration Today.* It was either boring or too technical for me. Fortunately, Poynter was ready to go more quickly than she'd promised.

She commented, "You know, I've never really talked with you despite the many times that you've been in these offices. How did you ever get to be a Professor at Hogwarts?"

"Well, it's a long story. I doubt I can even get a good start on it before we reach the Minister's floo."

She stared at me. "You don't think I ever get to use her floo, do you? I've got to go down to the Atrium to use one of those floo's. We've got lots of time—especially if we walk down the fire escape."

"OK. Here's the story." I gave her the dragon's eye view, and I was finished just as we reached the main floor. I asked her, "I notice that you don't wear a ring—on either hand. Seems unusual for a very capable, attractive woman not to be married."

She shook her head, "I was married. My husband was lost in the war with Riddle. I just never could think of marrying again."

"Why not wear a ring then?"

"Oh, I guess you don't notice how I'm dressed."

I looked at her critically for the first time. I shrugged. "Well, you seem to have simple, elegant tastes. So?"

Her eyes sparkled for a moment. "No, I'd say I have simple, plain tastes. I don't believe in ornamentation. I never had an engagement ring, and wearing a wedding ring when I'm not married seemed . . . oh . . . extravagant." Then she looked at me more carefully. "You've been married before, I know. It was Minerva McGonagal."

"Right."

She said, "You don't wear a wedding ring."

I said, "I gave it to someone."

"Too extravagant?"

I chuckled. "No, too hard to wear. It was a constant reminder of what I'd lost."

She said, "You know, if we'd met in another life . . ."

"Yes, IF, the true magic word that no person can control. Only God can."

We had somehow walked down the entire length of the Atrium full of floo connections without realizing it. Poynter took my forearm and said, "How did we reach the end of the line?"

I said, "It's the scintillating conversation."

She smiled and said, "Yes, 'IF'. Well, let's take this one. I'll drop you off in the Great Hall. It must be about time for dinner there."

I agreed. She continued to hold my forearm, picked up a handful of floo powder, and walked me into the floo. We walked out in the Great Hall. She said, "I'm sure you'll be showing up at the Minister's Office in the future."

"And I'm sure you'll be there to greet me."

She smiled and nodded. Then she took up some floo powder and disappeared.

⊓⊔

The new term started as they always did. Slughorn gave the beginning of term announcements. I rated a mention as a returning professor who had been on sabbatical for a term. The sorting hat recited a little ditty. I couldn't imagine how it managed to keep coming up with new apropos lyrics after all the years that it had been composing them.

There was the beginning of term teacher's meeting in the teacher's lounge. There were the never-changing list of extra-curricular duties that all teachers had to volunteer for: sponsoring clubs, chaperoning Hogsmead weekends, etc.

The one thing that didn't happen that I'd grown quite accustomed to was the visit from Aurora to announce her new harebrained scheme for Halloween. Maybe she didn't know that my new office was shared with Filch and Dursley. Of course, maybe it was that pulling a prank on my wedding day was something that was fun once, but pales into mere bad taste after the first time.

Sharing an office with Filch had both advantages and disadvantages. One of the disadvantages was that he would occasionally "borrow" some of my good whiskey. On the other hand, sharing the office was wonderful for discipline in class. All I had to do was remind students that having detention with me meant going to Filch's Office. The result was that very few would risk taking the long hike down into the basement to my office. After all, Filch might just be there with his own ideas about appropriate detentions.

The first week of October was bright and cool. I enjoyed the crisp walks that Ginevra and I took in the late afternoons when I didn't have a class or office hours. One late afternoon when I did have office hours, there was a knock on Filch's door. With a moment's foreboding as though someone had stepped on my grave, I didn't answer at first. Then I said, "Come."

For a second or two I thought it was Aurora. I half worried that she'd hatched some plot for my discomfort around Halloween, but the woman who entered was Ginevra. I stood and walked around my desk to greet her.

She gave me a peck on the cheek and sat. "Let's talk," she said. I had an idea what she wanted to talk about. She'd been bugging me about it for over a week, but I just sighed and waited for the shock wave to hit. She didn't disappoint. "We're less than a month away from our wedding. You know that we need to get a commitment from Brewster to a one year cycle rather than three."

She was right, but I was exhausted with all that had happened this year. I really didn't want to make that effort but I knew that I'd have to. I agreed. "Yes, I have to talk with him." As I was saying that, I realized that I'd have to do something more than that. Genevra was starting to ask for a date certain when it would happen. I cut her off when I said, "Give me a minute." I reached into the desk and pulled out a sheet of parchment. I began writing.

My head was down, but I knew she was about to say something. I held up a hand to forestall her. When I'd finished writing, I handed the parchment to her. I said, "Edit it."

She started to read silently and then decided to read aloud. Filch wasn't in the office, so I wasn't disturbed by that:

Mr. Brewster,

I want to meet with you and Cecilia to discuss the agreement that we have been living with for the last five years with a view to renegotiating it. Please don't fear that I have any intent to come up with a deal that will be prejudicial to your rights.

One other thing, I'd like my fiancée to be there to see what is happening and participate in the negotiations. May I suggest this Saturday, perhaps meeting at a restaurant of your choice. Please reply at your earliest convenience.

Best regards,
James Wendt

I asked, "What do you think?"

She nodded slowly as she read it a second time. "No problem from me. I'll send it by owl immediately." She got up, walked around the desk, and gave me a quick kiss. Then she opened the door, turned, and said, "See you for dinner."

The next day, there was a peck at the door of my office that I shared with Filch. It was not unexpected. Filch opened the door. He watched the owl hop over to my desk and leap up onto it scattering the papers that I was grading through the room. Filch's first reaction seemed to be happiness, but when he saw it was for me, he said, "Never liked those messy rodents with wings."

I worked the message off his leg. He didn't leave immediately, so I deduced that a reply was expected. The note was from Brewster. He simply said, "Come to my house at noon on Saturday if satisfactory." I scrawled under the message, "Accepted."

Ginevra and I decided that our continued attendance on dinner in the Great Hall would be a distraction for students—especially if we ate at a house table—and possibly for the staff as well, so we decided to go down to the kitchen for meals that we didn't prepare in our tent. We still had MRE's left. Every now and then, we would joke about missing the old staple of our life in the other world. We even shared one for lunch occasionally. But we began eating in the kitchen.

The first meal that we had there was dinner. Kretur came over to us immediately as we entered the kitchen. "What is we able to do for the Professor and Mrs. Potter?"

I corrected him gently, "It's actually a distant relative of Mrs. Potter. Allow me to introduce Ms. Ginevra Weasley."

Kretur bent over so far that he seemed to be kneeling and begged forgiveness for his mistake. Ginevra immediately took him by the arm and lifted him. "Don't be embarrassed. It's a mistake that many wizards have made. But I don't know you. What is your name."

Kretur smiled and said, "I am being Kretur. I used to be the slave of the House Black, but Mr. Potter is inheriting me. He is loaning me to Hogwarts."

I said, "Kretur, Ms. Weasley and I would like to take meals here in the kitchen with the permission of the house elves."

Just then Filch showed up. He normally eats in the kitchen. He said, "Well, it's good to see you Ms. Weasley and Professor." He then figured out that we were there to have dinner. He added, "Will you be eating here reglar-like?"

I said, "With the permission of the house elves, of course."

"Great. We. That is, when Dursley and I were eating here, we ate normal-like over at this table." He led us to a table on the side where I'd frequently eaten under different situations.

During the meal, I told Ginevra, "We've been invited to the Brewster's home this Saturday at noon for lunch. Can you make it?"

She glanced over at Filch and said, "Of course, we'll disapparate from the Shrieking Shack at . . . oh, a quarter of if that is OK with you."

I agreed. Filch commented, "Sounds nice." I immediately regretted mentioning it while he was present. I made a mental note to invite him out with Ginevra and me for lunch sometime.

Saturday morning came. I'd been putting off thinking about lunch and what I'd say. Now, I had to. Ginevra and I gamed out what Brewster might say.

She was playing the Brewsters. I thought she did far too good a job of objecting to everything I said. For example, I started the conversation by saying, "I propose that we change our agreement so that Jaimie and I each get to have one year at a time rather than three. I think that makes things better for both of us."

Ginevra, playing Cecilia Brewster said, "Doesn't that mean that Mum won't be here while Ted Jr. is two years old. That's the most critical year for children forming character."

I sat there, mouth open, dumbfounded. Ginevra laughed and said, "You might say that the third year is important too. Jaimie would be there for that."

"Thanks, that's good. I'm glad you're not the solicitor for the Brewsters."

She just laughed.

The hour arrived. We traveled to the Brewster house by disapparation. We rang the doorbell. Even before my finger was off of the button, the door was opened by Mr. Brewster. He invited us in. I said, "I don't think that either of you has met Ms. Weasley." I then introduced Ted Brewster and Cecilia Brewster to Ginevra.

Ted invited us to have lunch right there in his home. Sissy had made sandwiches and potato salad. We sat around the kitchen table that was just large enough for the four of us. When we finally were finishing, Ted said, "Are you sure. Isn't she an Auror?"

I answered, "No. A distant relative is an Auror. Coincidentally, her name is Ginny."

Ted chuckled. "Your Ginevra has the same fiery red hair." She was wearing her hair up in a tight braided bun at the nape of her neck, but you couldn't hide its color.

We went to the dining room for lunch. We stayed away from business while we were eating. Then, Ted asked us to come to the point of our visit. I said, "Well, it's pretty simple. Ms. Weasley and I are engaged to be married. It will happen on Halloween. You should receive an invitation shortly. It will be clearly better for us if we don't have to wait three years between getting to see each other. I think that might work better for your family as well. What do you think?"

Sissy said, "It's been just over two years since I've talked to Mum. That's an awfully long time. I'd sure not want to have to wait three years at a time for that."

Ginevra looked troubled. I started to ask her what the problem was. She said, "A thought just occurred to me. We're going to be married at the end of the month. We might get pregnant in the first couple of months. The baby might be born in late summer or early fall. Her dad wouldn't get to be there for the birth. I don't like that idea."

Ted frowned. "I wouldn't mind put off Jaimie's return for a month or two, but longer than that . . ." He left unsaid his obvious reluctance to agree to giving me more time than that.

I said, "That theoretically could happen, but I don't think that we'd let that happen. We'd get pregnant right away or not until after I return, right Ginevra?"

She didn't exactly smile, but she said, "I'd be willing to agree to that."

Ted looked back and forth between Sissy, Ginevra, and me. A smile broke on his face, and he said, "I think it would be good to see Jaimie more often. I agree." We shook hands all around. Then conversation turned to happier topics.

I asked Sissy, "What's going on with chess? I'm afraid that I've been out of touch with the real world for quite a while."

She sort of grimaced. "Well, the good news is that I did get to the first round of the World Championship. Unfortunately, I met a Norwegian in the first round, named Carlsen. He was the best player that I'd ever played. He was my downfall. If it weren't for losses to him, I might have made it to the next round."

Ginevra patted her hand and said, "Keep on it. You'll have more chances against him. Isn't that right, Jim. You eventually got back against your nemesis."

I tried to smile as I said, "Right. It's never the same as the first time though, is it?"

Ginevra shuddered and just shook her head.

We talked for a while about Hogwarts and how Dursley had taken his old friend's post as potion-master of Hogwarts. Sissy asked, "Who took the house cup last year?"

I laughed and admitted that I didn't know. After a while, we left. When we arrived back at the Shrieking Shack, Ginevra said, "That Cecilia is a pretty girl, don't you think?"

I tried to remember what she looked like. I had to admit, "I'm afraid I was so worried about getting them to agree to our new schedule that I really didn't pay much attention to her. I guess she's not bad looking. I hope you aren't jealous of her. Your beauty is incomparable."

She scoffed. "That's just what you say. We should get an independent opinion."

The final week before the wedding arrived. There were only a few people coming from the US for the wedding. We'd invited everyone in my family and even offered to buy airfare and pay for people's stay in a hotel. Those who had accepted were my Mom and Dad, who were now just retired and my Aunt Nan. Dad had insisted on paying his own way. Aunt Nan had accepted our offer. I paid for first class airfare for her and offered to upgrade my parents to first class, but Dad wasn't having it.

Mom and Dad were arriving the weekend before. That was good because I still had to teach. They would arrive on Friday morning and take the day to nap and recover their equilibrium. Then I could spend a lot of time with them on the weekend. I'd been getting my lesson planning finished for the week of the wedding. I'd still take Friday and Halloween off. Jaimie would cover my classes on those day. That disappointed my students greatly. Of course, it wasn't because they didn't like Jaimie (sometimes I thought they liked her better than me) but because they wanted the day off.

Ginevera would pick my parents up at the airport. Nan, who didn't want to spend a whole week here, would arrive on Tuesday and just rest up for a couple of days. She'd join us on Friday. Ginevra and I had discussed her plans for entertaining my parents until I was free. She had the whole week planned. She'd bite the bullet and take them by cab from the Edinburgh airport to their hotel and help them get checked in. The next day, she'd take my parents and me on a tour of Hoggsmead. I gritted my teeth at that. They'd been here before and had a little experience with magic, but I didn't want them to have to jump in the deep end of the pool on the very first day.

Ginevra argued, "Oh, come on! Your dad's very sensible. Your parents and I have been doing a little correspondence."

I growled, "Please don't tell me it's been by owl post."

She stared me as though I were a troll. "Of course not. By regular post. I had a little trouble getting the postage right. The first was returned marked 'insufficient postage', but once I got past that, we've been having a good correspondence."

I relaxed a bit. "Still, a full day of Hoggsmead is a bit much."

We were sitting in our Edinburgh flat discussing it. She got up and walked around behind me. She kneaded my shoulder muscles that were a bit bunched up. "That's why I want you there. It will make it so much more fun."

I was afraid to ask what was on the docket for Sunday. She said, "They're Methodists aren't they?"

"Sure."

"Well, there's a beautiful Methodist church not far from their hotel. We can go there for services. Then I thought we'd have lunch at Hogwarts."

"Stop right there. That's right out—especially if the rest of the day is someplace like Diagon Alley."

She was still behind me massage my tight muscles. "Are you a legilimans? That was just what I had in mind. You'll be along. There's so much to see. If they're willing, we might just return on Monday. That is, if they're up for it." My muscles had tightened again.

She was babbling on. "You can't go to Diagon Alley and not see Weasley Wizard Wheezes, even though it's not my George." She had stopped talking. I knew she was trying to hold back tears. After a while she went on. "Your Dad loves books. There's Flourish and Blotts. How can you go to Diagon Alley and not see Olivander's. It's so much fun to see a young witch or wizard get their first wand. I hope someone does while we're there. Of course, we'd want to visit where you do some consulting." She hadn't named Gringotts, though that was what she obviously was talking about. I suppose she thought it would make Gringotts more acceptable by not naming it.

I replied, "Oh, come on! You'll scare Mom to death with goblins. It took me years until I could walk in without having to suppress a shudder when I saw a room full of them."

She scolded. "You know that's just prejudice."

"It's straight up honesty. We will not set foot in Gringotts and that's final. Maybe the next time they visit, but not this time."

She gave in. "All right. You can lead the tour. Pick whatever boring places you want. But wouldn't they like to see your humongous vault with all the gold?"

I frowned. "Didn't I tell you that I'd cashed in all the gold for paper galleons as a symbolic gesture to help the Ministry."

She said absently, "Oh, yes. That's right."

"One other thing. You know, there's more to England than magic. There's a ton of places that are very interesting with absolutely no magic. There's St. Paul's. There's Wesley's church. There's the British Museum. There's the city of Bath. There's the Cotswolds. The list goes on and on."

She laughed. "Oh stop with the travelogue. The next thing, you'll be talking rapturously of the changing of the guard at Buckingham Palace."

"I would never do such a thing! You know that I couldn't give a brass knut for all the Royals wrapped together and tied up with a pink ribbon."

She laughed at that. "I think I may have heard such an opinion once before."

"So, what's on the docket for Monday?"

She reflected and said, "Well, I thought we might go take a peek at Hogwarts and have lunch with you. After all, they have to be there starting Friday. They should get a little inoculation to it. They could meet a few teachers."

"I suppose that's alright."

She said, "Tuesday we could see a few of your cultural treasures. And . . . if your mum wanted to see the changing of the guard, I wouldn't stand in the way.

"On Tuesday, we'll pick up your aunt. What's she like?"

I smiled at the chance to talk about her. "Well, she's wonderful."

Ginevra complained, "You used to say that about me."

"Used to! That's my third most frequent adjective for you."

"Oh, what's number two?"

"Classic." I changed the discussion. I wanted to save my favorite adjective for the bedroom. I went on. "Anyway, Nan is brilliant. She used to write for some American national magazines. She is always funny. She makes awful puns. I think she'd be able to see Gringotts, BUT don't you dare take her there."

"Aye Aye, sir." Then, Ginevra added, "Of course, that's the eve of the big day. We'll have last minute things to do."

Things went pretty much to plan. We visited Hoggsmead, had lunch as planned, and visited a few businesses. Hoggsmead was probably a good place to start a magical tour. Most of the businesses are not that different from Muggle businesses. After all, if you're serving food, what are you going to do that's all that strange? We did some walking. Both Mom and Dad have kept themselves pretty fit.

We went to the Shrieking Shack. Dad was impressed by the setup. His first comment was, "I thought that electronics didn't like magic very much."

I answered, "Well, the Shack is pretty far from the concentrations of magic. I think they've done some things to harden the electronics. You'd have to ask the owner of this business, Nicholas Brahms, for details. He's off with his wife somewhere, I think."

There were still a couple of his staff there running the shop. Dad asked, "How do these employees get around. There isn't a road for miles and miles."

I decided to kid him a little. "Oh, they're all runners. They live in a town about four miles away."

He looked at me as though I'd blown a gasket. I assured him, "Just because they're wizards doesn't mean that they can't learn Muggle technology. They have to check their wands at the door, of course."

Ginevra said, "You're going to teach them never to believe you, Jim."

My Mom asked, "Do you let her call you Jim? I always insisted that my son's name was James."

I answered her but was looking at Ginevra, "Believe me, Ginevra can call me anything she likes."

That was the highlight of Saturday.

My dad enjoyed all the walking we did. My mom tolerated it.

Sunday was a big step for everyone. For one thing, we disapparated outside the Cauldron. We walked through to Diagon Alley. I had the visit planned so that we'd start with the least magical and work our way up. I wanted to start with Flourish and Blotts. Ginevra wisely suggested that Madame Malcolm's would be a better start. She commented, "Your Mum can see all the latest in wizard fashions."

It was a good suggestion, although pretty quickly Dad and I got bored. He commented to me, "I thought a magic mall would at least be exciting." He added, "Hey, why don't any clothing stores have chairs. Magical ones are as bad as Muggle ones." I could only shrug.

After an endless wait, we moved on to Flourish and Blotts. The shoe was on the other foot. I think, though, that Mom does like to browse magazines. Dad insisted on buying a couple of magical primers. I said, "We'll just have to drag those around for the rest of the day, you know. I will not carry your water for you." Of course, it didn't work out that way.

From there we went to Olivander's. Ginevra wanted to save it for last. I argued that we were easing the parents into magic. Weasley's would be saved for last. Olivander's was not as interesting as I'd hoped. No one was buying a wand. We decided to return later.

When we approached Weasley's, Mom asked, "Are you related, dear?"

Ginevra said, "Distantly. There's a marked family resemblance though. The proprietor George sometimes mistakes me for his sister." Ginevra had done everything to distinguish herself from Ginny. She wore her hair in a long braid and her clothes were particularly Mugglish. George greeted us when we entered the store. He said, "Is this your Dad and possibly a sister, Wendt?"

"You know perfectly well that she's my Mom. Of course, you've met Ginevra."

He smiled. "Yes, I've heard a lot about your misadventures together, Ginny is fairly a font of information about your little escapades."

Dad asked, "James, you've not told us about them."

"Oh, we will, but frankly, those are stories best told after we all know each other better. Let's just leave it that we have shared some dangers and come through them at least as whole as we entered them."

He nodded. "Well, we'll hold you to that promise of revealing all later."

The tour actually went well. There weren't a lot of customers, so my parents were trying out some of the more jokey things. Mom saw a display of vials of love potions. She asked, "These things don't actually work do they?"

George said, "Really! Do you think that I'd sell defective products? Of course, they do. They only last for a night. Really, they just make people act goofy. Nobody is in danger of doing anything particularly physical. If we had truth in advertising, we'd probably have to label them 'Platonic Love Potions.'" He then led us over to a display of various skyving products. He commented, "Now these can have real physical consequences—strictly short term. For example, the 'Puking Pastiles' . . ."

I interrupted him to get him to move on to his "Muggle Magic" section. It had a lot of the standard Muggle magic devices—cards, magic rings, etc. George commented, "These are a real hoot at parties. Seeing people who can do real magic try to use these Muggle products, especially when they've had a little too much." He mimicked someone drinking from a bottle. "It has got to be seen to be believed."

That turned out to be the highlight of the tour. We then went back to Olivanders. This time, there was a family picking out a wand. We saw a little of the process, but before they'd settled on a wand, Mr. Olivander came over to us and said softly to me, "Would you mind leaving, Professor Wendt? A wand choosing its witch is a very personal process."

I nodded? "Of course."

We had dinner at the Cauldron. The day had pretty well exhausted my parents, so we took them to their hotel. Ginevra and I walked in the cool night air for a while before returning to our apartment.

I wasn't present for most of the rest of the events of the week before Friday. Ginevra told me that they actually had seen a few cultural things, including the changing of the guard. They'd had to stand out in the rain for an hour to get close enough to actually see anything. On Tuesday, they'd gone to see a movie. Dad had really wanted to see *Star Trek*. He sort of coerced the ladies into seeing it with the promise that they could go to Harrods the next day and spend the whole day there if they wanted.

That night, Ginevra asked me, "What in the world is it with you men and action science fiction?"

I replied, "Said the woman who lived out an action science fiction adventure with me."

223

"At least it was believable." She paused, "You know it was grindingly, oppressively real most of time. All we did was spend hour on hour at gun ranges shooting at cardboard boxes."

I interrupted. "Don't forget shooting at pillows."

She ignored me and went on. "It was the most boring four months of my life. And then, we had about ten minutes of terrifying, deadly adventure."

I nodded. "That's what life usually is."

She said, "Au contraire. We're about to spend hours of exhilarating fun in our bedroom."

"You say that now."

I didn't see my aunt Nan until Friday. She put in a brief appearance for dinner at the Three Broomsticks where she was staying. Ginevra reported that she'd taken her first disapparation very well.

On Friday, we had lunch at the Broomsticks. We did a lot of visiting over a very long lunch. There was a last minute review of the plans for the rest of the day and Halloween. At the mention of Halloween, Nan said, "I hear that you usually have adventures at the annual Halloween party at Hogwarts."

I frowned at Ginevra. "You've been telling tales out of school."

She just smiled. I commented, "Well, most of the time they were boring for me, followed by ten minutes of terror."

Nan insisted that I tell her one of the stories, so I told her about my first Halloween at Hogwarts when I impersonated Professor Snape and met my first Deatheater. When I finished, I said, "See. Hours of boredom followed by ten minutes of absolute terror." She was adequately impressed.

The wedding rehearsal that night didn't happen until the school's meal was over. The house elves quickly converted the head table area for the ceremony. It went without much to comment on other than the presence at the far end of the Great Hall of some students who looked to me like fourth and fifth year girls. They giggled most of the time. When we finished and moved down to the Gryffindor table to have the rehearsal dinner, they disappeared.

The house elves did their usual extraordinary work on the meal. It was delicious beyond what you would find in any restaurant other than Michelin three-stars.

Ginevra made a point of saying that I would, of course, not see her after the rehearsal. She would stay in the Girls side of the Gryffindor House. Of course, I'd not see her tomorrow until she walked down the aisle.

I said, "I've seen you in your wedding dress before, right?"

"You have, but you have not seen me as I will be tomorrow."

I twisted my head a little to look directly at her. "This isn't gong to be an X-rated appearance, I hope."

She stared at me, puzzled, and said, "I don't know what X-rayed is, but from your tone, I think I can confidently say, 'No.'"

I commented to Nan. "You see. Just another example."

She played the straight woman and asked, "Example of what?"

I said, "Life. Hours on end of tedium followed by ten minutes of absolute terror."

She asked, "You've been married before. What is there to be afraid of in the ceremony?"

"I'm talking about the first dance with Ginevra. I have never danced with her before."

Nan nodded. "You always were shy about those things."

That night in my apartment was very lonely. That is until 9 PM.

Dursley showed up a little before 9 PM. We disapparated directly to the main gate of Hogwarts. We walked in and Dursley suggested that I go with him to our joint office. When I got there, I found Filch with an open bottle of vodka. He said, "Since we didn't have a bachelor party yet, we'll have one tonight. And don't worry about smelling of alcohol. This is vodka."

I agreed to one drink. The wedding wasn't until three in the afternoon the next day. I could afford one drink. As the time approached 10 PM, the rest of the members of the Old Boys Club came in.

The vodka flowed like water—literally, vodka flows like water. I stuck to my one drink pledge, though. At midnight, we went over to the Three Broomsticks to continue the OBC meeting.

Filch immediately insisted that since we were, "at a new venustus your pledge to have only one drink doesn't hold. First, because we were talking vodka there. Here we're talking Dewars or Jameson or something. Second, because we're at a new venusian. So drink up." With that airtight logic, I could hardly resist. I still didn't get stinking drunk—just odorous drunk.

Everyone talked about the last wedding of mine that they'd attended. That raised the question of the possibility of something strange happening at Aurora's behest. I shook my head. "I think she's truly reformed."

A couple of wizards had volunteered to stay with me at the apartment and bring me back in the morning. I declined their offer with thanks. However, I accepted Dursley's offer to take me home and pick me up at 9 AM.

# Where in the World is Sharpenhoe

Dursley and I arrived at my apartment around 1 AM. I unlocked the door and was about to enter when he asked, "Care for a nightcap?"

"Are you crazy. I'll be lucky to be over a hangover by the time of my wedding as it is." I took a step over the threshold and suddenly found myself face down on damp turf. I felt around my body to make sure that I didn't have any broken bones or anything. I didn't inspect myself visually because it was pitch dark. I rolled over and hoped that my eyes would dark adjust enough to see something.

The first words that I said were, "You miserable moron, Dursley!" On cooler reflection, I decided that he must just have been the agent of the OBC to play a little bachelor party prank on the groom. Well, I was glad that they had left a coat for me. It was almost November. It wasn't particularly cold, but in the middle of the night, I was already feeling the cold until I put the coat on.

As I was doing that I realized that there was a paved road that was next to where I'd landed. I'd rolled onto it. I lifted myself unsteadily to my feet and felt around. On one side of the narrow road was a tall hedgerow. On the other side was a short hedgerow. I had enough night vision to make out the road and the hedgerows along the edges of it. I chose a direction and started walking. In a short while, I reached a small knot of houses. There were lights on some porches. I went to a mailbox that had an address on it. It fortunately had the street name as well as a number. The street was Sharpenhoe Road. Where the heck was that?

I then had to make a critical decision. Did I knock on a door and try my luck with the inhabitants or did I walk along the road, hoping to find a town where I could catch a cab somewhere. I could make a phone call, but whom would I call? More important, what would I say when I called them? "I'm located on Sharpenhoe Road, would you please send someone to pick me up?" I suppose that might work with the police, but then there'd be all sorts of inconvenient questions to answer. That would probably be true if I just knocked on someone's door. But then I might be answering the police questions not as someone who had called them for help but as someone who showed up on the porch with no explanation of why I was there. I decided to pick a direction and start walking.

As my eyes adapted to the dark, the choice of direction became easier. There was clear light in the sky near the horizon. It was much closer to one direction of the road than the other. Roads, particularly country roads twist and turn, so it wasn't a no-brainer to go that direction, but I decided that I'd go along that direction and adjust if I seemed to be getting farther away from the light. Anyway, what was my other option—flip a coin?

I glanced at my watch and discovered that it was 1:45 AM. Well, I had time to find someplace bigger than Sharpenhoe. My walk was pretty much boring. That is, except for the occasional stumbles over junk on the road. There were no cars on the road. That didn't surprise me in the least. I didn't find a sign of a farm house for quite some time. After a couple of trip-ups I decided that I wasn't going to walk fast in the dark. In about an hour I reached a fork in the road. Right or left?

I mentally flipped a coin and went right. I considered the old left-hand rule for solving mazes and decided that the roads didn't much seem like a maze to me. After about another hour, I reached another fork in the road. This one had a sign. One choice took me to Upper Sundon and the other to Lower Sundon. I opted for Lower Sundon to the left.

I then had the longest stretch of uninterrupted road that I'd had so far. It took an hour and a half to reach a roundabout. The intersecting road was Luton Road. There was beginning to be some light in the sky. I decided to take the left turn to Luton. I'd heard of Luton, I was sure. It must be a decent - sized town. Besides that, I just crossed over a railroad line before reaching Luton Road. The line went parallel to Luton Road. Maybe I'd find a rail station where I could go somewhere.

Luton Road was pretty desolate. After a short while, I was walking beside some sort of large factory. There was just enough light by then that I felt pretty confident of not tripping on anything. I made pretty good time walking. Shortly after passing the factory, I encountered another fork in the road. This time, it was easy deciding which fork to take. The one to the left was wider and carried on with the highway I'd been walking along—B579.

By this time it was well after 5 AM and there was a good bit of light in the sky. I was walking along Toddington Rd. I began seeing signs directing me toward British Rail.

I eventually reached the station around 6 AM. I discovered that there was a train bound for London. It was to leave at 7 AM. I managed to find a

227

fast food restaurant and had some breakfast. Then I hurried to the station to catch the 7 AM to London. It didn't take long for us to reach St. Pancras Station. At St. Pancras, I found a cab—eventually. It dropped me at the street outside the Cauldron.

I had no hope that I could enter on my own. I only hoped that someone would happen along who could enter and that I could tailgate behind him or her. It didn't happen very often, but I decided that I could invest a half hour or so waiting and hoping. That would take me to 8:30. If no one showed up, I'd move on to my backup. It was the Ministry of Magic. The good news was there was a visitor's entrance. The bad news was that I didn't know what the new visitor's entrance was. Another issue was what I would find if I got in. Would I find a welcome desk that was manned.

I had been thinking about it off and on from the moment that I found that I could get to London fairly quickly. I knew that it must be something that a Muggle could use. I knew that it must be some common everyday thing, like a phone box.

8:30 came and went but no wizards or witches did. I sighed in resignation. I trudged out to the main street and started looking for a cab. Fortunately, in a great deal of London, you usually don't have to wait long to find a cab.

One showed up. I hailed it and named the address. The cabby heard the address and he started his banter. "Well, I used to hate to go to addresses around there. It always seemed to me to be really spooky. But now! It's almost like the Ghosts cleaned that area up. It doesn't feel spooky at all. People actually want to go to the park that's right there."

After walking and riding most of the night I was not in a great mood. I just grumbled, "Right, you wouldn't believe the number of times I'm in that very neighborhood."

When I arrived at the park, I began searching for a visitor entrance. It was already after 9 AM when I arrived. I began searching the park, which covered almost a city block. I walked around the park casually, as though I were just enjoying a cool fall morning. I stopped at a newsstand at the edge of the park to buy a *Times*. I briefly considered it as a possible entrance. I tried to see if the newsstand might be it by using hints with the newsie who was on duty. I asked, "You don't happen to sell the *Prophet* do you?"

The newsie asked, "What was that magazine again?"

"You know, not a magazine. It's a paper."

He asked, "Are you talking about *Profit & Loss*?"

I frowned. "No. Sorry."

It was immediately clear that no phone booth existed in the park or next to it. I kept walking and looking for innocuous structures that might be the entrance. There was a loo in the park. I looked at it long and hard. I vaguely remembered that in the bad old days with Riddle, the normal entrance to the Ministry was through loos. I also remembered the disgusting way that you got in through them.

I decided that I had to try the men's loo. I entered and was almost immediately sure that this must be it. For one thing, the loo was the cleanest public loo that I'd seen outside of a four star Hilton. Secondly, the place was the best lit loo I'd ever seen, bar none. Third, the waste basket had absolutely nothing in it. I opened a stall and gazed at the commode. I wondered if I should try to step in it. I decided that it would be the very last resort. So, I turned back to the rest of the loo hoping that I'd see something that I could try.

Then I found it—maybe. In a corner in the back was an old-fashioned scale. It was one that required that you put a coin in to get your weight. I went to it, hoping for a miracle. I stood on it gingerly. Nothing happened. I decided to try a coin. I got out a pence. Somehow, I couldn't force it in the slot. Then I began to feel really confident about it.

I decided that it needed a wizard coin. I bypassed the gold galleon and the silver sickle. I went directly to the brass knut. I had to open my purse to find one. It was full of paper money. There was a moment when I was afraid that I only had paper currency. Then, seemingly at the bottom of the purse, I found a knut. I said a quick prayer and inserted it into the slot.

□

The scale glowed green and suddenly, I was seemingly sucked into the ground. However, I ended up in a fireplace in the atrium. I was pretty close to the Visitor's Desk. Hurray! It was manned or in this case, witched. I ran over to it and was greeted by a witch whom I thought I recognized.

She said, "Well, long time no see, Professor."

I was smiling and tempted to laugh like a loon. However, I said, "You can't imagine how happy I am to see you."

She perked up at that and leaned forward over her desk. She said, "Well, it's really good to see you, too."

"I'm sorry. This is going to sound crazy."

She quickly replied, "Oh, Professor, nothing you had to say would seem crazy to me."

"Yes. Yes. Well, could you tell me what offices are open this morning?"

She seemed a bit disappointed but said, "Certainly. There's the Auror Office." At that, she giggled a little. "But then, you know that. It's always open. Then there's the Magical Travel Bureau. You can get a Port Key there, of course. It's only open Saturday morning until noon. Then, there's the Owl Post Office. It's technically open all the time, like the Auror Office, but off hours and weekends, it's self-service."

My face must have shown how downcast I felt. She said, "Oh, of course, there's also Gringotts. It's open until noon. But I'm sure you're not interested in it."

I confounded her by deciding that Gringotts was probably my best bet. Of course, there would probably be someone in the Auror Office who would at least recognize my name if not my face, but there would probably be a run-around trying to prove who I was. They might not even take me to Hogwarts because it didn't fall in their official duties. So, I said, "Good. I'll just drop around Gringotts to do a little business."

Her reaction was disappointment, but she tried to recover something. She said, "I notice that you're not accompanied." Of course, she meant not accompanied by someone magical. "I could take a break and take you somewhere if you needed a . . . uh, launch. Is that what you Muggles call it?"

I said, "Close enough. I might just take you up on that."

That made her smile. She added, "If you need someone to help you find the Gringotts Branch, I'd be happy to."

I knew where the Gringotts Branch was, so I said, "I've been there before, but thanks anyway."

I hurried to the Gringotts Branch. I was immediately greeted on entering by a chorus of "Good Morning, Professor Wendt" from the half dozen staff who were there. One asked what they could do for me.

I said, "Well, to be honest, I sort of need help getting back to Hogwarts."

One of the goblins had come over and drew me aside to ask the embarrassing question, "How is it that you don't have one of your friends along?"

I said, "Well, it is a little embarrassing. You see, today is my wedding day. Last night, a few of my close friends threw a little bachelor party for me. They had a little practical joke that they played on me. They disapparated me to a remote area and dropped me off there. I had to walk and use Muggle transportation to get somewhere that I could get help to take me back to Hogwarts."

Backshish (that was his name) nodded sympathetically, but said, "Well, here's the thing, Professor. I would love to take you to Hogwarts, but I can't leave Gringotts property during my shift."

My face fell. I guessed that I might have to take up the Visitor's Desk witch's offer or try the Auror Office. Before I left the bank, Backshish said, "Wait a moment. I might be able to help you even if I can't take you to Hogwarts. The main office is still part of Gringotts. I could take you there through the floo. The main branch is open Saturday mornings as well. There are always bank officers there. One of them could take you to Hogwarts."

230

I shrugged. "It sounds good to me. Let's go—as long as it won't get you into trouble."

"OH, no. I'm sure that would be OK. Let's go."

He led me into the back room where the floo connection was. We stepped in and came out in a room of the main Gringotts Bank that I'd never been in before. It seemed to be some sort of break room. Backshish said, "I'll go find a secretary to one of the bank officers and see if anyone would be available to take you to Hogwarts."

I thanked him and leaned my back against the table. I was facing the floo connection. I was totally exhausted and was not thinking about anything in particular when I suddenly felt a sharp poke in my back. A voice that I should have recognized but didn't said, "Well, well, a Muggle thief caught unawares in the Break Room."

I swung around to find the familiar face of Javeen. She was holding a fire poker that she had somehow magicked without my noticing from the floo. I held my hands up and said, "Guilty."

She said, "I heard about your predicament and came to rescue you. You want to go to Hogwarts?"

I nodded mutely. She asked, "Your office floo?"

"No. It's not my office. My office doesn't have a floo connection."

She was puzzled, "What office is that?"

"I'm sharing office space with Mr. Filch and Mr. Dursley."

Her eyes bugged out, and she asked, "Filch, the Janitor."

I corrected, "The Facilities Engineer."

She added, "And Dursley, the Squib's Apprentice?"

I corrected, "The Professor of Potions."

She asked, "Then where do you want to go?"

I shrugged, "It might as well be the Great Hall floo."

She nodded, walked to the floo, put the poker back in its stand, and held out her hand to me. "Well, then, let's go."

I glanced at my watch. It was now almost 11 AM. I thought, "Too late for breakfast, it must be lunch time."

We walked through into the Great Hall. It was too early for lunch. The only people in the Great Hall were the other members of the OBC. They were sitting at the Huffelpuff table talking. When I appeared, Hagrid jumped up and said, "Pay up!" All of the others at the table reluctantly reached into their pockets or purses or whatever and got money out.

I asked, "I suppose that you fellows had a pool going?"

Hagrid focused on his feet—no mean feat. He said, "Well, it was like this Professor. We were waiting for you here and it was beginning to be boring, so we decided that a little wager would make the wait interesting.

I shook my head. "Boring! Boring? You should have been out there in the wild walking with me. You'd not have been bored." I laughed. It was kind of funny I had to admit to myself. Then, I said, "OK. Since you've profited at my expense, the least you can do is tell me what time each person had."

Hagrid looked up from his feet and said, "I had 11 AM."

Filch growled and said, "If you'd only gotten here a few minutes earlier, I'd have won. I had 10:30."

Dursley said, "I had noon."

Slughorn said, "You never cease to amaze me. I had 12:30."

The B. G. said, "Sorry. I didn't peg you as a runner. I had 1 PM."

Then Dursley said, "We'll stand you lunch somewhere else besides Hogwarts. You have to go back to your apartment to change anyway."

I couldn't help chuckling as I said, "Is there anyplace to go other than the Cauldron?"

Slughorn said, "Done."

Hagrid took me, Dursley took the B. G., and Slughorn took Filch through the floo to the Cauldron. We were greeted by Tom. I said, "Tom, it's before the lunch rush. Will you join us to dine my last as a single man?"

He asked, "Open bar?"

I replied, "Of course! The treat is mine."

Slughorn interrupted me, "No. The treat is mine. I claim the right as his boss."

No one argued. I drank very responsibly. One Jameson on the rocks. After lunch, Dursley took me to my apartment. I had a couple of hours before I had to be back to Hogwarts, so I asked Dursley if he minded if I caught a nap before he took me back.

"No problem, Professor. You have a TV. I'd like to catch up on the news and maybe a soap opera."

"Be my guest."

# Every Little Thing She Does is Magic

I dropped directly to sleep. I had strange dreams. I was in a large lecture hall or maybe it was the Great Hall. There was someone with a strange machine gun who was randomly killing people. I could escape by flying away. I did, but I came back to attack him. I awoke at that point and was invincibly awake. I showered and waited until 2 PM to dress. I wasn't going to stand around in my nearly new wedding suit just to get sweaty.

We returned to Hogwarts and took our places, since it was approaching three o'clock. I was back in an anteroom where I could only talk with my fellow groomsmen. At three, a string quartet began playing some of the music that I'd selected: Bach, Albeniz, Brahms. During the wedding, Ginevra had selected some sappy love songs to be sung by Aurora. I reflected that maybe the ten minutes of absolute terror had already begun.

At 3:30 the groomsmen and I walked out onto the stage. The mothers of the bride and groom had been seated already. The bridesmaids came.

Then, the moment of maximum dynamic stress arrived. Ginevra was absolutely right. I had never seen her dressed this way. She didn't wear a veil. She was in the white dress. Her flaming red hair was coiled around and above her head in a regal fashion, like a diadem. Her expression was incomparable. I discovered as she reached the stage that I'd been holding my breath from the moment that she had appeared.

The rest of the ceremony was a blur. I could remember all the details later, but it seemed at the time to me that all of time was bound in a nutshell. Then, I was kissing my wife. People were applauding. We walked down to the floor of the Great Hall, and though I knew that everyone was watching us, I felt totally alone with Ginevra. We were quickly ushered back into the Great Hall for pictures. I was in a lot of them, but there was a period when it was Ginevra with others.

Harry Potter came up to me. We shook hands. He congratulated me. Then he said, "I know that we were once rivals. I'm happy now that you have the woman whom I consider to be my Ginny's twin sister."

I laughed. "Not so happy as I am. I'm happy that in a sense we are now brothers-in-law."

He agreed. As I said that, a dozen comments came to my mind. It is sometimes the curse of the literature teacher and writer that all sorts of things come unbidden into one's mind. It has been an occasion of grief for me more than once that I'd let loose one of those comments. This time things occurred to me like: "I'm happy to say I got the better," or similar. Instead I said, "I hope you've had a wonderful marriage."

"You bet."

The wedding banquet was, if anything, a notch above the rehearsal banquet the previous night. We cut the wedding cake, and I was beginning to wonder if the evening would ever end.

□

I found Dursley at one of the other tables. I pulled him aside and asked him to come with me to the Potions Classroom.

"Why in the world would I want to do that?"

I smiled inscrutably (I hoped) and said, "Maybe there's something in your inventory that you're not aware of."

He scoffed. "If this is some sort of revenge for that little prank that we played on you, you'll really . . ." He paused and laughed. "You'll really have to go some to beat it."

I just continued smiling. He followed me on the way down to the classroom. When we got there, he took some elementary precautions. He had me enter the classroom first. He used the *revellio* spell to see if there were other people around prepared to jump out of the supply cabinets.

I said, "Oh, come on. If I wanted to get back at you, I'd arrange something for your bachelor party, not do something now."

"OK. You said, there was something new in inventory. Are we talking about chemicals?"

I shook my head. He said, "Then, equipment?"

I said, "Look, if you like, but I'm pretty sure it's not equipment."

None-the-less, he looked around the room, but he didn't find anything. He asked, "If not supplies and not equipment, what in the world could be new here?"

I shrugged. He thought a moment and then smacked his head. "Of course, there's a new book." He went to the book cabinet and looked high

234

and low. "There's no new book here. As a matter of fact, they're all ancient used copies of *Advanced Potionmaking.*" He turned back to the cabinet and said, "One of those copies looks really old." He picked up one and then with shaking hand opened the cover. His eyes first widened and then filled with tears. "How in the world did you find this? Did Snape have another copy in his office or . . ."

I shook my head. "No. You know that Ginevra and I were in another universe from this one. It was one where you didn't become Filch's apprentice. That book was never found until she and I found it in the Room of Requirement."

He asked, "How did you find it?"

"We were looking for a horcrux there. We accidentally happened upon that book. But, you know, I wonder if it was really accident. After all, we'd searched only a small fraction of the Room before we found the horcrux. Maybe we were meant to find it, and thus, you were meant to have it."

He just shook his head in disbelief. Then he said, "You've been away from the party too long already. Let's get back before we're both sorely missed."

⊓⊔

We returned.

Eventually the band that I'd hired tuned up and we had the first dance. Ginevra commented, "What in the world did you have to fear about this dance?"

"Oh, just that you'd decide that we'd never dance again after my weak-kneed performance."

She scoffed. "I would dance with you again anywhere, any time."

Then, other couples came to the floor. I danced with my Mom. I danced with Aurora. She was the best-behaved that I'd ever seen her. Maybe she was afraid of the wrath of Ginevra.

After a while, Ginny approached and asked for a dance. I involuntarily gritted my teeth and said, "You can always have a dance whenever you want one."

She smiled. "Don't be so glum. I'm not going to tread on your toes—or Ginevra's."

We danced for a moment or two. Then she said, "I'm really happy for you and Ginevra."

I nodded. "You know that I've always wanted the very best for you that is conceivable."

She said, "You know I almost envied your Ginevra. For some reason I thought that her Fred lived longer than mine." She choked on tears.

I said, "It's good to be with someone who has lived with deep grief. There are so many things you don't have to explain."

"Yes. There must be points where this marriage brings up old grief."

I nodded.

She smiled and put her head on my shoulder. My arm was around her waist. We danced that way for a while. Then at the change of song—or was it after the next—she pulled back and squeezed my hand. "You know that if you ever need help gallivanting about the galaxy, I'm available."

I smiled. "You know how much choice anyone has in that, but if I had any say in the matter, you'd be near the top of my list."

I noticed that Ginevra had danced with Harry. When we got together for a dance near the end of the evening I asked her, "I hope that wasn't diffi-cult."

"It was sweet. We hardly talked at all. He wished you and me a wonder-ful life together."

The evening ended with fireworks courtesy of a company that I'd hired for the occasion. No one else other than Slughorn knew about it. He'd signed off on it when I assured him that we'd thoroughly clean up the mess and that there would be a substantial contribution to the Hogwarts scholar-ship fund (which would have happened anyway). Of course, Ginevra and I had another sort of fireworks scheduled for our apartment a little later.

Throughout the night, people wanted to know what we were going to do for a honeymoon, since school continued the following Monday. My almost true answer was that we would not have a honeymoon, since we'd already had one in Monaco during the Summer Holiday.

It was almost true. Halloween night we were going to go to Paris, spend the night in a small hotel overlooking the Seine. Sunday night was dinner on the Eiffel tower at sunset Then late Sunday night it was back to Hogwarts and work.

It worked out as planned. I would have liked to have taken the express train to Paris, but with Ginevra, it was just not in the cards.

Our room was "compact"—a word that normally covers a multitude of sins, but when you only are interested in spending the night in bed . . . well . . . you just don't care that much. The hotel had room service. We used it. We checked out and walked the Seine randomly. There was a small cafe with street seating that we chose. It was November, the weather was cloudy and almost cold. Nobody else wanted to eat on the street regardless how fashionable it was. We couldn't have cared less. There was a warmth about us that was indefatigable. We disapparated to the Tuileries. Again, the weather didn't encourage casual strollers other than us. We didn't talk much. At one point, Ginevra said, "We really should come back here some-time."

"*D'accord.*"

Over dinner on The Tower, Ginevra asked me what had happened at the bachelor party. She said, "I'll never be to one, so I'm intensely curious about what they're like."

"Well, there's really not that much to them. The guys just take you out to drink. They buy. You maybe have a hangover the next morning. Every now and then, they play a little prank on you."

She looked at me with a sort of quizzical expression on her face and asked, "What sort of prank?"

"Oh, they might have a scantily clad woman jump out of a cake and em-barrass you."

"Did that happen to you?"

"No. Oh, they might disapparate you to some remote town in the middle of the night and leave you there."

She nodded. "That did happen to you, right?"

I nodded. Then, a thought occurred to me. "What about the bride? Do you have anything like that?"

She smiled slyly. "Maybe."

I smiled. "Give! What happened with you?"

"All right. Well, our little 'hen party' starts with a few drinks, too. Then . . ."

Sally had organized the party. She reserved a meeting room at a Hilton hotel in a London suburb. We had a great meal, and then we played party games.

The ladies that Sally invited were: Aurora, me, your Aunt Nan (we in-vited your mom, but she declined with thanks), Madame Pomfrey, Ginny Weasley, Pamela Moertl (yes, Aurora invited her, and she came!), and Sally's particular friend, Haley Poezl.

Besides getting stinking drunk—well some of us did—we played party games. There were silly games like ring toss. We had beer bottles in a car-ton. You couldn't have a beer until you landed a ring over a beer bottle.

Then there was groom trivia. This is usually played as bride and groom trivia, but since so few people knew me, we just made it groom trivia. Your mom declined to attend because of the drinking, but agreed to supply trivia questions. Another game was "Wedding phrases." You go around the room saying words or phrases that apply to weddings. When someone is stumped, they drop out of the game. Sally had brought a white board. We wrote phrases as they came up. That way there would be no question about whether a phrase had been used before. The last woman standing is the winner. I won that one.

Then there was "Never have I ever." That's a drinking game where the object is to get everyone else stinking drunk before the night's over with the bonus of revealing embarrassing facts about the players. The way it works is that each person makes a statement of something that she's never done. If anyone else in the group has done it, they have to take a shot of tequila. An example would be, "Never have I ever eaten haggis." I actually used that. It turns out that Madame Pomfrey had eaten haggis. She got me back, though. She said, "Never have I ever gone fishing." Ginny said, "Never have I ever used a love potion on a man." At that, Haley's eyes dropped to the floor and she seemed on the point of tears. She took a sip of her drink.

But toward the end of that game, after everyone had had a good bit to drink, they started being sexy. Aurora said, "Never have I ever disapparated into someone's bedroom." That caught Ginny. She blushed at that. I wonder whose bedroom it was. Haley said, "Never have I ever slept with a wizard." That caught Ginny, of course, and your Aunt Nan. There must be a story there.

The game ended when Sally said, "Never have I ever slept with James Wendt." That should have caught Ginny and me if we were honest, but nobody took a shot. That was pretty much the end of the party. It was getting late and everyone had had more to drink than they ought. We didn't want the Muggle ladies to have to navigate on their own, so Aurora took Sally with her. There was an argument about who would take your Aunt Nan and Haley home. I assumed that I, as Nan's hostess, would take her home, and Ginny would take Haley home.

Haley started the argument. Now, you have to bear in mind that everyone had their inhibitions down. Haley said—and I quote directly—her very words, "That bloody bitch isn't taking me anywhere. I'd rather walk."

I immediately said, "Of course, I'll take you." I then turned to Nan and asked, "You wouldn't mind going with Ginny would you?"

Nan is a perceptive old girl. Later at the reception, we were talking. She said, "I don't know, of course, but I would bet dollars to donuts that Haley and Ginny were rivals for Wendt. He never mentioned Haley ever. There must be a story there."

I pretended ignorance, but that sharp aunt of yours said, "Well, it's good that James has a wife who is discreet. I've a feeling that he's been in a lot of scrapes that he's never admitted to us. He needs a wife who will stand beside him and keep those incidents out of general circulation."

I tried to pretend modesty, but of course, she saw through me and just "tut-tutted." The truth is that when I arrived at Haley's apartment building with her, she asked me to come up with her. I thought it was probably a good idea in any case. After all she might have trouble with her key.

She got the door open. When she crossed the threshold she turned with tears in her eyes and asked me to come in for a drink. I decided that it would be a good idea, but I'd substitute coffee for something hard. She didn't object, so we went into the kitchenette to fix a pot of coffee. She told me some of her story.

This was not my first wedding at Hogwarts. Several years ago, my particular friend, Sally, had gotten married at Hogwarts. She married another wizard whom she'd met during the War with the Ghosts. He was an American, but got himself permanently posted here in England as a liaison to the English Auror Office.

I was the Maid of Honor for that wedding. You wouldn't guess it to see me now, but there was a time when I was frightened to death of magic and witches. I know what you'd say. If I knew Sally, I ought to have known that I'd be as safe as houses with you witches. I couldn't help it. I was just terrified of magic. I didn't know how to deal with it. Fortunately, Sally had an idea.

She promised me that she'd have her old boss, a non-magical, to accompany me whenever I had to be with witches and wizards. She claimed that he was something of a wizard himself in the way that he could explain totally insane things so that anyone could deal with them. Oh, she was so, so right about that.

I first met him when the other bridesmaids and I went with Sally and her Mum to shop for a wedding dress and bridesmaids' dresses. What I was dreading so much that I almost refused to go turned into the most glorious day of my life. I fell in love with James the moment that I saw him. Yes, it was YOUR James. God, in that moment, I swore to myself that I would make him mine.

After we shopped for dresses, I insisted that I needed more reassurance about magic. He agreed to take me to lunch, and he'd do what he could. We went to a restaurant and had lunch. During that lunch, we talked about our deepest secrets—at least, I did. I told him something that I've never told anyone else—not my Mum, not Dad, not Sally, no one. I told him about how I awoke after a Ghost took over my body.

You wouldn't know, but almost everyone who was possessed by a Ghost was unconscious the whole time. I woke up. It started as a hideous experience—being awake but not being able to control your body. With time, it changed. I won't tell you how, but at the end, I was truly sad when my Ghost had to go. I don't know what happened to her. She must be traveling somewhere in interstellar space even now. If I could have, I'd have brought her back, but you witches made that impossible.

Anyway, that long, long lunch that turned into dinner turned what might have been infatuation into committed love. I almost tempted . . . well, no matter. Every time that we were together for wedding events, I did everything that I could to capture his heart. Yes, I knew that he was married. I couldn't have cared less.

That other Ginny did everything she could to sabotage my work to win his love. At the time, I thought she was just being loyal to that witch wife of James. I now know that it was because she loved him as well.

That final weekend of the wedding, I was there the day before the rehearsal dinner. James spent a lot of the afternoon giving me a tour of the school. It included the Janitor's Office. You might think that was not significant. It was.

I learned that the Janitor's Helper had invented some sort of super love potion. He even showed us a vial containing some of it. When I heard that, I was determined to steal some and use it on James.

There was some sort of end-of-term party for the school that night. I attended and managed to sit across from James. I had an idea that turned out to be brilliant. Not only did I put some of the potion in his tea when he was sure to be looking at me, but I put some in my own.

The result was glorious, endless, mutual love. It was not just a slice of heaven. It was the whole thing. It was better than heaven. We sneaked away and went to the Astronomy Tower. From its Empyrean heights we could see the lake illumined by the quarter moon and the bright stars shining on our love. Your James was still ethical—pretty much. We kissed and caressed, but we didn't make love.

Then that other Ginny showed up and put an end to our joy. She forced us to take the love potion antidote. I had been in heaven. From that moment on, I've been in purgatory forced to atone for my weakness.

You're a witch. You can punish me in a million ways for loving your James, but you can't make what I now suffer any worse. Wait! No, you can make it worse. You could force me to attend your wedding.

I have a temper. I was beginning to feel my anger rise while she spoke. By the end, I had agreed with her. She had made a bad mistake, but she was now paying for it with a wrath that I couldn't bring myself to increase. I hugged her and told her, "You've suffered far more than I could wish. I could end it with a spell to make you forget—forget your terrible sin. You know that what you did was almost as bad as what the Ghosts did."

She nodded and sobbed, "Yes, you're right. But, please, please, don't take that gorgeous memory from me. It's the only thing that I have to cling to in the long, late, sleepless stretches of the night."

We burned the coffee while we stood and talked in the kitchen. Then I made another pot, which we actually drank. It was a late night when I finally left her apartment. I offered to stay the rest of the night, but she was ex-hausted and just wanted to go to bed.

I said, "Well, I guess your ordeal that morning was just as difficult as mine."

She scoffed. "As difficult! If you don't think it's really hard to hear that story from a woman who loved your husband and still does, then you're . . . you're . . ." She seemed lost for words. Then she finished, softly, "Just wrong."

We ate in silence for a while. Then, the sun was dipping near the hori-zon. There were just enough clouds to light the west in pink as the sun set. The lights of Paris are always wonderful. The gendarmes practically had to arrest us to get us off the Tower.

About the Author

William Wilkin lived in a small Southern Ohio town until he began his college career. He has a Bachelor's degree in Physics from The Ohio State University and a Master's degree in Physics from The University of Chicago. He had a career in corporate Information Technology and currently lives in Nashville, TN.

He enjoys music, both "serious" and "classic Rock". He reads classic Detective fiction and science fiction & fantasy as well as trying to stay current in physics.

He began writing seriously about 2005. He has a blog, in-mid-world, where he writes about Science Fiction & Fantasy and remotely related topics.

www.ingramcontent.com/pod-product-compliance
Lightning Source LLC
Chambersburg PA
CBHW060132130626
46556CB00006B/2317